Le Carré's Landscape

The reality of espionage isn't easily disentangled from its mythology – and somewhere at the uneasy confluence of these dimensions is the fiction of John le Carré. A former British intelligence officer, le Carré has captured the shadows and textures of the covert world with a sure eye for its nuances and a deep appreciation of the human factor. And while intelligence work may be far removed from the experiences of most of us, its grand themes – loyalty and betrayal – touch everyone.

In *Le Carré's Landscape* Tod Hoffman, a former intelligence officer, juxtaposes his own experiences and extensive research with le Carré's fiction, shedding light on those dank recesses where spying is done. Taking the reader through the countries and continents of le Carré's fiction, Hoffman reflects on the political causes and personal effect of spying – secrecy, manipulation, deceit, treason.

Le Carré's Landscape is a unique look at the master of the spy genre – a man who has captured the imaginations of millions of readers and perhaps enticed more than a few into the real world of espionage.

TOD HOFFMAN, a former intelligence officer with the Canadian Security Intelligence Service, is the author of *Homicide: Life on the Screen*. He lives in Montreal, Quebec.

Le Carré's Landscape

TOD HOFFMAN

McGill-Queen's University Press
Montreal & Kingston · London · Ithaca

Legal deposit fourth quarter 2001
Bibliothèque nationale du Québec

Printed in Canada on acid-free paper

McGill-Queen's University Press acknowledges
the financial support of the Government of
Canada through the Book Publishing Industry
Development Program (BPIDP) for its activities.
It also acknowledges the support of the Canada
Council for the Arts for its publishing program.

**National Library of Canada
Cataloguing in Publication Data**

Hoffman, Tod
Le Carré's landscape
Includes bibliographical references and index.
ISBN 0-7735-2262-x
1. Le Carré, John, 1931–   – Criticism and
interpretation. 2. Intelligence service.
3. Canadian Security Intelligence Service.
I. Title.
PR6062.E42Z68 2001   823'.914   C2001-900396-x

Typeset in Palatino 10.5/13
by Caractéra inc., Quebec City

For those who guided me through the landscape
and taught me
For Sally, who led me out

Contents

Preface   ix

1   In le Carré's Landscape   3

2   Introducing George Smiley   39

3   Out in the Cold   62

4   Karla   111

5   A Different Landscape   158

6   Changing Times   183

7   Other Wars   215

Conclusion   255

Epilogue   258

Notes   263

Bibliography   279

Index   287

Preface

"It's an odd game, turning a man's life inside out without meeting him."[1]

Yet that's precisely what an intelligence officer (IO) does: gathers odd bits of disparate detail, hearsay, and opinion, filling them into an indistinct outline he or she builds around a target – an object, the subject of a file, not even a person – until a human impression has been created, like a pointillist painting, where the dots give the illusion of connecting but don't quite. In large measure, it's what a writer does as well, taking characters, real or imagined (and often the supposedly real ones are only who the writer imagines them to be), and rendering them in such a way as to convey an impression of who they are. In either case, the measure of proficiency is how close the likeness stands to reality. Maybe this similarity of task is what inspires so many spies to become writers and writers to act like spies.

What is it about writers and spies? Like the spy, John le Carré has said, the writer will "prey on the community to which he's attached, to take away information – often in secret – and to translate that into intelligence for his masters, whether it's his readership or his spy masters. And I think that both professions are perhaps rather lonely." He goes on to explain how "you must abstain from relationships and yet at the same time engage in them. There you have, I think, the real metaphysical relationship between the writer and the spy."[2]

It's the sense of separateness they share: of observing events without fully participating, of eavesdropping on conversations without contributing. Also, there's the ability to create and bring characters to life, to constantly assume new voices. For writers, those characters act out only on the page; for the spy, they are roles to play. Take me for instance: under ordinary circumstances, I might be reticent to make a cold approach on someone, to just walk up to a stranger and engage that person in conversation. But in the guise of intelligence officer, I never hesitated. All I had to do was slip into the persona. I wasn't myself soliciting cooperation or fearful of rejection for who I was, but a character performing for the intelligence service. That character was whatever I thought an io ought to be: confident, friendly, overtly forthright, but with something obviously held in reserve. It sold to some – those who agreed to be interviewed and, eventually, to collaborate with my Service – not to others.

Of himself, le Carré has said, "I knew I was a writer first and everything else after that."[3] In his most autobiographical work, *A Perfect Spy*, he has a cia agent say, in reference to his alter ego Magnus Pym, "I think if Magnus's writing ever worked for him, he'd have been okay. There's just too much inside him. He has to put it somewhere."[4] All the withholding causes a pent-up desire to confess. And the most comfortable confessor is the blank page addressed in solitude. You can rehearse until you get it just right in your own mind, figuring out how best to explain things you might only half understand yourself. I think, for spies as well as for writers, eloquence comes more easily in print than in conversation. So we become inveterate and introverted scribblers and note-takers. An experience seems more real – or at least easier to control – when you see it laid out. If you can write down the what and how, maybe you'll come to understand the why and the who.

Le Carré wrote, "For the novelist, as for the counter-intelligence officer, motive concerns the possibilities of character."[5] Most of my service was spent in counter-intelligence, so I must be forgiven if I still think like a ci man, if I can't shake the impulse to suspicion or to seek refuge in secrecy. In fact, as of this moment, I was longer in ci than I've been back in the overt world. And that's another point: there's something disconcerting in surfacing from the protective, if stifling, fold of the covert world. The lies and subterfuges I hid behind were oddly reassuring. It was a relief never to have to be myself; exhausting to be someone else. In the end, not even I could easily tell who I was. Unless I confront my own motivations, the possibilities of my character, it is impossible to discuss those of others, even when the others at issue are the creation of a novelist.

I never intended to write a biography of David Cornwell, the former British intelligence officer who created John le Carré and lives the private life that parallels the literary one. This book is about how le Carré views and represents the profession that Cornwell once practised and how, in turn, that view has coloured perceptions of who spies are and what they do. Otherwise put, it is an operational critique – as distinct from a literary critique – of his fiction, and as such, it draws heavily upon my own career in intelligence with the Canadian Security Intelligence Service (CSIS).

My original plan was to conduct extensive interviews with le Carré. However, he declined to meet with me, stating that he is uninterested in the critical process. He added a further reason which no writer can fail to respect: "In order to function as a writer, I need my seclusion." So, following a brief exchange of faxes when I first embarked on this project, I have had no personal contact with him. I should add that I certainly bear him no ill will for his rejection. As a matter of fact, it appealed to the solitary in me.

However, his decision forced me to refocus, perhaps for the better (or so I hope, at any rate). I was put in the position of having to turn le Carré's life – though not Cornwell's – inside out without ever meeting him, only ever getting to know him from a distance. I wouldn't have occasion to test out my thoughts on the subject. Everything would have to be gleaned from how I read his work, what I could cull from interviews he'd granted to others, and what I've learned from my time among the spies pursuing the Cold War mission and fighting the post–Cold War malaise.

So it would be a more introspective book: my own journey through le Carré's landscape, or how he came to map such a big portion of my life, from my aspiration for a career in intelligence to how I perceived my role once I got there. This is the subject of the first chapter. Since leaving CSIS, I haven't entirely escaped. I'm still preoccupied with the essential mysteries of espionage: its seductive allure and heedless manipulation, the power of loyalty and those forces that encourage betrayal, the willingness to deceive ourselves and others. I've ended up turning myself inside out, discovering things I would otherwise have left unexplored. And as odd as it is examining a stranger's life, it was frequently more unsettling to delve into my own.

For eight years (1988–95) I was an IO, what espionage aficionados sometimes mistake for a spy. The distinction is crucial yet often overlooked, and it needs to be made. An IO is a salaried, full-fledged employee of an intelligence service, a pension-awaiting civil servant. It is the person we called a "source" (an agent in le Carré's parlance, an asset in the lexicon of the CIA), on the other hand – whether active in a target organization or close to a member of such an organization, or someone who shows him or herself (for any variety of reasons) to be a good prospect for infiltration – who spies. The distinction between IO and source is not merely academic; it is essential to any consideration of who becomes involved with intelligence services. For that is the most interesting question surrounding espionage: who participates in this strange trade? Are they motivated by the great expansiveness of their character or do they only indulge its puny limitations?

My becoming an IO was very much a result of being exposed to spies in pop culture. That experience created certain expectations which, no matter how much reality I saw, were and remain tough to shake. Where did reality fall off the cliff and plummet into the romantic image I'd wanted for myself? How much of my angst was genuine and how much artificial, just because it seemed like the thing to affect? As I compulsively looked over my shoulder, was I expecting to see anything? Could I have spotted it if it had been there? And what would I have done?

Ironically, whatever answers I arrive at will still leave you wondering at my conclusions concerning reality. Maybe they aren't reality. Six years after leaving intelligence, I can say that what follows is how I see the covert world, what drew me to it, and what pushed me out. The hardest thing about writing this book was to breach the line where ambivalence meets honesty. I'm not certain I've succeeded in doing so. I still want to believe all the myths I know in my heart are untrue. But right now this is as close to truth as I can come.

John le Carré was my companion before, during, and since my spy days. In the chapters that follow the first, I've used my experiences, as well as events of the postwar era, to get to know him as best I could. My secret landscape overlaps his, and in my mind, the two become inseparable. This, then, is as much the story of how I was drawn into intelligence as it is about what I found once I got there. I don't know if David Cornwell will ever read this book. If he does, I hope he recognizes some of the landmarks.

A word of warning is in order. Don't look to this book for revelations of secret information, for there are none. No sources or members of CSIS, past or present, are mentioned by their real names. All the specific incidents I describe have their basis in fact, but they are sufficiently disguised that none of the participants or circumstances could ever be identified. Methods of intelligence collection are discussed in terms already known to the public from other sources. Indeed, except for highly specific details, most intelligence methodology is familiar to fans of spy literature.

Because this is strictly a work neither of autobiography nor of history, I didn't feel constrained by absolute fidelity to events. However, neither is it fiction. Where details have been altered to protect sources or methods, the impression I mean to convey has been kept intact, and that's the real purpose of this book. It's not a text on intelligence but a discussion of ideas. Throughout, I have remained faithful to the spirit of each incident and have accurately reflected how I was affected and the effect I perceived in others who were involved. So while, for example, I have changed the nationality or occupation of an individual source, I have not changed that person's motives or my interpretations of his or her character. By allowing myself the freedom to conceal the superficial, I gave myself the freedom to be more honest on a more provocative level.

Another disclaimer, this one concerning my research method: there are seven or eight book-length critiques of le Carré's writing. I purposely avoided them because I didn't think it necessary to support my own interpretations with other's; nor did I want to put myself in the position of responding to others' analyses. The exception was David Monaghan's encyclopedic *Smiley's Circus: A Guide to the Secret World of John le Carré*, which is a valuable reference. I also used few reviews of le Carré's books, referring to them only when they raised particularly original points.

Some of the ideas I explore at length in this book were first addressed, at least in preliminary fashion, in articles I published in *Queen's Quarterly*. I am thankful for having been given the opportunity to confront them in its pages. I also gratefully acknowledge the generous support of the Canada Council for the Arts.

Le Carré's Landscape

Which is worse, the true believer who continues to believe
despite all the evidence of observable reality; or the person who admits
such reality yet continues to claim to be a true believer?

Julian Barnes, *The Porcupine*

"But I don't want to go among mad people," Alice remarked.
"Oh, you ca'n't help that," said the Cat:
"we're all mad here. I'm mad. You're mad."
"How do you know I'm mad?" said Alice.
"You must be," said the Cat, "or you wouldn't have come here."

Lewis Carroll, *Alice in Wonderland*

CHAPTER ONE

In le Carré's Landscape

Good books reflect their times; great books define them. No writer has captured the shadows and textures of espionage over the past four decades with as sure an eye for its nuances or as deep an appreciation of the human factor as John le Carré. So much of what has been assimilated into our collective understanding about intelligence work has actually been derived from his novels. When it comes to illuminating the dank recesses where spying is done, fiction suffers fewer constraints than fact. Memoirs are either stifled by residual obligations to protect information and people or embittered tirades to settle scores; in both cases the glare of hindsight tends to brighten a person's outlook on his or her own past. Outside researchers and journalists not only face limits on what they can find out but, more often than not, lack the subtle insight and expertise to separate the landscape from the fog that obscures this inhospitable environment.

However, it has always been a mistake to cast le Carré as a spy or thriller genre writer. He argued in an interview that "the spy novel is as flexible, as valid a theme in our time as any other major theme, as valid as the love story."[1] He has used and broadened the genre as a means of delving into the question famously put by Graham Greene: "who among us has not committed treason to something or someone more important than a country?"[2] He pits betrayal in unforgiving tension with love and watches while it exacts its bitter toll, whether in guilt, remorse, uncertainty, or simple fear of detection. Deciding what to betray amounts to a fundamental decision about oneself. E.M. Forster once confessed, "I hate the idea of causes, and if I had to choose between betraying my country and betraying my friend, I hope I should have the guts to betray my country ... Love and loyalty to an individual can run counter to the claims of the State. When they do – down with the State, say I, which means that the State would down me."[3] Still, he was honest enough to doubt that he had the courage to take the right choice.

This is the timeless theme that has consumed le Carré through eighteen novels, a stint with British intelligence – where betrayal's causes and effects were to be observed first-hand – and even before that, being abandoned by his mother and growing up the son of a frequently absent confidence trickster, early betrayals that made significant impressions on the child. Questionable motives, moral ambivalence, disillusioned heroes, and capricious villains have been the distinguishing features of le Carré's landscape. Behind the shrouded bastions manned by Cold War spies he found his ideal setting.

By 1961, when his first novel, *Call for the Dead*, was published, the world was settling down with the decidedly unsettling doctrine that chronic instability fostered stability. While nuclear bombs dangled over our heads threatening imminent holocaust, the great and not-so-great powers played cynical games of cat and mouse for nebulous advantages. Over the next thirty years, while the planet tilted precariously between not-peace and not-war, le Carré produced twelve of his books. The Cold War, as the defining feature of the international condition, served as the magnetic north of his compass, pulling his spies along and giving bearing to his plots. He was not, however, in the least put off course by its termination. His six post–Cold War novels demonstrate that his ability to balance daringly on the uncertain edges of the international arena has not been upset. Espionage remains the vehicle through which he explores greater, transcendent themes. The spies, whose skirmishes came so much to personify the Cold War, continue in their cloistered, secretive world (if anything, the domestic battles they fight to preserve their influence are as fierce as any ever waged against foreign enemies). Through their lives le Carré reveals something about the machinations underlying all our loyalties and betrayals, faiths and disaffections, loves and hostilities – in other words, our humanity. Espionage takes these abstractions and uses them as tools for fabricating elaborate schemes and manipulating people or situations as expediency demands.

Whether in Cold War Russia or the Middle East, the restive post-Soviet Caucasus or Panama, the spy's brief remains the same – to make the present simpler and the future less fearsome – because, in fact, the mere termination of the Cold War has done neither. And since the old dogs of espionage are unlikely to learn new tricks, the espiocrats – the brilliant term le Carré coined in reference to the bureaucrats running the intelligence organs – continue to rely on the usual textbooks for instruction on how to relate to the world. They do not so much strive for victory as try to preserve the game.

Why spying? "Spying was the passion of my time. I was there, I felt some of it on my own body. I reported on it. And as I grew away from it, and recollected it in tranquillity, I made it my bit of earth, my context, my way of looking at life."[4] Le Carré knows that espionage is a pitiless taskmaster of dubious morality, and he has sympathy for the toll it takes on the people who do its bidding. People do not grope through this murk without touching something from which better judgment would have them recoil; they have just lost the natural inclination to do so.

There is an unintended romanticism that attaches to all this. The notion of the lonely individual with a mission, engaging in dubious activities for an ultimately just cause is nearly irresistible. People who are denied comfort and security are easily envied from afar. Hardship, loneliness, fear all carry about them a quixotic ambiance when borne by someone else. Put them in a book that can be picked up and set aside at will or a film that will roll predictably to a close after a couple of hours, and you have an alluring situation. Whatever romanticism there is in le Carré's spies is projected from ourselves. By that, I am not referring exclusively to readers with no first-hand experience of spying. Participants, too, desperately cast about for the romance they expect of their profession.

Soon after I was transferred into ci – with barely a year's total service – I attended a seminar on agent recruitment. "Ladies and gentlemen, counter-intelligence is the greatest game there is," began the opening address, given by a grizzled officer whose every mannerism was studied to convey that he took it as anything but a game, "and you are all privileged to have the opportunity to play. It's a game of chess without pawns. Every gambit is engaged for a potential checkmate. There is no job more challenging, lonely, or likely to end in failure. But to participate in one of those rare successes is a reward unmatched, a reward to savour."

Going through a drawer of old keepsakes, I found a photocopied sheet of paper given to me by an FBI agent I had had occasion to work with. It read:

The Counter-Intelligence Officer's Motto –

So these intrepid officers,
heroes all, must go in silence
and in secrecy, their only
badge the stout heart which
swells with pride when they
do their job well.

I well remember when I believed these things with all my stout heart.

Outsiders try to relate to the IOs' solitude and doubt, to understand what drives them on. In most cases it is part of a personal quest more than it is a political objective. As any soldier will attest, once the shooting starts, you're fighting for yourself and your unit – what you can touch – not some abstract notion of flag and country. Spies are invariably searching for something: belonging, love, truth, a way out of one thing and into another. Intangible as these concepts may seem, they are immeasurably more real, and infinitely less corruptible, than grand political causes.

Great writers affect their readers. They make them feel, compel them to think, and occasionally inspire them to act. I first came across le Carré when I picked up *The Honourable Schoolboy* at the age of fifteen, unaware that it was the middle book of what would be the trilogy of George Smiley's quest for the Soviet spymaster Karla. I bought the book off the paperback rack in the newsstand at Montreal's Central Station while preparing to board a train to visit my best friend, who had recently moved to Ottawa. This, my first trip on my own, foreshadowed the same journey I would take more than a decade later as a neophyte spy.

The book rescued me from the trepidation of being alone. I was captivated by its exotic Asian settings, its complexity, its fluid and finely orchestrated conspiracy. I was also completely confused by its plot. I was drawn into the mood of the book, but the rest escaped me. I came away certain that only those privileged by initiation into the secret realm could fully get it, could even begin to imagine the intrigues being concocted in the elusive and embattled cause of national security. I knew that I wanted to see all that was hidden from those too timid to peek behind the curtain, to know what outsiders did not even dream. I wanted to get in on the game. The solitude and dangers braved by the characters were nothing but romance to a boy who had experienced neither. Their cynicism and regret seemed the well-earned campaign ribbons of the hard, stoic man I hoped to grow into. Only with maturity, of course, would these emotions come to reveal their true meaning.

Le Carré left the British intelligence establishment following the international success of his third novel, *The Spy Who Came in from the Cold*, in 1963. *The Spy* was acclaimed for its dismal and haunting portrait of Cold War skepticism long before skepticism became a commonplace response to the superpower standoff. Because of its original vision and the stark contrast in which it stood to existing spy literature, it was perceived to be a documentary-true representation of the intelligence world, a perception that has attached to all le Carré's work. Did he draw his title from jargon peculiar to spies, or did it become jargon from his using it? By the time I entered CSIS a quarter of a century later, it was really impossible to differentiate what he extrapolated from the real world to his fiction and what we appropriated from his imaginings to glorify our world. Someone returning to the office from lunch would be greeted with "Look who made it back from the cold"; or, on the way out to an operational assignment, would hear "Heading out into the cold?"

Le Carré resents how the attribution of realism to his work has caused his creative accomplishments to be undervalued. "What I had really done, as everybody who had been in the secret world with me knew perfectly well, was that I had invented a different secret world. I produced a place with its own ground rules and ethic and language and so on. The trouble was that my bluffs and fabulations were taken as gospel about the secret world. And while that was very flattering, it was simply untrue."[5]

Well, yes and no. His work should certainly not be mistaken for documentary, and his fictions are unencumbered by the constraints of actual events, organizations, or people. The Circus, for example, does not adhere to the strict delineation that exists in fact between the domestic responsibilities of MI5, or the British Secret Service (BSS), and the foreign activities of MI6, the Secret Intelligence Service (SIS). His realism is on a different, artistic level: through his rendering of scenes and characters with the nebulous and idiosyncratic qualities of atmosphere and temperament, he represents the true soul (or soullessness) of the covert world. He gives expression to the elusive psychology of distrust and disillusion and shameless connivance. Therein lies a reality he does not fabulate. And therein is the achievement of his stated objective: "It has always been my concern not to be authentic but to be credible, to use the deep background I have from the years I spent in intelligence work to present premises that were useful to my stories and that I knew were rooted in experience."[6]

The mentality of le Carré's spies and counter-spies is as honest a representation of espionage as is to be found in fiction. Living a life of secrecy – with all the deceits that imposes – for the purpose of unearthing those secrets held most closely guarded by an opponent exacts a price. Probing for weaknesses in a person for the purpose of preying on him or her to further some ill-defined objective is fodder for crises of conscience in those inclined to think such things through. Manipulation – as much for the manipulator as for the manipulated – has a corrupting influence. Take Aggie, a customs agent in *Single & Single* (1999). She finds a child witness to a murder and induces him to tell her all about it. Afterwards she "wondered what she thought of herself, the twenty-five-year-old daughter of her parents, worming secrets out of a kid of seven who believed she was the woman of his life."[7] This is not fabulation but insight into the effects of a peculiar territory on human nature.

As for me, I can't remember ever wanting to be anything but a police officer or an IO. This was remarkably convenient in Canada, where the path from one led to the other – until 1984, that was. Before then, the Security Service was a branch of the Royal Canadian Mounted Police (RCMP). Every aspiring intelligence officer could look forward to roughly the same career path: join the police force, barracks training at Depot in Regina, assignment to general policing duties for some number of years, and if all went well, an eventual transfer to the Security Service. That all changed the year before I finished my undergraduate studies in political science at McGill University.

Following the 1979 Macdonald Royal Commission inquiry into a series of wrongdoings by the Security Service and several more years of the sober – in the figurative, if not literal, sense – reflection and general dawdling that distinguishes government (in)action, it was boldly decided that Mounties were unsuited to perform intelligence functions. Civilian 1os, went the argument, would be less prone to the feeling of separateness from the society they were entrusted to serve than are police officers. Furthermore, since applicants would be recruited expressly for intelligence work, they would be selected on the basis of aptitudes and skills specific to this task, as opposed to those desired in prospective police officers. All those suitable candidates who might have been discouraged by the prospect of several years of uniformed policing would seek a career in the new, dedicated intelligence agency.

Thus was csis born, as a sometimes uneasy mix of experienced Mountie hold-overs from the old Security Service and rookie civilians. Many of our former police members were uncomfortable with their civilian status. They clung to their Mountie pedigree the way that deposed royalty clings valiantly to its discredited titles, regretting the fact that they could investigate but not arrest, missing the reassuring weight of a gun on their hip, feeling acutely the loss of the authority it conferred. Understaffed at the outset, the Service launched a concerted recruitment drive. Upon reflection, upper management conceded that individuals with police backgrounds displayed the most valuable training and skills to quickly adapt to the challenges of national security investigations. Right from the start, csis was back at square one, augmenting its Mountie complement with experienced cops almost as much as with civilians. Going so far as to recruit cops from outside the old Security Service ranks to fill out the organization, it caused grave distress among the civilians, or "Csoids," as we came to be known, because these recruits were taken on at the full working pay level, while we had to go through two developmental stages, not to mention the fact that we recognized – even if our superiors didn't – how this practice contradicted our very raison d'être.

Concluding that the substantive differences between cops and 1os were less than had been hoped for, csis managers focused on semantics. We, civilians and ex-cops alike, had taken to referring to ourselves as "members," in the tradition of the RCMP. Inevitably, we assimilated much of police culture, to the dismay of the functionaries who thought they had created something altogether new, counter to the truism that government never renews – it only recycles. Excluded from the work of intelligence, they never grasped its culture. Outsiders, they would never understand the insiders, even as they tried to eradicate the distinction.

"Member" was a term that especially rankled. It embodied all that divided "us" from "them." It smacked of exactly the elitist, exclusionary mentality that civilianization was intended to undermine. Whenever we referred to ourselves as members, we were supposed to be corrected; we were "employees." We were nothing special, nothing unique. We had a job; we were civil servants, grey figures in the great tradition of the faceless sameness of the bureaucracy. The objective was to cut the swagger right out of us. In my early days the effort failed. The more the bosses insisted on the "employee" designation, the more we delighted in membership. By the time I left, however, the ranks had enough eager youngsters determined to assimilate whatever notions would impress the higher-ups and secure their status as good corporate conformists that membership had been effectively undermined.

"The psychological culture of an espionage service resembles that of a clan or tribe, in which individuals are united by some greater goal and a shared sense of identity, ideology or otherwise,"[8] writes Markus Wolf, who headed the East German external spy service, the HVA, for nearly forty years. Ideology is alien to the majority, I'm tempted to say all, of Western intelligence officers. But identity is crucial. If we were going to sustain the casual dissembling we did on a daily basis, denying who we were and what we did to the outside world, we needed an inside world to which we belonged. We needed our own symbols, rites – maybe a handshake. We could only be grey on the outside if we kept a true sense that we were actually something very different within.

No validation of who you are comes when you constantly deny. Recruits are warned of this from the outset. Those needing praise and recognition are advised to seek them elsewhere. Validation, then, becomes an internal matter. You're proud of who you are, and you take a perverse pleasure in the restrictions with which you live. Your circle narrows, and eventually it consists, almost exclusively, of fellow IOs.

From the moment of separation, as the division of the intelligence service from the RCMP was known, I was faced with a decision: police or intelligence officer. About to complete my BA and, frankly, put off by the prospect that I would conceivably spend most, if not all, of a career with the RCMP patrolling isolated stretches of highway and small towns, I saw CSIS as the reasonable choice. Here, after all, was the opportunity to step directly into the position I'd always set as my objective anyway, to investigate sophisticated activities without ever having a disorderly drunk vomit on my shoes. I couldn't help but recall an old professor's pithy, if demeaning, description of the RCMP's responsibilities: "patrolling between Nowhere, Manitoba, and Elsewhere, Saskatchewan."

Why did I want to devote my working life to police/intelligence? Why had I never seriously entertained other prospects? Because I wanted to help people? That would be a satisfying answer, but I confess, no. If that was the case, why not medicine, social work, an aid agency distributing food to the starving or educating the illiterate? I never considered such options. I was never any sort of ideologue. Devotional anti-communism makes me uncomfortable, as does any unconditional faith. It tries to force all that is messy about human affairs into being neat. Since human thought and action cannot be coherently orchestrated without the most intensive manipulation and oppression, if we celebrate freedom, we celebrate an element of disorder.

George Smiley, the character with whom le Carré is most readily identified, despised "the fabulous impertinence of renouncing the individual in favour of the mass. When had mass philosophies ever brought benefit or wisdom?"[9] "*Man*, not the mass, is what our calling is about," he advises a group of trainees at Sarratt, the Circus's academy. "It was *man* who ended the Cold War in case you didn't notice. It wasn't weaponry, or technology, or armies or campaigns. It was just *man*. Not even Western man either as it happened, but our sworn enemy in the East, who went into the streets, faced the bullets and the batons and said: we've had enough."[10]

Ideology is artificial, something human beings invented that fails to deliver on its promise to systematize the erratic and make the random predictable. In the hands of benign philosophers and academics, it is an exercise in explaining. Adopted by megalomaniacs with insatiable power lust, it becomes a rigidly cruel exercise in sensory deprivation. There is a wonderful passage in *The Spy Who Came in from the Cold* where Alec Leamas, the British agent, is dismissive of the East German 10 Fiedler's questions regarding the philosophy of the members of his service. "'What do you mean, a philosophy?' he replied; 'we're not Marxists, we're nothing. Just people.'" Fiedler is perplexed by anyone who will do battle without some underlying conceptual doctrine, since his own actions are ordered by the logic of Marx and Lenin. He says, "I myself would have put a bomb in a restaurant if it brought us further along the road. Afterwards I would draw the balance – so many women, so many children; and so far along the road."[11]

Such thinking is too self-assured, too automatonic for my sensibilities. My ideological indifference is eerily similar to that of Jerry Westerby, le Carré's honourable schoolboy: "At Sarratt, they have a very worldly and relaxed attitude to the motives of a fieldman, and no patience at all for the fiery-eyed zealot who grinds his teeth and says, 'I hate Communism.' If he hates it that much, they argue, he's most likely in love with it already. What they really like – and what Jerry possessed, what he *was*, in effect – was the fellow who hadn't a lot of time for flannel but loved the service and knew – though God forbid he should make a fuss of it – that *we* were right. *We* being a necessarily flexible notion."[12]

Most 10s are driven by pragmatism: decent job, average pay, full medical and dental, good pension. Shallow though that might seem when set beside lofty philosophical concepts, there is little good to be said for the excesses committed in the name of ideals. I cannot think of a single case where someone was liquidated over a pension. And from what I observed, few communist agents were any more high-minded than the rest of us. Most of those posted to Canada devoted greater energy to scouting out discount electronic and appliance outlets than secret information.

So why? Vanity as much as anything. I was conscious that literally millions of people filled their leisure hours reading books and watching movies about how I would spend my days and earn my living. *I* read those books and watched those movies. But more – an inchoate sense that this was something important; the prospect that I would be the one who stood between danger and safety. To rise to that challenge, to be held up to such a responsibility was breathtakingly exciting. There were hazards out in the dark, tentacles probing over the horizon against which only a few of us stood ready to respond – men in black. The Cold War was my generation's war. We were engaged in what passed for combat.

When I was twenty-three, I toured the Allied landing beaches and military cemeteries in Normandy – row upon row of grave markers, and hardly a single casualty older than I was then. Never before or since have I felt more moved and less adequate. Whether they had fallen clear-eyed or teary, brave or cowering, they had been called and had answered. All of us who belonged to succeeding generations owed them a debt of honour and service. In the climactic scene of the film *Saving Private Ryan*, the mortally wounded Captain John Miller pulls Ryan, the man for whose rescue he and his detail had spilled their blood, close and with his dying breath beseeches, "Earn this!" Well, I felt, each of us shared the obligation for their sacrifice.

It was taken for granted that a real, prevalent, and imminent threat existed; our target was clear and present. I wanted to be a part of the battle. And – for Canadians since the Korean War, at any rate – it never deteriorated into a shooting war. It was subtler than that: a spy's war where victory would be had through stealth and cunning. I simply wanted to participate in what was the most substantial issue of the day. And I didn't want to be drilling for a shooting war I never expected would come. Nor did I envision myself joining any other government department to sit in some conference room debating policy or the niceties of diplomatic protocol. I wanted to be out on the front lines, to be where means had an end, actions had consequences, and the going would be tough and dirty.

I suppose I thought that I knew a lot about life, loyalty, and politics at twenty-five. In retrospect, I suffered from the sin Wolf attributes to all intelligence services: "too much professionalism untempered by the raw edge of ordinary life."[13] The isolating effects of intelligence are a recurring theme in le Carré's writing on the subject. Many factors come into play. First and foremost is that you find yourself joining an already isolated organization. This factor alone pulls you out of ordinary life. Secrecy is stressed from the moment you become involved in the recruitment process, as though you're being groomed for a role in a major conspiracy. "In case you get the job, it's best from the outset if you don't tell anyone you're interested in joining CSIS. If you feel the need to tell anyone you're being considered for a government job, say it's with the solicitor general's department," I was told by the personnel clerk who processed the first of my paperwork. She smiled slyly, "It's not a lie, since the Service falls within his ministry, but it obscures what you'll *really* be doing. Less questions are asked about the SolGen than about us."

I smiled in return, conspiratorially, no doubt. This was the first crack in the doorway behind which was the secret world. I'd begin building my legend immediately, just in case. Happily, I filled in the personal history form (PHF), listing previous addresses where I'd lived, jobs I'd held, schools I'd attended, clubs and associations I'd joined, places I'd travelled, references I could rely on. The PHF is the cornerstone of the process required for anyone to hold a federal job that requires a security clearance. I signed off on permission to launch an investigation into my background, my character, my finances. The intensive security screening that precedes employment with an intelligence service, when performed diligently, is supposed to reveal those weaknesses of character or telltale indicators that would sound alarms of a proclivity for unreliability.

Vetting is all about deciding who is loyal and who might not be. It is rarely about finding traitors because new entrants will seldom have had occasion to commit treason. It is trying to find in people's character those quirks, flaws, or appetites that *may* signal unreliability. Every investigator develops his or her own subjective means for measuring a person's reliability. Optimally, these means will have some basis in a common-sense appreciation for human nature. Often they do not. William Skardon, an MI5 officer who participated in the investigation of the notorious British traitor Kim Philby, had the ludicrous idea that "even a person's hobby gave him a clue to that person's susceptibility to treason. He had divided hobbies into 'constitutional' and 'non-constitutional.' Gardening was 'very constitutional'; ski-ing was 'doubtful'; motor racing 'very suspect.'"[14]

CSIS procedure was a little more logical than that. The information on the PHF would be confirmed through records checks and a field investigation consisting of interviews with long-time neighbours, friends, and professional acquaintances. The applicant's past would be probed for dimly remembered acts of folly and embarrassing sexual trysts; practices and preferences discussed, documented, and dissected. Once we had dispensed with the possibility that I might be homosexual, the investigator assigned to my case was especially preoccupied with whether I was inclined towards sex with more than one woman at a time. When he put the question directly, I resisted the temptation to reply, "As many as I can get," taking the more tactfully self-effacing "One is usually all I can handle" approach.

Drug use and alcohol abuse is duly considered and measured, your psyche pecked at for those nibbling little sores that threaten malignancy. Fingerprints are taken and compared against criminal dossiers. Finally, you're fluttered, as the Americans call it: strapped into a lie detector, a machine that many hold in disrepute – unless it measures a deceptive response; then, suddenly, everyone becomes a believer. You're interviewed by security officers and psychologists, all in the elusive quest to decide who will be faithful and who will betray.

My first posting in the Service was to analyze the results of these very security screening investigations. It was a job of desperate boredom, notwithstanding our being assured that we were truly on the front line of national security. After all, the logic goes, the most effective way to get at government secrets is to get an agent into a government position where he or she will be cleared for access to classified documents. We weren't only after spies but something even more elusive: the security risk, which is another thing entirely. It calls for measuring whether people, given the opportunity, might reveal sensitive government information to another power to which they felt some allegiance; or whether they could be easily bought; or whether something hidden in their past might leave them susceptible to blackmail should exposure be threatened.

No objective standard by which to judge a person's susceptibility to blackmail exists. I had a superior who delighted in telling what he referred to as "The $1.99 Chicken Story." A background check for a government employee's clearance revealed that she had been charged with shoplifting a chicken worth $1.99 from a grocery store. When confronted with her record, she readily admitted the incident. However, she added that it would kill her if her husband ever found out about it. The intrepid investigator to whom this confession was made became concerned. Suppose an enemy agent was to learn of her crime and threaten to reveal it to her husband. Would she violate the trust about to be imparted to her by the government? He requested that she volunteer the information to her husband so as to remove this vulnerability. After a couple of days she asked to be withdrawn from consideration because she couldn't bring herself to tell him. Needless to say, she wouldn't have been denied a clearance on these grounds. But the moral of the story was, according to my superior, that you could never tell what a person might be willing to give up to avoid having some, albeit insignificant, secret revealed.

Day after tedious day was spent in security screening reviewing the PHFs of civil servants, wondering what spies on earth would be stupid enough to allow anything remotely suspicious to slip onto a form they themselves had filled out. Those very rare occasions when some oddity caught your eye would positively be cause for rejoicing, not only because they broke the monotony but because they promised the possibility of that coup of coups, the launch of a full-scale investigation.

There is an undeniable seductiveness to being initiated into the lairs of secrecy that distinguish the subterranean geography of intelligence. Knowing no better, I equated secrecy with importance; ergo, if something had to be kept secret, it must be important. Since virtually everything that passes through an intelligence service is secret, it must all, I reasoned, be important. This misconception is the foundation upon which so much government activity wobbles. Knowledge is power, and secret knowledge consolidates power among a few worthies. Bureaucrats assiduously slurp up every piece of information like anteaters turned loose on an ant farm. The idea of being entrusted with information bearing "secret" and "top secret" caveats is exciting. It wasn't the power that might come from secret knowledge that I craved, but the sense of purpose and gravity that came with secrecy.

Secrecy gives itself to excess as well as to absurdity. What unsettles about secrecy is that we can never wholly trust having touched bottom. A little more digging, we suspect, and another layer will be revealed, one that will unbalance all existing concepts of reality. This is why intelligence services never achieve equilibrium. Disbelief becomes a self-fulfilling – and quite dispiriting – prophecy. If there is a choice, the Byzantine explanation always wins out. The conspiracy theory can never be definitively rejected, for that is the nature of conspiracy. The danger in this peculiar thought process is that the most reasonable and obvious explanations are dismissed out of hand as an elaborately crafted set decoration obscuring the elusive truth. During a 1993 interview, le Carré said, "If you live in secrecy, you think in secrecy. It is the very nature of the life you lead as an intelligence officer in a secret room that the ordinary winds of common sense don't blow through it."[15]

An early lesson in secretiveness came in training, but outside the classroom, when I casually discarded a telephone message in the nearest trash can. "What are you doing?" One of the training officers bounded after me with genuine alarm. Sensing a loaded question, I resorted to the tried and true response: "Nothing." He reached gravely into the garbage and plucked my discarded note from among the spent coffee cups, doughnut remains, and soiled napkins. He uncrumpled it gingerly. I stood by wondering if I was about to be fired for violating some recycling statute. "Your name is written on this." He pointed to the offending script. I nodded vaguely. There was no denying it: my name was clearly visible on the "To" line. Was I not permitted to receive phone calls during business hours? "Your name is protected, so you've gotta run it through the shredder," he explained. "If anyone went through our trash and found this slip, they might be in a position to identify you as a member of the Service. Normally, you'd get a security violation, but I'll let it go this time."

Whew! A bullet dodged. I felt relief just for not having a reprimand put into my file in my first week on the job. Only later would I marvel at the farcical contradiction of being required to keep my identity secret while being mandated to identify myself by name whenever I conducted Service business. That is to say, when interviewing someone in the course of a national security investigation, I had to use my real name, produce identification, and pass out business cards while guarding the true nature of my employment from all but my closest friends and relations. So our acquaintances supposedly don't know what we do, but those we confront in performing our duties are informed from the get-go. At the time I was too impressed and gratified at having been inducted into the world of secrets to dwell on such technicalities. I was also rather flattered by the prospect of someone suffering the indignity of rifling through reeking garbage just to learn my name.

The business cards are worth mentioning because they were the focus of lengthy debate in the early 1990s. IOs were originally supplied with cards bearing an embossed CSIS crest – a garish palisade of blue, gold, and white with a red maple leaf at the centre, topped by a royal crown – their names, direct office lines, and post office box address. These were revoked after an incident in which, if memory serves me, a rather unsavoury character who was interviewed in Toronto and handed a card proceeded to flash it as identification supporting his impersonation of an officer. This episode caused an uproar over the improper use of cards, rather than derision towards any moron who would accept a business card as proof of identity. But that's neither here nor there.

The ensuing crisis over what sort of business cards should be issued to IOs went all the way up to the Executive Committee. I can just imagine the committee convening solemnly, all the executives come to bask at the director's feet, each harbouring his own fantasies of impressing the great man. Of course, it's just my imagination since I never attended one of these summits. The highest that my career soared was a single day spent as acting/head of unit, nominally supervising four officers who, on every other day, were my colleagues. When the actual head took a day off, she had to go through the motions of appointing a stand-in. The sum of my authority was to countersign a single report.

The business-card kerfuffle would fall under the auspices of the deputy director of operations (known in the trade as DDO) because it had been one of his people who had had his card misused. The deputy director of administration and services (DDS) would certainly insist on a say, for it was his responsibility to print and distribute the cards. In other words, it was one of *his* cards that had been misused. The deputy director of human resources (DDH) would get his two cents' worth, since one of the Service's human resources had been involved. I suspect the official languages coordinator, too, would have demanded equal time, since the cards were printed in both English and French.

The DDO would hem and haw the matter to the committee's agenda, "A problem has arisen for which there was no precedent, and in that regard, I think, perhaps, in the long run we might be grateful for the opportunity to address it at this juncture because it isn't something that was foreseen by my predecessors, and now that it has occurred we are in the fortunate position of being able to devise a coherent policy we can adopt and communicate to all our employees to serve as a directive as to how to behave in the event it arise again, as it conceivably will, since it is something that, though unforeseen, as I said, is not something that will necessarily not come to pass again in the future, unless we take action to devise a coherent policy which we can adopt and communicate ..."

About here he would have to either pause for breath or spit out the foot that was threatening to choke him. No one would come to his rescue naturally, instinctively recognizing that the wounded wildebeest is the one that gets picked off, giving the others a chance to thrive. The director, like Caesar, would allow the performance to continue for as long as it so pleased him, munching peeled grapes and revelling in the power that made grown men cringe – and not just any grown men, but those powerful enough to have lesser men cringing before them. Eventually, he would become bored, clap his hands, give a backhanded on-with-it wave, and insist on learning about the crisis, at which point he would be told some story that was gentle on the teller and harsh on someone absent from the room.

Depending upon the generosity of his mood, the director would either growl his disapproval or benevolently forgive, confident that he could store the transgression for future use. Needless to say, no decision would be forthcoming on the spot. The incident called for a thorough mulling-over. Best to convene a task force in Policy Branch to conduct a study and submit recommendations as to the type of business cards an IO should distribute. Also, have a brief prepared for Communications Branch in the event that the press got hold of the issue and called with questions. The Branch would inevitably come back with the tired and true "CSIS neither confirms nor denies ..."

Such were the issues that came to the director's attention. I'm not suggesting that his entire day was spent at trivial pursuit, but it's hard to imagine the CEO of any comparably sized corporation – CSIS at the time numbered more than 2,500 employees – concerning himself with the style of business cards. The end result, after months and months of careful executive pondering, was to issue plain cards bearing a name and telephone number and nothing else. They looked like something you could instant-print out of a coin machine in a dollar store. I once handed one to the president of a private security firm, and he turned it this way and that before asking, "How do I know these weren't made in Beirut?" I couldn't argue.

After enough officers had complained about the amateurish cards, the problem wended its way back up to the director. Another round of meetings and task forces were convened until he finally got around to pronouncing his decision on this weighty issue of issues. After what I'm sure were many sleepless nights – they must have been since more months passed – he took a stand and proclaimed that we would forthwith carry two sets of cards, one with a crest and one without. It would be left to each member's discretion as to which contacts would be given which card. Dubious people would get the plain one, of course. This happy compromise found the director to be decisive but still in the position to lay blame on anyone who made the mistake of giving the crested card to someone who could use it to meet women or otherwise convincingly impersonate a spy.

The official identification card, too, was cause for much deliberation at the very highest levels. A real badge – any type of metallic shield – was rejected as being police-like and therefore unbecoming to the new Service. In its place was issued a sheet of paper bearing the IO's photo and the CSIS crest encased in a plastic sheath and bound inside a folded green wallet of the tackiest plastic. It should have carried a warning against being flashed in the rain, for the slightest moisture would cause the wallet to crack and disintegrate. Because of its colour, it was quickly dubbed the Kermit. The Service has since adopted a badge; but in keeping with civilianization, it is not referred to as such, but as a "metallic authoritative device" – fittingly, MAD.

When you're immersed in something every day, when you assimilate the particular behaviour demanded by your circumstances, you cease being surprised by it or take it for anything but granted. That's how race-car drivers become acclimatized to extreme speeds: only on acceleration do they actually feel the rush of velocity; once they reach race speed, their reactions become attuned to the severe demands. Doctors aren't born with a heightened tolerance for gore; their resistance is built up over time and exposure until they're equipped to handle what regularly confronts them. And so it is with IOs. We relish the secrecy. Becoming incapable of determining what ought, or not, to be secret, we conceal everything. And we adopt suspicion as a ready reaction to absolutely everything. These are the trademarks of the well-adjusted IO, in contrast to the well-adjusted person: secrecy and suspicion. What is held within can never be betrayed. Conversely, what is shared is forever at risk.

It is an unavoidable fact that with each additional person taken into the loop of a secret, the potential for exposure increases exponentially. In response to my pledging that our relationship and any information coming out of it would be guarded in the strictest confidence, a very wise source chuckled, "Forgive me if your promise fails to move me. I realize – even if you are unwilling to admit it – that as soon as I reveal a secret to you, it is no longer secret, and I no longer have control over where it goes. So, understand, anything I tell you, I am accepting that it is out of my hands from that moment on."

IOs would greet each public revelation of Service business with horror. When then-director Reid Morden launched a campaign of "demystification" in the early 1990s, we trusted that he meant some empty pseudo-initiative that would have him giving lots of speeches filled with the kind of non-revelations for which savvy public officials are famous. We could barely contain ourselves when the 1992 *Public Report* issued by the Service exposed the information that our establishment consisted of 2,760 people and our projected budget over the coming two years would peak at $229 million.[16] We shuddered at the operational advantages the opposition would attain from these dramatic revelations. How could we possibly function when everyone knew how many of us there were and how much money we had at our disposal?

Well, obviously, the information brought no catastrophe. In all probability, it was dismissed by hostile services because the source, CSIS itself, could not be trusted. "What clever disinformation," they would marvel. "What a bold ploy to mislead us with false data. As if a security service would ever release such classified information." Breathing in the same obsessively secret air as us, they assuredly suffocated themselves.

It is at the conjunction of your private and professional selves that the aberrance of the subculture becomes hardest to bear. Imagine coming home after a debilitating, frustrating day and not being able to unburden yourself to your most intimate. Maybe that doesn't sound like much. But try eliminating all talk about your work from daily conversation, and you'll get a sense of how great a portion of your life gets sealed inside. A CSIS agent from Toronto told a reporter that his fiancée had no idea what he did for a living and never asked.[17] That seems rather excessive, not to say difficult to believe. On the other hand, who I am to judge the trustworthiness of another man's wife? Mine knew from an early stage in our relationship what agency I worked for. I never revealed specific information concerning targets or tradecraft, but I wasn't afraid that Canada was endangered from her knowing the source of my paycheque. However, the fact that day-to-day trivialities were repressed is symptomatic of a lifestyle, one where deception instinctively comes before truth. For most people, this would be an unusual way to live. After a while, the IO forgets that; when abnormal becomes the norm, you've got a problem. You don't even notice how the job is corrosive poison to relationships.

Casual acquaintances can be the most awkward. What you do for a living is the first or second question people ask when they meet you. It's not usually considered a tough one. Yet the IO double-hitches, choosing what he or she wants – or ought – to be on that occasion: doctor, lawyer, Indian chief; tinker, tailor, soldier, spy. Once, I was at a university campus bar in Montreal with a friend and a group of his friends, who were strangers to me. I should point out that CSIS prohibits itself from operating or recruiting sources on campus for fear of being accused of interfering with sacred academic freedoms. CSIS members, however, are perfectly within their rights to attend universities, use their libraries, or drink in their pubs. Talk turned to politics. The discussion was of a pretty general nature – opinions on current affairs and the like. Somehow it got around the table that I was with the Service. I presume my friend had whispered it to someone, who had passed the news along. Suddenly, the individual who was talking went still. I hadn't really been paying attention to what he'd been saying, being more enraptured by the girl sitting next to me, but apparently it was something subversive. He took it upon himself loudly to challenge me. At first, following my training, I laughingly denied being what I was, but that failed to win me any friends or influence people. After all, the more fervent the denial, the more likely that it's disingenuous. As he became more menacing, all I could see flashing in front of my eyes was the headline "CSIS Agent in University Punch-up." Win or lose, I'd lose. I meekly left.

Whenever someone casually asked what I did for a living, I lied. When I worked in Montreal, telling people that I was with the

SolGen was a sufficient answer. The federal bureaucracy is distant enough from most people's lives as to engender little follow-up, and the only department anyone finds threatening is Revenue Canada. But when I worked in Ottawa, the problem was more acute. Ottawa is the quintessential government town where everybody is, or is related to, a plodding civil servant, striving politician, earnest executive assistant–consultant–policy-adviser, or whatever other job description she or he goes by, or a journalist covering one or all of the above. While people in other cities are oblivious to CSIS, so many Ottawans hold security clearances or have friends or relatives who've been screened that everyone knows what CSIS does. The SolGen cover is the equivalent of climbing up Parliament Hill and screaming CSIS as loud as you can. Since it became common knowledge that CSIS members casually identified themselves as SolGen, all legitimate employees of the ministry were quick to specify the precise branch in which they worked. Only those from CSIS stumbled and sputtered when asked specifics, and shrunk away when pressed.

Another attribute I equated with secrecy was urgency. I wanted everything I dealt with to be perpetually, unrelentingly, energizingly *urgent*. I intended to take personal responsibility for protecting Canada's security, to be the last knight errant holding disaster at bay. How deluded was I? In retrospect, I realize how very much I had to learn.

The first lesson was that an intelligence service is a bureaucracy. And the first lesson of bureaucracy is that *nothing is urgent*. These were lessons I never expected to internalize. In fact, I intended to make a career defying them. I was an aggressive charger when I started out, impatient, anxious to confront everything and anyone. I was a man with a mission and a badge (in fact, as I explained, an ID card, but you get the picture), believing there was no such thing as *over*zealous. What an oxymoron! How could one be *too* zealous? You were either zealous or you were negligent. On the first performance evaluation I was issued at the completion of my entry training, my supervising trainer was generally complementary but less than enthused about my "action-oriented approach." He tempered the criticism with an expression of confidence that "experience will moderate" this tendency. I took this rebuke – that my approach *should* be tempered – as a challenge: to never allow myself to be compromised by complacency. Of course, my trainer was a man of wisdom and experience who knew people and, of greater relevance, knew the system. With time, my approach was so thoroughly moderated as to advance beyond complacency to positive lethargy. I lost all motivation and sense of purpose. That fact, combined with growing personal displeasure, caused me to resign. Actually, I'd become so lethargic I probably could have sleepwalked indefinitely through my career, if I had not been pushed by an unwanted transfer to either relocate or depart.

To my own discredit, I should have picked up on early indications that inertia prevailed over urgency. Indicator one was that it took three years from the time I initiated contact with the Service until I was engaged. As tortuously slow as this sounds by real standards, those who handled my file would undoubtedly object that they had proceeded at warp speed in bureaucrat time. During this three-year interlude, I had gone ahead with my life, including a year of study in Paris and three months working in Edmonton, both moves necessitating further-flung inquiries than if I'd been less mobile, since the Service would now have to satisfy itself that I hadn't been subversive in either of those locales. Unaware – at the time – of what such an investigation entailed, I had no basis for impatience. It did strike me as odd, though, that an organization which insisted on its determination to recruit the best and brightest would take a chance that a desired candidate would still be available years after first seeking employment. On the other hand, I suppose it says something about me that I was.

I might have been alerted to the fact that the process was prone to getting hung up on trivialities when my PHF was returned from HQ as incomplete because it was missing my father's middle name (it's crucial to have full names and dates of birth in order to conduct comprehensive criminal and security records verifications). I explained that my father doesn't have a middle name. I don't know how many memos this fine point engendered, but it seemed to be the source of great confusion, if not suspicion that I was deliberately trying to obstruct efforts to ensure his proper vetting. The matter was cleared up, but I've always been curious about the debate it must have generated over what I might be trying to hide – sort of like when people pull the old stunt of mailing out a misdated or unsigned cheque to stave off an aggressive creditor they can't afford to pay.

Furthermore, if I'd been more attentive to the points of reference to which CSIS referred in the 1980s – and probably continues to refer – I would have picked up on the clues that the intelligence service wasn't exactly breaking news at stop-press speed. We have to go all the way back to September 1945 and the defection of Igor Gouzenko, a military intelligence (GRU) cipher clerk at the Soviet Embassy in Ottawa, to unearth the major coup. Following a comedic – though potentially tragic – mishandling of Gouzenko's defection, during which journalists, the police, and the minister of justice all turned him away, the magnitude of his revelations became clear. Information he supplied disclosed as Soviet agents Dr Allan Nunn May, a British scientist conducting atomic research in Canada, Alger Hiss, an assistant to Edward Stettinius, the United States assistant secretary of state, and an employee of the British High Commission in Ottawa, as well as several Canadian citizens.

Members of the Service still speak with pride about Gouzenko, conveniently omitting any reference to the initial reluctance to take him in. He's part of our tribal lore and as relevant to us as Moses's flight from Egypt is to the Jews. Gouzenko was, in large measure, our reason for being. His revelations were proof positive that Canada was right at ground zero of the Soviet espionage offensive against the West. We owed him our entrenchment in the bureaucracy, our place in the Western intelligence community. And though there were many desks dealing with all manner of counterintelligence and counter-terrorism threats, the Soviets were always *the* hot target. However, all the East bloc countries maintained active offensive services that could be counted upon to serve as Soviet proxies. Never again, though, would there be a Canadian spy case with such sweeping repercussions as Gouzenko's.

The lasting significance of his defection was its demonstration that the Soviets would conceivably aim their espionage assets against even the smaller members of the Western alliance. Thus secrets shared across NATO would be vulnerable not only in Washington, London, and Bonn but equally so in Brussels, The Hague, and Ottawa. Technologies that were restricted from sale to Warsaw Pact states might be accessible by covert means in Stockholm or Johannesburg or Singapore, the point being that no place was immune from espionage attack. Consequently, no state could afford to stand out as a soft target. All were obliged to erect safeguards around their sensitive information and undertake counter-intelligence measures to deter and, when that failed, uncover spies and traitors. Gouzenko proved that the threat was ubiquitous.

Similarly, we reached into the past for our arch-villain, Kim Philby. His espionage shook all participants in the Western alliance. Since it had only been some twenty-five years since his hurried defection to Moscow, this event constituted comparatively recent history. He died on 11 May 1988, barely a month after I began training. I arrived at work that morning, and of course, his passing was all the talk that greeted me. "About time that fucking bastard died," spat out one of my training officers with unexpected venom. What Philby had done was still a very personal issue for the tribe. Our memory, of necessity, was long.

I suppose it's heartening that my contemporaries in Soviet intelligence likewise depended upon the long view for perspective. Historian Christopher Andrew writes, "Even in the Gorbachev era, operations in Britain during the Second World War and the quarter century afterwards were still held up as a model for young intelligence officers at the FCD [First Chief Directorate, the KGB's foreign intelligence branch] training school."[18]

Nobody commits to a profession with greater ignorance than an IO. "All in good time," you're assured in answer to every question. "Need to know, I'm afraid," you're told. Soon as you need to know, you will. Fair enough. Part of the mystique. Ironically, once it's built up, every effort is made by senior managers to scale it down. By then it's too late. You can intellectualize it away, but in a stubborn part of your ego you play it up. Of course, we're not James Bond – well, not *really*; however many files get stacked precariously on your desk or days go by without your chasing anything more elusive than a records clerk who'll willingly track down the infinite cross-references that cause paper to avalanche and slice savagely into unprotected skin, leaving tracks of deep, razor-fine cuts on the inexperienced. You see, I could later impart to wide-eyed youngsters, I'd begun in the primitive days before comprehensive computerization, when the work was done with hard copies, reports were handwritten, and we were lucky if we had access to one terminal per unit. Still, by the time you made it over to the Dill Pickle, the Service watering hole of choice in downtown Ottawa, you were Intrepid, the tireless spy doing things you just couldn't speak about.

Every time I'd entered RCMP C Division in Montreal, where CSIS had office space at the time, as an applicant, I'd get the cold eyeball I thought was reserved for car salesmen in Amish country. Even those managers and investigators who'd participated in my screening ignored me as if we'd never met – until, that is, I'd made it. The transformation was as dramatic as it was instantaneous. I was family. One of the executives who had sat on my final board came bounding out of his office upon hearing I was in signing some forms. After not acknowledging me as anything more worthwhile or welcome than a derelict at a glitzy charity fund-raiser to aid the homeless, now he practically threw his arms around me in greeting.

"Congratulations, great to have you aboard," he beamed like a proud father.

"Thanks," I sputtered, unsure how familiar I should behave; also still a little uncertain about whether I'd boarded a luxury liner or a tramp freighter.

Moving from Montreal to Ottawa to attend the three-month Entry Training course was a leap into the unknown. And like my eleven classmates, I was happy to close my eyes and jump. Though it was grandiosely designated the Sir William Stephenson Academy in honour of Intrepid himself, the training centre was an isolated corridor in the main building at RCMP Headquarters, located at the confluence of an expressway and a major thorough-fare in the city's east end. The austere buildings, as grey as a gloomy winter day, concrete-paved campus grounds, and isola-tion were fitting for our cult-like induction. I remember how apprehensive I was on my first day. After my years of waiting, fulfillment was at hand. I stood on the brink of a new world.

Within the main building, how far an individual got along the passages marking each stage of penetration towards the inner sanctum was determined by the colour of the access passes every-one was required to wear. Without any pass at all, I was greeted at the entrance by one of the trainers, who had an especially soothing presence. I was the second of my class to arrive. The first was Jacques, a blasé young French Canadian. More slightly built than I, he sported the same style of cop-short hair and wore the same nondescript, cheap dark suit and bus-driver-blue shirt. We were set to work filling in forms for building access and identifi-cation cards. Jacques affected casual boredom, while I signed with momentous flourishes. I soon learned that his father was a thirty-year veteran of the Security Service and CSIS, so he was well prepared for the drill and already had the what-me-worry attitude perfected by postal clerks, bank tellers, and civil servants the world over.

Early on, he would raise considerable ire among some of our veteran colleagues for a comment he made in a newspaper article. As part of one of the Service's periodic reach-outs to the public, an interview was set up between an *Ottawa Citizen* reporter and six of my classmates (I wasn't among them). "We're just normal Canadians who are seeking a satisfying career and trying to make it big in the world," he said, in keeping with the overall theme of denying that anything set IOs apart from others. "It just so happens it's with CSIS and not with Canada Post or General Foods."[19]

The thought that we could just as easily be sorting mail or packing processed foods didn't sit well with devoted defenders of the national interest, who had long ago convinced themselves they were nothing like clerks or other mortals. Some made noises about finding out who the fictitiously named Dallis was and getting a personal explanation. Funny to think that everyone knew the interviewees were in the entry class, which meant there were only twelve possible suspects. Yet as far as I ever learned, he wasn't uncovered. Again, this was a clue of something to be gleaned.

Of all le Carré's books, *The Secret Pilgrim* (1990) touches me most deeply for its poignant exhumation of those souls lost to espionage and the memories they revive in me, who once dove into the covert never expecting to re-emerge. At once, it evokes the giddy elation of my early save-the-world days and the worn-out disillusionment that followed. Maybe it's true, as James Ellroy wrote: "Disillusionment Is Enlightenment."[20] I like to think so anyway. It makes the transition an achievement rather than a capitulation.

Ned has been purged from the elite Russia House and banished to the dumping ground of Training Branch – not physically a gulag, in that comfort isn't lacking, but the psychological equivalent for a fieldman who firmly believes that teaching is for those who never could or no longer can. Ned, in reality, is an unlikely candidate for Training, because he is the type to whose care young, impressionable recruits are rarely entrusted. Training is for the docile corporate citizens who will convincingly impart the word according to the policy manuals without resorting to their own opinions. They are hardly the best but are far from the worst. Many are really disillusioned, but they generally refrain from expressing it, recognizing that holding disaffection within is the better part of discretion, though hardly valour.

Ned invites his mentor, the great George Smiley, to address his graduating class, to bless it with his wisdom. Listening, Ned is moved to recall some of the highlights and lowlights of his long career and, in the manner of all people who have reached a certain age or a significant turning point, to evaluate what he has made of his life. For Ned is on the precipice of retirement; my turning point came when I decided to resign from the Service.

Smiley enchants with his human presence and fatherly advice. He is held in reverence, not only by the students, but also by his old protégé. He sends them off with hope, tempered with sage caution: "if the temptation to humanity does assail you now and then, I hope you won't take it as a weakness in yourselves, but give it a fair hearing."[21]

My own trainers were jaded, but I think we could sometimes infect them with our enthusiasm and bravado. Maybe *you* had failed to save the world, we thought (and occasionally said), but do us the favour of teaching us well, and we'll undoubtedly make up for it. Oh, and by the way, we'll never end up like you. I remember with embarrassment how cocky I was. The trainers surely found the idealism amusing and didn't quite know what to do with it. Behind my back I imagine they must have laughed it off as futile. After all, they couldn't openly chastize me for being gung-ho. No reason for them to take that responsibility: leave it to the system to break me.

When I arrived at the Quebec Region field office in Montreal after nearly three years behind an HQ desk, I was jumping with eagerness to bag a spy. Taking it as a given that spies were out there, it stood to reason I only had to be diligent in my pursuit to wrestle one down. Throughout my first – I don't know – days, weeks, months I constantly tingled with anticipation. A morning outing with desk mates for coffee and a doughnut released a free flow of adrenalin enough to keep me on alert for the rest of the day. I was first to check on the arrival of fresh batches of reports – classified "secret" regardless of content – and examined them with the concentration and care of a sapper defusing a mine. I would check and cross-check the most obscure references for the elusive clue that would reveal treachery and deceit. Just let me find one spy, foil one plot, save the country just once, and I'll be irrefutably content. It seemed like little enough to ask.

Ned recalls his first opportunity to break free from his London desk. He was assigned to the watchers – what we called physical surveillance units (PSU) – to assist with surreptitious protection of a visiting Arab princess. Surveillance is usually a numbingly tedious chore that nonetheless demands uninterrupted concentration. The most difficult skill for the new surveillant to acquire is the ability to surrender his or her own rhythms to those of the target. Everything moves at other people's pace: you wait for them to do whatever they do and move at their speed, maintaining a tempo that keeps you on their periphery, close enough to see, far enough away not to be seen. Ned is going about the task when he spots a man following the princess through a department store. Expecting an assassination attempt, he prepares to spring into action. Fortunately, he advises Monty, the head of his team, before doing anything. Calmly, Monty holds Ned back when the man reaches into his overcoat and withdraws, not a weapon, but a wallet with which he proceeds to pay for items she has taken the liberty of shoplifting. "That's the trouble in our job, Ned," counsels Monty. "Life's looking one way, we're looking the other. I like an honest-to-God enemy myself sometimes, I don't mind admitting. Take a lot of finding, though, don't they? Too many nice blokes about."[22]

Yes, the trouble indeed. Spies would have you think that their greatest talent lies in their perceptiveness, their ability to divine the subtle moods which inspire human nature, and to ascertain how it registers on the political scales. But this is an illusion. Spies react to all people with the same instinct: suspicion. This isn't perception, it's reflex.

My first operational outing was even less auspicious than Ned's. A telephone trace on a target diplomat who was married showed that he had attempted to call a Canadian woman at her home. I was positively dizzy with anticipation as I considered how I would first approach the woman, charm and impress her so that she'd tell me all she knew of the diplomat, then recruit her as an access agent and have her actively report on him, eventually setting him up for a direct pitch that would lead to his working in-place or defecting. Such were my plans. However, life was looking the other way.

The preliminaries for such an ambitious plan would deplete the patience of an archaeologist accustomed to rooting through a desert to find a shard of pottery. I am not that patient. The first duty was to scout out the address to which the telephone number was assigned so as to size up where the woman lived. It was to be my first time out of the office all on my own for an operational purpose. With excitement, I signed out a car and pulled out of our underground garage, as jumpy as Don Knotts on caffeine overload. Our office was downtown, the address in the northeast suburbs of the island. In other words, the *operation* amounted to driving across town, looking at a three-storey walk-up apartment building, stepping out of the car, verifying the name of the occupant on the mailbox, driving back to the office, filling in the mileage and amount of gas used on the run sheet, and writing out a report.

I arrived at the appropriate block and circled once, checking the plates on all parked cars to see if I recognized any from the contact sheets that recorded cars visiting East bloc or otherwise targeted consulates. Nothing. I circled again to check for anything else that might trigger my spider sense. Nothing. I parked and stepped gingerly out of the car as if afraid I'd trip an explosion. I checked up and down the deserted working-class street of low-rises and low-price retail outlets selling broken-down furniture and outdated appliances. Nothing. I approached the address I had carefully recorded at the top of the first page of my black imitation-leather flip-open notebook. Luckily, the buzzer on the front door was out of order, as it so frequently is in seedier buildings where upkeep is neglected. I checked the appropriate mailbox. A heady complication arose: a name other than that of the woman in question was scrawled on the plastic label. I double-checked to make certain and, seeing no one around, recorded the name in my book so that I could run a check on it back at the office. Exiting the building, I scanned carefully for signs that I'd aroused interest. But still there was nobody around.

I drove back to the office filled with the euphoria of a mission accomplished. All my training had been to good purpose. I was capable of finding an address and checking a mailbox. Upon my return I reported to my supervisor all the intricate details of my sortie. "Excellent work," he gushed. He checked his watch. It was 2:00 p.m. "We've got to inform HQ. See if you can get your report together before you leave." My workday didn't end until 4:00. I'd do what I could.

TO: HQ
FROM: Quebec Region Counter-Intelligence
As per our previous communications (appropriate report numbers and dates cited), the undersigned checked address at issue. Subject's (the woman's) name did not appear on lobby directory. Individual whose name is registered (name provided) is not known to Service. Inquiries will continue to locate subject and identify the above named.
SIGNED: T. HOFFMAN, CI.

I presented it to my supervisor for his counter-signature. "Excellent," he marvelled as he applied his name with flair. He checked his watch: 2:20. "Have it sent out immediately." I galloped excitedly to one of the clerks (those were in the days before "clerk" had any pejorative implications and they were redesignated "intelligence assistants") and stood over her while she typed and transmitted immediately – 2:25. Before I left that day, I had a response:

TO: Quebec Region Counter-Intelligence
FROM: HQ
As per your previous communication (suitably cross-referenced for future retrieval), HQ recognizes your efforts and looks forward to the results of continuing investigation.

Thus did I receive my first official attaboy for investigative acuity. At the time I suspected these were at a premium, a reward for distinguished service. Of course, they were no such thing; merely a means of keeping paper flowing back and forth; in that flow was the tangible evidence of activity – not accomplishment, note, but activity.

So did I ever locate the woman and make contact with her? Yes, I did. And she turned out to be most cooperative and even drawn to the possibility of participating in a spy caper. However, my masters were shocked at the optics of setting up a target with a woman. Without saying it in so many words (or at least, not putting so many words on paper), they thought it smacked of pimping. On the positive side, the region and Headquarters succeeded in firing plans and counter-plans at each other over a period of months, amply demonstrating the frenetic activity of which we were capable.

And why did I leave? Such a momentous decision wasn't taken rashly, nor was it the result of a single factor, though it was precipitated by a single event. On 15 November 1994, the chief of counter-terrorism, where I'd been assigned for just around a year, called me at 9:10. "Could you go up and see the DG at 9:30," he said rather curtly. This request was unprecedented. In all my time in Quebec Region I'd never exchanged more than a dozen words with the director general, let alone been summoned to his office. He was the sort who would steam past you in the halls with a sparkling smile and an over-the-shoulder "How are you, chief?" or "Everything going well, guy?" because he had no idea of your name. And he would keep moving so that, even if you were inclined to give him more than a "Fine" or an "Okay," he would be out of earshot by the time you spat it out. But he had good hair, wore nice suits, and spoke English and French flawlessly, thus meeting all the qualifications for a position in senior management.

"Uh … yeah … sure … what's this all about?"

"I don't know. Something about a transfer I think." Before I had a chance to say anything more, my boss had hung up.

Perturbed. Confused. Transfer? What the hell was going on? I hadn't requested a transfer. The DG wouldn't call me in to discuss a transfer within the region. I'd been moved around before, and it was always handled informally through the chiefs. The next twenty minutes dragged by while my mind raced.

I went up to his office with trepidation. I couldn't imagine any good coming from this meeting. I wasn't responsible for any recent revelations for which he might want to congratulate me or seek elaboration. If he kept himself well informed of operational goings-on, it was conceivable that he wanted to ask me about why I'd failed to be responsible for any revelations worthy of congratulation or elaboration. But if that was the case, three-quarters of the investigators would be lined up. More importantly, I hadn't done anything to warrant complaint or cause trouble.

There was nothing to be read in his mood when he greeted me and invited me to sit down. He flashed his wax-imprint smile, the kind that shows full frontal teeth without creasing the cheeks or glistening the eyes. His desk was pristine except for a single sheet of typed paper.

"How are you?"

"Well, I guess you'll tell me," I replied with, I hoped, light-hearted friendliness in my voice.

"You've been transferred," he announced stiffly, smile still firmly in place.

"I didn't request a transfer," I said dumbly, as if that counted for anything. I thought he stifled a chuckle at my naïveté.

"Where?" I managed as my throat dried and tightened up.

"Ottawa." I might have visibly shuddered. "RAP," I slumped dejectedly – Research Analysis Production, a group of analysts who prepared papers based on a combination of intelligence product and open source information. These are thick and nicely bound and invariably say nothing, the kind of attractive bundles of paper that bureaucrats love to circulate, but never actually take the time to read. For all the useless chores associated with oper-ational intelligence gathering, at least I had the pride of doing genuine intelligence work. And, albeit less frequently than I would prefer, occasionally I would participate in some genuine operational action.

"When?" I croaked.

"August 31, 1995," he recited from the paper before him.

"Is this open for discussion?"

"No." He paused. "Is there anything you'd like to say?"

"Not if it isn't open for discussion."

We were at a place this DG always tried to avoid. He ought to say something; he could be consoling or commanding. He elected to be didactic.

"The Relocation Planning Committee met several weeks ago to identify appropriate candidates for transfer to HQ. They carefully studied the operational needs of the Service and matched them with personnel possessing the knowledge and skills that would enhance our analytic capability ..."

Bullshit. He went on to quote the administrative policy that gave the Service arbitrary power to transfer officers anywhere in Canada as operational considerations required. We had all agreed to it as a condition of employment. However, there was a counter-doctrine, very popular with management consultants, asserting that all employees were empowered with the responsibility to guide their own careers. As good as it sounded, this was just a positive spin put on the failure to devise a coherent personnel development policy. It was supposed to mean that employees could decide their general career paths for themselves. The assumption on our part was, logically, that our decisions would be respected. In practice, it worked better as a theory.

The DG was droning on. "An in-depth review was commissioned of our resources and needs and you were identified because of your master's degree as an exceptional candidate for RAP. We believe your operational experience, both at Headquarters and in the field, will be a huge asset to the section."

Here, I thought, was the key: I had an MA in political science. For several years, people with graduate degrees had been hired directly into RAP without having to attend training. They were appointed to supervisory ranks, with commensurately higher pay, rather than having to spend four years at developmental pay levels and, on average, an additional four to five years before being able to compete for the next level. Nominally, these RAP-pers, as they were known, were limited in their career prospects to that section. But of course that proved not to be the case, and they competed for operational positions against those of us from the ranks. In me, I presume, they saw the graduate-degree qualification and the opportunity to move me into a slot at $5,000 or so less annually than they were paying others with similar education, but less Service time and no operational qualifications.

"Equally important to the Service is our belief that a few years in RAP will nicely round out your resume and have great benefits for your career," the DG continued.

"How?"

"Huh?"

"You said it will benefit my career. I want to know how. What position can I expect next?"

"Of course, we can't promise what will be available in some years from now, but the broader the range of experience you possess, the more valuable an employee you'll be." In other words, there was nothing waiting for me on the other side.

Barely seven years earlier, my classmates and I had been greeted by the DG of Training: "For every one of you sitting in this room today, two thousand applicants were rejected. You have survived a rigorous, highly competitive process designed to measure your aptitude for the tasks ahead. I have no doubt that many of those we rejected would make competent IOs. But you are the ones we wanted. You are the cream of the crop. Congratulations and welcome." Now I was hearing the DG of Quebec paraphrase these sentiments: "Don't think you're irreplaceable. If you leave we have two thousand people just waiting to step into your place." How quickly do we descend from chosen to expendable.

I appealed the transfer in accordance with Service procedure. My grounds were twofold: first, the professional grounds that this was not how I wished to see my career proceed, and second, on the personal grounds that three of my and my wife's four parents had been diagnosed with cancer in the preceding year. None of their prognoses were certain at that time, and under the circumstances, neither of us was comfortable with moving away. I felt as though I was being forced to choose – unnecessarily – between my job and my family, not a position one expects to be placed in by an employer so preoccupied with loyalty.

Amusingly, one of the board members who heard my appeal told me, "We don't want to lose someone of your calibre over this issue." Several weeks later the appeal was rejected by the director. A couple of months after that, facing the deadline for my move, I submitted my resignation. I felt that RAP would be intolerable. I was demoralized at the prospect of being thoroughly removed from my family and operational work. After eight years I felt I deserved a little more respect in having my career aspirations and personal needs addressed. I wasn't bluffing, but I was open to any discussion this action might provoke. The DG called me in.

"You're sure you wish to do this?"

"I don't feel I've been left any alternative."

"I expect you'll regret this." He extended his hand. Stupidly, I shook it.

My career in intelligence was over. I felt no catharsis, only deep remorse. Cynicism drained from me. I found myself in one of those classic situations where, when a chapter is over, however difficult it has been to get through at times, you recall only the positives. Even as the experience failed to live up to my hopes, I had been living my dream, fulfilling my identity. And I only realized how inseparable my identity was from my job in the weeks and months after I left CSIS.

Of course, there was more going on in my head than just an aversion to headquarters routine or living in Ottawa. If I'd been generally content, the prospect of giving a couple of years in a thirty-year career to a unit that I found distasteful should not have represented a huge sacrifice. And Ottawa was only two hours by car from our parents. I certainly had enough time to consider the big picture: you take the job you don't want, let it be known that you don't want it but will submit for the good of the Service, work hard, build credit in the favour bank, and parlay it on the next posting. That's how the system worked for anyone who knew how to play it. As well as I knew it, I was never capable of playing.

My decision wasn't entirely impetuous. I had been dissatisfied for some time. I was keeping an irregular journal, and in April 1993, on the occasion of my fifth anniversary in the Service, I wrote:

Apathy has settled over me and I'm having an increasingly difficult time handling it. This should be an optimistic time in my career, a point at which I've absorbed enough to be productive and confident, and am young enough to enjoy an endless array of opportunities and exciting prospects. My evaluations have been consistently positive. I have several operational successes. And, still, I keep thinking about getting out.

I've seen no evidence that hard work and success correlates with advancement. The back-room policy hacks get ahead and the hard-nosed operational officers languish under their thumbs. I'm stifled, enslaved by administration. There's no pressure to get on with the job, so it goes undone. Sometimes I go days without doing a single thing just to see if anyone will say anything, challenge me to account for all the hours in the day, but it never happens. If I announce to the weekly operational meeting that I submitted a single request to Liaison Section to verify a license tag and nothing more, I'm congratulated for my initiative. It's insane.

I won't be able to survive another twenty-five years of this. It's like living with a slow, rotting disease.

The transfer order gave me the push I'd been waiting for. Far from my attitude accounting for the transfer, it came more than two years after I recorded these thoughts. Never was my attitude questioned; never did I receive subpar performance evaluations or reprimands. If my superiors had any complaints about how I went about my duties, they never raised them to my face. The heart of the matter was that I desperately needed to expand my horizons, to breathe fresher air, to be allowed more creative expression. As Ned phrases it, spies "have seen too much and suppressed too much and compromised too much, and in the end tasted too little."[23] This was what I was afraid was happening to me. I was not unlike Smiley, who "found himself shrinking from the temptation of friendship and human loyalty; he guarded himself warily from spontaneous reaction. By the strength of his intellect, he forced himself to observe humanity with clinical objectivity, and because he was neither immortal nor infallible he hated and feared the falseness of his life."[24] You know that your own terms of reference for normalcy are skewed when you routinely check your rear-view mirror for tails, note the licence plates of cars parked in the vicinity of your home for future reference, lie about your whereabouts as a matter of course, suspect every new acquaintance of ulterior motive. That's really no way to live. I had had enough.

Smiley joylessly takes the Cold Warrior's bow in *The Secret Pilgrim*: "The purpose of *my* life was to end the time I lived in. So if my past were still around today, you could say I'd failed. But it's not around. We won. Not that the victory matters a damn. And perhaps we didn't win anyway. Perhaps they just lost. Or perhaps, without the bonds of ideological conflict to restrain us any more, our troubles are just beginning. Never mind. What matters is that a long war is over. What matters is the hope."[25] And though I was only thirty-three, far younger than Smiley, I suppose my time had passed. My generation's war was over.

CHAPTER TWO

Introducing George Smiley

He looked most distinguished in his regulation dark blue suit and muted red, but still undeniably power, tie. He might have been there to sell insurance, only we knew he wasn't. He strode to the front of the windowless classroom noiselessly – you could imagine, stealthily, if you wished. The television and VCR were already set up beside the lectern. He inserted a cassette, and on his discrete nod, the lights were dimmed. With a click and a whir, the tape began playing. It was black and white and grainy, like the playback of a convenience store's video surveillance camera, except that the angle of focus was extremely narrow. The sound was muffled beyond understanding.

The scene was of two men obviously in a hotel room – no place else is furnished with those distinctively uncomfortable straight-backed upholstered chairs and awkward-sized coffee tables, too low to eat from, too high to step over. One man was doing most of the talking. The other was writing copious notes on a pad he balanced on his lap. Occasionally, he would stop writing, look intently at the other man, and pose a question. Or so I guessed, since he would immediately go back to writing when the first man resumed his narrative. The climax of the seven or eight minutes of film came when the talker handed the note taker a sheaf of papers. At this point, the distinguished man stopped the tape, and the lights suddenly blazed back on.

"Did you find that exciting?" He looked around the horseshoe conference table at which we all – twelve spanking-fresh recruits in our first week of entry training – sat, deliberately making eye contact with each one of us in turn. "If you didn't" – he was daring us to be negative, despite our obvious undiscriminating eagerness – "you're in the wrong business. Because what you've just seen is a surreptitious video of a covert meeting between a high-level source working in place at a Sov-bloc diplomatic establishment and a CSIS field investigator. This is, ladies and gentlemen, as good as it gets."

He paused to let that sink in. "You don't see James Bond here. The meet's in a standard hotel room, not some sumptuous villa. And our guy drove there in a Reliant or a Hyundai, not a 'Vette. Nothing explodes and no guns are fired. In fact, neither man in this video is armed. What for? You don't listen or write with a gun."

He continued: "An intelligence officer is, far above all else, a source recruiter and handler. If you're good and if you're lucky, you'll have the opportunity to handle a source like the one in the video. You'll arrange and participate in secure debriefings to collect the intelligence such a source has to provide to this Service. That's an 10's job: to find someone with access to relevant information, establish contact, cultivate, recruit that person, and, ultimately, direct him or her to find out exactly what the government needs to know. No guns, no glamour, and precious little glory. But this is what we do."

Whatever technology accomplishes, the human source has always been, and always will be, the highest aspiration of an intelligence service. No satellite photo or eavesdropping equipment can measure thoughts or intentions. Only a person trusted by a target can pose the questions that will elicit a specifically coveted nugget of information.

Technical coverage mounted against people will never be so absolute as to account for their every action, let alone their intent. Only in novels can a target be truly blanketed. In real life, your knowledge is always patchy. There is essentially no such thing as twenty-four-hour-a-day, seven-day-a-week surveillance. An exception may be an imminently life-threatening situation when the person whose life is threatened is suitably important. Otherwise, no overtime budget could accommodate anything near total coverage. Nor are there enough human resources. Nor could a single operation win out against all the other operations being championed by other sectors, all of which believe their priorities to be paramount. Therefore you compromise, attaching surveillance when you expect the target to do something, or for those hours when you know least about his or her actions. And you hope against hope that something actually occurs during those precious, random hours when someone is watching.

Wiretaps are fine as far as they go. However, often there is a backlog of tapes to be translated and transcribed. Only in emergencies will you receive real-time reporting. Otherwise you could be reviewing reports of conversations several days old. Besides, no one who is doing anything significant talks over the phone. When the person does, it is cryptic and brief. And unless you manage to recruit an actual co-conspirator as a source, you will only learn so much: a lot of gossip, the odd peccadillo, plenty of innuendo, and more speculation than you could possibly process. Individuals who want to keep what they do a secret do not confide lightly. Bugs planted in homes, offices, or cars are better, but they are still limited in that they are merely a conduit for what is voluntarily said aloud within their limited range. They cannot direct a conversation or elicit information, and they certainly cannot evaluate a person's thoughts or feelings. Besides, you can't bug every place the target might hold a conversation, so you're always left to wonder what was said out of range.

Toys and gadgets are peripheral. Spying is an intensely human activity. Our training focused on how one builds rapport with people, creates bonds of trust, and projects empathy. The most Bond-like thing I ever did was to speed or burn a red light while conducting surveillance. But I did so with a very un-Bond-like dread about being ticketed by the police. Few things are more degrading than flashing a CSIS ID to a city cop and having the officer nonchalantly continue to scribble the citation, while sneering, "If you're so important, I'm sure you know someone who can take care of this."

But no matter how many times you repeat the obligatory repudiation of Bond and all he stands for, there is not a spy alive who did not sign on without a Bond complex, the faintest fantasy that he or she would not have something of the same experience, nor a rookie recruit who does not have to curtail a swagger mimicked from Sean Connery. That is why so much time is spent disavowing Bond. You can denigrate him all you want, but there is no denying his place as a cultural icon with resonance far beyond the domain of espionage. There is not another profession that can point to a single fictional representation that is so universally recognized. And yet Bond is very much an every-hero, a suave, courageous, resourceful man of action. He is a flamboyant action-adventure cartoon who is almost coincidentally a secret agent, more commando than spy. His very nature makes him unsuited to Cold War conditions: Bond "was a man of war and when, for a long period, there was no war, his spirit went into a decline."[1]

I am more partial to the Bond movies than the books. The character only comes alive in my imagination with Connery's wry grin or Roger Moore's bemusedly cocked eyebrow. Left to Ian Fleming's prose, he is stilted and lacks dimension. Both actors brought an essential sense of fun and frolicking panache to their portrayal. Fleming was far more serious about Bond, and as a result, the print version is humourless and affects a gravity that detracts from what are mindlessly fun pulp thrillers. Actors could put tongue in cheek playing Bond where Fleming could not in writing him because, according to his biographer John Pearson, Bond "is Fleming's dream of a self that might have been – a tougher, stronger, more effective, duller, far less admirable character than the real Fleming." Pearson refers to *Casino Royale*, the first Bond adventure, as "an experiment in the autobiography of dreams."[2] And say what you will about the misogyny and the violence, it is an imaginative and richly atmospheric dream.

Fleming did take a glancing blow at realism in introducing little-known SMERSH as Bond's nemesis. SMERSH was a special counter-intelligence unit established personally by Joseph Stalin in 1943, whose Russian acronym meant "death to spies." Its mandate was to follow advancing Soviet troops and hunt down, arrest, and often kill suspected deserters and traitors within recovered territory. Any Russians who had fallen into German hands – as prisoners of war, for example – were suspected collaborators. SMERSH was disbanded in 1946 and its functions absorbed into the CI Directorate of the MGB, the predecessor of the KGB. That it had not operated outside the USSR or ever been implicated in executing foreign IOs was something of which Fleming, "who always knew a good thing when he met one, took no notice and continued to base himself on his outdated conception."[3] Realizing that no run-of-the-mill villains would suffice, at the end of *Casino Royale*, when Bond vows revenge against them, Fleming admits, "Without SMERSH, without this cold weapon of death and revenge the MWD would be just another bunch of civil servant spies, no better and no worse than any of the western services."[4]

No less a literary figure than Anthony Burgess was a great fan of Bond. Surprisingly, he praises Fleming's villains – "they strain credulity, though only just" – and the terrain he made his own: "the ingenuity is always plausible, the technology comparatively primitive, and dreams of power unremarkable in the age of Hitler and Stalin."[5] In contrast to these entertaining fables, he finds le Carré's work to be "rather heavy-footed studies of the true espionage situation, books written without humour or fantasy though said to be reliable in matters of intelligence procedure."[6] I think that Burgess has unintentionally struck an important point: Fleming and le Carré are not really comparable. They have been forced together by those who like to think in terms of genre; both authors use espionage for plot and framework, but there the similarity ends. Fleming wrote entertaining fantasy-adventures untroubled by the fetters of reality, while le Carré has fashioned our fears and insecurities – sensations foreign to Bond – into a world reflective of the real one.

Le Carré despises Bond; he has referred to him as "an absolute travesty of reality; it was an absurdity and a vulgarity."[7] Exacerbating his spy-as-superhero nature, Bond loves all those things of which le Carré is so contemptuous: "England, or England as it was, or an idea of England; men without women in a London club, savoring their claret and losing their unearned money with good grace at the gaming tables."[8] This simple vision is accompanied by an equally one-dimensional grasp of Russia and a lament for England's decline. Bond, in *From Russia, with Love*, suggests that Russians "simply don't understand the carrot. Only the stick has any effect. Basically they're masochists. They love the knout ... As for England, the trouble today is that carrots for all are the fashion. At home and abroad. We don't show teeth any more – only gums."[9]

In at least one respect, however, Anthony Lane credits Bond as a precursor of le Carré: "what matters about the Bond novels is the central duel of wits between compulsives ... an increasingly single-minded conflict between Smiley and Karla, recalling the great set pieces of Bond versus Blofeld, Bond versus Largo, Bond versus Drax."[10] There may be an element of truth to the argument, but of course the nature of the conflicts is completely different. Smiley and Karla engage in an environment of bureaucratic quiescence, whereas Bond's quarrels are settled on the lawless frontiers of a middle-aged man's – Fleming was forty-two when he created Bond – dreamscape, where violence is followed by sex is followed by violence, and no predicament is too inescapable to ruffle our hero. Fleming was not aiming to explore the psychological or political complexities of espionage: he was writing thrillers. His spy world is no more a counterpart to real intelligence than Mickey Spillane's private eyes resemble the real thing, much as we all wished it did.

The ideal carriage is one that will allow the spy to go unremarked. Le Carré elaborates about Smiley: "Obscurity was his nature, as well as his profession. The byways of espionage are not populated by the brash and colourful adventurers of fiction. A man who, like Smiley, has lived and worked for years among his country's enemies learns only one prayer: that he may never, never be noticed. Assimilation is his highest aim, he learns to love the crowds who pass him in the street without a glance; he clings to them for his anonymity and his safety. His fear makes him servile – he could embrace the shoppers who jostle him in their impatience, and force him from the pavement. He could adore the officials, the police, the bus conductors, for the terse indifference of their attitudes."[11]

If Smiley the man is inconspicuous, Smiley the character is remarkable. More than anything, it is the accumulation of small moments of truth that bring fictional characters to life and give credence to the situations in which they find themselves. In writing about a profession as disconnected from common experience and as confused by myth as espionage, such moments are particularly gratifying. Everything about the manner in which George Smiley is described reveals a truth regarding intelligence officers and their natural habitat. Fat, short, middle-aged, with thinning hair and thick spectacles, Smiley is likened, by turn, to a toad or a mole. Three lines into his first novel, Call for the Dead, le Carré proclaims him "breathtakingly ordinary."[12] Thus the first truth: that spies strive for anonymous ordinariness. As William Colby, the former director of the CIA, so effectively observed, the ideal operative "is the traditional gray man, so inconspicuous that he can never catch the waiter's eye in a restaurant."[13] The successful ones, at any rate, do not strut about extravagantly with look-at-me showiness. Nor do they lurk and skulk in so theatrical a fashion as to call attention to themselves. Bond would have had his cover blown well before uttering his trademark greeting,

"Bond. James Bond." As Allen Dulles, one-time CIA director, friend of Fleming's, and fan of his books, put it, "I fear that James Bond in real life would have had a thick dossier in the Kremlin after his first exploit and would not have survived the second."[14] Indeed, as if to prove the point in *Casino Royale*, Mathis of France's Dieuxieme Bureau jovially advises him, upon his arrival at Royal-les-Eaux, where he is to face off against Le Chiffre over baccarat, that he is "blown, blown, blown."[15] Within pages an attempt is made on his life; it is not enough, however, to convince him to lower his profile.

A little of Smiley's history is in order. He was recruited into the secret service by his Oxford tutor in 1928. Using his research into the arcana of seventeenth-century German literature as cover, he was sent to a small German university, where he taught while talent spotting potential agents. It was from this vantage point that he witnessed Germany's descent into fascist savagery. When World War II was declared, he stayed behind enemy lines running an agent network under the thin disguise of a representative for a Swiss small-arms manufacturer. His was a harsh and difficult war. "He had never guessed it was possible to be frightened for so long."[16] In 1943 he was brought back to England, where he married Lady Ann Sercomb, for whom it was generally held he was totally unsuited. He took her to Oxford, where he was set to resume his research. Then Ann divorced him, and the Gouzenko defection caused men of Smiley's experience to be called back into the service.

Vetting government employees assumed a heightened priority following Gouzenko, given the proof he presented about communist infiltration. In Canada the Cabinet Security Panel approved new guidelines in January 1947 that would see the RCMP Intelligence Branch conducting background investigations on individuals accessing classified information. Similarly, a special cabinet committee in Britain established procedures to examine the loyalty of civil servants. More than confirming the presence of Soviet spies under diplomatic cover, Gouzenko made it clear that they were aggressively, and successfully, recruiting locals in a position to further their intelligence objectives. "The automatic assumption of bureaucratic loyalty to the nation had been shaken," according to historians Jack Granatstein and David Stafford.[17] Thus it was recognized that anyone could prove disloyal. At this point even those who might have been predisposed to favour the Soviet Union for its role as a wartime ally began to see its hostile intent. If gentlemen were not expected to read each other's mail, surely states enjoying friendly relations should not be spying on one another.

Ann is Smiley's raw nerve; he cannot keep himself from clawing at it, causing the pain to flare predictably. She hovers on the outskirts of his life, popping in between this lover and that, reminding him of his humiliation at being cuckolded, tempting him to try once more to satisfy her. Her reckless affairs so impair his judgment at a crucial moment that he unwittingly tips Karla to his most glaring weakness during an interrogation in India. So preoccupied is Smiley with Ann's betrayal of him that, rather than working out what Karla holds dear and appealing to whatever fears he harbours at its loss, he makes the cardinal error for an interrogator; becoming consumed by his own lonely anguish and thereby turning his interrogation into a confession, not an extraction. What he reveals of himself will be spun to advantage by Karla at a later date (to be discussed below). When a person speaks, he informs; when he listens, he discovers.

According to Anthony Cave Brown, Smiley's marriage to Ann was based upon that of Sir Stewart Menzies to Lady Avice Sackville.[18] Menzies, reputed to have been the model for M in Fleming's Bond novels[19] and for Control in *The Spy Who Came in from the Cold*, was head of MI6 – or C, as the occupant of the position was known after the original head of service, Sir Mansfield Cumming – from 1939 until 1952. His marriage to Lady Avice ended in scandal after she embarked on a very public affair with Captain Frank Spicer, whom she married as soon as Menzies divorced her in 1931. Notwithstanding the very substantial blot that divorce made on the record of a senior civil servant in that era, Menzies's career survived intact. Upon Lady Avice was laid the blame for the rupture, and she was forever discrete about her time with Menzies. In her total retreat from his life, their relationship differed substantially from that of Smiley and Ann.

It has been speculated that Smiley was based upon Sir Maurice Oldfield, a career MI6 man who served as C from 1973 until 1978. But Oldfield's biographer, Richard Deacon writes, "I never thought that the character of Smiley had more than a superficial and incidental resemblance to" him.[20] Physically, for instance, they did share certain characteristics. Oldfield was unassuming, short, and portly. His most tellingly Smiley-esque trait was to clean his thick glasses with the end of his tie.[21] Le Carré concedes as much, but denies any greater connection.[22] He did introduce Alec Guinness, who played Smiley so effectively in the BBC productions of *Tinker Tailor Soldier Spy* and *Smiley's People*, to Oldfield when the former asked to meet the genuine article. Le Carré marvelled at how keenly Guinness observed the man, how "Oldfield's orange suede boots, the quaintly didactic waddle, the clumsy cufflinks, the poorly rolled umbrella, were added to Smiley's properties chest from then on."[23] However, these details were merely stage dressing for the character.

At the time of Oldfield's death in 1981, the *New York Times* and the *Times of London*, among other sources, identified him as the model for both Smiley and Fleming's M. The television program *News at Ten* wrongly quoted le Carré saying as much. He responded with a letter to the *Times*, insisting, "The truth, once and for all, is this. I never heard of Sir Maurice either by name or in any other way until long after the name and character of George Smiley were in print. I knew him, whether by reputation or personally, scarcely at all. Our social contact, such as it was, occurred after his retirement, and amounted to a couple of lunches, over which he was inclined to rebuke me, albeit amiably, for what he regarded as the unflattering portrait I had given of his former Service."[24] Indeed, le Carré's argument makes sense. In 1961, when Smiley debuted, Oldfield was serving as SIS liaison officer at the British Embassy in Washington, a post he had taken up the year before and would hold until 1964, when he returned to London as deputy to C. Prior to that, he had done two tours in Singapore, interrupted by a spell at Headquarters in London. None of this would have put him in extensive contact with young agent Cornwell, whose work centred on Germany. A further point: unlike Smiley, Oldfield spent the war with military intelligence in the Middle East. He himself denied being either Smiley or M, saying, "When Fleming was writing the Bond books I was a minor cog in the organisation in Singapore. I don't *think* I was the model for Smiley – perhaps some characteristics are mine. But, Cornwell (le Carré) did ask me to lunch with Alec Guinness."[25]

Le Carré has since revealed that he drew principally upon two individuals in creating Smiley. One was John Bingham, a thriller writer with whom he worked early in his intelligence career. He described Bingham as "an extremely good intelligence officer, a moleish, tubby fellow. He gave me not only the urge to write, but also a kind of outline of George Smiley."[26] The other was the Reverend Dr Vivian Green, a senior tutor at Lincoln College, Oxford, where le Carré was a student. Of him, le Carré said, "He has the gift of quiet and a *tremendous* shrewdness. To me Vivian really was a kind of Father Brown, a natural confessor." Green, by way of response, suggested, "Smiley's perceptiveness and general intelligence, his idealistic side, his slightly detached view of the world and his love for German literature" belonged to his creator.[27] Stafford writes on the subject, "More convincing as a model for Smiley is David Cornwell. Smiley, le Carré has confessed, is a fantasy about himself."[28] Though the physical dissimilarities are marked – le Carré is elegantly tall and slender, and born in 1931, he is far younger – he used Smiley as a puppet through whom to express his own attitudes and sensibilities.

Le Carré's first two efforts of writing were first-rate murder mysteries. They follow the conventions of the detective genre: a crime is committed at the beginning of the novel and a detective – Smiley – is introduced to restore order and bring the criminal to light. The classic detective story is frequently likened to a morality play,[29] in which some evil has caused turbulence and the detective serves as the force of good who re-establishes calm. The sources of the evil in le Carré's books are distinctive. *Call for the Dead* features an original spy angle, whereby the disorder is attributable to merciless East German intelligence agents and worsened by bureaucratically apathetic and self-absorbed British intelligence. In *A Murder of Quality*, disorder emerges from what is supposed to be the very preserve of British order: the upper class and its own peculiar sense of propriety.

Le Carré has often repeated the story of how he wrote these books while commuting by train from his suburban home to his intelligence job in London. He admitted to George Plimpton that he was shortchanging the British taxpayer from early in his career as he devoted his best efforts to literature: "To give the best of the day to your work is most important. So if I could write for an hour and a half on the train, I was already completely jaded by the time I got to the office to start work. And then there was a resurgence of talent during the lunch hour. In the evening something again came back to me. I was always very careful to give my country second-best."[30] With all the IOs who maintain outside interests, whether time-consuming hobbies or second-income businesses, it is a wonder that any spying gets done at all.

Smiley is on the brink of retirement when he is sent to conduct a routine security interview in *Call for the Dead*. Samuel Fennan, a Foreign Office employee, is the subject of an anonymous letter accusing him of having been a Communist Party member while a student at Oxford. The interview is friendly, including a walk in the park and a stop at a coffee bar and ending with Smiley assuring Fennan that he sees no cause to doubt his loyalty. Nonetheless, that night Fennan is found shot to death beside a suicide note bemoaning the ruination of his career. Maston, the post-war head of intelligence – officially an adviser to the cabinet on security – sends Smiley to talk with Fennan's widow in search of clues as to why he killed himself.

Elsa is a German Jew, a survivor of the Holocaust. She spews contempt at Smiley for all her suffering, for all the suffering that a state is able to inflict on its citizenry. "It's an old illness you suffer from, Mr. Smiley ... The mind becomes separated from the body; it thinks without reality, rules a paper kingdom and devises without emotion the ruin of its paper victims. But sometimes the division between your world and ours is incomplete; the files grow heads and arms and legs, and that's a terrible moment isn't it?"[31] Elsa taunts him, making a good point: judging a file is easy, condemning a human being is difficult. She claims that her husband was despondent following the security interview, and that is why he took his own life.

IOs intrude on people's lives without a second thought. Just doing my job, you tell them and yourself. And it's true. Routine inquiry, that's all. And this is true too. But what is left behind? What is the anxious government job applicant or desperate refugee claimant left wondering? You listen to their stories, their explanations, with bland indifference, diligently writing down what they say, keeping the mood congenial because that encourages them to open up. You've heard it so many times before, but they've never been in the position of having to tell it. At the end, they always ask what conclusions you've drawn. You respond evasively, denying the power to influence decisions that are taken far above your lowly station. I just record what you say and submit a report to my headquarters, where it's an analyst's job to make an evaluation. My job isn't to offer opinions, you lie. Never does anyone caught in the jumble of bureaucracy receive the satisfaction of sitting across from an official who will personally take responsibility for a decision. That Smiley told Fennan that he had nothing to worry about was an uncommon act of kindness.

By chance, the phone rings while Smiley is speaking with Elsa, and he answers, thinking it might be his office calling. In the event, it is the local telephone exchange calling to give Fennan the 8:30 wake-up call he requested the previous evening. It is hardly logical that, at the same time he is contemplating suicide, a man would order a wake-up call for the following morning. Thus does Smiley begin to suspect that Fennan was murdered. His suspicion is increased when he returns to his office to find a note from Fennan postmarked just hours before his death urgently requesting Smiley to meet him that very day. Smiley promptly composes a letter of resignation, pins Fennan's note to it, and submits it to Maston, who is interested only in having the matter neatly disposed of, not pursued into any disorderly complications.

Smiley's interest becomes all the more purposeful after an attempt is made on his own life. His assailant is traced to the East German Steel Mission and its resident diplomat, Hans-Dieter Mundt, through a car hire he arranged with the shady agency of one Adam Scarr. Two weeks after Fennan's death and soon after Smiley gets on to him, Scarr is found dead. Three weeks later Mundt is reported to have left England under an assumed name. The timing puzzles Smiley. There seems no reason why Fennan should have been murdered while Elsa, who claims to have disapproved of his spying, has been left unharmed. Why did Mundt remain in England for weeks after the two murders and the assault against Smiley? And what has happened since then that has convinced him to leave? These questions are left dangling, to be taken up in *The Spy Who Came in from the Cold*.

That Smiley's continued inquiries are undertaken on an unofficial footing places him in the English literary tradition of the amateur sleuth. He partners with Arthur Mendel of Special Branch, whose imminent retirement affords him the luxury of playing an unofficial role in the affair. Unfettered by decreed procedures, the amateur, in this tradition, customarily exhibits far more efficiency and creativity than does the professional. Recall, for example, Sherlock Holmes's running circles around the plodding, uninspired Scotland Yarders in so many of Sir Arthur Conan Doyle's classics. Holmes dismisses Inspectors Lestrade and Gregson as "the pick of a bad lot. They are both quick and energetic, but conventional – shockingly so."[32] In tirelessly assembling vast knowledge, Holmes the private detective far outshines the less-questing professional: "I flatter myself that I can distinguish at a glance the ash of any known brand either of cigar or of tobacco. It is just in such details that the skilled detective differs from the Gregson and Lestrade type."[33] The amateur is shown to have an abundance of imagination and to eschew the conventional interpretation that, at first sight, seems to offer a plausible solution. Indeed, that is precisely what happens in *A Study in Scarlet*, among other Holmes exploits, when he sarcastically debunks the theories put forth by the Yard and solves the crime on his own. So too is Smiley dissatisfied with the convenient explanation behind Fennan's death because the details simply do not mesh.

Maston, on the other hand, will take any answer that gets the problem off his desk. He has a body and a suicide note: case closed. Maston is Smiley's antithesis, "the professional civil servant from an orthodox department, a man to handle paper and integrate the brilliance of his staff with the cumbersome machine of bureaucracy."[34] Smiley's incompatibility with Maston is owing to the fact that, contrary to Elsa Fennan's accusation, he is too conscious of the human dilemmas of espionage and not enough preoccupied with the paper. Smiley has so much doubt and instinct: "suspicion, experience, perception, common sense – for Maston these were not organs of fact. Paper was fact, Ministers were fact, Home Secretaries were hard fact. The Department did not concern itself with the vague impressions of a single officer when they conflicted with policy."[35] The irony is that once, in the not-so-distant past, the intelligence service had thrived upon the wits and inventiveness of individual, swashbuckling officers.

The short history of America's Office of Strategic Services (OSS), established in 1943 in response to intelligence needs that arose from wartime conditions, and its rapid transition into the CIA gives a clear illustration of the evolution of the spy from romantic to bureaucrat. Wild Bill Donovan, its legendary head, recruited a band of "inspired amateurs [and] offered them a chance to live out their teenage adventure fantasies, to display their courage, to win the acceptance and approval of their fellows. They had to be action people ... The more hell they raised, the better Donovan liked them."[36] Le Carré used similar words to describe wartime British intelligence – "the inspired amateurism of a handful of highly qualified, under-paid men" – going on to note how they "had given way to the efficiency, bureaucracy, and intrigue of a large government department."[37]

Such was the image that the oss carried into peacetime as it enthusiastically traded anti-fascism for anti-communism in a bid to survive. Initially uninterested in continuing intelligence gathering after the war, President Harry Truman abolished the service in September 1945. However, the following January he reversed himself and established the Central Intelligence Group to coordinate all intelligence being gathered by other government agencies. The lesson of the cig, Phillip Knightley has argued, is "that there can be no such thing as a *small* intelligence agency ... In one year the cig expanded six times over," seizing collection responsibilities from the departments of State, War, and Navy.[38] As it expanded further, becoming the cia, it also took responsibility for covert action, which entailed its own financing avenues and airline, not to mention greatly inflated numbers of operatives and massive administrative support. Other Western intelligence agencies experienced similar, though less dramatic, degrees of bloating.

Bureaucratic culture conspires to smother initiative and impose its own peculiar measures of success and effectiveness. It turns talent inside out and expends it on the *appearance* of doing the job, as opposed to the actual *doing*. The skilfully crafted memo proposing an operational plan is a highly appreciated art form to the bureaucrat's eye. It represents solidity and reliability, like a well-executed copy of a familiar masterpiece, whereas an operational plan in action is a dubious avant-gardist adventure teetering on the precipice of daring originality.

The principle upon which democratic bureaucracy was founded is sensible – noble, even – ministerial responsibility; that the minister ultimately bears direct responsibility for whatever is undertaken by his or her department. When government was small and ministers knew all their senior officials, who, in turn, knew those beneath them, this was not so difficult. But in the multi-faceted conglomerate of the modern administrative state, it is not surprising that ministers and those deputies reporting directly to them are terrified by the multitude of decisions taken without their knowledge as part of the routine functioning of the department. The defensive strategy adopted to protect their careers against junior officials with a penchant for independent action has been to pile layer upon layer of authority to authorize every action. Sometimes fortune intervenes to save a senior official from accountability. The October Crisis was "the most momentous event that occurred during my career with the RCMP," claims John Starnes, the first civilian appointed director general of the Security Service. However, while the Front de Libération du Québec was murdering a provincial cabinet minister and holding a British diplomat hostage, Starnes "was struck down with a severe bout of pneumonia on 8 October and remained out of the picture until 23 November."[39] He goes on to insist that those officers who visited him at his sickbed were merely concerned with his well-being and that he was in no shape to be consulted about business.[40] Hence the highest ranking intelligence official in the country managed to be in absentia during the only apprehended insurrection that Canada had experienced since the Riel uprising.

Within the CSIS rank structure an operational plan would generally be prepared by an investigator in the regional office intending to carry it out. Just the act of writing such a proposal was proof positive that the IO was either too inexperienced to have the political savvy to flee such an obviously burning house or too fireproofed by past mistakes to care. He or she would forward it to the desk head. Wiser – wise enough, at any rate to have attained one promotion – the desk head would review it with a view to plausible operational advantages. He or she then pushed it up to the section chief. With both eyes cast resolutely upward, looking out for personal advancement, the chief looked skeptically on any action that would not conveniently fit the routine task of monitoring – though not necessarily interdicting – opposition activity. The chief had the discretion to kill the plan, pass it a level or two up the regional chain of command, or support it and forward to headquarters.

At HQ the plan, with as many reams of supporting files and precedent-setting case histories as could possibly be assembled, tumbled back down the chain to be reviewed by a desk analyst, of the same rank as the originating investigator. He or she would assess its usefulness and express an opinion on the likelihood of success. The decision to approve or deny carried on up through the HQ chain of command, which paralleled that of the region. Invariably at some point along the way, somebody would decide to call a meeting so all participants could discuss the issue. The result was a road trip – four hours of driving (Montreal to Ottawa return), a gruelling two-hour lunch, and a few hours of socializing, catching up with old friends, assurances all around that the matter was enjoying everyone's fullest attention, and a passel of congratulations for all the effort expended. Six months later nothing had happened, but the plan was under active consideration, all have added their minutes to the file, which was expanding like so much pent-up flatulence. And we were all busy, busy, busy.

Even superficial contact with the Service quickly reveals the constricting power of its serpentine bureaucracy. When Mitel Corporation, a Kanata-based firm that develops leading-edge telecommunications systems, reported its suspicions that the Vietnamese government was conspiring with one of its employees to steal sensitive technologies, it found CSIS unable to help. Said security chief Darell Booth, "Frankly, I don't understand how they can work, the way they are set up with all that red tape."[41]

Notwithstanding the multi-layering of this house of cards, action and decision occured in much the same fashion as in the old days. The working level initiated and implemented; senior management authorized and advised – which begs the question: what did middle management do? Ostensibly, it supervised; a rather generic, nondescript activity. In practice, the term "middle manager" deserves pride of place in the pantheon of oxymorons. Middle managers are denied the authority to take meaningful decisions, and their function is not to go out and participate in operational work – thus the predicament of finding them some avenue through which to contribute, as opposed to merely obstructing those who work from contact with those who decide. This challenge confounds all large, bureaucratic organizations, not just government, and certainly not just intelligence services.

The war was an extraordinary time, one that Smiley recalls with a mix of remorse and relief. It was a time that le Carré missed, but about whose lore he would have been versed, having been fourteen when it ended. The ascendancy of the Mastons over the Smileys was a post-war phenomenon. If the world was not a simpler place, they would certainly treat it as such. Purpose would surrender to perpetuation. Victory ceased to be an objective because the new war was so ambivalent. What constituted a win? The spies recruited for World War II understood that they would give up the game once the war ended. For the post-war spies, the game was the thing. The grand irony of *Call for the Dead* is that the mastermind behind the entire affair turns out to be Dieter Frey, a Jew from Dresden who served in Smiley's anti-Nazi network. A socialist hoping for a better world, Dieter has remained in the East after the war.

Smiley has an epiphany that it was Elsa Fennan who was under the control of the East Germans, not her husband, and that he wrote his own letter of denunciation to provide a means for contacting British security. He fabricates circumstances whereby she and Dieter will arrange to meet. Under surveillance, they sit side by side at the theatre, their usual spot for surreptitious contact. When Dieter realizes he is in danger of discovery, he murders Elsa to ensure her silence. He then flees, but is confronted by Smiley on Battersea Bridge and, in a confrontation reminiscent of Holmes and Moriarty at Rickenbacher Falls, is pushed into the fog-shrouded Thames. Convinced that Dieter could have killed him instead, Smiley concludes that he "had remembered their friendship when Smiley had not."[42] This scene is an effective metaphor for the Cold War as it was: old confreres who had once stood as brothers-in-arms now prepared and sometimes forced to do unspeakable violence to one another.

Through the remorse that Smiley feels at killing Dieter comes the bitterness over how the communist vision has been so savagely deformed in implementation. Of Dieter, Smiley says, "He was one of those world-builders who seem to do nothing but destroy: that's all."[43] Whatever good Dieter set out to accomplish has been distorted and bent beyond recognition. Indeed, that is the irony of the communist experiment. An ideology conceived with the best of intentions, it was hijacked and perverted along the way. Dieter was largely Smiley's creation, his best agent. He spent his formative spy years working for the British, going over in adulthood to the side that promised a better, more-certain future. The Soviets were least likely to permit German resurgence or, thanks to their ideological rigidity, make expedient compromises. Stalin's preparedness to conspire with Hitler was excused as a reaction to implacable Western hostility. If Smiley begot Dieter, then Dieter begot Mundt. Smiley finds it "odd to think of

Mundt as Dieter's pupil ... It was as if Dieter's brilliant and imaginative tricks had been compressed into a manual which Mundt had learnt by heart, adding only the salt of his own brutality."[44]

Le Carré was educated in the English public school system, at Sherborne, and went on to teach at Eton after completing his university studies at Oxford and Berne. The public school is one of the most venerable, if not always venerated, of Britain's upper-class institutions. It is where those of breeding are groomed with the superior education that will secure them their destiny in the higher echelons of society. Birth preordains much in this nation still very much conscious of bloodlines. And while le Carré insists that his dictatorship over England would see the abolition of the public school system, he admits that "like all good hypocrites I've sent my children to public school. But I just wish it was not there."[45]

Carne School, the setting for *A Murder of Quality* (1962), has sufficient reason to hold its chin at a haughty, aristocratic jut: it "had property, cloisters and woodworm, a whipping block and a line in the Doomsday Book – then what more did it need to instruct the sons of the rich?"[46] Its masters and old boys hold themselves in great esteem for being Carnians and, by extension, reserve a particular disdain for all who have been schooled elsewhere, especially if they have suffered the indignity of attending a grammar school.

This, at any rate, is their external pose. Terence Fielding, Carne's senior housemaster, hosting a dinner during his last Half before retirement, compares himself – not at all favourably – with a street sweeper: "Something is dirty, he makes it clean, and the state of the world is advanced. But I – what have *I* done? Entrenched a ruling class which is distinguished by neither talent, culture, nor wit; kept alive for one more generation the distinctions of a dead age."[47] This might be le Carré speaking from his own heart, and as is clear from his later works, he could just as well have written this passage about an intelligence officer as a teacher. Towards both professions he expresses incredulity at the possibility of their witnessing any tangible accomplishment. The institutions of intelligence and public education share the same elitist manners and exclusionary attitudes, content to meander along with the good manners of aristocracy. Both are insular, and their members –

those chosen few – regard that as a positive thing, for they know best and thus should be left to their own resources. The truth, expressed only in whispers, is that they realize their arrogance is undeserved, and they live in persistent terror that others will find out. Indeed, they are surprised that nobody has seen through the facade. The fear makes them dangerously protective.

Le Carré rejects the strictures of England's entrenched institutions. Having studied and taught at private schools and then served in the intelligence service, he "really had decided I did not like institutional life, and I wanted to be a freelance soul."[48] The creative mind runs every risk of going maddeningly stagnant in institutions. You see your own decline reflected in the dead-eyed apathy of colleagues and it is terrifying. Fielding sees it clearly when he says, "Carne isn't a school. It's a sanatorium for intellectual lepers. The symptoms began when we came down from University; a gradual putrefaction of our intellectual extremities. From day to day our minds die, our spirits atrophy and rot. We watch the process in one another, hoping to forget it in ourselves."[49] There is no fighting it: you either run or surrender. Le Carré ran, but he has been firing shots back over his shoulder ever since.

Carne is an effective metaphor for an intelligence organization. In both these institutions le Carré found a similar inbred, desultory reclusiveness. They share a sameness in the institutional rhythms to which they sway, recoiling from progress in the hallowed name of tradition. Fielding reflects, "We just got a little older. We made the same jokes, thought the same thoughts, wanted the same things. Year in, year out, Hecht, we were the same people, not wiser, not better; we haven't had an original thought between us for the last fifty years of our lives."[50]

Having undergone a transition similar to le Carré's, from institutional life to freelance existence, I deeply appreciate the differences. In my case, however, I never considered myself a freelancer misplaced in an institution. I've often felt misplaced since being cut loose from the secure tethers of the institution and trading a lifetime of guarantees for uncertainty. The institution automatically issues a paycheque every two weeks. The freelancer constantly scrambles for assignments and is paid only when a designated task is satisfactorily completed. The institution is complacent in terms of quality. The freelancer must validate his or her worth every time out. The institution clings to its people, if for no other reason than that they're there. The freelancer hangs unprotected out on a very unstable limb.

"Absolutely secure people are idiots," says writer and semiotician Umberto Eco. "Insecurity is the key to an honest job."[51] Our government bureaucracy stands uncomfortably close to the old Soviet economic model: show up for work, get paid, do nothing abnormally stupid, and be assured of a job for life. Incentive and censure are essentially unknown. Trying to stave off falling victim to the idiocy of security is a losing battle. It is not that institutions attract only idiots, but they do shelter those they have attracted from the ceaseless winds of productivity. Freelance souls, of necessity, sustain a nicely destabilizing sense of urgency.

The great pinata of institutional life is the pension plan: whack away long enough at a career and it bursts open with dole for the rest of your life. The long countdown to retirement begins almost immediately. Under the RCMP pension, to which all ex-members of the force within CSIS were entitled, retirement could come after twenty years' service. The rest of us were governed by the so-called eighty-five factor: we qualified for our pension when our age and years of service equalled eighty-five. In my case, that meant putting in thirty years, at which point I would have been fifty-five.

Pension is a daily topic of conversation, as casual a refrain as the weather. "How much more time do you have to put in?" It was interchangeable with "What's new? How're you doing?" "Just fifteen years to go, and you?" I found it debilitating, at barely thirty years of age, to have no milestone on the horizon grander than getting to the end of my working days. Our battle cry to cover every contingency was "It's all pensionable time." Got to track down a misfiled piece of paper – it's all pensionable time. Backlogged on filling out monthly time sheets and submitting overtime claims – it's all pensionable time. Spent a week in bed with the flu – it's all pensionable time. That was the spirited attitude that infused every job. Of course, there were a select group of flyers designated by some unseen force on high for upward mobility. For the rest of us, forty wasn't the professional prime, a time for experience to be parlayed into promotion. It was an age at which to calculate the annuity you would have to supplement whatever new interests you could pursue. And if it didn't amount to enough, there was always the option of staying with the institution and putting in ... more pensionable time.

The action in *A Murder of Quality* surrounds the killing of the wife of a Carne teacher. Stella Rode has remarkably predicted her own murder just days before it happens, sending a plea for help to Miss Ailsa Brimley, editor of the *Christian Voice*, to which she subscribes, for no other reason than that she cannot think of anywhere else to turn. The *Voice* is just that kind of publication. It reflects a gentle spirit and treats, and is treated by, its readers as family. Stella fears for her life, she writes, at the hands of her husband, Stanley. Brimley, who worked with Smiley during the war, appreciates the danger of discarding intelligence and takes the note seriously. Assuming that Stella will have contacted the police herself if that is her preferred course, she realizes that she will have to go another route if she is to be of assistance. She calls upon Smiley, the only non-police officer she knows who might be able to help. He agrees to contact Fielding, whose acquaintance he made through his brother, another wartime counterpart. Via Fielding, Smiley hopes to be able to surmount the motes and battlements that Carnians have so carefully erected around themselves and their institution. Again, the parallel with intelligence is striking. Carne is a world loath to admit outsiders, prone to distrust them, prepared to expect lesser behaviour from those not of the fraternity, and thus reluctant to answer to them. The division between town and gown, as the expression goes, is comparable to that between overt and covert. The comment of the very competent local police inspector Rigby – that "neither side knows nor likes the other. It's fear that does it, fear and ignorance"[52] – apply equally to both situations.

Unlike so many of the staff at Carne, Rode is not an old boy. Worse still, he previously taught at undistinguished Branxome Grammar. This background makes both him and his wife rather unsound – she especially, for she makes no effort to assimilate Carnian ways. She worships at the town chapel, while he turns Church of England to further his career, to make himself more socially acceptable, and, as much as possible, to obliterate his unseemly antecedents. Smiley is overcome with compassion for Rode because he "had tried so hard – he had used Carne's language, bought the right clothes, and thought as best he could the right thoughts, yet remained hopelessly apart, hopelessly alone"[53] – not unlike the intelligence officer operating in a hostile foreign land.

In the eyes of the local chief constable, himself a Carnian, the folly of bringing a grammarian to Carne goes a long way to explain the murder. "Experiments never pay, do they? You can't experiment with tradition," he asserts. "Like Africa. Nobody seems to understand you can't build society overnight. It takes centuries to make a gentleman."[54] We never learn his reaction when Rode is proven innocent and Smiley shows that the motive for Stella's murder derives from a prevalent, yet unspoken, peccadillo common to all-male public schools and prisons.

As it turns out, she was a miserable and ruthless individual who delighted in gleaning gossip about other people's vulnerabilities and then tormenting them with her knowledge and the threat of exposure. Fielding, the consummate Carne insider, has suffered the disgrace of having his affections for a young boy at another school result in his dismissal many years earlier. He has succeeded in hushing up the matter, and a friend gives him the appointment at Carne. However, when Stella learns about it and holds it over him, he becomes fearful of the consequences of publicity and resolves to kill her. He has been forced, as well, into killing his own head boy, Tim Perkins, because, desperate at the prospect of failing the term, he has gone into Rode's writing case and cheated on his exams. Fielding's excuse depends upon nobody having seen inside the case, for he will claim to have himself seen the murder weapon in that very case, a damning piece of evidence against Rode. However, Perkins knows that it was not there, thus poking a huge hole in Fielding's story.

There is no espionage element in *A Murder of Quality*. It is more a straightforward murder mystery. That Smiley has been a spy is his way into the affair, since it provides his connection to Brimley and Fielding. It also makes him a credible investigator (unlike so many of literature's amateur sleuths), and his link to Fielding causes him to be held in higher esteem by Carnians than an ordinary policeman such as Rigby.

With these two novels, le Carré established his touch with plot and character. He showed himself to be deft at crafting an effective thriller, and he developed what would be his most enduring figure in George Smiley. What he had yet to do was to lay claim to his own unique domain. That would come with his next novel, in which he ventured down espionage's most secretive passage – not the protected corridors of classified information, but through the underbrush of the spy's mind, the barely acknowledged place where spies question and wonder.

CHAPTER THREE

Out in the Cold

Germany occupied a singular place in the geography and psychology of the Cold War. "No other country had the line between East and West running through its middle. Germany was the divided centre of a divided Europe. Berlin, Germany's once and future capital, was the divided centre of the divided centre," writes Oxford historian Timothy Garton Ash.[1] It was divided first into four occupied zones and then into two when the Americans, British, and French consolidated their territory under a single currency in 1948. The Soviets responded in October 1949 by officially proclaiming the German Democratic Republic. This action resulted in a new Maginot line, a new European standoff, and the most flagrant point of friction between American and Soviet forces. On 7 April 1952, Stalin told a Kremlin meeting of senior Soviet officials and East German leaders, "The line of demarcation between West and East Germany must be seen ... not as a simple border but a dangerous one."[2]

The West German economy was flourishing on Marshall Plan money. The population was thriving under a new regime that refuted Germany's authoritarian past in favour of democracy and tolerance for nonconformity. West Berlin was developing into a vibrant and decadent international city. Quite the opposite was happening across the street in East Berlin, where the Soviet Union established a tight grip over its territory. It inserted and propped up a communist government that allowed for no dissent. It would rehabilitate East Germany as it saw fit, expunging the Nazi past and ensuring that Germans would never again pose a threat to Mother Russia.

The bright lights of the Kurfurstendam were proving irresistible to so many in the East that huge numbers of people fled over the dividing line. As Soviet ambassador Mikhail Peruvkhin ruefully conceded, the "uncontrolled border ... prompts the population to make a comparison between both parts of the city, which unfortunately, does not always turn out in favor of Democratic [East] Berlin."[3] To staunch the hemorrhage, the Soviets erected the Berlin Wall on 13 August 1961, creating what became the most enduring symbolic – as well as physical – barrier of the Cold War. A latter-day incarnation of the great fortifications of the Middle Ages, the wall, with its stolid harshness – its cinder blocks and razor wire and floodlights and guard towers – represented the permanent intractability of the superpower standoff. Unlike earlier walls, the one in Berlin served, not to keep hungry invaders out, but to keep a captive populace in.

Many, on both sides of the wall, were distressed at the concretization of the division of Germany. They held out the hope that a rehabilitated Germany would eventually be reunited, something that seemed far less likely the further the Soviets went toward dividing it. Among some West Germans who had opposed Hitler, East German communists enjoyed legitimacy in recognition for their having been at the forefront of the anti-Nazi movement. Therefore there was a reservoir of political and financial assistance from the Western side. Conversely, many in the East felt trapped by circumstance and geography. Having expected that a post-Nazi Germany would be a free Germany, they were anxious to do what they could to give advantage to the West. Thus did Berlin become the great souk of the intelligence profession. It was, in le Carré's words, "thronging with second-rate agents: intelligence was discredited and so much a part of the daily life of Berlin that you could recruit a man at a cocktail party, brief him over dinner and he would be blown by breakfast. For a professional it was a nightmare: dozens of agencies, half of them penetrated by the opposition, thousands of loose ends; too many leads, too few sources, too little space to operate."[4] Says Magnus Pym of Berlin in *A Perfect Spy*, "What a cabinet full of useless, liquid secrets, what a playground for every alchemist, miracle-worker, and rat-piper that ever took up the cloak and turned his face from the unpalatable constraints of political reality!"[5]

The East German Ministry of State Security had two essential components: the domestic side, known commonly as the Stasi and the external, also the Stasi, but distinguished under the German acronym for Main Intelligence Directorate, HVA. The Stasi was a fearsome, pervasive organization, made up, according to statistics from 1989, the last year of the GDR, of 90,000 full-time employees (of whom less than 5,000 were HVA) and 170,000 unofficial collaborators, or conscious sources. Of the latter, 110,000 were regular informants. In perspective, one in fifty adult East Germans had direct links to the secret police.[6] Consequently, "the Stasi lives up to its reputation for being everywhere and watching everyone," writes Ash in *The File*, his memoir about being the target of Stasi interest.[7]

Five unofficial collaborators, or IMS in the German shorthand, were tasked against Ash, who lived in East Berlin for ten months in 1980 while working on his Oxford doctorate. As his interests carried him beyond the strict confines of his research on Berlin under the Nazis and into the taboo precincts of contemporary dissidence, the authorities suspected that he might be a British agent or at least a source. Though he was not supplementing his studies with spying, he was doing something almost as threatening: publishing critical articles in the *Spectator* under a pseudonym, about which the Stasi never learned.

When the GDR disintegrated and was absorbed into a united Germany, the government opened up its files to public scrutiny. All citizens could apply to see what information had been recorded against them. Ash obtained his file and discovered who among his intimates had been informants, who had given every appearance of being a friend, only to pass along whatever they had learned or surmised about him to a Stasi officer. He found their general coverage of his activities fairly good. But "[s]ome of the small details are wrong. The interpretation is paranoid."[8] It is in the minutest of details and twists of interpretation that suspicion is aroused and innocence becomes perfidious.

Soviet interpretations of intelligence were certainly no less paranoid. The documentary evidence smuggled out of the KGB archives by Vasili Mitrokhin when he defected to the British in 1992 paints a picture of a regime governed by institutional paranoia. Notwithstanding the volume of information being passed over by Kim Philby and the other Cambridge spies in the time leading up to and following the outbreak of the Second World War, "Stalin's understanding of British policy was so distorted by conspiracy theory that no amount of good intelligence was likely to enlighten him."[9] In fact, right through 1944 these most committed of spies "were to be seriously suspected by the Centre of being double agents controlled by British intelligence simply because their voluminous and highly classified intelligence sometimes failed to conform to Stalin's conspiracy theories."[10]

Soviet paranoia was not exclusively a feature of Stalinism. Between 1981 and 1984 residencies were ordered by the Centre to gather intelligence in support of the expectation that the United States was planning a nuclear first strike. Dubbed Operation Ryan, it tied up both the KGB and the GRU in a futile quest for information that did not exist because the plan did not exist. It was "a delusion which reflected both the KGB's continuing failure to penetrate the policy-making of the Main Adversary [the United States] and its recurrent tendency toward conspiracy theory."[11]

As far as interpretation goes, it is here that genuine, unintentional harm may be done. We would boast about being paid to be suspicious as if only we truly knew how pervasive subterfuge and treachery were. I fear that my interpretations probably tended at times to be as paranoid as those to which all other IOs were inclined. How could it have been otherwise? Intelligence work is premised on endeavouring to expose that which the most precautions are taken to keep secret. To every vagary you encounter, you can impute something devious. In every act, you strain to find malice. You cannot perform counter-intelligence work with any degree of proficiency unless you learn to think like a conspirator, focus your eye until it adjusts to the flash-pop of inconsistency, and tune your ear to the false quaver of equivocation. I suspect first, absolve later – it's instinct. And it is entirely in keeping with the demands of investigating and exposing espionage.

You deliberate incessantly over motive. And in the end, you come up with something nefarious. Why? Because you so very much want to. That's right – *you want to*. You know it's out there if only you can detect the hair's weight off balance in the scale between truth and falsehood. Properly conducted, espionage is observed by no uninvolved witnesses and leaves behind no forensic traces. Nothing need be stolen: papers can be photocopied and replaced, a verbal exchange can suffice, a high-speed burst of encrypted radio signals may be broadcast. A chalk mark or a blast of graffiti on a wall may be the only physical evidence that a spy has something to pass to his or her handler. Or a pre-arrangement has them meeting on an ascending or descending date during any designated month at quarterly intervals at locations that are visited once and never after. To catch a spy, you rely on defector information, confessions, allegations of varying reliability, and intensive investigation to follow up on every conceivable lead. Even after all available sources and methods have been exhausted with the utmost care and integrity, invariably you still come away convinced that something has been missed, that somehow more should have been done. Guilt and innocence know boundaries; suspicion is infinite.

During the Cold War, Canada's Department of External Affairs (as it was then known) had a list of scheduled countries – primarily those of the East bloc, as well as China and Cuba – to which travel or contact with citizens was restricted for government employees occupying positions requiring a security clearance. The personal history form included the question, "Have you ever visited or had contact with officials of a scheduled country?" If yes, the details were to be specified.

Only a few months on the job and still convinced that I was the shield guarding the free world, I received the file of a veteran of some twenty years in the public service whose "top secret" clearance was up for renewal. It was a rush job because she needed topping up prior to being assigned to a new post. To the question concerning travel to or contact with scheduled countries she responded, "I don't know what a scheduled country is, but any travel/contact in which I might have engaged would have been on behalf of the Government of Canada." When I think back on this response – look at it in print here – it seems so innocuous – an offhand attempt at humour; or, at most, an insolent swipe at the intrusiveness of the security screening process; an expression of arrogance from one accustomed to sipping cocktails with the mighty, ministers, deputy ministers, and the like, or scurrying about in response to the needs of her superiors, not troubling herself with the base queries of simple-minded and unrefined police types (there is no shortage of such attitudes in le Carré).

At the time, however, it set my mind sizzling over the hidden meaning behind such a response. How could a long-serving bureaucrat who had been through the process before not know what a scheduled country was? It didn't make sense. Was she hiding something? Not likely. A straight no would have been the logical answer in that event. But maybe she couldn't resist the temptation to be too clever. Was she simply trying to make a point by showing contempt for csis? Was she trying to show me up? That was not a good idea, for it suggested an unhealthy attitude towards the seriousness of security in general, not a good trait for a woman with potential access to top-secret material. Surely it was my duty to intercede and help her improve her attitude and awareness of security risks, or at any rate, educate her about the government's practice of naming scheduled countries and its policies towards them. Another alternative was to grin indulgently at her petulance, sign off on the form, which gave me no other cause for concern, and move along – not likely.

My recommendation was that security clearance be withheld until such time as she could demonstrate an awareness of what constituted a scheduled country. Without an appropriate clearance, she would be frozen wherever she was. I argued in my report that it constituted a danger to national security to have senior personnel who could not recognize a potentially hostile state, let alone know the appropriate behaviour when faced with an official from such a country, an official likely to be interested in learning – by hook or by crook – Canadian secrets. My supervisor upheld my decision.

So had I contributed anything to protecting Canada? Well, I'll never really know. Most likely, I just reacted badly – vindictively, even – towards someone guilty of nothing more than boredom. Faced with the mindless task of filling out one of the infinite number of forms a bureaucrat fills out in the course of a day, she had tried to keep from going insane by amusing herself. At a later time in my career, I might have done the same. But when this incident occurred, I was sincere in my concerns. I was adhering to policy. I was being earnest. Innocence comes hard to the guilty mind. Because there is always something hidden in the secret world, we anticipate double-dealing in the overt. Like a little boy in the woods, we cannot resist giving the topsoil a good kick in order to tramp through what lies below.

An early briefing that new entrants to the Service receive from Internal Security includes this golden rule: "If it looks too good to be true, it is." In a world where catch phrases pass for philosophy and fortune-cookie writers masquerade as gurus, this is a useful aphorism. It is apropos of everything. If you're chatting up a girl in a bar and she's too anxious to take you home to bed, she could be a hostile agent on a mission to compromise you. Young and impressionable, I came away so paranoid that I feared compromise every time I made eye contact with a woman. On the other hand, I was unmarried and could hardly be blackmailed for a conquest I would eagerly boast about back at the office. We were cautioned to be on guard against everyone. Any person you meet who seems curious about you may be gathering information to prepare a character assessment for the files of an enemy service. Don't give up too much; always be circumspect. Someone who asked too many questions was an obvious threat; someone who asked too few required greater caution, for he or she was obviously more cunning. A financial or commercial opportunity that promised unparalleled returns could be less than legitimate and was to be avoided at all costs. When illegal drugs appeared at a party, even though you might not partake, you were advised to leave. Actually, you were advised to report the incident, but I doubt that anyone ever did. In most instances, I doubt whether anyone left either. Every wrong number to my unlisted home phone sounded like a finely executed attack. Was this any way to live?

When every good encounter is greeted with the suspicion that it is somehow *too good*, no encounter is taken at face value. When every conversation is pressed through a tight filter of mistrust, when you are constantly wary of another's motives, you never achieve intimacy. This is the debilitating cold to which the spy is consigned even when living on friendly ground. To compensate, the relationships you cultivate within the Service become forcedly intimate. How else could it be? We all gravitate to those from whom we can expect understanding and empathy, with whom we can be most at ease. Because we find companionship within the intelligence fraternity, the isolation is inadvertently enhanced. In time your ties outside become more tenuous. When you cease to know any other way, what is most familiar seems to be most reliable. Unless you are drawn back from the cold, you will retreat further and further into it, until the way back is totally obscured as in a blizzard.

The Spy Who Came in from the Cold (1963) established le Carré as a major writer and provided him the wherewithal to leave the intelligence service. He was, however, not compelled to leave. Though the book clearly presented an impression contrary to how his superiors would have wanted the service to be seen – if it needed to be seen at all – he says that they "seemed able to live with it. They were broadminded, you see. They were sweet."[12]

Graham Greene applauded the novel with a cover blurb: "The best spy story I have ever read." Without a doubt, it still stands among le Carré's best works. Anthony Cave Brown asked Sir Stewart Menzies his opinion of the book. "'That fellow,' declared 'C,' 'knows something.' What John le Carré knew, 'C' did not say."[13] Philby, however, dismissed the plot as "basically implausible."[14] This is one of the few points upon which le Carré might have found common ground with Philby, as he himself concedes, "The story was entirely imagined. I knew very little about the kind of spying I was describing. I had never been in East Berlin, let alone East Germany. I was certain from what I had seen of our intelligence services that they possessed neither the wit nor the ruthlessness to mount such a fiendishly ingenious operation." He went on to relate that a senior officer in the SIS remarked that it was "about the only bloody double-agent that ever worked."[15]

The first unsolicited operational proposal I ever contemplated was to stage a double-agent scheme. I was inspired by the knowledge that most of the great spies have been walk-ins, people who have presented themselves to opposition intelligence services and volunteered their secret knowledge and access. For all the hours devoted to developing profiles of potential agent recruits, few cold approaches bring success. Even the best IOs rarely recruit anyone; by understanding their targets, they pick out those likely to be amenable to recruitment and make themselves accessible – most often through access agents, those friends of the target willing to spy on them – in the event that they will want to make contact. It's good for your humility to realize that those who come over have invariably convinced themselves to jump before you ever came along.

I was working the China desk at the time. My idea was to contrive a situation that would see a CSIS member of Chinese heritage initiate an approach to the Chinese Embassy. The benefits for us would be derived from learning who would be assigned to handle the double and the tradecraft they would employ. By analyzing the queries they put, the information they most sought, we would gain insight into the areas where they placed emphasis, and in analyzing what they needed to know, we might be led to people supplying them with information on subjects about which they expressed no curiosity. Furthermore, controlled doubles offer a ready conduit for disinformation. The plan was, I thought, well conceived and relatively sophisticated. My unit head read it once and scrawled across the last page, "Good idea. Should never see the light of day." And it didn't.

Admittedly, the risks in dangling a double are considerable. Whenever you send double agents out, you can never be entirely sure how they will come back. If they possess enough information you don't want leaked, any deviation from the script is dangerous. If they're blown and that fact is successfully masked, the whole affair can be turned to the advantage of the ostensible target. So much of the operation has to be improvised along the way that you can never be sure of the course it will follow in the end. Furthermore, there was no imperative for effecting such an operation at that time. If discovered, it could have been interpreted by the Chinese as a provocation, the repercussions of which were difficult to predict: a cancelled agricultural or high-tech sale, scotched trade talks, interrupted diplomatic contacts. Our spy initiatives simply fell behind such concerns. It has been reported that a joint CSIS–RCMP probe into Chinese intelligence activities and their links to Asian criminal gangs was terminated in 1997 after two years because "CSIS anticipated political resistance." The newspaper article noted, "Prime Minister Jean Cretien has poured a great deal of energy and political capital into cultivating improved trade links with China, and CSIS managers worried that news of the project would draw his ire."[16] CSIS director Ward Elcock denies political interference, saying the study – known as Sidewinder – was scrapped because material that was originally taken as fact proved to be mere allegation.[17] Other, unnamed sources, however, insist it was "so controversial that it was watered down and rewritten before a sanitized version was circulated to other government agencies."[18] Furthermore, the RCMP reportedly does not accept the revised report as submitted by CSIS.[19]

Another double proposal during my time involved giving a member some information taken from an obscure foreign military journal and reprinted on Department of National Defence stationery bearing a "top secret" caveat. The member would walk in to the target embassy and hand the document over as an indication of the intelligence at his disposal. The proposal was referred to Legal Branch for an opinion on, of all things, the legality of misrepresenting previously published material as a government document. Reading the law with all the care of a particle physicist at a microscope, the lawyer decreed that we could not undertake the operation because it would have us infringing copyright.

The IO who drew up the plan exploded: "Who's gonna complain?"

"That's not the point," the lawyer sniffed, looking down his nose all the while at his Gucci loafers. "The csis Act expressly forbids the Service from engaging in *any* illegal acts in carrying out its official duties. Copyright infringement is an illegal act."

"I guess you're right," replied the IO in a tone of sweet agreement. "Besides, we would also have been guilty of rape ..."

The lawyer deigned to make eye contact, looking perplexed.

"... 'cause if this had worked, we'd have fucked them." With that, the IO got up and walked out not looking back.

The Spy Who Came in from the Cold is an intensely sophisticated and dense book. The plotting is exact, all the ingredients blended together as subtly as in a delicately simmered sauce. However, in terms of reality, the novelist – as he admitted – may have outsmarted himself by devising an operation of higher complexity than most intelligence managers would ever have the confidence to authorize, let alone conceive and commit to paper, not to mention carry to fruition. For this operation to succeed, not only would all the clues so assiduously laid have to be found, but – and this is more problematic – they would depend upon a refined interpretation if they were to have their intended effect.

Alec Leamas watches helplessly as Karl Riemeck, the star and last surviving agent from his network, is shot down just yards short of the final barrier at the checkpoint between East and West Berlin. His death is the work of Mundt, last seen fleeing London in the wake of the Fennan case (*Call for the Dead*). He has come out well from that fiasco and risen to deputy director of operations at Abteilung headquarters. Bitter and weary, Leamas returns to London, where Control, the head of British intelligence, offers him the opportunity for one last mission, one last expedition into the cold: to eliminate Mundt. He agrees and begins the process of fabricating a legend that has him leaving the service under a

cloud of missing funds, impoverishment, and frequent drunken-
ness – all this to attract the attention of the opposition, who will
read in his behaviour the signs of a desperate man ready to cash
in on the only commodity left in his possession: his secrets. The
problem facing agents in building a legend is that it becomes their
life; consequently, their life becomes the legend. They must
always bear in mind the probability of being observed and must
therefore always buttress the facade they have made for themselves. Doing so entails an inhuman capacity for solitude, control,
and awareness. No human contact, no relationship, is – or, rather,
is supposed to be – shared above the level of the lie. The psychological torment of such an existence is excruciating: the spy "must
protect himself not only from without but from within, and
against the most natural of impulses; though he earn a fortune,
his role may forbid him the purchase of a razor, though he be
erudite, it can befall him to mumble nothing but banalities;
though he be an affectionate husband and father, he must under
all circumstances withhold himself from those in whom he should
naturally confide."[20]

The most sustainable, and therefore the best, cover is the one
closest to reality. One fabricated out of whole cloth will not stand
up to the scrutiny of opponents who, like yourself, look askance
at every approach. Don't send someone who can't hold liquor to
strike up a conversation in a bar with a boozer. Don't take a man
who's never suffered losses and pose him as disgruntled. Don't
give a woman a background she can't discuss proficiently.

In a moment of concern for Alec's plight, Control says, "We
have to live without sympathy, don't we? That's impossible of
course. We act it to one another, all this hardness; but we aren't
like that really, I mean … one can't be out in the cold all the time;
one has to come in from the cold … d'you see what I mean?" To
which Leamas can only reply, "I can't talk like this, Control."[21]

Of course he can't, because Control is right, and if Leamas
thinks too much along these lines, he won't be able to steel himself
to the mission at hand. The sad fact is that once you pretend at
hardness for so long, you do become like that – not really, maybe,
not at the furthest extremes, but in all the recognizable ways, in
all the ways you dare reveal. Often as you remind yourself that
it's a game, you still don't know how to stop playing.

Not being impermeable, Leamas recklessly falls in love with Liz, a girl he meets at the library where he manages to get a clerical job following his dismissal from the service. An apparent complication is that she is a member of the Communist Party. But then, every association is a potential liability for a man headed on a solitary journey to an unknown destination. He cannot resist telling her that he may have to leave suddenly and that on no account is she to follow. Further, he reveals that there is someone with whom he must get even, but he will try to make his way back to her eventually. And he tells her all this on the night before he hits rock bottom, assaulting a grocer who has refused to extend credit and ending up in jail for three months.

Immediately upon his release, the opposition are convinced that Leamas is ripe for the plucking, and his recruitment is rushed as they attempt to cash in on his resentment. He agrees to go to The Hague for debriefing. There the papers get wind of the news that a British agent has disappeared and report that he is wanted for violations under the Official Secrets Act. Leamas realizes that the story must have been leaked by Control and that he has been cut off, with no choice but to continue the journey to East Germany. Closing off the return bridge was not discussed with Leamas, but it has obviously been Control's plan from the first: the "terms had been too generous, he'd known that all along."[22] He has failed to take heed of the admonition that anything too good to be true, without exception, is. He has never been explicitly told how the scenario will play, but he has understood it implicitly, saying to Control, "I know how these things go – all offensive operations. They have by-products, take sudden turns in unexpected directions. You think you've caught one fish and you find you've caught another."[23] Indeed, this turns out to be the essence of the case.

On arrival in East Germany, Leamas is met by Fiedler, the Abteilung counter-intelligence interrogator supreme. There is nothing that he needs to withhold, his network having already been blown sky high, his agents exposed or dead. But Fiedler is convinced that the information known to Leamas is too extensive to have been collected solely by the agents about whom he is already aware. There must have been somebody even higher, and all the evidence aims a hair-trigger squarely at Mundt. The risks of openly alleging such a thing are not insignificant. Mundt has a considerable power base, and furthermore, Fiedler is a Jew, not a comfortable thing to be in the early post-Nazi German Democratic Republic. After some twists in the plot, Mundt is brought before a Presidium tribunal to answer for his crimes. Fiedler's evidence is damning, if circumstantial. He is troubled by the ease with which Mundt slipped out of Britain following the Fennan debacle. Fiedler contends that he was, in fact, arrested and that, faced with the choice of turning double or a long prison term for murder, he chose the former and has been a British spy ever since. Mundt's subsequent operational visits to the West have coincided with Leamas's depositing large sums of money in accounts meant for a very high level source whose identity has been kept from him. He demonstrates how every advance in Riemeck's career has been owed to Mundt and that he was ordered shot rather than captured because Mundt knew his arrest would result in his own exposure.

Meantime, Smiley is flitting about London tidying up on Leamas's behalf, settling his outstanding debts, introducing himself to Liz, and arranging for her to be taken care of financially. This action would appear to be an inexcusable sabotage of Leamas's cover. Together with the fact that Leamas has, in effect, told Liz that he would be leaving her suddenly, it forms the crux of Mundt's defence: that Leamas is a British plant working in conjunction with Fiedler to defame him and open the way for Fiedler to move up as his replacement. To Leamas's horror, Liz is lured to East Germany and forced to testify about their relationship.

Mundt succeeds in convincing the tribunal that Leamas's defection was a British put-up. For what is at worst complicity and at best a gross defamation of a loyal protector of the state, the tribunal will condemn Fiedler to death. In a wonderfully startling turn, this is revealed to be the objective of the operation all along: for Leamas to discredit Mundt by establishing what is the truth; for Liz to discredit Leamas; for Mundt to demonstrate all of this, thereby pointing the finger at Fiedler and eliminating him, while vindicating himself. It has been brought about by Fiedler's astute assessment that Mundt had indeed been turned prior to his return from London. The trial was needed to definitively absolve Mundt of all blemish of disloyalty and to dispose of Fiedler, thereby enhancing Mundt's ability to continue his deception.

The final danger comes when Mundt has to arrange for Leamas and, at his insistence, Liz to make their way over the Berlin Wall and in from the cold to the West. Only a brief gap can be pried open in the tight security perimeter with which the East has reinforced the wall. Leamas mounts the wall first, and while he is pulling Liz up, shots ring out and she is felled. This outcome was to be expected: with her knowledge, she represented an additional threat to Mundt's continued security. Instead of following the urgent voice of, among others, Smiley, Leamas goes to her on the East side and is himself shot down.

Le Carré gives a fascinating account of how he came to create the Leamas character. He was in the bar at the London airport when a "very rough-edged, kind of Trevor Howard figure" sat down beside him and ordered a large Scotch. He paid with several coins of sundry currencies. He drank up and left. Le Carré goes on, "I thought I picked up a very slight Irish accent. And that was really all, but there was a deadness in the face, and he looked, as we would have said in the spy world in those days, as if he'd had the hell posted out of him. It was the embodiment, suddenly, of somebody that I'd been looking for. It was he, and I never spoke to him but he was my guy, Alec Leamas, and I knew he was going to die at the Berlin Wall."[24]

The Spy Who Came in from the Cold is a work of profound disillusion. The supposed greater good to which individuals are so casually and callously sacrificed is so feebly defined as being – for all intents and purposes – non-existent, or at least unrecognizable. Leamas, thinking he is out to get Mundt, has identified with Fiedler, with whom he has assumed common cause. When he finally clues in on the truth that Mundt is London's man and Fiedler the threat, he adjusts his perspective and – albeit grudgingly – accepts the outcome. He tells Liz, "People who play this game take risks. Fiedler lost and Mundt won. London won – that's the point. It was a foul, foul operation. But it's paid off, and that's the only rule."[25] This is precisely how Fiedler summarizes the operation that has brought Leamas's supposed defection: "it was a good operation. It satisfied the only requirement of our profession: it worked."[26]

It is at this point that the novel is most radical: in the moral equivalency that it draws between spies on both sides of the Cold

War. Speaking hypothetically while still under the impression that Mundt is the operation's true target, Fiedler asks Leamas whether the British would kill him if the circumstances demanded. Leamas concedes that "it depends on the need." To which Fiedler replies, "We're all the same, you know, that's the joke."[27]

This observation put me in mind of a conversation I once had with someone who had been an informant for an East bloc service and had subsequently cooperated with Western intelligence. I asked him how interacting with our side differed from his relationship with the other. He laughed heartily, and taking a sip of the drink I had poured him, a bite of the lunch I had bought him, he said, "You behave exactly the same. It's as if you all study the same textbook. Make small talk, offer a drink, pay for a meal, pose a series of questions that are interesting for you in a clump of mundane questions that are meaningless. It's all the same."

One minute Mundt is the ruthless murderer of Samuel Fennan, and Fiedler the professional intelligence man correctly interpreting complex innuendo and circumstance to root out a dangerous traitor; the very next, Mundt is the treasured double agent desperately in need of protection, and Fiedler the menacing obstacle on the verge of liquidating a valued source. Fiedler is by design the more sympathetic character throughout. A Jew who survived the Nazis by fleeing to Canada during the war, he has returned to East Germany to build the Stalinist utopia in which he believes. The ruthless Mundt, a proven killer, whose open hatred of Jews suggests a Nazi bent, has nothing to recommend him except that *our* side has enough against him to coerce him into becoming *our* man. Nothing else matters. The relative merits of each individual are inconsequential. It is an apt metaphor for our willingness to forge allegiances with the nastiest dictators, never taking ethical soundings.

At the end of the affair, Leamas expresses angry contempt for his profession, asking rhetorically, "What do you think spies are: priests, saints and martyrs? They're a squalid procession of vain fools, traitors too, yes; pansies, sadists and drunkards, people who play cowboys and Indians to brighten their rotten lives."[28] He makes no distinction between his side and the other because, when all is said and done, he finds no distinction to make. Fiedler is an honourable man whose cause it is Leamas's duty to oppose. Mundt is a detestable man with whom he turns out to have been in league. Leamas goes on, "I'd have killed Mundt if I could, I

hate his guts; but not now. It so happens that they need him ...
They need him for the safety of ordinary, crummy people like you
and me."[29]

Le Carré has constructed a cynical, remorseless landscape that
depicts the Cold War of the time and projects an attitude that
would not prevail for many years to come. Cold War fatigue was
a long way off in 1963. Our spies were supposed to be good, theirs
bad. Ours would not commit murder, theirs would (Bond killed
but never murdered). Certainly, the rectitude of our side established our moral superiority. However, in *The Spy* Fiedler can
speak of believing in something, while Leamas finds the question
of faith unfathomable. For Fiedler's part, he cannot understand
how Leamas can fulfill his role without belief. Fiedler, who admits
being prepared to commit any atrocity so long as it advances the
communist cause, has faith that he is serving the common good,
that he is destined to improve society. The question, then, becomes
whether it is nobler to behave vilely for something than for nothing? Maybe the end can justify the means; maybe the means are
only defensible by their end. Espionage verges on the frighten-
ingly abstract. As Graham Greene argued, "the spy takes more
interest in the mechanics of his calling than in its ultimate goal –
the defence of his country. The 'game' (a serious game) achieves
such a degree of sophistication that the player loses sight of his
moral values."[30] East German spymaster Markus Wolf echoes
those sentiments: "Whatever my doubts about the system I served,
such a life of privilege, responsibility, and occasional fascination
would be hard for anyone to give up to campaign for change."[31]

If anything, le Carré's next offering, *The Looking Glass War* (1965),
was even more biting and condemnatory towards the Cold War
intelligence industry, prompting a former colleague to greet the
novelist at a dinner party with "You *bastard*! ... You utter bastard."[32] His is an uncompromising attack on the arrogant and
cold-blooded bureaucrats who are content to make martyrs of
others while nesting themselves snugly in the safety of secrecy
and the bonhomie of pretended hardships and the pretensions of
their second-rate clubs. The men of the Department, a faded
remnant from the war, are venal and inept – though they recognize neither trait in themselves – and frustrated at having run out
of combat. Once upon a time, twenty years earlier, during the war,

they handled their share of operations behind enemy lines, or so legend has it. Somehow – probably through sheer oversight and the propensity of bureaucracies, once given life, to live on in perpetuity – they have retained their brief to collect military intelligence. But they have had precious little to collect in recent times. They languish, usurped by the Circus, with their mandate for political espionage, an inflated budget, a chauffeur-driven fleet of cars, and a more reputable address.

Turf wars are as common between government departments as among dogs, where the last one to urinate on a fire hydrant wins. Jealousies over perceived sleights or encroachments are as consuming as the fear of a rival intruding on a marriage, reaching the point where the rivalry becomes reason enough to sustain the union, no matter how desultory and dissatisfying it is. The director of the Department, Leclerc, grudgingly acknowledges with regard to the Circus, "They've more money and more staff than we have. They do a bigger job. However, I doubt whether they do a better one. Nothing can touch our Research Section, for example. Nothing."[33] However, researchers are to intelligence what stewards are to air travel: hardly the macho glamour boys of the industry.

We in CSIS had a similar relationship with the RCMP as the one between the Department and the Circus, made all the more provocative by our shared roots. The annual report of the CSIS oversight committee, the Security Intelligence Review Committee (SIRC), for 1986–87 addressed the issue, concluding that "senior managers in both CSIS and the RCMP seem increasingly comfortable within their respective boundaries," while at the working level the "term 'healthy tension' has been used to describe the situation, but we think it would be even healthier if it were a little less tense."[34] Naturally, senior managers got along. Their careers were not tied to the fortunes of individual cases. As far as top RCMP officers were concerned, they had already achieved what advancement they could hope for, while senior CSIS managers were often parachute drops from other departments who had no intention of making a career in the Service. They gazed longingly on prizes elsewhere in the civil service – prizes they were most likely to attain by exhibiting cooperation, not by winning conflicts. Only among those who lived and breathed their case work did it matter how the work was divvied up. More recent reports suggest that the situation has not much improved over the years. Turf wars continue, and as a result, information is not readily shared between the two agencies. A 1998 SIRC report noted, "Police complain that CSIS agents do not share their information, while the spies complain the Mounties undermine their intelligence operations and sources by trying to bring CSIS evidence into court."[35] With regard to the Sidewinder case discussed earlier, SIRC reported that the RCMP ceased sharing documentation with CSIS because of their dissatisfaction with revisions the Service made to its original report concerning Chinese espionage activities.[36]

IOs tend to imagine themselves sophisticated, creative investigators, unbridled by paramilitary, command-structure clumsiness, and police as lead-foots who can't see farther than an arrest. In turn, cops deride the IOs' impotence, questioning the rationale behind interminable information collection culminating in nothing. Both sides are reluctant to share with the other for fear of losing control over a file. If a CSIS case is presumed criminal, it goes to the RCMP; if one of theirs touches upon national security, it comes to CSIS. Because the Service mandate is narrower than that of the RCMP, CSIS lives in greater fear of the police than vice versa: losing a case to the Service will not affect the RCMP's position, while CSIS is concerned that too much RCMP infringement could show it up as superfluous. This is precisely the shadow cast by the Circus over the Department. In our case, the problem is rooted in the RCMP's pain over the amputation of one of their divisions and the humiliation of being told they were incompetent to perform a task that had been theirs for forty years, and in CSIS adapting to new rules and tentatively placing down roots.

The Looking Glass War opens with a chillingly prescient scene. A commercial charter flight loaded with school children, bound from Dusseldorf, is anxiously awaited at a small airport in Finland by an Englishman of military bearing. Despite the blinding snow, he is not disconcerted when a delay is announced. He knows the plane will be late. He knows that it has inexplicably veered two hundred miles off course over the Kalkstadt region. He knows that it is fitted with a camera to snap air-to-ground surveillance photos of a Russian missile base reportedly under construction. Inconceivable? The fantastic imagination of a clever novelist seeking a plot device? Never would the lives of innocent civilians be endangered in so cavalier a fashion.

Or would they? David E. Pearson lists seventeen commercial airlines as having had CIA ties: Air America, Air Asia, Air Ethiopia, Braniff Airways, Bird Air, China Air Lines (Taiwan), Civil Air Transport, Continental Airlines, Evergreen Aviation, Fairways Corporation, Flying Tigers, Intermountain Aviation, Korean Flying Tigers, Page Airways, Pan American World Airlines, Southern Air Transport, and Transocean Air Lines. He identifies several national airlines that reportedly perform "special missions" for their governments, among them the Soviet Union's Aeroflot, Czechoslovak Air Lines, Cubana, Israel's El Al, Finnair, Lot Polish, Libyan Arab Airlines, and Korean Air Lines (KAL).[37] Of the last, he writes, "KAL served as an asset to the Korean Central Intelligence Agency (KCIA), which was established, designed, provisioned, and trained by the U.S. CIA in the early 1960s."[38]

This intelligence connection may have been the cause for tragedy on two occasions. On 20 April 1978 KAL902 out of Paris, bound for Seoul via Anchorage, strayed some three hundred miles into Soviet airspace, overflying the sensitive Kola Peninsula, home to the Northern Fleet, a nuclear submarine base, and eight air bases before it was fired upon by fighters and forced to land on a frozen lake. Two passengers were killed. This flight, Pearson writes, "was a major intelligence boon for the U.S. and allied intelligence services that followed it every step of the way. Every detail was known: when and where the airliner entered the Soviet territory, when the interceptors were scrambled and from which bases, what orders were given, by whom and using what channels, and when the orders were executed."[39] There was little fallout from this incident, presumably because of the low loss of life.

In the early morning hours of 1 September 1983 another KAL aircraft, flight 007 en route from New York to Seoul via Anchorage, wandered into Soviet airspace over the militarily sensitive Kamchatka Peninsula and Sakhalin Island. This time, when fired upon by Soviet interceptors, the plane crashed, killing all 269 aboard. At the time of its destruction, KAL007 was 365 miles off course and had flown through approximately 250 nautical miles of Soviet airspace. On the question of whether the crew of 007 had accidentally and unwittingly drifted off course or had deliberately penetrated Soviet air defences, Pearson concluded, "Not only is the number of coincidences, errors, acts of incompetence, and so on that an accidental model of the flight has to incorporate unacceptably high, but it would also be necessary to accept that all of these problems occurred in redundant, independent components of that system."[40] In other words, the navigation systems at the disposal of a Boeing 747 crew are so sophisticated as to make such a gross – and catastrophic – error next to impossible.

Journalist Seymour Hersh disputes the contention that navigational accuracy, sophistication, and redundancy makes pilot error almost inconceivable. Of the navigational systems aboard the Boeing 707 involved in the 1978 incident, he contends that "none of it [was] state-of-the-art, but more than adequate, if properly monitored,"[41] thereby implying that the crew was negligent. And as concerns the 1983 tragedy, he asserts, "to get as far off course as they did, the crew members must have had to ignore or rationalize many obvious clues that something was wrong."[42] His theory is that the crew did just this. He concludes that a series of innocent errors, followed by what can only be described as wanton negligence in failing to recognize those errors, sent flight 007 far off course. He finds no evidence to suggest the aircraft was performing an espionage task. Furthermore, he believes the Soviets legitimately failed to identify the plane as a civilian airliner.

To pursue the theory that 007 was deliberately off course: what would be the purpose of using a commercial passenger jet for espionage? Photo surveillance is unlikely, given the sophistication of existing satellite capabilities in this regard, not to mention the potential for severe embarrassment were the plane forced to land and such equipment discovered. Both Pearson and R.W. Johnson favour the possibility that 007 was being utilized as a probe to test Soviet radar and anti-aircraft responses in the area. During its flight it succeeded in inducing the Soviets to activate every electromagnetic transmitter in their arsenal over a four-hour period and a 7000-square-mile area, allowing American electronic intelligence monitors to determine the scope and nature of their air defence capabilities.[43] What is the importance of this data? Pearson explains: "The United States wants to know where Soviet radar stations and antiaircraft missile bases are located and how the Soviets will react if their air defenses are penetrated. We want to know the power, pulse rates, and frequencies of the radars, the procedures used in operating them, and the ranges at which aircraft flying at different altitudes come under surveillance. When a plane is detected, we want to know who talks to whom.

This information ... hopefully will also enable our bombers and missiles to evade Soviet air defences on the way to their targets."[44] As for the risk, the expectation was that the Soviets would never actually destroy a confirmed civilian airliner, as opposed to a military plane that attempted a similar penetration. If this was, in fact, what happened, the conceptualization of the mission was almost fantastically callous: 269 innocent civilians were flown unknowingly on a mission designed to trigger a military reaction.

Likewise in le Carré's novel, as when the hapless Korean aircraft drifted off course, MiGs are scrambled to investigate the intruder as it passes over the purportedly sensitive Kalkstadt region. They fly alongside for a time, only to peel off and allow it to proceed. Still shaken despite his safe arrival, the pilot tells the courier Wilf Taylor, the military man who has been awaiting him, that he won't ever undertake such an assignment again. He says, "It was OK when we just stayed on course photographing whatever there was; but this is too damn much, see?"[45] Without making so much as a passing concession to the rudiments of tradecraft, he disgustedly tosses Taylor the film canister.

Because of the bad weather, the airport is virtually deserted as Taylor leaves. He cannot even get a taxi. While he is walking to his hotel, a car bears down on him out of the swirling snow, striking and killing him. The film rolls down an embankment. Has Taylor been deliberately murdered? Is he simply the victim of an accident? Has the film been lost in the snow or recovered by hostile parties? What is going on in Kalkstadt?

Taylor's death is greeted with perverse elation by Leclerc, not so much out of brazen heartlessness but in expectation that the Department's status can only be enhanced since Taylor has proven important enough to kill. "Perhaps the Ministry will believe me now. Perhaps they'll finally accept we're an operational department," he muses while contemplating the fleet of cars that the minister will allocate him in light of the circumstances.[46]

With its recurring overlay of bureaucratic and administrative machinations on genuinely tragic operational misdirections, *The Looking Glass War* is le Carré's most blackly comedic writing. It is so, at any rate, to anyone who has worked in the intelligence community. Absolutely hilarious is a scene in which John Avery, on his first run abroad, to claim the body of the unfortunate Taylor, attempts to destroy some papers in his hotel room by burning them. The ashes clog the drain, and when he finally gets them washed down, he finds a brown stain etched into the enamel of the sink. He opens the window to allow gusts of freezing air to clear the smell just at the very moment the reception clerk knocks on his door.[47]

I know of a situation in which a long-time source was being introduced to a rookie handler in a hotel room and was determined to impress him with his grasp of tradecraft. He insisted on demonstrating for the handler the proper technique for destroying documents if they should ever be interrupted. Rather than dissuading him, the handler went along, perhaps in the interest of building rapport with the source, and followed him into the bathroom. There the source took a stack of papers and proceeded to set them alight. The flames created so much smoke that the smoke detector was triggered, emitting a shriek piercing enough to wake all but the deepest sleepers. Luckily for all concerned, they were able to silence the device with determined, frantic fanning. The meeting was quickly adjourned, and they escaped without having to explain to hotel personnel the acrid stench of fire left behind.

A pathetic craving for importance is what inspires the faded fantasists of the Department, who "would draft projects which were never submitted, bicker gently among themselves about leave, duty rosters and the quality of their official furniture, give excessive attention to the problems of their section staff."[48] Such is the typical, uneventful day of the average intelligence officer.

Not once did I ever hear of a manager volunteering that his or her section was overstaffed and that personnel might better deploy people elsewhere. Just the opposite was the case: managers battled with the intensity of sharks in a feeding frenzy, snapping up bodies whenever and wherever they could be found. Size of empire was a significant measure of status – size was often all that mattered. A large unit would give the manager the appearance of being important. After all, the logic goes, if a section wasn't important, it wouldn't be so big. To have an employee transferred out and not replaced was a definite sign of decline. Other managers would smell the blood in the water and agitate for the scraps; if a section could be stripped of one person, surely it could make do with two less. Access to secondary resources – vehicles overnight and on weekends, so that officers could theoretically be recalled to the office on a moment's notice, or cellular phones and beepers, premium items, the possession of which signalled the imminent communication of *something* – was, like conspicuous consumption, indicative of bureaucratic wealth.

Operational paperwork was always in heavy demand, especially when there was some element in the case that obviously precluded action. Soon after the demise of the Soviet Union, I was pursuing the investigation of a mysterious foreigner who was in contact with suspect Russian diplomats. Once we had succeeded in fully identifying him, background checks revealed that he had done jail time in Asia on drug and weapons related charges. All the indicators were that he would make for a most interesting conversation. It could prove very useful to find out what he was doing in Canada and, more specifically, what business he had with the Russians. Since Russian intelligence was a mandated target, we had every right to speak with people who met with suspected intelligence personnel. This individual, however, promised not to be routine, a prospect I found intriguing and exciting, but of which my supervisor was abjectly – and quite obviously – terrified.

I wrote up a standard report summarizing the information at our disposal and stating my intention to interview the subject. My boss looked it over and gave me the laudatory platitudes he used for all proposals of which he wanted no part. "Fabulous idea, really wonderful work," he puffed. His eyes were flickering uncontrollably around the room and he was licking his lips incessantly, unable to keep them moist. Little beads of sweat popped out along his receding hairline. "You make some excellent points about the potential for obtaining interesting intelligence."

Praise invariably foretold stall tactics, usually the forwarding of the report to HQ for its "input," even though it was within my boss's purview to authorize such routine activity as an interview. I was not proposing anything more intrusive, involved, or confrontational than that – a simple, friendly chat. The bottom line was that he wanted his signature to be buffeted from below by mine and from above by someone from HQ, so that blame could in no way settle on his head. By referring the matter to Ottawa, he could point to me as the initiator and to HQ as supporter in the event that anything backfired. At the same time, his signature would be visible to all, smack in the middle, should any glory attach to the initiative. Transferring paper to the HQ desk could be counted on to effect a delay of anywhere from three to six months as the higher-ups wrestled with the complexities of pre-emptive blame control. And who knew, by that time my boss might have been transferred or, better still, I might have been, thus making the whole mess moot. It was the classic cover-your-ass manoeuvre.

His forwarding comments were rather less positive than his oral comments. He blandly wrote, "Action held pending your evaluation. This interview could possibly result in operational benefits, but has degree of risk potential. Subject's background indicates low probability of cooperation and attention is drawn to criminal past. However, regional office will approach on your recommendation."

With the file safely at HQ and me doing busy work until a decision was taken, information came via another channel that the subject had left Montreal and was in, of all places, Moscow. My boss had a brainwave: write up a proposal that would have me flying there to interview the subject at the Canadian Embassy. With the Cold War over, this was a time when it was fashionable to imagine we might move so close to the Russians that our intelligence activities would no longer automatically be adversarial. My boss initiated the idea and put it on paper over his own name. Why? Because he knew that there wasn't a lightening-strike chance that HQ would approve sending an identified CSIS officer to Moscow on an operational assignment. But it was so boldly proactive to suggest such a thing that he would show himself to be operationally forward-thinking, yet in a way that would assuredly never be put to the test.

The victories and defeats preoccupying the intelligence mandarinate in *The Looking Glass War*, as in real life, do not involve engagement with the enemy but with the hierarchy its members are scrambling to ascend in competition with other mandarins. The pitch is steep and toeholds at a premium. Envy and competition are fierce. What becomes farcical is the indicators of success – access to secrets, subsistence allowances, allocation of staff and money, and availability of government Humbers with chauffeurs – in an environment supposedly consumed with the weighty responsibility of assuring national security.

Taylor's death gives each member of the Department "a moment's optimism, like a rise in pay."[49] Leclerc develops a particular spring in his step, hearing a call to action, though, as with an echo bouncing around a vast canyon, he cannot quite trace the source. But surely something big is up. After all, he has the vague-as-vapour report from Jimmy Gorton – whom, like everyone else, he distinguishes as "one of our best men" – in Hamburg that Russian rockets have been seen in Kalkstadt. That Gorton is in need of an operational coup to ensure the renewal of his contract is dismissed as irrelevant in the growing climate of threat. And what better confirmation than Taylor's killing? Undaunted by the hour at which he learns the sad news, Leclerc rushes to the office and ecstatically decides to create an ops centre and have a bed put in his office so he can monitor the situation around the clock. This information, too – that the director is sleeping in the office – will quickly circulate through the Department, further imbuing everyone with a sense of urgency.

Thus they are catapulted, like Alice, through the rabbit hole and into a fantastic Wonderland, where they "got so much into the way of expecting nothing but out-of-the-way things to happen, that it seemed quite dull and stupid for life to go on in the common way."[50] So enthralled have they become at the prospect of adventure that they summon all their resistance against wake-fulness for fear of ending the dream and returning to the other side of the looking glass (if metaphors may be combined from Lewis Carroll's two classic Alice tales). It becomes, then, a choice, not between sense and nonsense, but between common or extraordinary. This is the lure onward through the topsy-turvy world of illusion, where nothing is prescribed or constrained for having been named. Possibilities are endless and apt to encourage insupportable flights of fancy. (CSIS responded similarly when-ever given the opportunity. When the Gulf War broke out, for instance, emergency operation centres sprung to life across the country, kept open round the clock. Those assigned to staff them did not miss a CNN broadcast or a newspaper article. If the war spilled beyond Kuwait and across the Canadian prairies, we were standing on guard for thee.)

The minister is supportive of the Department's new crisis footing, especially of its determination not to share with the Circus. He, too, must be concerned with his place in the broader scope of government activity. However, he forbids the use of additional overflights. This order suits Leclerc fine, for it gives the Department a perfect excuse to mount the grand operation of infiltrating a man behind enemy lines – just like in the war. It even has a candidate in mind, Fred Leiser, a man it used back in the day. There was no reason why he should not be able to saddle up and ride again. War is war. Adrian Haldane is the only skeptical voice in the Department, but even he succumbs to the blind enthusiasm of the moment, not least of all when Leclerc appoints him to head Special Section, which will control the operation, designated Mayfly.

What drives the men is a desperately held desire to give themselves over to a faith and win back their self-esteem. These are the squalid fools about whom Leamas speaks. War promises ordinary people the occasion to partake in extraordinary moments as little else can. For Leclerc, Haldane, and Leiser it is the irresistible desire to recapture a past that was probably less than they recollect. The big wartime operation that involved Leiser in fact ended in failure, with his barely evading capture. For Avery, the only participant too young to have been in the war, Mayfly is a chance to play the war rules. He feels an enveloping glow of gratitude at being included in this exclusive cabal. He "thanked Leclerc, thanked him warmly, for the privilege of knowing these men, for the excitement of this mission; for the opportunity to advance from the uncertainty of the past towards experience and maturity, to become a man, shoulder to shoulder with the others, tempered in the fire of war; he thanked him for the precision of command, which made order out of the anarchy of his heart."[51]

But his wife, Sarah, sees through the wall of secrecy that Avery has built around his job, as if the fact of its being secret is proof enough of its significance. Even the tidbits he lets slip fail to convince her. Finally, she demands, "Are you a martyr, John? Should I admire you for what you're doing? Are you making sacrifices?" He replies, "It's nothing like that. I'm doing a job. I'm a technician; part of the machine." Further on in the exchange, she concludes, "Then you're not responsible, are you? Just one of the team. So there's no sacrifice."[52]

This comment points to the crux of a recurring criticism in le Carré about intelligence officers: their deft manipulation to avoid personal sacrifice or penalty, the moral vacuum in which they insulate themselves (and each other) from the consequences of their actions. Those who brave the more cluttered world beyond, such as Leiser and others yet to be discussed, are apt to be destroyed.

I can't claim innocence from these very sentiments. I participated in operations that implicated human sources who took
actual risks while I hid in the shadows. One source in particular,
who I'll call Doe, was an absolute marvel of reckless abandon. At
no time of my involvement, however, was I anything but safe and
sound – more than might be said for Doe.

He wanted money. He let it be known through channels that
he had every reason to expect would bring him to our attention,
in the grand tradition of those who, in effect, walk in. Our
approach was simple: an access agent already under control was
tasked to advise Doe that if he was serious about earning some
money, the agent "knew some people in the government who
would pay for the opportunity to speak with him." To anyone in
the business, this was a clear euphemism for "the local spooks
would like to chat." Doe agreed without hesitation. He was a
street-savvy and shrewd man with keen intuition for how to
survive and thrive, all talents refined in the harsh environment of
a dictatorship. Operating in Canada was a cruise for him.

For the first meeting, it was arranged that he would come to a
certain room at a downtown hotel at a designated hour. The
carefully selected room was positioned in such a way that all
approaches to the hotel could be watched from the window, but
it was obscured in such a way that those inside could not be
observed. Ten minutes after the appointed hour, he still hadn't
shown. The investigators began to get uneasy. They had thoughts,
not so much of Doe bailing out, but of his intentions having been
detected. A few more minutes passed, and his dark sedan was
recognized as it careened down the street and slid precariously
into a no-parking zone, its front wheels bouncing into the curb,
leaving the rear end of the car sticking out a good three feet. The
driver's door flew open and Doe flung himself out, dashing at
full gallop for the entrance. The investigators stayed by the window, uneasy that his haste might be precipitated by a fear of being
followed. The last thing on earth they wanted on their hands was
a defection. It occurred to one of them that the Son of Sam was
undone by a parking ticket he had got near the scene of one of
his killings, and that Doe may have made a casual, but ultimately
fatal, error if a vigilant meter attendant should happen past.
Arriving in the room, sweaty and breathless, but with rock-steady
hands and gleaming eyes that bespoke neither desperation nor

apprehension, Doe presented himself with an "I'm here, what do you want me to do" attitude and an apology for being late.

The investigators introduced themselves, first names only. Doe was offered a drink. He declined, which was both surprising and impressive, given the circumstances. However nervous he might feel, he wouldn't risk alcohol dulling his senses. What he was being offered was explained: cash for secret information. He would be paid according to quality. They wanted to begin with what was readily at his disposal – details and opinions of diplomatic personnel he knew, positive identifications of intelligence officers, diagrams of diplomatic establishments to which he had access, the contents of selected documents that passed his desk. Eventually they might wish to task him to seek out specific information they desired. "Yes, yes, yes," he agreed impatiently. "Whatever you wish." He added that he could spare an hour without being missed and would answer any questions in order to confirm his knowledge and trustworthiness. Several were posed – questions to which the investigators knew the answer, so they wouldn't have to await an analyst's evaluation to judge his truthfulness. They were satisfied with how he responded. Most promising were his admissions of not knowing when such was the case. He didn't invent to impress. But he did, in every instance, promise to find out. He was instructed on security procedures to follow if he should ever have to reach a member on an emergency basis. These consisted of coded numeric messages to be phoned to a beeper that would signal a meet at a preestablished time and place. The investigators also set a schedule for subsequent debriefings so as to circumvent telephone contact. Doe quickly committed the system to memory.

The operation was off and running. Not once did Doe demur when tasked. Occasionally, he had to be restrained from acting foolhardily. He assumed the danger of discovery alone. While nothing could conceivably have befallen me as I flitted about in the background, I envisaged sharing it with him. The tension was real, as was the relief when he arrived at each meet to assure us that there was no indication he had aroused suspicion. Consulates and embassies are officially the territory of the country that occupies them, and if he had been caught snooping around, it would have been extremely difficult for us to come to his aid – that is, assuming our government would have even wanted to concede our activities by making the effort. Although I don't think I would have admitted it to myself at the time, Doe would probably have been abandoned in the event of exposure. And like the good members of the Department, I would have moved on to the next file.

Thankfully, my response to a catastrophe was never tested. Doe went about his tasks undetected and, as far as I ever knew, unsuspected. As with the bulk of operations in which an IO participates, I was not privy to how it concluded. I was moved on to my next assignment, Doe moved on to different handlers. Such is how operations proceed. They are depersonalized over the long run. Source and handler bond while together, but never so much that the relationship between people supplants the knowledge that the source is being directed by an organization, rather than an individual. Handlers are replaceable; good sources often are not.

In a passage that presages sentiments he would express later (i.e., regarding Kim Philby, as will be related in the next chapter), le Carré writes that the Department "provided shelter from the complexities of modern life, a place where frontiers still existed. For its servants, the Department had a religious quality. Like monks, they endowed it with a mystical identity far away from the hesitant, sinful band which made up its ranks."[53] The religious analogy is appropriate. Like priests or monks, intelligence officers are initiates, set apart as keepers of great mystical suppositions (if not truths), protectors of a way of life. Just as religion depends upon faith without proof, so too does intelligence. Before Haldane bestowed his support, Leclerc had chastized him: "For Heaven's sake, Adrian, do you think Intelligence consists of unassailable philosophical truths? Does every priest have to *prove* that Christ was born on Christmas Day?"[54] In other words, what one fundamentally *knows* must sometimes be taken on faith.

Leclerc fondly reminisces about the wartime experiences that Mayfly has resurrected: "We had to face situations where we had one rumour, John, no more. One indicator and we'd take the risk. Send a man in, two if necessary, and maybe they wouldn't come back. Maybe there wouldn't be anything there. Rumours, a guess, a hunch one follows up; it's easy to forget what intelligence consists of: luck, and speculation. Here and there a windfall, here and there a scoop. Sometimes you stumbled on a thing like this: it could be very big, it could be a shadow … You get instructions: find a man, put him in. So we did. And many *didn't* come back.

They were sent to resolve doubt, don't you see? We sent them because we didn't know."[55] Leclerc is conspicuous for doing the *sending*, as opposed to being *sent*. The pride he derives from *their* failure to come back is dangerous, not to mention contemptible, for a man of his mentality is surely prepared to take extreme risks with others that he would decline for himself.

Smiley warns a new intake of trainees against the vicarious thrills that 10s can mistake for genuine action: "The joes [sources] live out our dreams for us, and we case officers sit safe and snug behind our one-way mirrors, telling ourselves that seeing is feeling. But when the moment of truth strikes – if it ever does for you – well, from then on we become a little more humble about what we ask people to do for us."[56] I like to think that I maintained my humility in Doe's presence. On one occasion I argued against a proposal put forth by an analyst who watched Doe from behind a desk; it would have had him planting a listening device in a piece of furniture to which he had access before it was delivered to an office that we had targeted. Since a limited number of people shared his access, I feared that it could too easily be attributed to him if it were ever detected. Fortunately, my warning was heeded.

Unfortunately, Leiser's assignment isn't tempered with humility. Accepting inadequate training and planning, outdated equipment, and virtually no support once the operation is underway, he agrees to infiltrate East Germany, make his way to Kalkstadt, and confirm or refute the presence of the missile emplacement. Why does he agree to do this under such suicidal conditions? "'I mistrust reasons. I mistrust words like loyalty. And above all,' Haldane declared, 'I mistrust *motive*. We're running an agent; the arithmetic is over. You read German, didn't you? In the beginning was the deed.'"[57]

Maybe the deed is Leiser's reason. Only in the deed can he hope to recapture the daring of his youth, the fellowship that a man can share only with the men beside whom he faces danger. But it's all a delusion. The danger will be his alone. And nothing is really shared with him. Leiser isn't a member of the Department, just an agent. His handlers learn everything there is to know about him, but divulge nothing of themselves. He is a tool to be used and discarded when the time comes. But if you want something to be badly enough, you imagine that it is. So Leiser conjures up love for his handlers, particularly Avery. He allows himself to think only the best of them, in the face of any suggestion to the contrary.

He does this for the chance to belong. He does it to hear exactly the words that Avery says to him just before he heads over the frontier: "You're one of us, Fred. You always were; all the time your card was there, you were one of us. We don't forget."[58] Of course, it's all a lie. His name has been dredged up from the past. He never was or ever will be one of them. No source ever is. For one thing, there's a strong class dimension to the book. Leiser isn't even English, but a Pole, as is clear whenever he speaks using expressions that are out of date or otherwise slightly off. When Haldane approaches him, he notes how Leiser's "voice carried the slightly impertinent assumption that he was as good as Haldane,"[59] something he never could be. Leiser is merely an agent, someone to be used and discarded when no longer needed.

Haldane employs a pseudonym, while Avery refuses to reveal his last name and even lies when Leiser asks his age, claiming to be thirty-four. So badly does Leiser want to love them that he accepts the war rules that protect their identities even as they strip him of his. And he refuses to be swayed by Avery's petty untruths. After he arrives in Kalkstadt, alone, woefully unprepared, frightened, and exposed because he has had to kill an East German sentry at the border, he "remembered Avery: the warmth and English decency of their early comradeship; he remembered his young face glistening in the rain, and his shy, dazzled glance as he dried his spectacles, and he thought: he must have said thirty-two all the time. I misheard."[60]

The relationship between handler and source is complex. It has a peculiar intimacy characterized by apprehension and a mind warily keyed to detect any false notes. The trick is to know the source without exposing too much of yourself. If the source needs a confidant, the io is there with an open mind. If he needs a drinking companion, the io always pays and always keeps up. If she needs attention, the io has eyes for no other. It's really all a cruel game. At the end of the day, the io walks away, while the source falls deeper into the fantasy. I don't believe I ever shared a genuinely true moment with a source, regardless of how intimate the person's confessions. In at least one instance, I was the prime confidant of my source's life, yet he knew little or nothing about me. As the spy Maurice Castle comes to realize in Greene's

The Human Factor "with a sense of revulsion: The situation's impossible, there's no one in the world with whom I can tell of everything, except this man Boris whose real name even is unknown to me."[61]

It's rather amazing what a source will confide to a handler. I suppose that it's a manifestation of the relief he or she feels at dropping the cloak. There the source sits – a spy – and the other person in the room not only knows it but is the instigator. If secrecy seems onerous to the 10, it's positively oppressive for the source. Sources enjoy no release, none of the exaggerated camaraderie of the intelligence service proper, where 10s can toast each other for a cross well borne. No, their lot is true isolation. That's why the best handler is one who creates the most seamless illusion of intimacy, much like the best prostitute, who can make a john believe, fleetingly, that a genuine connection exists. Not without reason did Michael Barrett, a one-time CIA assistant general counsel, write, "Espionage is the world's second oldest profession and just as honorable as the first."[62]

Your mission is to tweak whatever nerve is most sensitive in order to extract secrets out of sources, to cause them to betray some trust they have undertaken. You promise them affection, protection, dignity, material gains, or whatever else they are most in need of. In return, they expose to you the intimacies of their friends, colleagues, lovers, even. And you flatter them and pay them, all the while soothing their conscience, telling them that they're doing the proper thing, that they're serving some purpose higher than any personal bonds they're violating along the way.

All the while, you suppress the contempt that screams in your head: "There are no higher causes. They've all been corrupted. It's people you should be clinging to. They are what keep us human." But you say nothing. This is how you serve what you have sworn loyalty to. You need the sources because you need the information, but you wonder. Beyond reliability, beyond motivation, you wonder what they feel, whether betrayal comes easy or tears into them a little bit each time. I would watch their eyes – whether they bore straight into me or danced agitatedly without fixing on anything – and their hands – whether they rested comfortably or fidgeted or gripped on for dear life. Some had no qualms whatsoever, convinced they were doing the right thing, either because of the personal benefits they derived or because they believed in helping their government. Some clearly revelled in the exercise, gloating with mean-spirited pride because they were putting something over. Others were so ashamed that they left an aftertaste. They were the ones who fought a constant internal battle over who deserved the best of them.

Do they sleep easy? With whom does their heart rest when they drop their guard? What is their *rosebud*? Until you can answer those questions, you wonder. To bestow loyalty is to honour a debt. Whether to one's country, God, family, friends, or self, the notion of a duty to serve and, when necessary, to sacrifice is explicit. Normally, one would not expect core loyalties to clash so extremely that the obligation to one depends on the betrayal of another. But what is one to do when such a situation does present itself? Deciding which faith to sacrifice is every bit as macabre as selecting which limb to amputate, and surely as traumatic. Le Carré acknowledges that his books "are about the peculiar tension between institutional loyalty and loyalty to oneself; the mystery of patriotism, for a Brit of my age and generation, where it runs, how it should be defined, what it's worth and what a corrupting force it can be when misapplied."[63]

Out of faithlessness towards those on whom they inform, sources are prone to manifest an exaggerated faith in their handlers. Yet for all the comfort a man may find in the company of a prostitute, it's not a liaison he would happily divulge to the world. Ironically, in both instances, things may evolve to the point where this is the only relationship in which he participates as a whole, undivided person, where his filthiest secrets are laid open. Even when the source is sincere, however, the 10 is calculating. And the incisive question in the 10's calculation remains: Is the source sincere?

Where the source may (and this too is open to question) trust the handler unconditionally, the 10 will always retain doubts about the source. Information is never taken at face value. You incessantly seek confirmation for whatever a source says. No doubts are too far-fetched to entertain. I once ran a source about whom another source advised that he was making inquiries regarding the purchase of a gun. I was told this on the same morning that my source had contacted me insisting on a meeting for late that night. Coincidence? Was he planning to kill someone and expecting me to assist after the fact? Was he setting me up for the kill?

You can knot yourself into insanity with such conjectures. Needless to say, I wasn't killed. Nor, to my knowledge, had the source intended to kill anyone else. Why did he want a gun? I don't know. Did he ever get a gun? I have no idea. Not everything is knowable. Nor, in point of fact, do you want to know everything. If the information being offered is good and the source does more or less as instructed, the io's job is done. Talk of guns only serves to panic managers.

The very best sources display a predisposition for risk-taking and adventure. They have an enviable freedom of spirit that lets them flaunt those rules that constrain the rest of us. A lot of well-meaning, perfectly loyal people refuse to cooperate when approached by the security service. They simply cannot accommodate the split loyalties the task entails. Really, that's how it is: you nurture confidence with one face, while betraying it with the other. You develop relationships with the intention of manipulating them at the behest of a handler, ever lurking just offstage.

Once over the frontier to the East, Leiser makes the fatal mistake of failing to change the frequency on which he is transmitting his reports back to Avery and company, who have taken up residence in a farmhouse in Lubeck just west of the border. Doing so is fundamental to eluding the listeners who scan the ether for suspect broadcasts. The East Germans pick up his signal and are shocked to hear an exact replication of the transmission format used by British agents during the war. By his second transmission they have pinpointed him and moved in.

Not that it even mattered anymore – the enigmatic Smiley has already been dispatched to Lubeck to advise Leclerc et al. that the East Germans are on to their man and that they had better clear out, lest the West Germans catch them in the act of running an offensive operation from their territory. Smiley is appalled at the amateurish work of the Department and expresses suspicions to Control regarding the Circus's role in the affair. After all, the Circus has volunteered help with false documents as well as the transmitter. He wonders aloud how the Germans knew which frequencies to scan.[64]

Avery is utterly aghast at the total disregard for the man they are about to abandon to the enemy. "'The war rules,' Leclerc spoke proudly. 'We play the war rules. He knew that. He was well trained.'"[65] For Leclerc the operation is a complete success. No,

he hasn't found out whether or not there is a new missile installation. No, his man hasn't made it back to the West. But the
Department has been re-established as an operational player at
Whitehall. Other operations beckon. And that was the whole
point, wasn't it?

Bonn in the late 1960s was the capital city of a wealthy, restless,
chastened West Germany. Yet the title of le Carré's next novel, *A
Small Town in Germany* (1968), defines its character; it was the
"waiting house for Berlin," "permanently committed to the condition of impermanence," housing ministries and foreign missions
"discreetly temporary in deference to the dream, discreetly permanent in deference to reality."[66] Germany had entered a phase of
rebellious teen age, too mature for, and growing resentful of, the
close supervision of the four-power occupation, not yet dependable enough for total self-reliance. Germans were beginning to
grow restive at their continuing vilification for Nazi atrocities they
were desperate to consign to their forgotten and forgiven past, and
they were annoyed that their burgeoning economic power had
failed to win them parallel boosts in other aspects of sovereignty.
Into this breach came the nationalist leader Klaus Karfeld, advo-
cating a united Germany ahead of a united western Europe. His
appeal was mounting at a particularly sensitive time for the British
Embassy, engaged as it was in negotiations to secure Britain's entry
into the European Community. Britain would not gain admittance
without German approval, and Germany was hard pressed to
approve with Karfeld mustering anti-British rallies across the country. One in Hanover turned particularly ugly as crowds rampaged
against the British library, killing the librarian, a German woman.
    Karfeld was precisely the charismatic nationalist that the Allies
had feared when they decided to divide Germany following the
defeat of the Nazis, the kind of leader who "did not understand
what was so *very* wrong about Nazism that it should be punished
eternally with the whole world's hostility."[67] Today that view
regarding eternal punishment is widely accepted, but a scant
twenty years after the war it was heresy to promote a strong,
independent, and united Germany. Karfeld rejected the Western
alliance's insistence that Germany be "*docile* towards the West and
hostile towards the East."[68] He championed a Germany that would

choose its own place in the world – a freedom Britain was yet ready to concede – as befitted its economic power.

Amid these political complexities, Leo Harting goes missing, along with forty-three Chancery (political section) files, none classified below "confidential" and one, a so-called green file, classified to the highest "maximum and limit" level. It contains reports on the most delicate official and unofficial discussions between the embassy and German officials over the previous six months. Alan Turner is dispatched from London to find out where and to whom Harting has run. He is told to tread lightly, not to create a stir, and under no circumstances to let the Germans know a leak has been sprung. Indeed, he is to do nothing that could further stress the embassy or cause difficulties in its position vis-à-vis the Germans and the EC negotiations.

Turner's arrival is greeted as a distasteful intrusion; as he puts it to Head of Chancery Rawley Bradfield, "I'm the abortionist. You don't want me but you've got to have me. A neat job with no aftermath, that's what you're paying for. All right; I'll do my best."[65] Bradfield wants, somehow, for the whole matter simply to go away. Harting is gone and has been so for three days before anyone has taken notice. Files have been mysteriously vanishing, but it is natural to explain them away as misplaced, not pinched by a traitor. His disappearance has not been revealed in a dramatic thunderclap but in a series of absences, beginning on Friday and only confirmed when he fails to appear at church on Sunday.

Bradfield's attitude seems to be that whatever damage Harting can do, whomever he can show the files to, has already occurred, even if the specifics are unknown to the embassy. The crisis will pass, but will the scandal? "Crises are academic. Scandals are not. Haven't you realized that only appearances matter?" Bradfield demands. He goes on, "I serve the appearance of things. It is the worst of systems; it is better than the others. That is my profession and that is my philosophy."[70] That is the effete battle cry of an embassy, all linen napkins and correct place settings and the proper burgundy and dare-not-offend. Whatever the hostility, politesse must be sustained because the form long survives the substance. As le Carré would write in *A Perfect Spy,* "in diplomacy nothing lasts, nothing is absolute, a conspiracy to murder is no grounds for endangering the flow of conversation."[71]

Turner is not given to such delicacies. He attaches great urgency to the crisis of Harting's flight; diplomatic niceties be damned. The green file was the most secret in the embassy, and he has got to determine into whose hands it has been delivered. First in any pursuit is to know what – in this case who – is the object. From where Harting has been will follow an indication of where he is likely to go.

Harting is not a real diplomat but a temporary who relies on his contract being renewed annually. By seducing Bradfield's wife, he has gained an ally who will argue for his renewal. Bradfield succumbs to her supplications ("I'd shown Rawley what I wanted him to buy me!" Hazel confesses to Turner).[72] Nor is he really English but a German refugee from the Nazis. As Lumley, Turner's boss, put it with distaste, "There's a smell, that's all. A foreign smell. Refugee background, emigrated in the thirties … Professional expatriate. There was one in every mess in Occupied Germany in those days."[73] He implies something unsavoury and untrustworthy about Harting because he's not of the club. In retrospect, he suggests, these are the predictable results when the lower ranks infiltrate.

Like so many marginals, Harting has found a way to survive by making himself useful, taking on the drudgery that others shun. Of course, when your purpose is to collect information, the most tiresome chores can be those that yield the greatest rewards. He offers himself up to handle those jobs – such as the destruction of outdated files from Registry – that will allow him to root through the deepest cavities in the embassy's archives. Arthur Meadowes, head of Registry, gives Harting free run, explaining to Turner, "Anyone can look at anything, that's my rule. Anyone sent up here, I trust them. There's no other way to run the place. I can't go sniffing around asking who's looking at what, can I?"[74]

Get to the archives and you decipher the genetic code. Nobody can learn more than the squinty-eyed wretches who toil in the musty crypts where the files are given their final resting place. When the KGB's First Chief Directorate began relocating its headquarters from the notorious Lubyanka in central Moscow to Yasenevo in the suburbs, Vasili Mitrokhin was assigned the monumental task of sealing and transporting the archives to their new repository. As a result, he had the opportunity to browse at will through files dating back to 1918.

Unknown to anyone, he had become seriously disaffected. He took notes from the files, using his decade among them to build up a massive private archive of top-secret data. When he defected, he took with him the largest single haul of intelligence ever: "Few KGB officers apart from Mitrokhin have ever spent as much time reading, let alone noting, foreign intelligence files. Outside the FCD archives, only the most senior officers shared his unrestricted access, and none had the time to read more than a fraction of the material noted by him."[75] In other words, the lowly archivist can be a better catch than just about anyone else when it comes to learning background information and the identity of agents. The crucial factor missing from the files is an indication of the intentions or thoughts of operational and senior officers.

When vigilance becomes routine, it invariably suffers. No one can be on guard constantly; no one can suspect without respite. Naturally, a colleague, one who is seen daily and with whom one exchanges pleasantries and idle chatter about family, cars, sports, the weather, is not someone we mistrust. Otherwise, a very antagonistic environment would prevail. For instance, within CSIS buildings, photo access cards were to be worn in plain sight. Most staff dangled them from chains around their necks or clipped them to their belts. Others thoughtlessly – or rebelliously – tossed them onto their desks, where they lay throughout the day. These people weren't constantly challenged to identify themselves. How could they be? Most you would recognize at least by sight. Those you didn't, well, you'd figure that someone else must know who they were or they wouldn't have gotten inside in the first place – which certainly didn't mean they were free to wander, but it did confirm that identification was someone else's responsibility.

Classified documents were so plentiful and were innocently lost at such a rate that a couple of times a year, a half-day would be set aside for all staff to thoroughly search their cabinets and drawers for missing files. Invariably, several 'secret' and 'top secret' dossiers that had been given up for lost resurfaced. And there was nothing treasonous about these episodes, just carelessness. Nobody analyzed the recovered files for patterns and nobody really believed that the carelessness was feigned to mask concerted deception. This is precisely how spies survive undetected for years, when hindsight plainly reveals all manner of clues. Those admitted into Fortress Intelligence have passed through the ring of fire of suspicion and come out the other side into sanctuary. What accounts for this phenomenon? More an aversion to confrontation than anything conspiratorial. There's no great wall of silence, only a see-no-evil ethic.

And what is Harting after? Why would he steal files? Spies never steal; they memorize, they copy, but they never steal. And what is in those files?

A Small Town in Germany spends considerable time trying to be enigmatic. It lacks the tense excitement of *The Spy Who Came in from the Cold* and the sardonic wit of *The Looking Glass War*. Turner is without the finesse of other le Carré characters; he knows no middle ground. Lumley explains why he chose him over another man for the job: "Because you'll find him and Shawn won't. Not that I admire you for that. You'd pull down the whole forest, you would, to find a man. What drives you? What are you looking for? Some bloody absolute. If there's one thing I really hate it's a cynic in search of God."[76] Here le Carré hits upon the consummate definition of a cynic: someone searching for God but doomed to disappointment for never finding sufficient proof of his existence.

Leo Harting remains a ghost, as Karla will in later novels. Le Carré cleverly builds the symbiosis between hunter and hunted. Of his quarry, Turner thinks, "Come on, Leo, we're of one blood, you and I: underground men, that's us. I'll chase you through the sewers, Leo; that's why I smell so lovely. We've got the earth's dirt on us, you and I. I'll chase you, you chase me and each of us will chase ourselves."[77]

Just as Turner sees his other self in Harting, so le Carré saw himself in both men. "'Externally,' le Carré once explained, 'Leo and I lived in the same house, worked in the same building, ate in the same canteen, drank at the same parties, and we felt perhaps, for different but related reasons, the same intense alienation from the environment of which we were a part. But there,' he concluded, 'the analogy ends. Perhaps I have more in common with Alan Turner, and have set one part of my nature in pursuit of another.'"[78]

Where the book succeeds best is in its conclusion. With the dexterous sailor's touch that is his hallmark, le Carré faultlessly knots all the strands of the narrative. Harting hasn't been working for the other side; he has been working all along for the side he imagined himself to be on. He hasn't actually stolen files but cached them in a hidden nook of the embassy. There he has laboured, gathering up a case against Karfeld. He has found in the embassy's own files evidence of a grotesque Nazi past that Karfeld has succeeded in covering up. Karfeld was the administrative supervisor at a factory where toxic gas experiments were carried out on humans. But the evidence is largely circumstantial, and besides, the statute of limitations on such common Nazi crimes has expired. Only not for Harting: he recognizes no such statute. He has become a dangerous man; he has found a cause. Nothing so frightens the non-believer as the zealot. Bureaucrats' great talent is to believe in nothing to the point that they cannot convincingly adopt the opposite stance when so instructed.

Indeed, Bradfield argues, "He should have grown out of it; the rest of us did."[79] With Karfeld ascendant, prudence calls for overtures to be made towards him. If he should ever come to wield political power, it will not be possible to ignore and wish him away. He will have to be engaged, accommodated, perhaps even won over. To that end, the green file reveals, secret talks have already been held between Bradfield and Karfeld as the British hedge their bets against exclusion from the EC. Perhaps they can still play some role in central Europe nonetheless. Bradfield justifies his actions in the time-honoured fashion of the representative of a nation on the wane, but still covetous of international glory: "I would rather fail as a power than survive by impotence. I would rather be vanquished than neutral. I would rather be English than Swiss."[80]

Having seen legal recourse prove inadequate and the British abdicate their responsibility, Harting resolves to assassinate Karfeld. Turner sees Harting as a victim of British heartlessness. His quest to capture him becomes a mission to rescue him. Karfeld, however, enjoys protection at high levels, no match for the likes of little Leo Harting. Turner urges Bradfield to help: "It was us who put it into his mind back in those days: the notion of absolute justice. We made him all those promises: Nuremberg, de-Nazification. We *made* him believe. We can't let him be a casualty just because we changed our minds."[81] (This is precisely what happened to Leiser.) But of course politics creates such victims all the time. If truth is the first casualty of war, integrity is surely the first – and most frequent – casualty of politics. And those who insist on upholding integrity over expediency are obstacles that cannot be tolerated.

Harting faces the classic philosophical dilemma: if you knew Hitler was going to take power, knew what he would do, would you have been justified in taking extreme measures to prevent it? Would it be morally right to assassinate him? Or, being a civil servant, would you follow the orders of your superiors and appease them? And if you followed orders blindly without reference to any standard of morality, how would you be different from those Nuremberg defendants who claimed innocence on the grounds of obedience? In the face of nascent neo-Nazism in the person of Karfeld, Harting will not choose complacency. The embassy, on the other hand, has its orders, its protocol, its interests to be served and preserved in the polite tones of diplomacy – at all costs. Tacitly, at any rate, it allows the Germans to flush out Harting at Karfeld's Bonn rally and leaves him to their disposal, to be disposed of brutally. Once again, cynicism is victorious.

And once again, le Carré's prescience has been demonstrated. A recent study of wartime documents conducted by historian Richard Breitman shows that the British, in particular, were unenthusiastic about the prospect of convening a tribunal to hear charges of war crimes for World War II atrocities. From 1943 on, no evidence of crimes against humanity was gathered from German police and ss intercepts.[82] Bygones, maybe? There are always political considerations overriding morality. The repercussions of action always seem much more severe than those of inaction – hence the attraction of a promise of peace in our time as an alternative to standing firm; hence the preference for letting criminals go free.

World War II was only latterly, even peripherally, about justice and evil. It was first and foremost a battle against an aggressive power that demonstrated insatiable ambition. This is the way of all international relations, every unpalatable alliance and each distasteful compromise, and all suppressions of, or failures to respond to, intelligence. In Karfeld, Harting sees history repeating itself, from the rise of xenophobic nationalism through international appeasement. The question becomes one of who will learn from history? Will Karfeld learn that he can go far but not quite as far as Hitler? Or will the British learn that such men cannot be tolerated? Fearing the penchant of the British for finding excuses to be reasonable, Harting cannot count on their being moved to outrage. Therefore, in answer to the question of whether he would have moved to prevent Hitler, Harting utters a resounding yes.

In *The Naïve and Sentimental Lover* (1971) le Carré ventured away from international espionage and deeper into his own life to find his plot. Thematically, however, he continued to ruminate on questions of loyalty and betrayal, love and isolation, faith and trust, all elements that touch the spy's modus operandi and are crucial to the modus vivendi of mere normals such as Aldo Cassidy.

A self-confessed private man, le Carré usually braves the public spotlight only for the obligatory post-release round of interviews and appearances and then retreats to his home in Cornwall. One can only imagine how difficult and painful it must have been when his affair with Susan, the wife of his friend James Kennaway, the Scottish novelist and screenwriter, exploded with enough celebrity messiness to spawn books from all three of the principals. Le Carré had met the Kennaways in 1963, following the publication of *The Spy Who Came in from the Cold*, through his prior friendship with Susan's brother and sister. Susan Kennaway wrote that the success of the novel "had taken David by surprise and he was quite unprepared for it ... David felt isolated from the people he had been working with and living with for so long."[83]

The intelligence community is at once isolating and embracing. Part of its allure is the intense feelings of belonging that it inspires. Yet to belong is, at the same time, to exclude. And excluded are all those who do not belong. Strangely though, the social attachment between spies is rather like meeting people on a package holiday in a country where you don't speak the language. You may not like everyone you're thrown in with, but there's a certain seductive ease to the relationship, so you tend to become very close in a very short time. You always have common experiences to recount, acquaintances to gossip about, and a barrier against having these conversations with anybody else. But if you ever run into these people later in another context, you find yourself trapped in a long awkward pause with nothing to say, no easy banter. What was shared belongs to a particular time and place and set of experiences, and it can't be replicated in any other circumstances. This is how it is between ios. Our bond is ultimately limiting. When a member's interests begin to extend beyond the secret world, it can be as disorienting an experience as it is refreshing. There's a childlike excitement in meeting new people without the predisposition for withholding, of living in a bigger world than the one you've grown accustomed to.

Leaving the secret confines is like giving up an addiction cold turkey. In a very literal sense, you're cut off. All the cryptic confidences into which you once fit so comfortably are removed. You can't talk to old colleagues the way you once did; soon enough, you can't really talk to them at all. The holes punched through the official need-to-know principle by the unsanctioned need-to-vent principle are suddenly closed up in your presence. The community that was the only place where you felt truly at home becomes alien. I can only imagine how this experience is compounded by fame.

By Susan's account, James Kennaway lived an uninhibited life of emotional extremes. She writes of "his crazy ebullience, his wickedness, his introspection, his unfailing ability to surprise me, to make me laugh, to make me sad and to make me love. Above all I think I, and probably most of the people who knew James, will remember his zest for life and the way he entertained us when he chose to."[84] With a burst of self-awareness, James opens *Some Gorgeous Accident*, his fictional account of the affair, by describing Link, the character modelled on himself in the following terms: "Link's love, his speech, his actions, why even his thoughts had overtones of violence; of pain experienced and pain inflicted purposely. He was a man who arrested attention and invited passion with dangerous facility; dangerous because, as he welcomed life, seized it by both hands and pulled it in the door, he let destruction in as well."[85]

Such people inspire turbulent attachments because they live with passion. They have a rare talent for banishing complacency from their lives. They are responsive to the demons of action and deaf to the gods of consequence. Who wouldn't want to live their lives with wild abandon, especially after years of introverted dissembling for fear of open sincerity?

In *The Naïve and Sentimental Lover*, le Carré's role is played by Aldo Cassidy, a staid pram manufacturer living the unexamined life of those who have succeeded in conventional terms. Indeed, in "both build and looks he might have served as an architectural prototype for the middle-class Englishman privately educated between the wars; one who had felt the wind of battle but never the fire of it."[86] He has a wife, two children, a home at a fashionable address, and a retreat in the exclusive Swiss resort of Sainte-Angèle, and his company is doing very nicely, thank you. But there's certainly no fire. It's all so dreary and stagnant. There is no spontaneity or passion about him. Nor is there love. And without that element, in particular, he is reduced to going through the motions; he has fallen back on being reliable, devoted – in his way – to the family and company that depends on him. So blasé is Cassidy that he is not even aware anything is missing from his life.

Then one day he happens upon Shamus and Helen, le Carré's stand-ins for James and Susan. Cassidy is everything they profess to hold in contempt, for he is decidedly among the "Many-too-Many, the compromisers for whom freedom was a terror; these were the backcloth for the real drama of life."[87] This description is similar to Link's opinion of his friend Dr Fiddes, who acts le Carré's part in *Some Gorgeous Accident*. Link tells him, "You and the grey ones are scowling at the empty sky, I'm buzzing about and boozing about, ignoring its emptiness. The same game. Just a question of styles. Your tension lies between the fear of pain and pain itself. Mine is the wild pursuit of pain for pain's sake."[88]

Cassidy takes to the couple because he mistakes them for charmingly seedy aristocrats, the proprietors of Haverdown, the country manor he visits with the intention of purchasing. By the time Helen confesses that they are actually penniless squatters, Shamus has already won him over: Cassidy has fallen in love. After all, they are not actual deadbeats. Shamus is a writer, an artist, and therefore entitled to his eccentricities, for in them lies either the source or the result (one isn't quite sure) of artistry. "If he didn't make hell he wouldn't make books,"[89] Cassidy says, making excuses for him. This comment accurately reflects James Kennaway's own attitude, as expressed in his journal: "Let me scream like a child if I write like a man: let me die if I write like a god."[90] If truth be told, Shamus has not done a whole lot of book making. He has had his great triumph with a debut novel now ten years in the past; since then his output has been nil. In this sense he may be the writerly equivalent of the Department in *The Looking Glass War*, which has to squint back twice that time to find triumph.

Just as espionage novels are essentially stories of pursuit, so too is *The Naïve and Sentimental Lover*. And just as le Carré describes

Turner and Harting as representing one part of his nature chasing after another, the same is true of Cassidy and Shamus. Listening to Shamus's irreverence and watching him in the light of the lantern he uses to illuminate their trek through Haverdown, it appears to Cassidy "as though the figure behind the lamp were not a separate figure at all, but his own, mysteriously reflected from the depths of the liquid twilight; as though his swifter, freer self were examining, by the light of that unusual lantern, the features of his pedestrian other half."[91] This is the essence of the attraction Shamus holds for Cassidy: the chance to see himself as he might otherwise be. It is the same attraction as Fiddes feels towards Link: "Fiddes loved Link … He waited for Link's next outburst; for the indiscretions, the prejudice, the jokes. He fed on Link's energy, of course he did."[92] And it is likely the same attraction that Kennaway held for le Carré. While the latter always thought of himself as a writer, he had not long lived as one. In Kennaway he found the living epitome of the free-spirited artist. Shamus asks the question, "Who can write about life and run away from it at the same time?"[93]

Shamus has this theory that the world is divided between two types, the naïve and the sentimental. He, being an original, is the former, while Cassidy falls into the latter category because he longs to be like Shamus. Just as the original reflects the imitator, the two are alike, yet utterly different. They resemble Joseph Conrad's narrator and his secret sharer, the cast-off murderer Leggatt: "He was not a bit like me, really; yet as we stood leaning over my bed-place, whispering side by side, with our dark heads together and our backs to the door, anybody bold enough to open it stealthily would have been treated to the uncanny sight of a double captain busy talking in whispers with his other self."[94]

Following his first breathless binge with Shamus and Helen, which included much drinking and the constant threat of property damage, Cassidy counts himself lucky. Shamus's volatile behaviour carries with it the promise of danger, and the sexually charged Helen brings what's forbidden disconcertingly close. He thinks, "I have visited Bohemia and got away unscathed."[95] And unscathed is how Cassidy was determined to emerge from all situations, be it his marriage, parenthood, or whatever.

But no longer is this enough. From this time on, his life seems puny. Shamus is larger than life, Cassidy is smaller. Nothing satisfies him, least of all his wife, Sandra, about whom he thinks, "I would call you an inexorable bore. You block me. I could be a writer if it wasn't for you. As it is I'm stuck in prams."[96] For her part, like Avery's wife, Sarah, Sandra is far more perceptive than Cassidy gives her credit for. She suspects that his frequent trips in pursuit of various charity initiatives are a sham, which of course they are. Philanthropy is his cover for having an identity all to himself and for his carousing with Shamus. When Cassidy suddenly informs her that she can't accompany him as planned to a Paris trade fair, she threatens to leave him.

In fact, Cassidy is replacing her with Shamus. From their first parting, he has waited impatiently for Shamus to call. When he finally does, Cassidy invites him to Paris, relieved at the chance to fulfill the role of patron and audience to the great writer. Shamus swings erratically from gratitude for Cassidy's indulgence and generosity to scorn for someone he denigrates as "[t]errified of everything in life except the perpetuation of it"[97] (just as the espiocrats were terrified of everything in the Cold War except the perpetuation of it).

Cassidy endures the harangues, suffers the indignity of having a jug of water emptied on his head in a restaurant, and nurses Shamus through his drunken jags of vomiting. But why? Because Shamus takes him to "a Paris which Cassidy had not dreamed of, not aspired to even, since it answered appetites he did not know he had, and showed him people he had not imagined"[98] – a Paris of whores and brothels, low bars and back alleys. This episode is based on a real trip to Paris enjoyed by James Kennaway and le Carré in August 1964, during which – in Susan's words – James "took it upon himself to show David the darker side of Paris and the darker side of his own character."[99] In gratitude for this experience le Carré wrote in Kennaway's notebook, "JIM, you have done more for me in a week than I have done for anyone else in a lifetime."[100]

Cassidy is very much like Leiser in his insatiable desire to believe. As is so often the case in le Carré's world, the object of faith proves unworthy, and Shamus well knows it: "You really believe that crap I tell you? Listen, I am the lousiest fucking conjuror in the business and you fall for every fucking trick ... You want to throw me out, pramseller: that's what you want to do. I don't work, I don't write, I don't exist! It's the fucking audience that's doing the magic, not me."[101] Nonetheless, the effect that believing in Shamus has on Cassidy is very real. He becomes more free-spirited, more daring. He begins seizing from life what he desires, including Angie, his secretary, Heather, his wife's best friend, and Helen, with whom he falls in love.

Shamus is enraged when he learns of Cassidy's affair with Helen. He beats her and induces Cassidy to join them at Sainte-Angèle, where he threatens them at gunpoint. The plot risks unravelling at this stage, and le Carré's frantic efforts to hold it together are forced. Shamus gives Cassidy the opportunity to profess his love for Helen, forgiving their transgressions only when he does so. He then holds a mock ceremony to wed them.

Cassidy and Helen then depart from the chalet in a snowstorm for the railway station, but arrive too late for their train. Helen proceeds to berate him, sounding less like the idealized object of his passion than the ever-nagging wife. In the event, Shamus has followed them and he takes a shot at Cassidy. In an epiphanous moment, one he can't fully explain, he turns Helen back to Shamus. "It's just that the main axis is between you two," he stutters. "Maybe it's between us two, him and me."[102] Either way, their relationship is inextricably tied to the dynamic of the threesome, of Shamus being the original and Cassidy striving to emulate him, of Shamus being naive and Cassidy sentimental. By winning Helen, Cassidy has achieved equality with Shamus. He can no longer serve as his undiscriminating audience. They have ceased to depend upon each other.

This mad climax is not unlike the real denouement of le Carré's affair with Susan Kennaway. James's frequent affairs and many mistresses – and his insistence on bragging about them to her – drove her to seek her own lover. That it should be their mutual friend was not mere accident. She writes, "James was a great manipulator of people ... he enjoyed playing with people's lives and it was inevitable that sooner or later he would need to begin to play with my life and with David's life and it was inevitable too the turn that that would take. The only mistake that James made was that I would actually fall in love with David. To complicate matters further I still loved James. I believe also that David fell in love with me and I know that James and David loved each other in the way that David and Jonathan were brothers."[103] In James Kennaway's account, he concedes that Fiddes feels driven by Link to Susie (Kennaway used this name for his female lead):

"How can you blame me? You told me to grab. You told me that life was for living. You told Susie too. You brought us to this – not that we're doing anything. You breathed on us your boozy, acrid, smudgy breath and we must have found in it fresh air."[104]

What is Cassidy to do after Shamus? Going back to the "boss-cow" – Helen and Shamus's name for Sandra – seems like a defeat. Helen begs him to go forward: "For a while you really *did* care … You put a value on *yourself* … That's something you never did before … Find someone else. Don't go back into that awful dark."[105] But it isn't that easy to cast off one's character, to embrace a new faith, to embark on new loyalties.

Cassidy does return to Sandra, though he makes some significant changes. He retires from his pram business and purchases Haverdown, to which he retreats to live as a country squire. In his new home he installs Heather, with whom he sleeps when Sandra visits London. On his own visits to London, he has trysts with Angie. He gives writing a try, but finds it causes him to think of things he has convinced himself are better left unconsidered. "For in this world, whatever there was left of it to inhabit, Aldo Cassidy dared not remember love."[106]

In real life, James Kennaway became hysterical at the prospect of Susan running off with le Carré and suffered something akin to a breakdown. Le Carré, whether from obligation to his wife of the time (they would later divorce) or loyalty to James, encouraged Susan to return to him. They remained together until his untimely death in a car accident in December 1968 at the age of forty.

Spies tell lies; it's an occupational requirement. The idealized response has it that this constitutes a hardship. In reality, many experience it as liberating, a state-sanctioned freedom, a cover for every infidelity. All responsibility is absolved by the job, any excuse reinforced by secrecy.

When we were driving back from a three-day conference in Ottawa once, my partner was at the wheel. He asked where I wanted him to drop me off.

"At my house," I answered, a little nonplussed by the question. "Where else?"

"I don't know," he grinned slyly. "I told my wife I'd be gone for a week, so I've got four more nights to spend where I please." Chuckling with glee, he shrugged at the lack of imagination that had me condemned to just going home.

Likewise, artists claim immunity from normal conventions on the grounds that creativity cannot thrive within boundaries. James Kennaway wrote in his diary, "I guess I've a duty to talent more than to the family."[107] He used this duty as a rationale for cheating and cruelty. Does lying really confer freedom? Or is infidelity nothing more than a broken bond of fidelity? Is Shamus really freer than Cassidy? What is Shamus's behaviour without an audience? In other words, life forces choices regarding fidelities and freedoms upon each of us, but it never releases us from our own nature.

A friend, a lover, a wife, and family; conflicting and incompatible loyalties; choices and treasons – the principles at stake in a personal infidelity are not dissimilar from those encountered by the traitor to a country. Against whatever it is committed, treason demands subterfuge, a premeditated plan to minimize the probability of being found out. This can range in complexity from the subtlest intelligence operation to the mundane lies emanating from a casual romp with adultery. The difference between intelligence officers and other people is that ios anticipate – and, over time, expect – lies and faithlessness. This attitude colours their perception of the people they meet and the world they inhabit, creating a grossly distorted and sourly bilious universe. Constant manipulation and defence against being manipulated turns them cold to the warmth of genuine intimacy.

Do public responsibilities supersede personal loves? Does society's prescription for justice override other conceptions of right and wrong? When that final line in the sand is to be crossed, to what or to whom will we remain faithful? And so long as we hold true to that faith, have we really committed treason at all? These questions are not remote from any of us. We constantly define and refine our loyalties. And in so doing, we commit our share of treasons. Everyone pledges tacit or explicit oaths: the fealty of religious consecration; the commandment to honour one's parents; the code of silence, whether of a fraternity, corps, or the Official Secrets Act; the commitment of love or friendship; the vows of marriage; a personal perception of morality. Some of these are imposed, others adopted by choice. Often our resolve will be challenged. How we respond is a measure of who we are and what we aspire to be.

CHAPTER FOUR

Karla

Something changed in 1963: not the world, perhaps, but our perception of it. Portentously – and fittingly, given the peculiarities of intelligence – we would not even know the implications of what had happened for another four years. Conceivably, we still do not know. When Kim Philby defected to Moscow on 23 January, confirming the accumulated suspicions of a dozen years, he took with him our confidence in the reliability of our society's institutions. How, we have been wondering ever since, are they to protect us when they were so inadequate at safeguarding themselves?

We could refer to the post-defection era as Philbian in nature. Ron Rosenbaum has argued that "the Age of Paranoia we've lived in for the last half century – the plague of suspicion, distrust, disinformation, conspiracy consciousness that has emanated like gamma radiation from intelligence agencies East and West, the pervasive feeling of unfathomable deceit that has destabilized our confidence in the knowability of history – is the true legacy of Kim Philby." It was he who "revealed dark shapes beneath the surface only dimly glimpsed before, if at all – depths of duplicity, subzero degrees of cold-bloodedness that may not even have been *there* until Philby plumbed them."[1] Overstatement? In fact, maybe, but in effect, no. Of his Philby-esque creation, Bill Haydon, le Carré muses through the voice of Ned, "Sometimes I wonder whether that was the greatest of all Bill's crimes: to steal for good the lightness we had shared."[2]

Because the paranoia has extended beyond the world of intelligence to pervade our culture as a whole, it is particularly important that any discussion of espionage consider Philby and his legacy. The facts of his espionage per se do not concern us here;

they have been recounted – to the extent they are known – in detail elsewhere. What is of concern is the idea of Philby, the enigma of Philby. To this day, the notional Philby climbs, plummets, twists, rolls, loops, and blows more clouds of pure smoke than an aerobatics plane. Efforts to resolve outstanding questions, dissect peculiar inconsistencies, unusual turns of phrase, and seemingly uncharacteristic behaviour continue. Each tidbit is manipulated and magnified until distorted into a kind of Rorschach test, where the ink blotch is indisputably present, but it could be anything or nothing.

More than any of his infamous Cambridge fellow travellers, Philby personified the reliability of the British Establishment. Guy Burgess could be dismissed as a drunk, a homosexual, and a flagrant hedonist. Anthony Blunt, too, was a homosexual, and besides, he departed the hard world of intelligence soon after the war to immerse himself in art history, though he still aided the KGB. Donald Maclean, once an indisputable rising star of the Foreign Office, was also an indiscreet and volatile drunk whose career was peppered with erratic outbursts (it has been argued that he supplied information of greater value to the Soviet leadership than Philby did).[3] And John Cairncross, the last of the Cambridge recruits to be publicly confirmed as a Soviet agent, was not a product of the hallowed upper classes, and his civil service career was rather undistinguished.

But Philby? He was a gentleman, dashing and charming, the son of the flamboyant explorer and Arabist Harry St. John Philby and the product of the proper schools. He was, as le Carré wrote, "of our blood and hunted with our pack."[4] This is the crux of the consummate deception that was his. He was not the outsider who ingratiated his way in, not the stranger decked out in some elaborate disguise. He was able to penetrate to the deepest bunkers of state secrecy simply by being all that he appeared to be. The conceit of the Establishment was not so much that it could not be duped by one of its own, but that its own would never have cause to dupe it. When Philby formally joined MI6 in 1940, vetting was little more than word-of-mouth assurance from others who had already passed the test of pedigree – hence the shock when he was exposed as a communist agent.

That one conducts oneself with honour and integrity within one's own service is a much-cherished sentiment. An intelligence officer inhabits two distinct worlds: one within and the other without. Within is a world of civility and safety; without, one of subterfuge and menace. Each calls for a different set of rules and responses. However much one expects and accepts to betray and to be betrayed without, within one can drop the guard and ease the constant vigilance, finally taking things at face value. Within is supposed to be a refuge from the exhausting practice of tossing every incident over and over in one's mind like a coin, seeing first heads, then tails, then heads again, and on and on. When you come to believe – really believe – that nothing is as it seems, everything can seem to be anything.

Richard Helms, the former director of the CIA, was proud that his son, after interning for a summer at the agency, expressed the thought that he had been lucky to have worked in such a civilized environment. Reflecting on that story, journalist Bob Woodward wrote, "That was it. There was a sense of decency out there; it was the great barrier reef to the toughness, the deception, the impossibility of playing by the Marquess of Queensberry rules on the world stage. Inside the agency, among themselves, they were all Caesar's wife – no lies, straight dealing."[5] This is what Philby desecrated: the sense of decency, the illusion that the lies ever stopped.

"Philby's case has more to do with betrayal of class interests than with betrayal of country," writes Phillip Knightley, who was part of the *Sunday Times* investigative team that broke the details of Phiby's subterfuge in 1967. "No one pretends that if Philby had been the son of an accountant, a grey recruit from a north London grammar school and a red brick university, his treachery would still be under discussion nearly a half century later."[6] This is a fascinating idea, one that digs at the very foundation of our notion of loyalty. Was Philby's treachery worse than others' because, more than being just a British citizen, he was a member of the class bred to lead the realm? Le Carré embraces this question, and much of his disgust with the Philby case is directed to the Establishment, which, on a certain level, seemed to conspire along with him. He writes, "If Philby's relationship to the Establishment was ambivalent and paradoxical, the relationship of the Establishment to Philby affords an even richer study in English attitudes."[7]

The manner in which the attitudes of the British class system have permeated intelligence is one of le Carré's recurring themes. In *A Small Town in Germany*, Turner chides Peter de Lisle, Bradfield's number two in chancery, "who do you represent out here? Your-selves or the poor bloody taxpayer? I'll tell you who: the Club. *Your* club. The bloody Foreign Office; and if you saw Rawley Bradfield standing on Westminster Bridge hawking his files for an extra pension, you'd bloody well look the other way."[8] Quite different is the attitude when they think it is foreign, contract-appointed Harting selling out. In le Carré's later works, the confidence with which the upper class has its way and improvises rules suitable to its own interests manifests itself in the arms dealers Sir Anthony Joyston Bradshaw (*The Secret Pilgrim*) and Richard Onslow Roper (*The Night Manager*), the banking house of Tiger Single (*Single & Single*), and the multinational conglomerate ThreeBees of Sir Kenneth K. Curtiss (*The Constant Gardener*). There is something inviolable about them, an expectation that their impeccable manners are not a cover but an expression of their good intent, as if a proper table setting ensures a fine meal.

There are those, however, who dispute the impact of class. Historian Hugh Trevor-Roper, for one, rejects le Carré's argument that some ephemeral "Establishment" was responsible for Philby's ease in gaining admission to the state's sanctum sanc-torum. He dismisses reference to an Establishment as "so vague as to be meaningless." Instead, he blames "the effect of secrecy, of insulation, of immunity, of immediate circumstance – and per-haps also of a popular myth."[9] Le Carré, too, blames the nature of secrecy and all that attends it. Where the two differ is in le Carré's tracing a link between the insularity of a unified Estab-lishment empowered with recruiting its own and with keeping those secrets. Trust was something imparted, not by word or deed, but by belonging. The British secret services long regarded their American counterparts as suspect for lacking any screening method as allegedly foolproof as their own old boys' network of public schools, Oxbridge, and the peerage. Henry Kirby, a former member of Parliament who had been with MI6 in the 1920s, was positively horrified at the OSS for "drawing on the ethnic dregs of America for skill in languages and knowledge of foreign coun-tries. Their security was non-existent."[10]

The *act* of Philby's betrayal is less compelling than the *idea* of it because it is the latter that sets him apart from all the other spies and traitors who have blipped past the radar of international affairs, before, during, and since the Cold War. There is nothing shocking in his youthful attraction to communism or his earnest, if naive, longing to change the world. The turmoil of the late 1920s to the 1930s led many a young academic to question the intellectual foundation of capitalist society. Herbert Norman, a contemporary of Philby's at Cambridge who served in the Canadian foreign service and was hounded to suicide in 1957 by nagging suspicions that he was a communist, is representative of this generation. Deeply affected by the Depression, which convinced him that capitalism was undergoing chaotic, dying convulsions and that Soviet state-planned economics was the model for the future, and frightened by ascendant fascism, Norman joined the Communist Party in the mid-1930s. He wrote, "Better socialism by revolution than the Dark Ages of fascism."[11] Unlike with Philby, the evidence indicates that Norman was not disloyal to his country while in its service, though he was tainted by his leftist dalliances and destroyed by the paranoia of those years following the defections of Maclean and Burgess.

Philby was moved by the rightist violence he witnessed in Vienna in 1933. The drive to do *something*, to become involved in the momentous events of the day was irresistible. Since he saw no virtue in inaction and the communists were seemingly the only ones willing to meaningfully confront budding fascism, it is understandable that he embraced the politics of the left. Surely, too, his early marriage to a Jewish-Austrian communist could have been satisfactorily explained as an impetuous desire to save her from rampant anti-Semitism.

From our vantage point – that of the deceived – Philby, the betrayer, was despicably hard-hearted. But was he necessarily so, or did he merely choose to follow his heart in another direction? Denouncing Philby's treason is all too easy because he spied for Stalin, one of history's most reprehensible killers. However, the particulars of his case do not blur the overriding moral dilemma of treason. Greater understanding calls for an examination of the traitor more than the treason. Philby claimed to have served the Soviet Union out of a fervent belief in communism. Graham Greene appeared to accept this claim, writing, "He was serving a cause and not himself, and so my old liking for him comes back."[12] That Philby had not acted for personal gain was enough for Greene to forgive him. What he was applauding, I think, was that Philby had maintained a steadfast moral centre. Doubts, however, continue to abound as to his true motives.

Today, more than ever, it is hard to accept that anyone engages in grand gestures for the sake of ideology, lofty visions of truth, or noble principles of human betterment. An experienced intelligence officer is disturbed by anyone offering to spy because of a deeply rooted conviction. Cynics and zealots are as far apart on the food chain as koalas from polar bears. IOs – and this applies equally to the East bloc as to the West – would much prefer to deal with someone seeking to settle a personal score or demanding cash payment. Such people are more predictable. Beliefs are too much whimsy to appeal to the cynical mind – luxuries to be indulged only once the necessities are ensured.

A financial relationship is the one with which a handler feels most comfortable. After all, I was being paid to meet with the sources, I'd reason with them, and you ought to be paid to meet me. It created a symbiosis of purpose. Here we are in the same place for the same reason. Money gives one a tangible hold over the source, something the source can hold as well. The constancy of money's influence can be trusted; it's something the source will need as much tomorrow as today.

Across the divide from Philby stands Oleg Gordievsky, the most important KGB officer ever to defect to the West. In his autobiography, *Next Stop Execution*, he professes to have become disillusioned with Stalinist Russia while still an adolescent. Nonetheless, he joined the KGB, following in the footsteps of his father and elder brother. Once inside, he writes, "I have to admit that I was so absorbed in this new work, so carried away by the thrill of the material, that I worried less about ideology than in other periods."[13] Many are the innocent young spies who become mesmerized by the not-seeing-the-forest-for-the-trees syndrome.

The 1968 Soviet invasion of Czechoslovakia caused Gordievsky's emotional break from the KGB. His disaffection, compounded by mounting professional dissatisfaction, started him along the route of the double agent. His was an act of ideological transformation. Unlike Philby, he had begun by loyally serving a state whose philosophical underpinnings he claims to have already doubted. Also unlike Philby, his movement to the other side gave him every reason to anticipate an eventual material improvement (though he is adamant that money played no part in the decision). And again unlike Philby, who was never overly troubled by domestic attachments (his personal infidelities corresponded to his public ones), Gordievsky, in his emergency exfiltration from Moscow, faced the pain of having to surrender his family to the never tender mercies of jilted Soviet authorities.

His preparedness to abandon his wife and two daughters lends some insight into how the ubiquity of politics in repressive states dampens personal ties. Of his relationship with his wife, he writes, "Because Leila had grown up very much a Soviet girl, heavily indoctrinated by Communist propaganda, I had never dared tell her that I was working for the British [which he did, in place, for eleven years] for fear that she would denounce me. Inevitably this meant that we had never come as close as we might have in normal circumstances: always I had withheld a central feature of my existence from her. Is intellectual deception of one's partner more or less cruel than physical deception?"[14] The Soviet system encouraged suspicion such that even the closest of intimates were denied the sharing of their innermost despair. Those heretical thoughts that could not be spoken in public were equally taboo in private. For Gordievsky, his wife was not someone in whom he confided and to whom he owed devotion, but a further source of threat.

Nonetheless, he expresses great remorse over the loss of his family. He knew they would endure considerable hardship for his actions, including ostracism, intensive KGB surveillance, loss of opportunities, and general misery at the stigma of being connected with an enemy of the state. He tried repeatedly to win them permission to join him in the West following his defection, but to no avail until the disintegration of the Soviet Union. However, by then the marriage had been destroyed.

Philby and Gordievsky both committed treason for ideological reasons, if they are to be taken at their word. Each had the misfortune of being born into a political system he saw as so flawed as to be irredeemable from within. If we are to applaud Gordievsky for defecting to our side, we may be compelled – however grudgingly – to recognize the moral imperatives that drove Philby. Much as it is distasteful to argue the morality of betraying a liberal democracy in Stalin's favour, the playing field must be levelled. Otherwise, we stand for my-country-right-or-wrong against their-country-right-or-wrong; by this measure, Gordievsky is a hero because he was our defector, Philby a villain for belonging to them. In that case, each individual is condemned to blind allegiance to the government of the day in whichever country he or she was born, and that obligation reigns supreme. In too many circumstances, this argument is untenable.

Le Carré makes no allowances for Philby's supposed philosophy. He simply condemns him for approaching "society as something that had to be forced off, lied to and fronted to, penetrated and destroyed. The opportunities for overt protest were always available to him. Properly used, our Constitution supplies the channels of outrage and free speech you need to alter society. You don't have to go it sneaky and sly and do it all from within."[15]

What is interesting is how the British Establishment dates one's affiliation and, by extension, its due of loyalty from birth. Philby began paying his debt from the moment of his adherence to the Communist Party, his rebirth of sorts. Le Carré sees in Philby a sort of arrested development. Though he rejects Philby's political motives, le Carré allows that "the British secret service kept it alive as no other environment could have done ... Once entered, it provides no further opportunity for spiritual development. The door that clanged behind the new entrant protected him as much from himself as from reality. Philby, once employed, met spies, conundrums, technique; he had said goodbye to controversy. Such political opinions as sustained him were the opinions of his childhood. The cleaner air of the outside world would have blown them away in a year. Instead, he took into the soundless shrine of the secret world the half-formed jargon of his intellectual betters, the brutal memories of his father, Vienna and Spain; and from there on, simply ceased to develop. He was left with a handful of cliches whose application had ceased in 1931."[16] In contrast, Knightley applauds Philby's lifelong devotion: "he made a total commitment when he was only twenty-one and he had the strength of purpose to stick to it for the rest of his life. How many of us can claim to have done that?"[17]

Philby always bristled at being characterized as a spy or double agent, both terms implying one who is a traitor to his or her cause, one who changes sides for the purpose of betrayal. He did no such thing. "All through my career," he insists in his autobiography, *My Silent War*, "I have been a straight penetration agent working in the Soviet interest."[18] In other words, he never betrayed his true loyalty. He only joined British intelligence at the behest of the KGB. Therefore he was at all times, in his own mind, a Soviet intelligence officer. One of the great sorrows of his life was to learn that the KGB never thought of him in such unambiguous terms. In its view, he was a trifle unsound, never fully one of them.

It may be that, at some moment that is difficult to specify, Philby passed beyond the point of no return. Thus, however his beliefs may have evolved, whatever peace he may have wished to make, he was no longer in a position to do so – at least not outwardly. The KGB held ample proof of his treasons against Britain, and the tacit threat of exposure in the event that he experienced a crisis of conscience or some other change of heart would have been obvious to him. The Soviets would never even have had to whisper the threat. He was a professional intelligence officer, and as such, he well knew the game. Physical evidence of agent meets are usually collected – photos or signed receipts, for example – in order that the agent be tied to her or his handler by something more tangible than loyalty. It is always a good idea for the agent to be made aware that the consequences of withdrawing services could be grave.

When Philby was confronted in Beirut in 1962, during the interim following his departure from MI6 and prior to his flight to Moscow, he did make up a confession of sorts. Though the document itself remains secret, Anthony Cave Brown obtained the information that he revealed only that he had spied for the Communist International before World War II – in other words, before he joined the British intelligence service. The source of this information went on to suggest that the manner in which the British had handled Philby raised significant questions: "Was it an incredible series of botches, or was it an incredible series of operations to plant Philby in Moscow?"[19]

Is it possible that Philby was part of a grand triple agent strategy? Hard to say. Cave Brown writes that "Philby was a gentle man who feared violence, menace, and jail."[20] It was certainly within the arsenal of the British to play upon these fears to manipulate him at this late stage in his career. They knew that the Soviets would have to come to his assistance once it became clear that he had been blown and offer him sanctuary, for surely they could not abandon him in view of the services he had rendered.

However, what would have been the point? Surely, SIS expected
that Philby would be kept under quite a restrictive watch once in
Moscow, as indeed he was. Is it plausible to believe that the British
could have established a secure means of communicating with
him? They did demonstrate an extraordinary capacity for delicate
and dangerous operations in the heart of Moscow when they
succeeded in exfiltrating Gordievsky, who was under very close
surveillance following his recall from London under suspicion of
treason. SIS was able to receive his distress signal, have him elude
his watchers and make his way north from Moscow, connect with
him, and smuggle him over the Finnish-Soviet border to safety.[21]
Therefore, with this verifiable example of what was possible, it is
not utterly far-fetched to imagine that a secure communications
link – perhaps a dead or live letterbox – could have been established with Philby and that he might have served some British
purpose in exile.

Another theory is that he was turned much earlier. In this scenario, he would have had to accept withdrawal to Moscow or
blow a hitherto successful operation, and with it years of whatever
benefit it had derived. Were the doubts the KGB never fully sur-
rendered about Philby's allegiance nothing more than an expression of the instinctive suspicion with which every double agent is
held? The thinking goes that the very act of being a double agent
reveals a predisposition to disloyalty; hence no profession of loyalty on his or her part can ever be trusted. Or was something more
substantive going on? Philby did – possibly in total innocence –
exacerbate Soviet fears by exhibiting his overt Britishness.

Then there is the hypothesis that he, if not consciously turned,
was an unwitting conduit of disinformation aimed against the
Soviets. This scenario assumes that Philby was suspected far earlier than is commonly acknowledged and was left in place unmolested so that the British and Americans could confound and
preoccupy the Soviets with false and misleading intelligence. Cave
Brown speculates: "The entire affair *suggested* that 'C' [Menzies]
had indeed manipulated Philby in some great strategic deception.
Yet that solution to the mystery was the *one aspect of the affair that
was most violently denounced*. That, surely, suggested 'C' had known
the truth about Philby for a much longer period than he acknowledged, and his own almost complete silence and his appearance
of indifference to the implications, which he maintained from 1951

until his death in 1968, was surely convincing evidence that 'C' believed he had done his duty, that he had not been outwitted."[22] Consider, as well, the cryptic comment of Anthony Montague Browne, Sir Winston Churchill's private secretary from 1952 to 1965: "There is one secret left in the Philby case, and that I may not discuss."[23] Further, there is the matter of a 1982 freedom-of-information request submitted by a British author for CIA documents related to Albanian operations blown by Philby. The CIA counsel opposed the release because the "Soviet government would be able to make an estimate of the accuracy or otherwise of the intelligence provided by Philby while he was in Washington." The court agreed that the documents should be withheld.[24]

Are these tantalizing tidbits suggestive of something real, or are they part of an illusion meant to inject a measure of uncertainty in KGB minds about the worth of Philby's lengthy collaboration? Cave Brown ultimately rejects the notion of Philby as C's dupe on the grounds that he inhabited such sensitive positions that an operation of that nature would have inevitably caused more harm than good.[25] But if one doubts the value of the intelligence Philby passed along, this scenario gains credibility. Thomas Powers contends that Philby "betrayed many agents and informants, but aside from this, no one has yet shown that he gave the Soviets anything more than a secret sense of superiority."[26] If the agents he blew were judged expendable, they could have been a price willingly paid for the larger purpose of assuring his long-term acceptance into the Soviet fold.

Knightley concludes that Philby was exactly what he had claimed to be: a dedicated Soviet agent to the last. After meeting with Philby in Moscow shortly before his death, Knightley writes, "He made a new life in the Soviet Union and, after ups and downs that he had the courage to admit to, he died happy, fulfilled and unracked by guilt – his final coup. We are deluding ourselves and will have learnt less than nothing from the affair if we persist in thinking otherwise."[27] Or did Philby delude Knightley into thinking as he wished him to – his final deception rather than his final coup?

These are all questions without answers. Not only is he no longer around to reply, but we would find ourselves unable to believe him regardless of what he might say. The relevant intelligence services will never respond unambiguously because whatever advantage there is left to reap from the affair lies in the remnants of ambiguity. So we are all left to speculate and vacillate. Even Greene, who staunchly stood by his old colleague and friend, was moved to doubt at the very end of his life. In response to a question raised by his biographer, Norman Sherry, he spent his final days reviewing personal papers and books related to Philby in search for clues as to whether he might have ended up a triple agent.[28]

If it were the case that Philby was in fact a triple, even Greene would have been deceived and his reason for supporting his friend through all the tribulations of his exposure would have been unfounded. Or perhaps Greene, the old SIS man, was part of the grand deception. "I believe he was serving a larger purpose in remaining a close friend of Philby's," suggests Sherry.[29] In 1987 Philby was given permission to meet with Greene, and they saw each other on four occasions and exchanged letters. Sherry claims, "To the extent that he established contact with Philby after his defection, Greene was helping his country's intelligence services, and, in a larger sense, was patriotically defending its security."[30] Furthermore, he quotes an interview that Greene gave in which he declared that Philby would have known that he would pass anything of relevance along to SIS.[31] Thus, should we not believe that, if a triple game was afoot, Greene was in on it?

But should we give credence to the game at all? Of greater interest to me than a definitive yes or no is that the questions surrounding Philby still fascinate us. We still wonder at what he was up to and try to pin down the many loose and dog-eared edges to the case. When that proves impossible, we conjure up all manner of conspiracy and collusion. We are reluctant to accept the explanation that screams out at us, preferring the whisper of something else. This is, perhaps, a natural outcome of the obsessive shroud of secrecy pulled tight round the world of intelligence. And this secrecy plagues not only outside observers but those inside the shroud, for they too find themselves excluded. From the need-to-know principle, which demands that people be informed of only what they absolutely need to know for the performance of their function, to the bigot list, which specifies those few individuals permitted to access highly classified material, not even case officers or desk heads can be certain of seeing the whole picture. Compartmentalization fosters the notion of untold happenings elsewhere. It permits the propagation of innuendo and the possibility of snatching victory from defeat. Bureaucrats manipulate this situation to their own advantage, as C did in his cunning suggestion that he had one over on Philby rather than vice versa. Intelligence can rely as much on what is done as on what is thought to be done. If an operational proposal is rejected or an initiative stymied, the customary explanation from on high is, "If you knew all that was going on, you'd understand." Invariably, those other things going on are beyond the need to know. The illusion can be far more powerful than the reality.

The circumstances behind Philby's abrupt departure from Beirut after that final fateful confrontation with SIS, during which he offered a partial confession and promised to return the following day for a more in-depth debriefing, have been great fodder for conspiracy theorists. Did SIS allow him to flee because it feared the public revelations a trial would bring? Or was the entire scenario a set-up to infiltrate him into Moscow, either to protect a long-standing triple operation or for future activation? Or was it the result of outright bungling?

While we cannot be sure, a passage related by Cave Brown concerning Prime Minister Harold Macmillan seems very telling. Upon being informed by Sir Roger Hollis, head of MI5, that a Russian spy within the Admiralty had been caught, Macmillan replied plaintively, "Why the devil did you 'catch' him?" He lamented the impact upon his government of having to try a spy: "better to discover him, and then control him, but never catch him."[32] It must be recalled that it had been Macmillan who, as foreign secretary, had risen in the House of Commons in November 1955 to formally exonerate Philby from the allegation that he had been involved in the flight of Burgess and Maclean. Thus he would have been particularly loath to have Philby brought back for a very public repudiation of his words.

Bureaucrats thrive or founder largely on how well they satisfy the will and whims of their superiors. After he had made it clear that he did not want to see spies caught, the intelligence mandarins could only satisfy their prime minister by turning Philby or causing him to flee. While it is not impossible that the former was accomplished, it is certainly more plausible that Philby took advantage of the window left – maybe inadvertently, maybe not – open. More than this we may never know. And given our propensity for disbelief, what more we may learn will be treated with skepticism. There is no firm footing at the bottom of the conspiracy hole, just ever more slippery, better-concealed plots.

Following the public revelation of the Philby story, le Carré contributed his angry introduction to the book compiled by the *Sunday Times* investigative team, while Greene wrote his sympathetic introduction to Philby's memoirs. By this time, Greene had already begun writing *The Human Factor*, his novel about a mole deep within the secret service. However, he would put it aside and not publish it until 1978 because he feared that it would be taken as a Philby novel, when, as he pointed out, Maurice Castle "bore no resemblance in character or motive to Philby."[33] Nevertheless, the thematic inspiration is clearly Philbian. Greene, however, went out of his way to make Castle a more sympathetic individual, motivated by loyalties that would strike a wider chord than Marxism.

Castle is moved to disclose British secrets to the Russians out of love for his black South African wife, Sarah, her son, Sam, and his gratitude to the communist lawyer who spirited them out of the country after Castle's cover was blown. He is repelled by the complicity of his service with South African intelligence and, by extension, with the detestable apartheid regime. However, he is explicitly not a communist, and he tells his handler adamantly, "I'll fight beside you in Africa, Boris – not in Europe."[34]

He says, "I became a naturalized black when I fell in love with Sarah."[35] As an intractable enemy of his family, the South African regime is his to fight as well, by whatever means are at his disposal. When he divulges his activities to Sarah, she responds, "We have our own country. You and I and Sam. You've never betrayed that country, Maurice."[36] And an act of betrayal against that sacred ground is how he views collaboration with the hated South Africans. Even in England there is a certain isolation to the country he and Sarah share. The condescending courtesy, the unconscious racism confronting his family, distanced Castle from any claim it might have exercised over him. His own mother says, "I'm not at all racialist, though perhaps I'm old-fashioned and patriotic,"[37] as if patriotism explained or excused intolerance.

Castle is quite resolute in his loyalties. The moral quandary lies in his deception, his violation of the trust placed in him as an intelligence officer. Perhaps he should have resigned in disgust, submitting a scathing letter expressing his repugnance against Britain's Africa policy. That would have been acceptable, but also safe and ineffectual. Instead of abandoning his opportunity to do something, he takes advantage of it for the sake of love.

Race imposes allegiance in spite of oneself. It is one thing for Castle to think himself a naturalized black, with his diplomatic passport, and return to England secured; quite another is it for a white South African to identify with the brutally subjugated majority during the days of apartheid. Hard-line – and many less than hard-line – whites believed that the boot holding Africans down was the only thing stopping them from jumping up and slitting whites' throats. Their recurring nightmare was of an unrestrained race war. After much soul searching, crime reporter Rian Malan had to admit that no matter how fervently any white might sympathize with Africans, socialize with them, attend their protests, recognize their dignity, and yearn for justice – all the things he did – at the end of the day the white returned home white.

My Traitor's Heart is Malan's brilliant memoir of his experiences in apartheid South Africa. He is of impeccable Afrikaner pedigree, able to trace his roots in Africa back over three hundred years. Furthermore, he is a blood relative of two of apartheid's most notorious figures: Daniel Francis Malan, who, as prime minister, first institutionalized the idea of racial separation in 1948, and General Magnus Malan, who was minister of defence in 1976 when Soweto erupted. But Rian was not like his forebears. He wanted desperately to be the just white man. He smelt the stench of apartheid and wanted to defect from his Afrikaner tribe in order to stand with the oppressed against the oppressor. But one can't shed one's skin. "I am a white man born in Africa," he concedes, "and all else flows from there."[38]

For those less courageous than Malan, *My Traitor's Heart* is terrifying for its fearlessness in penetrating the dark caverns from which no answers are forthcoming, only the echo of tougher questions. He refuses to accept the platitudes of the politically correct or take comfort in good intentions, mocking his own youthful fancy that sporting long hair, for instance, or sleeping with an African maid struck a blow against apartheid. There came the time to demand honesty of himself. It drove Malan from South Africa. "I ran because I couldn't carry a gun for apartheid, and because I wouldn't carry a gun against it. I ran away because I hated Afrikaners and loved blacks. I ran away because I was an Afrikaner and feared blacks."[39]

He saw no way to reconcile his loyalties without betrayal, no way to be the moral Afrikaner in the midst of outraged blacks and vicious whites. Unable to discern to whom the largest debt was due, he fled. More than anything else, Malan was a traitor to his own heart, for – in his estimation – he failed to be the just white man. Conditions were too complex for definitive choices. To stand for something really did mean taking up a gun for one side or the other.

Malan explores the clash between narrowly defined race and an encompassing view of humanity. Thinking in terms of "race traitor" raises ugly, fascistic overtones of supremacy and inferiority. But the truth is, as Malan acknowledges, that tribal sentiments run deep. People tend to subdivide themselves, distinguishing those for whom they feel kinship from those they do not along lines of skin colour, place of birth, religion, and history. Few of us can muster a sufficiently universal spirit to reject narrowing our scope of loyalties.

When it becomes evident that information is spilling from a leak in Castle's two-man African subsection, the number of probable suspects is distinctly limited. Following the preliminary interview with the security officer Daintry, Castle says to Arthur Davis, his junior, "Colonel Daintry wasn't very difficult. He knew a cousin of mine at Corpus. That sort of thing makes a difference."[40] Since Davis is just a Reading man, he is clearly the more suspicious of the two. The British secret services held great stock in superficial acquaintance. Among those who had vouched for Philby was Colonel Valentine Vivian, deputy chief of sis, who had served with Philby's father in India. He commented, "I was asked about him, and I said I knew his people"[41] – enough said; reliability confirmed.

Anxious to avoid public disclosure of the treason, Dr Percival undertakes to dispose of Davis by slipping him a drug that will bring about a quite natural appearing death. All Castle need do to forever escape suspicion is to cease all reporting following Davis's death. sis will then be satisfied that it has liquidated the right man. But an operation of such consequence that he cannot ignore it comes to his attention. In passing it along, he knows he will have to activate his escape plan and flee, leaving behind the family he so adores.

The exile in which Castle finds himself is exceedingly lonely and bleak. Even the Moscow weather suggests despair: "This was not the snow he remembered from childhood and associated with snowballs and fairy stories and games and toboggans. This was a merciless, interminable, annihilating snow, a snow in which one could expect the world to end."[42] The picture presented of his life is morose and pitiful. He lives off the tenuous gratitude of the KGB, with no more than a token function to perform, waiting in desperation and depression for the day when Sarah will be able to join him. Defection is never the preferred outcome of an operation. It makes for wonderful headlines in the morning paper, but at the end of the day, once an in-place source's usefulness has been depleted, you want the person to go home – with a nice final bonus, surely, but home nonetheless. You definitely don't want to be saddled with responsibility for a defector for the rest of his or her life.

As Greene accurately portrays it, defection is, for defectors, a heart-aching choice. They will often be overcome by a dramatic sense of loss, which becomes particularly acute once the host service has run out of questions and shunted them aside. Suddenly they find themselves without the high status lavished on them immediately after the jump, when the media are enthralled by the daring of the whole escapade. Senior officers, who once sought them out as much for their celebrity as for advice, no longer receive their calls. Furthermore, as they try to settle in their new country, they are just another immigrant. All this can cause depression, remorse, and, in many instances, alcohol abuse and loneliness-induced troubles with the other sex. As well, they face adapting to a new language and strange ways of doing things, such as opening bank accounts, having a telephone installed, finding a doctor, and so on. Except for the most prominent jumpers who are sufficiently valuable to secure the rest of their lives, it is a pretty dismal existence, no matter which side one ends up on. Greene showed Philby the manuscript of *The Human Factor* prior to publication, and Philby objected to the portrayal of Castle's life in Moscow. He felt it left a misleading impression of what his own life was like. Nevertheless, Greene refused to alter the glum mood he had created.[43]

Yuri Modin, who got to know Philby following his defection, after many years spent analyzing the data received at Centre from the Cambridge spies, confirmed Philby's dislike of *The Human Factor*. Philby disparaged Castle as "a whining fool who ekes out his days in a Moscow hovel. His own circumstances were totally different, what with his huge apartment, his magnificent view, the copies of *The Times*, *Le Monde*, and the *Herald Tribune* to which he had subscribed, the videotapes of cricket test matches and the pots of Cooper's Oxford marmalade sent from London."[44] Quite unintentionally, Modin makes Philby seem every bit as pathetic as Castle. There we see him, perhaps in a more comfortable apartment than the one to which Castle is consigned, clinging feebly to the pleasures of an English gentleman. It is the Western press he yearns for, not *Pravda* or *Izvestia*; the cricket season he follows, not hockey; and premium marmalade he craves, not whatever gloopy jams are to be found at the head of the queue at GUM. Philby would conceal to the end any disappointment he suffered at living out those years in banishment. It is not inconceivable that he had sought to re-establish a relationship with Greene "as an antidote to *taedium vitae*. He would wish to continue his double life, if this were possible, in any country on any side – a double agent on the lookout to become a triple agent."[45]

It is impossible to overstate the devastation wrought by the suspicion – let alone the revelation – of a traitor's presence. One part of you never quite emerges from denial. To learn that the bond between those who keep the same secrets has been desecrated is a shock to the psyche. Your gut response to the suggestion that a mole is on the loose is disbelief. The shared confidences of the job preclude you from thinking the absolute worst of any colleague. There are so many reasons why an operation might go sour or an agent cease to be productive. That someone close to you, perhaps at the highest levels of your own service, is a double agent is usually the last possibility to be examined – until, that is, the evidence becomes irrefutable. And even then, you have to tread most cautiously. A full-scale mole hunt can decimate an intelligence service, turning officers against one another on the scantiest of evidence, turning people already unhealthily predisposed to distrust into raving paranoiacs.

The Philby operation succeeded in convincing some – in particular, James Jesus Angleton, the CIA's head of counter-intelligence from 1954 to 1974, and Peter Wright, an assistant director of MI5 – to tie up resources and undermine genuine intelligence in an endless witch hunt for ever-deeper, more furtive Soviet infiltrations. Wright became, and remained, convinced that Sir Roger

Hollis, the head of MI5 from 1956 to 1965, was a Soviet agent, the elusive and notorious "fifth man" of the Cambridge spy ring, and he expended considerable effort to prove that this was so, but because the suspicion was unfounded, without success.[46] The irony is that this was not a premeditated Soviet contrivance, just a happy by-product from the debris of a blown operation.

Indeed, by somehow convincing a service that it has been penetrated, the opposition can create conditions under which it can operate with near impunity, for any suggestion as to what it is up to will be treated as part of the grand deception. This was the dizzying logic that caused Angleton so to cripple the CIA that it was incapable of the adroit gymnastics necessary to manoeuvre in step with the KGB. Philby and Angleton had been close during the former's tenure as SIS liaison to Washington, and Angleton was irrecoverably traumatized when he learned that he had been deceived all along.[47] This was a perfectly understandable response. Here was a man who prided himself on his ability to mistrust enough to see through anyone's masquerade on the basis of instinct and an encyclopedic grasp of Soviet methodology. And yet he had been soundly hoodwinked, probably robbed blind of CIA secrets during the frequent and friendly exchanges they had had over alcoholic lunches.

Convinced, in hindsight, that the CIA was being manipulated by its own Philby, Angleton refused to accept the legitimacy of any operation, certain that each opportunity that presented itself was a ruse carefully designed, like a magician's sleight of hand, to misdirect his gaze from true Soviet intentions. Angleton became a virtual prisoner of these fears, and consequently, he took the entire CIA hostage with him. Being deceived by Philby was such a blow that he saw Soviet deception in everything, including the Sino-Soviet split and the Prague Spring, and he believed the mole could be anyone, including Secretary of State Henry Kissinger.[48] His decade-long mole hunt, launched in 1964 largely on the basis of vague accusations from defector Anatoly Golitsyn, was an unmitigated disaster, ruining careers and legitimate operations without ever finding the dreaded penetration. Golitsyn also succeeded in convincing Angleton that defectors following him would, in truth, be KGB plants sent to disrupt the CIA. Since bad information was far more dangerous than no information, in that it would steer the

Americans in the direction the Soviets wanted them to take, whatever they said was interpreted as purposeful deception.

The mole obsession took a marvelously ironic turn around 1973
when Angleton protégé Clare Petty took up the investigation and
concluded with 80 to 85 per cent certainty that Angleton was
actually the mole: "'I looked at CI cases that had failed ... examining why they went wrong, looking for overlaps and common-
alities,' he explains. 'I also reviewed Angleton's entire career,
going back through his relationships with Philby, his adherence
to all of Golitsyn's wild theories, his false accusations against
foreign services and the resulting damage to the liaison relationships, and finally his accusations against innocent Soviet Division
officers.'"[49] With an enemy like Angleton, the KGB could do very
nicely without friends. The CIA dismissed Petty's analysis, but
far-fetched as it is, it presents an intriguing idea. For all his
legendary status, Angleton caught no spies, unearthed no moles,
and was outwitted by the only bona fide KGB agent he encountered. To theorize that he was a mole was a conclusion worthy of
Angleton himself.

When he was finally pushed into retirement and the damage
he had inflicted was recognized, the CIA took an organizational
vow never again to be so spellbound by ghostly traitors that it
would fail to see the form for the shadows. This decision, in large
measure, explains its reluctance to acknowledge when there really
was a penetration of its Soviet Section. Accordingly, Aldrich Ames
succeeded in surviving undetected for a decade before his arrest
in 1994.

He should have set off every indicator light on the dashboard.
He drank to excess, lived ostentatiously beyond his means in an
expensive home, drove a Jaguar, and was disgruntled about
having been passed over for promotion – every indicator a CI
investigator is trained to watch out for. All this could – though
should not – have been ignored were it not for the fact that cases
were regularly going belly up and as many as ten Soviet sources
were captured and executed. The truth of the matter is that heavy
drinking is commonplace in intelligence circles. At one time it was
de rigueur. As for being disgruntled, who isn't? More than one
officer has gone into debt for the sake of a flashy car he had no
right to buy. And some members have outside incomes, from
working spouses, inheritances, family businesses, or any number

of other legitimate sources. However much one might believe otherwise in retrospect, "Ames's drinking did not stand out at the CIA. And neither did Ames. Conspiracy theorists might find some sinister aspects in the CIA's inability to see Ames for what he was. But there was no cabal of covert operators shielding him; he had never belonged to the old-boy clique at the CIA. His superiors in Rome and in Washington simply never took notice of him."[50] Or as Don Payne, one of the investigators who worked on the mole hunt put it, "There were so many problem personalities … that no one stands out."[51]

We had some old-time drinkers who were so brazen as to take business calls at the Service watering hole of choice, where our identities were the worst-kept secret in Ottawa. None of them were disloyal, and few would let the bottle get the better of their discretion. The point is that it's always easy to point out the risk cases after the fact. But treason is a thing apart from any overt character flaw. Optimally, the spy who is to remain undetected – every spy's objective – will exhibit none of the telltale signs that would arouse suspicions. Thus the man who cruises into the parking lot in his Jag or takes multiple martini lunches, inviting people to comment on his habits, isn't doing much for his cover. In his blatancy may reside his innocence – or not. The spy hunter quickly learns that character weaknesses are prevalent. Traitors are not. It is a gross oversimplification to imagine that drinking necessarily implies problems of loyalty. The drinking is merely an opening, but it is so endemic in the profession as to be nearly epidemic. Vladimir Kuzichkin, a former KGB officer who defected to the British in 1982, wrote of his five years at the Soviet Embassy in Tehran, "An air of permanent holiday pervaded the Residency. Everybody drank, from the resident downward. There were parties every day behind closed doors."[52]

I recall one operation against a communist official with a great thirst for beer, which he quenched in a seedy little out-of-the-way tavern whose most redeeming quality was the amplitude of its waitresses' breasts and the skimpy tops they wore to show them off. Night after night he sat alone at a stained table, gulping from chipped glasses, gawking in red-eyed fascination at the capitalist wonders laid almost bare before him. Analysts concluded that this was an unusual show of independence, since most officials were forbidden from going out drinking alone. These nightly excursions, we thought, might be indicative of an unhappy fellow who would welcome some convivial conversation. So a man was put into the tavern. After several occasions of making eye contact and exchanging nods, they struck up a conversation, as men will over a drink. A few more occasions and they shared a table. A few more and they began looking out for each other. They discussed the news, whatever game was on the television, and a few humdrum household matters. It never amounted to anything, proving that not every unusual act is a sign of impending treason.

Intelligence officers all realize that their secrets hold a certain value if offered up to the opposition. They are also aware – acutely so – that they will never get rich on their salary. The temptation is present, as is the opportunity. The thrill of the forbidden can be very alluring, yet few succumb. Any number of factors may explain their resistance: fear, devotion to duty, belief in the cause, satisfaction with their lives, pride, self-respect, a sense of honour.

The traitor, whether of the personal variety or of the arcane world of state secrets, enjoys a certain literary cachet. When viewed from a distance, the flawed character holds an attraction that fades only upon closer scrutiny. Actually living such a life, however, is rather less desirable, fraught as it is with the prospect of an unhappy ending. Maurice Castle did not seek the life he has found, nor does he find solace in his dreary exile in Moscow. What he most longs for is "a permanent home, in a city where he could be accepted as a citizen, as a citizen without any pledge of faith, not the City of God or Marx, but the city called Peace of Mind."[53]

Le Carré tackled the Philby legend with brilliant subtlety in *Tinker Tailor Soldier Spy* (1974), which he at one time called "the most difficult book I ever wrote"; he only arrived at the final version after "destroying in despair" two early drafts.[54] He did not soften the betrayal, as Greene had, by allowing Bill Haydon to spy for a purpose that could arouse sympathy. Indeed, Haydon never satisfies by confessing a resolute ideological creed. He freely admits to anti-Americanism and disillusion with Britain's insignificance in world affairs. In the event that either superpower were to best the other, he would simply prefer that the Soviets win the day. "It's an aesthetic judgement as much as anything," he concludes. "Partly a moral one, of course."[55] His is hardly an expression of ideological fervour. Worse than having him end up forlorn in squalid Moscow, le Carré has Haydon expertly killed before he is to be expatriated in a spy swap.

The psychological leap required to commit treason cannot be overstated. It is not like adultery, a finite act open to disavowal. Rather, it is more aptly compared to suicide. Greene's novel *The Heart of the Matter* is concerned with many of the competing loyalties he confronted in his own life. Police Major Scobie, a devout Catholic, is trapped in a loveless marriage. Taking as his mistress a lonely and vulnerable new arrival to Sierra Leone – the setting is where Greene was posted as a wartime 10 – he is plagued by guilt, not so much for betraying his wife as for his offence against God. His subsequent spiral towards suicide – with which Greene sometimes flirted – is not just a means to escape the conundrum his life has become but also an opportunity to avoid ambiguity by defying God with the most forbidden sin he can commit. No more treasonous act is possible.

Walking up the drive and into a foreign embassy is like slipping the barrel of the pistol past your lips and letting it glide into your mouth. To pass the envelope, irretrievably, to the enemy and take money in exchange is to squeeze resolutely on the trigger, sending the bullet unstoppably through the chamber and letting it seek purchase in your brain. Regret recedes beyond contemplation. Action overwhelms thought. What is done cannot be undone. You turn your back on all the comforts you've known, imagining something safer; not finding it.

At the same time, treason is a great expression of ego. Many who contemplate it are arrogant about their own sophistication, confident that they are so adept at the game that they can outsmart any pursuers. It is the supreme act of independence and defiance, just as suicide is an act of defiance against God. There is a principle which claims that life is a seamless garment, running uninterrupt-edly from the moment of conception until death. One is prohibited from taking into one's own hands the conscious choice to termi-nate a life, even one's own. So it is in the canon of intelligence that one guards the sanctity of state secrets without exception. In a profession marked by self-containment, treason is the only means of stepping outside the parameters of acceptable behaviour and distinguishing oneself as more clever than the rest. To betray is to best, to have the defence shift left while you run the ball right. With every day that you keep the secret of your true self, you have gotten away with something. Sources need intense flattery; they need their handler to tell them how superior they are. In most cases, nobody else will. What all spies have in common is the elation of being – for as long as they get away with it – cleverer than everyone else, smarter than all the combined forces of the state security apparatus. Anyone can acquiesce; the traitor is an outlaw who relies on his or her wits. Rosenbaum characterizes Philby as "a *personal* imperialist, an imperialist of the self, who used his power to impose his own vision on the globe, to make the Great Powers navigate by his charts. To make his own mischief on a grand scale."[56] Smiley attributes similar sentiments of grandeur to Haydon: "Standing in the middle of a secret stage, playing world against world, hero and playwright in one: oh, Bill had loved that all right."[57]

Perhaps, then, it is this godlike sense of being the grand manipulator that drives the traitor. Elevated from the mass of drudges slogging through their day, filing reports, monitoring events, they cause events to happen. At the mention of a name, hinting that a Soviet was a double agent, a Philby or an Ames could bring that person's death. And they did. It's heady stuff for a grey man to hand down a death sentence, just like that.

Control has come to suspect that the Circus has been penetrated. Too many cases are turning sour; too many sources are drying up. His search for the traitor is by necessity a solitary effort and by inclination an obsession. With his health in decline and his isolation growing, his hold on the Circus is waning, creating a perfect opportunity for Haydon to manipulate Percy Alleline's sense of being under-appreciated to undermine Control's position. In conspiracy with his Soviet handler, Karla, Haydon fabricates source Merlin, a magical window into the very heart of Moscow Centre. Whatever blanks there are on Britain's map of Russia, be they military or foreign policy or economic, Merlin can fill them in. Eventually, Operation Witchcraft, as it is christened, is the only worthwhile product being collected by the Circus.

The straw that breaks Control's back is Operation Testify. Launched in Czechoslovakia, it goes disastrously and – most horrible – publicly wrong. Jim Prideaux has been sent in to meet a General Stevcek, who has let it be known through channels that he wishes to speak with an emissary from Control. Control expects that Stevcek will offer up the name of Karla's mole. But when Prideaux arrives at the meet, he is greeted with fireworks.

Shot in the back as he tries to flee, he is taken prisoner and, as Smiley will learn later, interrogated by Karla. Much to Prideaux's surprise, Karla is uninterested in Stevcek, grilling him instead about Control's mole theory and who is suspected. Haydon capitalizes on this failure, convincing the minister that Testify is the proof of Control's incompetence. A good housecleaning, but not fundamental renovation, seems in order. He manoeuvres Alleline into Control's slot and sets himself up as head of London Station, through which everything that touches upon Centre and agent recruitment now has to be routed.

Enter Ricki Tarr, one of Peter Guillam's disreputable "scalphunters" (the section assigned to carry out murders and kidnappings and hit-and-run recruitment pitches too dangerous for the local resident). He is sent to Hong Kong to assess whether Boris, a Soviet trade delegate may be vulnerable to a recruitment approach. Performing a covert entry on his hotel room, Tarr comes face-to-face with Boris's wife, Irina. After a bit of bluff, Tarr seduces her, and she comes clean that both she and Boris are from Centre. Irina wants to defect and will reveal vital secrets in exchange for asylum. Following procedure, Tarr cables London Station and seeks its intercession. Time is short since the delegation is soon to return home, and Irina is increasingly fragile under the strain. Inexplicably, London stalls, requesting additional information. In the interim, a woman, bandaged and in a coma, is spirited away on an unscheduled Soviet flight.

Irina's fate was inspired by that of Konstantin Volkov, the deputy resident of the NKVD (precursor to the KGB) posted under cover to Istanbul, who offered to defect to the British in August 1945. Among the Soviet moles about whom he claimed to have information was a counter-intelligence section head in London. News of the offer arrived on Philby's desk, and he was certain it was to him that Volkov was referring. Philby obviously informed his handler of the looming defection. Through a combination of happenstance and manipulation, he arranged to journey himself to Istanbul to debrief Volkov. He took several days to reach his destination, by which time Volkov, heavily bandaged and sedated, had been loaded aboard a Soviet aircraft on a stretcher and returned to Moscow, where he was executed.

On a hope and a whim following Irina's disappearance, Tarr goes to clear the emergency dead-letter drops established for her in case she has managed to leave him a message. And so she has, revealing that most closely held prize she has promised upon defection: that Karla is running a highly placed mole in the Circus. Not certain who he can trust but knowing he has to avoid London Station, Tarr goes to ground, surfacing only to Guillam, who is out of favour with Haydon's inner circle. Guillam brings in Oliver Lacon, the minister's intelligence watchdog, who in turn calls in Smiley, who was among the casualties when Control's people were swept aside.

And so the game commences, a game as treacherous for the mole hunter as it is for the mole. Of the hunter is demanded a ruthlessness that may not be in his nature. He has to be willing to look into the graves where all the bodies are decomposing without flinching. He has to go unwaveringly wherever the truth takes him, regardless of the enemies he encounters along the way. The mole has made a choice, and part of that choice, on some level, is a resolve to confront the consequences. Not so the mole hunter – Guillam takes it especially hard: "for the first time in his life, he had sinned against his own notions of nobility. He had a sense of dirtiness, even of self-disgust."[58] Along the way he comes to suspect everyone and everything: "His friends, his loves, even the Circus itself, joined and re-formed in endless patterns of intrigue. A line of Mendel's came back to him ...: 'Cheer up, Peter, old son. Jesus Christ only had twelve, you know, and one of them was a double.'"[59] But for all that, in the end "it required an act of will on his own part, and quite a violent one at that, to regard Bill Haydon with much other than affection."[60]

How can that be? How can your psyche be so bent around that you loathe yourself while retaining affection for the real culprit? That you can no longer trust anything, but long so much to believe in the traitor? However cautious we may be, we take more on trust in our daily lives than we realize. Underlying whatever pessimism we may feel towards others, we have to operate on the presumption of fairness, if not on the part of individuals, then certainly on the part of the system or the norms that govern behaviour. When this trust breaks down, there is a genuine sense of disorientation. Back we go through the looking glass. Those of us inside intelligence were supposed to be acclimatized to the double and triple games, to be constantly on the lookout for deceit, to spot the hair displaced from the door jamb that signaled a covert entry.

But can one really live that way? I suppose you can if you are able to seal yourself off from all emotion that comes naturally. Philby was truly remarkable in that respect, even under the influence of alcohol, even when sharing apparent intimacies. The barren wasteland to which he banished his secrets when in the company of others was as boundless as the Empty Quarter plied by his father. The urge to confess, to experience the relief that comes with opening yourself up to another person, was absent from his personality. His every overt relationship, personal as well as professional, was replete with lies. Was he incapable of love? Did he not need love? Was the vulnerability that true love exacts a weakness he would not allow himself to indulge?

Deception calls for steely harshness, with yourself and with those around you. Knowledge of Haydon's affair with Ann is rife around the Circus, causing Smiley considerable anguish. In a conversation following his detention at Sarratt, Haydon confirms that he has pursued her on Karla's instructions. He tells Smiley that Karla has great respect for him and considered him Haydon's greatest threat. Haydon says, "But you had this one price: Ann. The last illusion of the illusionless man. He reckoned that if I was known to be Ann's lover around the place you wouldn't see very straight when it came to other things."[61] Smiley puzzles over this remark. "Illusion? Was that really Karla's name for love? And Bill's?"[62]

Perhaps love is incompatible with espionage. Certainly, trust and intimacy, love's closest companions, are. And without those qualities, love is an illusion. This personal emotional repression forms an apt parallel with Cold War politics. It took an immense effort to maintain hostility for nearly fifty years, especially when one considers that it was not directed primarily against a specific individual or nationality, the usual targets of hatred, but against an idea. Throughout this long war, "there was no German monster to fan the patriotic flame, and Smiley had always been a little embarrassed by protestations of anti-communism."[63] What, then, sustained it? A collective identity embedded largely in fear – fear by us of them and vice versa. We were afraid to fight – nuclear arsenals made hot war inconceivable – and we were afraid not to fight – gains by one side were perceived as costly defeats by the other. So we devoted great energy to finding creative means to square off. We probed each other's flanks and ended up with Koreas and Vietnams and Afghanistans and Angolas. The Soviets battened down their borders and ended up with Hungary and Czechoslovakia and a Berlin Wall. The Americans bolstered their outposts and ended up with fiascos in Latin America. We were so consumed by fear that nobody was able to see a way out of the maelstrom. The international system revolved around the Cold War stalemate, and it became routinized and bureaucratized. It became easier to reap the benefits of embracing the system than to find a way out. Symmetry ensued. A complex tango between skilled, if tentative, partners began.

The responsible minister fears the public scandal that will follow should the mole successfully flee to Moscow and Centre decide to use him to make British intelligence look foolish. Oliver Lacon doesn't allude to any irony when trying to set his mind at ease: "'I think that's always been a point the Russians accept,' said Lacon. 'After all, if you make your enemy look a fool, you lose the justification for engaging him.' He added: 'They've never made use of their opportunities so far, have they?'"[64]

Perhaps the development of this mutual dependence made treason easier, as the two sides came increasingly to resemble each other, as confrontation became a matter of complicity, as individuals showed themselves incapable of living up to the standards they were supposed to embody. I have written elsewhere that "le Carré's books don't climax; they anti-climax. The quarry most frequently turns out to have been unworthy of the hunt ... Reality never lives up to fantasy. The spies toil endlessly in a fallow landscape of disappointment, ending up as damaged and broken as the dust bowl farmers of the depression."[65] And so it is with *Tinker Tailor Soldier Spy*. Like Guillam, at the end of the affair Smiley "felt so bankrupt; that whatever intellectual or philosophical precepts he clung to broke down entirely now that he was faced with the human situation."[66] With Haydon safely in custody, he "felt not only disgust; but, despite all that the moment meant to him, a surge of resentment against the institutions he was supposed to be protecting ... The Minister's lolling mendacity, Lacon's tight-lipped moral complacency, the bludgeoning greed of Percy Alleline: such men invalidated any contract: why should anyone be loyal to them?"[67]

In contrast to this sentiment, Mathis in *Casino Royale* advises James Bond, "Surround yourself with human beings, my dear James. They are easier to fight for than principles."[68] Unfortunately, we rarely get to select the people who surround us. Principles, on the other hand, are of our own choosing, and they are our best hope for rousing our flagging resolve when people and institutions prove, as is so often the case, unworthy.

The pinnacle of intelligence work is to recruit an opposition 10. It is a delicate, exciting, ulcer-burningly tense exercise. Whether by blackmail or by bribe, by hook or by crook, you must compel the person to take a leap of faith in a faithless world. If you do your homework right, you get a fairly good idea at what level to cast your pitch. That, of course, is different from knowing whether it will be a hit or a miss. The great trick with a foreign diplomat or delegate is to manoeuvre yourself into contact with him or her in such a way that the person is undeniably conscious of meeting with an intelligence officer, even when the fact isn't specified. Doing so provides an immediate indication that he or she is prepared to withstand the risk inherent in contact with the enemy. Your concern in these instances is that the target may have informed his superiors of your approach and intend to report back regarding your methods and interests, or that he hopes to turn the tables completely and tempt you with a recruitment offer of his own. Once you ascertain that they have not told anyone about seeing you, you have a considerable hold over them: the threat that their side will come to learn they have engaged in a clandestine meeting with the opposing service.

The ideal setting for such an encounter is the hotel room. For one thing, it offers complete privacy and eliminates the danger of inadvertently being spotted. For another, there is no ready explanation for being with an 10 except that the target is being recruited. Whatever he or she might feign, there was not an East bloc citizen – let alone one who had finagled permission to travel to the West – who did not know the implications and consequences of crossing the threshold of a hotel room with a local 10. Nonetheless, being there only signals a preparedness to listen, no more. Yes, they've been hooked, but not yet landed.

You choose an approach carefully. If you have discerned a craving for Western luxuries or a need for money, it's pretty straightforward: information for cash, the amount determined by the quality of the information. Money is the most effective door-slammer. The source takes the money and is required to sign a receipt, proof that payment has been received. It's a bureaucratic procedure, a slip of paper to be attached to the cash requisition signed by the handler and his or her supervisor demonstrating that money entrusted to the handler was disbursed for its intended purpose. But it's more than that: it's a signed confession, really – nothing that you would ever want to use to pressure the source to continue supplying information, but …

A particular sexual predilection is slightly more difficult. In CSIS at any rate, we were not permitted to offer satisfaction of such needs. And while we could promise to look the other way if the predilection was of a nature likely to be frowned upon by the person's home security service, blackmail was not a weapon likely to bring about a positive relationship. We could, however, show ourselves to be far more open-minded and sympathetic about such things. If it's a matter of ideology, then you simply must express agreement. Whatever the motive, you must share it.

The most important thing is to keep talking about the target of recruitment, never about yourself, because the act of recruiting is all about the other person, not you. The trick is to bring targets to where they lose themselves in whatever fantasy they have created for themselves, not to try to sell your fantasies to them. This approach never works because, as discussed earlier, you don't so much recruit someone as make yourself available when the person is ready to jump. Since you won't make the decision for him or her, but can only confirm one that the person has taken for him or herself, it is especially important to be able to read what it is that brought the person to this point. If anything, watching the interrogator drift off into a fantasy strengthens the target's hold on reality and the peril of what he or she is contemplating. Nothing breaks the mood more decisively. Nothing shows the target more conclusively how weak you can be. This is the mistake that Smiley makes with Karla, though at the time he has no idea with whom he is dealing.

It is 1955, and Centre is in the midst of one of its periodic purges. A slew of officers lucky enough to be overseas think that the time is propitious for defection, rather than returning home to find out whether they are in or out of favour. Smiley is being dispatched far and wide to meet with likely defectors and decide if London needed to purchase what they are selling. In the case of Karla, he is not a volunteer, but a victim of a blown network. In Delhi he is informed that he is to return to Moscow immediately.

Given the circumstances and atmosphere at home, it is a certainty that his head will be on the block. He is detained by Indian authorities at the Circus's request, and Smiley is dispatched to offer him a better alternative.

Karla responds to Smiley's offer with stillness. Instead of giving him a take-it-or-leave-it, Smiley fills the silence with patter about the wife he supposes him to have back home. He rambles on about her predicament and how he can help get her to the West if Karla will only cooperate. But, of course, Smiley isn't talking about the wife he imagines Karla to have; he is speaking of Ann: "I exchanged my predicament for his, that is the point, and as I now realise I began to conduct an interrogation with myself."[69] He confuses himself with the target: "I would have sworn I am getting through to him, that I had found the chink in his armour: when of course all I was doing – all I was doing was showing him the chink in mine."[70] Without uttering a word, Karla learns more about Smiley than he ever gives away about himself. He knows, when the time arises, that Haydon will have to seduce Ann and that this will cloud Smiley's judgment.

The scene between Karla and Smiley in the Delhi jail is masterful in how effectively le Carré reduces the Cold War to a standoff between two very human characters. That, in effect, is what it was once one had broken away from the interminable political forums, committees, and study groups where issues were discussed but never acted upon. The bottom line in the espionage game is played out in claustrophobic rooms between individuals, one on the run, the other promising sanctuary. The currency is secrets, the consequences personal.

Karla personifies all that threatens Smiley's sense of propriety: his home, his service, his country. Exposing Haydon has not eliminated the danger, for he is merely Karla's puppet. There is nothing to say that his successor has not already been groomed against the eventuality that he is unmasked. After all, an in-place source has a distinctly finite existence. Karla has to think beyond Haydon. Therefore, so long as he continues unfettered, the threat remains. The entire thrust of the real-life investigation into the Cambridge spies had been to unearth those Englishmen who had penetrated the government. In the Karla trilogy the true quest lies in capturing the mastermind behind the penetrator. Le Carré's point is that the Haydons – or the Philbys – are not unique. The person with the cunning and guile to find and seduce them will always find another. Purging Haydon does not expunge the adversary. Karla himself has to be toppled.

As with other le Carré characters, Karla's true identity has been subject of much speculation. For a long time he was taken to have been modelled upon East Germany's Markus Wolf. In comments made in 1991, though confused, Wolf seemed to delight in the connection, saying, "I remember being surprised when I read *The Spy Who Came in from the Cold*. I have never been able to understand how he obtained the information that allowed him to describe me so accurately. Everything was astonishingly close to reality."[71]

The confusion here resides in the fact that Karla does not appear in that novel. Since Wolf would not be flattered to have been the murderous traitor Mundt, he must have mixed up Karla with the far more sympathetic Fiedler, for whom he has never (to my knowledge) been mistaken. Ironically, le Carré tells how he originally intended to give Mundt the name Wolf, after the brand of lawn mower he owned, but was advised that a real Wolf existed in East German intelligence, so he dutifully renamed him.[72] Interestingly, Wolf himself was more testy on the subject in 1993, when he complained, "I'm afraid I have been rather incorrectly typecast ... Unfortunately le Carré never consulted me or some of his Russian characters would have been drawn more realistically."[73] Wolf's delight or testiness would be of little consequence to le Carré, since he has always denied the connection. He writes, "What similarities Wolf could have with Karla is a total mystery to me. Both were communists, I suppose. Both served disgusting regimes. Both were competent agent runners. But that hardly makes them blood brothers."[74] Karla is not such a closely drawn character as to have needed real-life inspiration. Much of his strength lies in his vagueness, for in it he embodies all the inaccessibility of enemy spymasters who orchestrate the gambits of their covert emissaries.

Le Carré's next offering, *The Honourable Schoolboy* (1977), takes up Smiley's quest. It is a very long and meandering novel, in which he gives the plot a far looser rein than had been his custom. He describes minor characters at length, providing them with a presence far out of proportion to their importance to the story. Peripheral scenes are drawn out in details that portend things that never come to pass. I read the novel with the sense that it must be well tied up, but emerged unsure about exactly how it got that way. The reader is left under the impression of seeing the case precisely as it develops, with no more inkling of what will prove significant than have Smiley and his cohorts as they pursue leads and gather clues. Trails widen and narrow, angles sharpen and blunt along the way. Patience and vigilance are the watchwords. Without either, the beam upon which the entire case depends for support may be undermined.

Smiley has taken to referring to Centre as Karla, provoking a rebuke from Lacon: "I think it safer to stay with institutions if you don't mind. In that way we are spared the embarrassment of personalities. After all, that's what institutions are *for*, isn't it?"[75] Personalities are uncomfortable, lacking the stability that one expects in an institution. An institution is suitably abstract to defy resolution – like blaming crime on the Mafia. No one can pin down what the Mafia is, let alone expect it to be brought to heel for all the transgressions laid at its doorstep. Inconveniently, Karla, as a man, can conceivably be ensnared; whereas Centre, as an institution, will endure. Thus the specific objective of bringing down Karla can be judged as success or failure. Operations against Centre enjoy less precise measure. The grey men, like Lacon, fear precision, for it offers a yardstick by which they can be measured. Better the never-ending conflict than the decisive confrontation.

The distinction does not matter for Smiley. They are one and the same, Karla and Centre. Behind his desk he hangs a framed photo of Karla, taken from a passport and enlarged to grainy indistinction. He steers clear of explaining exactly why he has placed it there – one suspects as a reminder of what he is after. He holds Karla accountable for Haydon. Centre is too unattainable a concept, but Karla is within his grasp.

Once a double agent has been blown, those against whom he has conspired undertake a careful damage assessment – or "backbearing" in Circus jargon – to learn what they can about their opposition's priorities and, by extension, where their remaining weaknesses lie. By seeing which Circus investigations Haydon has gone to lengths to quash, Smiley can determine what Karla has been most anxious to conceal. In contrast, those that Haydon allows to proceed unhindered are tainted. To preserve his cover, he will have been selective and discrete. It is an exacting and exhausting process, complicated by the general disarray within the Circus. Haydon conspired to dismiss competent officers he feared might expose him, while harmless incompetents were promoted. Most damaging, agents deployed around the world against Centre have undoubtedly been blown and are therefore operationally worthless.

Surrounded by a cadre of loyalists – Connie Sachs, she of the infallible recall for Centre minutiae, the ever-faithful Peter Guillam, whom he has rescued from Haydon-imposed exile, Doc Di Salis, the China hand, and Fawn, the zealous factotum – Smiley sets about reviewing cases that Haydon pointedly suppressed. While Haydon was running the shop, a decision not to vigorously pursue an inquiry would not have caused a second glance. As Smiley acknowledges regretfully, "File and forget. We always have good reasons for doing nothing."[76] There is no obvious damage in intelligence that provokes outcry and demands immediate remedy.

That is one of the truly appalling features of intelligence services: an infinity of excuses for inactivity against little incentive to charge hard. Indeed, so frequently are operational proposals rejected from on high that it would be absurd to attribute the phenomenon to egregious obstruction, as opposed to normal sloth. This is not James Bond's world, where every incident threatens the destruction of the planet. In the real intelligence world, disinterest prevails over the sledgehammer. Dangers, where they exist, are incremental rather than imminent. And – most significantly – it all occurs in silence, meaning there are no external pressures to force one course or another. It is not only fear of an operation going wrong that might induce inaction. That it might go right can be an equally fearsome prospect. It is in the very nature of intelligence work that an investigation can lead to some sticky patches best left – in the minds of some – unexplored and can touch some people who enjoy the illusion of being untouchable.

Take Drake Ko as an example. "Short of a Victoria Cross, a war disability pension and a baronetcy, therefore, it is hard to see how he could be a less suitable subject for harassment by a British service, or recruitment by a Russian one," Oliver Lacon argues in response to Smiley's proposal to make him a target for investigation. To which George replies, "In my world we call that good cover."[77]

And herein lies the crux of the paradox: the secret world is like a dimensional warp of the overt one. Step through the portal and everything is filtered through a different prism. Truths are well-told lies, character a meticulously rehearsed role. Those furthest removed from suspicion present the most intriguing possibilities.

In light of his exposure, Haydon's every decision has to be re-evaluated. Conspicuous among operations that he terminated without explanation is an inquiry tapping into a Centre gold seam, the unexplained movement of funds from Moscow through Vientiane to Hong Kong via an air charter company called Indo-charter Vientiane, part of Ko's business empire. Sam Collins, the Circus's one-time fieldman in Vientiane, has requested traces on the money trail from London Station. Mysteriously, the response to his request is absent from the file. Through her researches, Connie concludes that this fact represents the visible trace of an operation by which Karla has financed an agent or agents in the Far East. Haydon cleverly kept Collins off the case by informing him that it was a matter already being handled by the Americans, while he kept the Cousins away by advising them the Circus had it well in hand, Hong Kong being its preserve. The net result was that everyone treated it as hands-off. Meanwhile, the money suddenly ceases to flow along the channel Collins discovered, indicating that Karla is aware that it has attracted unwanted attention.

Few field operatives survived Haydon's gutting. Purely from lack of time, however, he did not get around to blowing all the Occasionals, those individuals – not quite members of the service, not quite informants – who have been Sarratt-certified in trade-craft and can be consciously tasked and put on the ground to gather information. The Honourable Jerry Westerby, son of minor aristocracy, journalist by trade, spy through his devotion to Smiley, is among these still-useful operatives. Dubbed Operation Dolphin, he is activated and dropped into Hong Kong to dig around and pick up the trail of the seam. He learns that, though the flow of money to Indocharter Vientiane has dried up, it has continued to a company called China Airsea, whose owner is none other than Ko. Thus the connection between Centre and Ko has never been interrupted; it has merely been otherwise concealed.

The Honourable Schoolboy is tightly packed with character and setting as Westerby manoeuvres his way through Southeast Asia to the people and places linked with Ko in order to make sense of his

Moscow connection. It is as if, suddenly liberated from his familiar European landscape, le Carré experienced a reinvigorated enthusiasm for atmospherics. All the while, Smiley, Connie, di Salis, and Guillam are making sense of inconsistencies in Britain and fighting a rearguard action against the encroachment of the Cousins.

Just as nuclear reactors produce deadly radioactive waste, so the by-product of Westerby's necessary self-reliance is debilitating loneliness. Usually he takes solace from whores and bar girls. But that is temporary and does nothing to soothe more persistent – and perilous – longings. "There is a kind of fatigue, sometimes, which only fieldmen know: a temptation to gentleness which can be the kiss of death."[78] It is perfectly natural that Westerby should be smitten with Lizzie Worthington – who goes by the marginally more exotic moniker Liese Worth – Drake Ko's trophy blonde. His approach to her is part of Smiley's plan to let Ko know that the barbarians – though not necessarily the British secret service – are at the gate – to shake his tree, as le Carré puts it.

Lizzie has given herself to Ko as a reward for his allowing her former lover, the elusive Tiny Ricardo, a reckless pilot who will fly *almost* any mission anywhere with any cargo, to live. For Tiny has failed to fulfill his assignment to fly into Mainland China with a cargo of opium. He was to return with what Drake Ko values most – his brother Nelson. Westerby tracks him down and finds a Conradesque burnout in the Thai jungle living precariously on Drake's sufferance.

When Drake slipped out of Shanghai for Hong Kong, his brother stayed behind – willingly, since he is a devoted communist, though of the Soviet persuasion. He was educated in Leningrad, where Karla spotted and cultivated him. Notwithstanding the fraternal socialist feelings of any given moment, he recognizes the need for a reliable friend in the East. And though Nelson fell out of favour during the Sino-Soviet split, Karla is unshakably patient. Nelson is Drake's connection to Moscow and the gold seam, which is Nelson's remuneration for providing the Centre with China's secrets.

After some highly complex machinations, Drake does manage to ferry Nelson out of China on a junk plying the waters between the mainland and Hong Kong. As the two are about to be reunited on the out-island of Po Toi, American helicopters swoop in and scoop up Nelson. In the melee Westerby is shot and killed. The intelligence to which Nelson is privy was closely guarded by the Cousins and seemingly not subject to existing agreements for sharing with the Circus. To what degree the Circus's political masters have conspired with the Americans to give them Nelson remains a mystery. Guillam is left to wonder whether or not Smiley has partaken and how much he is affected by Westerby's death. In the end, he is no closer to Karla. As is his custom, he quietly fades from the Circus once the case is closed, replaced as chief by Saul Enderby from the Foreign Office.

It is almost as if, while devising *The Honourable Schoolboy*, le Carré was not quite sure which elements of the plot were going to prove crucial and which were not. The story is rambling and undisciplined. Although Karla's major Eastern penetration is foiled, the larger objective of bringing about his demise eludes Smiley. In fact, this is reduced to a peripheral element of the plot, a tool to intimate great moment, which is never delivered.

Discussing the books he wrote following the enormous success of *The Spy Who Came in from the Cold*, le Carré told a television interviewer, "I wrote two or three books that certainly took wrong paths, it seems to me so in retrospect. I think I also, out of a sense of insecurity, got too hung up on George Smiley and I shouldn't, perhaps, have put him into *The Honourable Schoolboy.* I always feel that was a book by itself."[79]

As usual, however, le Carré is fascinating on the subject of motivation: how intelligence officers cling to their souls in hells of their own creation. They need some constellation by which to navigate, a fixed point they can ever turn to for a sense of direction. Smiley is Westerby's motive.[80] It is a relief to have a person in whom you can believe and to whose care you can submit. The trouble is when the person who represents all that you hold to be right is tortured by his or her own doubts. Smiley has more than his share of demons. Guillam is sensitive to his turmoil. Of Smiley, he thinks, "He'll cease to care, or the paradox will kill him. If he ceases to care, he'll be half the operator he is. If he doesn't, that little chest will blow up from the struggle of trying to find the explanation for what we do. Smiley himself, in a disastrous off-the-record chat to senior officers, had put the names to his dilemma, and Guillam, with some embarrassment, recalled them to this day. To be *inhuman in defence of our humanity*, he had said, *harsh in defence of compassion*. To be *single-minded in defence of our disparity.* They had filed out in a veritable ferment of protest. Why didn't George just do the job and shut up instead of taking his faith out and polishing it in public till the flaws showed?"[81] It is because he has the strength of character to face the doubts. Indeed, he answers the question himself much earlier in the book: "A lot of people see *doubt* as legitimate philosophical posture. They think of themselves in the middle, whereas of course really, they're nowhere. No battle was ever won by spectators, was it? We understand that in this service. We're lucky. Our present war began in 1917, with the Bolshevik Revolution. It hasn't changed yet."[82] Smiley will not allow the flaws to paralyze him. He believes in what is most real to him: the enemy. And this reality is what allows him to care *and* to keep the paradox at bay.

Perhaps Connie best explains why Smiley believes in the enemy. One of the first sources Westerby approaches for information about Ko is the banker Frost. Soon afterward, the same Frost is found very badly tortured and very dead. Smiley is upset by the news. "'Karla wouldn't give two pins, would he, dearie?' she murmured. 'Not for one dead Frost, nor for ten. That's the difference, really. We can't write it much larger than that, can we, not these days? Who was it who used to say 'we're fighting for the survival of Reasonable Man'? Steed-Asprey? Or was it Control? I loved that. It covered it all. Hitler. The new thing. That's who we are: reasonable.'"[83]

Whatever you may say about Western intelligence over the years or how closely you want to shave the parallels between intelligence services the world over, you cannot argue with Connie's remarks. We never subscribed to the grand ideological crusade, but we always – as organizations – maintained a sense of reason, a cognition of excess. This gave us the feeling of being at a constant disadvantage, for those who feel no such constraints appear to operate from a position of greater strength. But then, we did defeat Hitler as well as the new thing, didn't we? That was because true strength derives from a moral wellspring. Despite the occasional inhumanity, the periodic excesses, and the episodic cruelty, we never deviated from our own commitment to democracy, the rule of law, and respect for human beings. As long as that remained a fact, and as long as this instinct won out over the others, the flaws remained subservient to the broader objectives.

Dolphin has left Karla unscathed, at least as far as the Circus is concerned. We never learn what use the Cousins make of Nelson's capture or how deeply it has wounded Karla. In *Tinker Tailor Soldier Spy* Smiley concludes, "Karla is not fireproof because he's a fanatic. And one day, if I have anything to do with it, that lack of moderation will be his downfall."[84] He is only partly correct: true, Karla is not fireproof, but it is not fanaticism that will bring him down: on the contrary – and surprisingly – it is a particularly human weakness to which he will succumb. Fanaticism is a perpetual blind rage, causing a single-mindedness of purpose and eradicating all other considerations that dare rise up to object. It does not give itself to sober reflection or compassion or alternatives. Like a volcanic eruption, fanaticism's instinct is to indiscriminately overwhelm all in its path.

Through two novels, coming into *Smiley's People* (1980), Karla is a sphinx, a half-drawn face clawed away by time and distance. As related above, Smiley has met him once and been outplayed. Whenever he sees Ann, Karla's spirit is there to taunt him: "Haydon's shadow fell between them like a sword."[85] Once Karla has infiltrated his life – his love – Smiley's quest becomes decidedly personal. It is fitting, then, that it will be Karla's one true love who will ultimately be his downfall; and it is striking of Smiley that this very thing makes him waver.

Smiley's People is a novel of tortuous ambiguity, brought out by the clarity of the synchronicity between Smiley and Karla. In this, their final confrontation emerges how closely they may identify with each other. "On Karla has descended the curse of Smiley's compassion; on Smiley the curse of Karla's fanaticism,"[86] le Carré writes of the transposition of their characters. Yet Smiley recoils from the idea of being just like Karla. He is positively incensed when Connie refers to him and Karla as "two halves of the same apple," deploring the notion that they share method or absolutism.[87] Yet in the end he concedes, "I have destroyed him with the weapons I abhorred, and they are his. We have crossed each other's frontiers, we are the no-men of this no-man's-land."[88]

Enemies become mirrors of each other. Much of what they think they understand about each other comes from the projection of their own perceptions. Karla the fanatic is not supposed to be susceptible to human impulses that might distract him from his war. After questioning him in that Delhi jail cell, Smiley reproaches himself for digressing into his own longings, rather than fastening onto Karla's, whatever those might be, when all along, Smiley has been correct in appealing to Karla's love for someone. In the event, however, it is not a wayward wife but a mad daughter whom he fathered with a mistress who was executed for anti-Soviet tendencies. Under the system he so ruthlessly upholds, madness is a matter of politics, not medicine. His daughter's anti-social behaviour puts her at risk and makes him vulnerable to his enemies. To save her he has to get her out, to get her the treatments that only the West can offer. Just as he would build a new identity for an illegal or deep cover agent who is sent to live abroad, he sets about using all the resources at his disposal to create a legend for her. Also, he takes the liberty of using all the funds at his disposal – in other words, state security funds – to cover the costs.

To build her identity, he dips into the Soviet émigré community. Maria Ostrakova, whose chance at freedom from the Soviet Union has caused her to leave behind her own daughter, is approached in Paris by Kirov, recruited by Karla for this one mission. He coerces her into applying for papers on the pretext that her daughter is being permitted to join her. A legend is best constructed with superficial respect for the life it imitates. Usually, identities are built for illegals from records of the deceased. Often, names are taken from the gravestones of infants for whom a birth certificate will exist but no other official documents, such as social security numbers or passports. Identity papers should be legitimate rather than forged whenever possible. And there must be no evidence to tie the bearer of the legend with those who conspired to create it. Any loose ends hanging from this last point must be snipped off by whatever means necessary – in this instance, by murder. Ostrakova is reluctant to believe Kirov's story, but hope leaves her no alternative. As time passes and her daughter fails to materialize, her suspicions are confirmed. Needing to confide in someone, she sends a letter to General Vladimir, a trusted associate of her late husband and leader in the Estonian exile community, expressing her fear, "They are putting the wrong egg in the nest."[89]

Vladimir sees in Ostrakova's letter a renewed call to arms. Once upon a time, long before détente, East bloc émigré communities were fertile hunting grounds for spies looking to bag friends and enemies alike. Western intelligence sought to exploit their propaganda value, using them to embarrass the East by hungrily gathering up their tales of oppression. Sometimes they could identify the local thugs who had arrested or interrogated them, thus increasing the West's database on who might be who behind the Iron Curtain. Occasionally, their underground networks provided glimpses into the dissident movements struggling valiantly in their homelands. They were quick to inform against anyone they suspected of having been sent from the East to infiltrate and sabotage their efforts to continue the fight against communism. And they suspected everyone. In their own minds they were soldiers still on active duty, alert to every opportunity to subvert the Soviet oppressors.

For the most part, their value lay in padding their handler's statistics for agent meets. You could always count on leaders of émigré groups to agree to a meeting. Usually you had to restrain them from telling others of your approach and discourage them from introducing you to all their sundry associates. Even when little or nothing of substance was forthcoming, it was good to keep in contact with the émigrés because regular sources are money in the bank for intelligence services. They would always pay lip service to secrecy, but their discretion was, more often than not, lacking. Émigrés, like some rare species of animal whose habitat is constantly being encroached, live in ever-dwindling circumstances. They need to talk to someone who will give their patriotism its due; only among their own or with their intelligence handlers can they hope for such validation.

Vladimir was once a prize Circus asset. But prize assets are discarded with as much sentiment as chicken bones sucked clean of meat. He has been reduced to living in squalid conditions, a relic of another time and other battles, which for him have never been resolved, but which his patrons have long since forgotten. He is not even afforded the dignity of an experienced handler with whom to maintain contact. He has been farmed off as a nuisance to any rookie unlucky enough to receive his summons. Once he receives Ostrakova's letter, he feels himself liberated from the junk heap, released from his fruitless vigil, and recalled to the front. From that moment on, he insists on "Moscow rules," those strict procedures employed to foil security services when operating behind enemy lines – the war rules of *The Looking Glass War*'s Department.

The Soviets contributed mightily to the émigrés' sense of grandeur by mounting considerable resources against them. Ready and willing to suppress dissent at every turn, they were always remarkably sensitive to criticism from abroad, inadvertently justifying the exaggerated opinion the émigrés held of their impact on the regime. If the Soviets fear our voice, the émigrés' argument went, we must be effective. Some thirty years into the Cold War, however, the West realized there were few dividends to be collected from support for the old soldiers, who by then were far removed from the politics of their homelands. Facing permanent exile, their services refused, they continued to play at politics, to fantasize about future battles and heroics.

With the aid of his comrade, Otto Leipzig, Vladimir assembles proof of the true identity of the girl who has exited Moscow with French papers in the name of Alexandra Ostrakova on Karla's most secret orders. For their trouble, both Vladimir and Leipzig will be murdered. Alive, such men could be easily disparaged and dismissed. But dead – death is confirmation that they were on to something. Smiley, as Vladimir's old handler, is recalled from a retirement spent yet again, in the company of his beloved German poets, to find out what they have learned that is important enough to be killed for.

Immediately upon being tasked, of course, he is disowned. Lacon is most explicit: "One, that you are a private citizen, Vladimir's executor, not ours. Two, that you are of the past, not the present, and conduct yourself accordingly."[90] And then later, as the final moves are being prepared, Saul Enderby, warns him he will not hesitate to excommunicate Smiley in the event of a scandal: "I'll say the whole catastrophe was a ludicrous piece of private enterprise by a senile spy who's lost his marbles."[91]

In *Tinker Tailor Soldier Spy*, Smiley tried bribery of a sort and watched Karla calmly board a plane to Moscow to confront his fate. By the time we get to *Smiley's People* it is to be a burn job all the way. The key to success lies in turning Anton Grigoriev, Karla's man in Berne, who pays Alexandra visits and reports back to him on a weekly basis. He also administers the bank account covering her expenses at the sanitarium to which Karla has arranged her commitment. To do this, he impersonates a Swiss citizen, something that would no doubt interest Swiss authorities if they were so informed. The Circus needs Grigoriev as a conduit to pass a message to Karla giving him the choice of defecting or having his embezzlement of public funds, his daughter's presence in the Swiss sanitarium, and the murders he has ordered to protect himself revealed to Centre.

Grigoriev, too, will have to be burned in order to ensure his complicity. Toby Esterhase's lamplighters – the watchers – are assigned to follow Grigoriev and get to know his routine. They snap compromising photos of him in the embrace of his mistress. Surveillance people get to see all the subtle little indicators that people emit suggesting vulnerability. Unaware of being scrutinized, people give themselves away in small ways: the scowl they direct at the back of their spouse, the troubled weariness they assume over a solitary drink, the lustful abandon with which they take a lover, the covetous gaze that overcomes them when they see goods they cannot afford. Still, uncertainties abound. There remains that last instant in which sober second thought can forestall action. As le Carré so magnificently phrases it, "In the world of a secret agent, the wall between safety and extreme hazard is almost nothing, a membrane that can be burst in a second. He may court a man for years, fattening him for the pass. But the pass itself – the 'will you, won't you?' – is a leap from which there is either ruin or victory."[92]

In the end, Grigoriev submits to the threat of exposure and the promise of haven in the West. So too does Karla, not, one suspects, because he feared what would become of him – after all, he had returned from Delhi at considerable risk – so much as to protect his daughter. This is what shakes Smiley; Karla "had acquired a human face of disconcerting clarity. It was no brute whom Smiley was pursuing with such mastery, no unqualified fanatic after all, no automaton. It was a man; and one whose downfall, if Smiley chose to bring it about, would be caused by nothing more sinister than excessive love, a weakness with which Smiley himself from his own tangled life, was eminently familiar."[93]

Waiting for Karla to pass through the Berlin Wall, Smiley is reserved, without a sense of great victory. Just the opposite: he behaves more like a man who has lost something. This sense of loss pervades the book. In the final lines, Guillam intones, "George, you won."

"'Did I?' said Smiley. 'Yes. Yes, well I suppose I did.'"[94]

Compassion is an amazing quality. It is the only obstacle in our nature that blocks off our worst – and frequently first – instincts.

It shatters absolutes and causes us to reflect on how we might be in other circumstances. One of the last interviews I conducted was with a Tamil scientist from Sri Lanka who had knowingly given money and technical advice to the Liberation Tigers of Tamil Eelam (LTTE), a group fighting a terrorist guerrilla war for a separate homeland in the northern part of the island.

The Tamils do not have an easy time in their country. They are treated as second-class citizens by the Sinhalese majority and face all the attendant hardships of discrimination. At the same time, the LTTE is a vicious group, responsible for numerous assassinations (including that of Indian prime minister Rajiv Ghandi) and suicide bombings that have taken thousands of lives. I am not claiming to know how the dispossessed might best improve their conditions and inform the world of their plight. I can only hope wanton massacre is not the way.

Investigations within Canada's Tamil community have revealed widespread support for the LTTE. Many of those fleeing Sri Lanka had ties, however loose, to the Tigers, and they remain anxious to funnel money back to their homeland to contribute to the struggle. Determined not to allow Canada to become a conduit for terrorist financing, we traced the gold seams. Fundraising efforts are extensive. It is estimated that between $1 and $2 million are collected annually, making Canada one of the largest sources of finances for the cause.[95] Collectors, who are not averse to applying pressure against those of their compatriots who are less than generous in their contributions, solicit door-to-door. One Tamil, who spoke to a journalist in Toronto, pointed out that he does not inquire what the money is used for. "We are here, having a good job, eating well, having a car, going for parties. When we are living like this and giving a little money, to ask questions, it's not correct."[96] Ruth Archibald, Canada's high commissioner to Sri Lanka, is less shy and admitted this capital may go towards the purchasing of arms.[97]

Reliable information had linked the scientist directly to money that was used to purchase arms in Europe, which were then shipped to rebel camps in northern Sri Lanka. He voluntarily came to our office for an interview when requested to do so. My partner and I had decided to keep it non-confrontational because we would never be able to link him to a crime against Canadian law, but we might convince him to supply information that would move us up the chain to those who had illegally acquired the weapons in other countries. Another reason was that many people from Third World countries are accustomed to brutal, heavy-handed security officers whose only tactic is to bully and intimidate. Such people are so taken aback by polite authorities, and so relieved, that they are sometimes lulled into saying more than they intended. In some respects, it can be easier to resist an antagonist than a friend.

The preliminaries over, we quickly realized that we were going to get a friendly, cooperative demeanor smeared over a litany of lies and a remarkably faulty memory.

"Do you know what the LTTE is?"

"No, I do not know of this. What is LTTE, sir?" His deference struck us as oddly condescending.

"The Liberation Tigers of Tamil Eelam," I said slowly, letting just enough sarcasm into my voice so that he knew I knew he was lying.

"Oh, yes, yes, I have heard of this, but I do not *know* of them," he replied in a self-satisfied tone, as if to say, "I can stretch this game out indefinitely."

"Who is the leader of the LTTE in Sri Lanka?" I asked.

"I do not know who that person is," he smiled meekly. Asking a Tamil who runs the LTTE is the equivalent of asking an American to name the president of the United States.

"Have you ever heard of Prabarakhan?" I came back with the leader's name.

"No, I do not know who is that person," the shit-eating grin never left his face, but his bald pate was starting to shine with moisture and his eyes darted around the room in mounting panic. His answer was as credible as hearing a South African claim never to have heard the name Nelson Mandela.

"I'm surprised," my partner interjected. "Everyone knows of Prabarakhan."

"Oh, Prabarakhan," he said loudly, in a voice spilling over with surprise, rolling the consonants deliberately in a pronounced Sri Lankan accent, as if my pronunciation had confused him. "Yes, yes, yes, I have heard of this Prabarakhan."

"Who is he?" I retorted, tired of pulling teeth, wishing that the people who lied to me would at least not treat me like an idiot.

"Oh, I believe he is in LTTE."

"How do you know this?" I asked, trying to point out the inconsistencies in his knowledge.

"Oh, everybody knows this."

"But, you just said you didn't know what the LTTE was and you'd never heard of Prabarakhan. Now you know that he's in the LTTE and that *everybody* knows this."

The sweat was starting to bead up on his head as if he had just stepped in out of the rain. "I have family in Sri Lanka," as if this was the answer to all my questions. And in a way it was.

"You've sent money to the LTTE," I said softly but with certainty, in order to pin him down and indicate how much we knew about him.

"I have family," he almost whispered, pleading for understanding of what this simple fact implied.

He never conceded giving money to the LTTE. He was helping his family the best way he could. I would never convince him that he was aiding a group the Canadian government thought of as terrorists. They were in the jungles acting on behalf of his people. I certainly wasn't. Under what circumstances would he forsake them to cooperate with me? After over an hour I knew: none. And I knew that because I could give him no good reason why he should. He was not in the least conflicted about his loyalties. At the end of the day, I went home and forgot about the plight that was never out of his mind. He had no home apart from his family worries, even though he lived on the other side of the globe.

I didn't win in this case. I had lost sight of what winning meant. Getting a truthful answer to my questions? Yes, but so what? It would change nothing, it would better no one. Sure, this feeling of hopelessness came when I knew I was about to leave intelligence. The emotions I felt had to do with more than this one interview. I had lost sight of the difference between winning and losing because neither had any consequence for me. And that's what being part of a bureaucracy means: *no consequence*. The truth of my life was so disconnected from the truth of his life. I was not unlike Anil, the protagonist of Michael Ondaatje's novel *Anil's Ghost*. She returns to her native Sri Lanka as an investigator on behalf of an international organization. After fifteen years living in the West, she "had come to expect clearly marked roads to the source of most mysteries. Information could always be clarified and acted upon. But here, on this island, she realized she was moving with only one arm of language among uncertain laws and a fear that was everywhere."[98] The scientist lived in a place of chronic violence and depravation; I wasn't going to change that. His family needed protection; I wasn't going to provide that.

In *The Honourable Schoolboy*, le Carré makes the point, "A desk is a dangerous place from which to watch the world."[99] In a related thought, Lacon comments to Smiley about how awful it must have been to see Vladimir with his head blown to bits. "No, it wasn't awful, it was the truth, thought Smiley. He was shot and I saw him dead. Perhaps you should do that too."[100] Like a writer, an IO should be gathering up pieces of truth. It's a demanding and messy commitment. You have to experience the truth in order to recognize it. I had nothing against which to measure the terror of knowing that my family lived under constant peril. Nor can Smiley fully appreciate the sacrifice that Karla will have to make to protect his daughter until the end-game is played out.

Like Smiley, I had come to realize the dilemma of playing with other people's lives. *Smiley's People*, like *Tinker Tailor Soldier Spy*, is a classic example of how le Carré uses anticlimax as a powerful device to undermine the expectations of a spy thriller and thus elevate his fiction above the confines of genre. He effectively subverts Smiley by denying him heroism in his moment of greatest professional triumph. Neither Smiley's unmasking of Haydon nor his entrapment of Karla permits him any satisfaction. Rather, at the moment of victory, he is plagued with doubt. I am convinced that espionage is a game most easily survived by absolutists. Whether motivated by belief or self-interest, it calls for tunnel vision, something to blind against the bigger world. There is no other way to stave off the insanity induced by the contradictions. You can only survive by thinking in terms of the zealot – the true believer – or the bureaucrat – the consummate self-server.

CHAPTER FIVE

A Different Landscape

The Middle East was a new landscape for le Carré. Explaining his rather dramatic shift in focus from Cold War Europe, he told an interviewer, "I'd like to stay as close as I can to contemporary reality. By the end of the Smiley books I'd gone too far into a private world."[1] It was time, he was suggesting, to come out and engage the world in a more overt fashion, to face the turbulent open currents of crisis when the Cold War had become a stagnant bog of conflict.

By the early 1980s the Cold War had been systematized and rendered emotionless. It had become confrontation without passion. Reflecting on the Cold War in a 1993 interview, le Carré referred to espionage as "a sideshow got up as major theater."[2] The same could not be said of the Arab-Israeli crisis. Where terror and subterfuge frequently pay greater dividends in the currency of politics than diplomacy or conciliation, the work of the secret agent takes centre stage.

Détente, or peaceful coexistence or whatever the buzzword of the day, had left the superpowers and their minions in Europe going through the motions. There was no fury, just endless sniping. The Middle East, on the other hand, was (and is) a region of unbounded passion, where the principals deal in life and death, not chessboard posturing, a shooting war as much as a spy's war. Indeed, the spies do a good deal of the shooting. With *The Little Drummer Girl* (1983), le Carré sought to turn cartwheels and somersaults at the same time: to defend Israel's right to exist and the Palestinians' right to redress. It, in his words, "propagated the heretical thesis that there are rights and wrongs on both sides"[3] of the dispute. Perhaps the best testament to his success is that members of both camps found elements of the book distasteful.[4]

What impressed me most on first reading – and continues to do so with each subsequent one – is the manner in which every minute detail of the operation (read, plot) is considered and accounted for by the Israeli intelligence service, how they succeed in making their presence ubiquitous. Not everything proceeds as they anticipate or intend; nor is every plan automatically confirmed in action. But they are so meticulous and attentive to all the possibilities of the situations they manufacture, as well as those presented by circumstance. Fortuitous contingencies, as well as the infinite possibilities of choice, are calculated, not by mathematical probability, but by instinct and experience with human nature. Happenstance is, by turns, the bane and the saviour of intelligence operations. Adaptability is a crucial weapon. You have to be like a medieval map-maker, working within broad outlines, gradually filling in the empty expanses, changing perceptions, refining and correcting.

What spies crave above all is a world they can control, one they can manipulate just so. The actress Charlie, who the Israelis talent spot and recruit as their penetration agent into the inner circle of the Palestinian bomber Khalil, gradually learns "to see the world that way: everyone belongs to someone."[5] The cycle of conflict and violence in the Middle East is such that enemies have been demonized, subhumanized. Irony is absent from the voice of Marty Kurtz, the Israeli operational leader, when he says that "in our view somebody has to be very guilty indeed before he needs to die ... Only those who break completely the human bond, Charlie."[6] There is a consoling certainty to this sentiment. It is enviable to have an enemy who has broken that bond and, moreover, to possess the confidence to judge his guilt. Le Carré set out explicitly to paint everyone's human face, to remind us that the best and worst impulses of all the players are undeniably human. He characterized *Drummer Girl* as being "about a balance of compassion."[7]

To assume the power to decide who has broken the human bond, and when, and whether this person needs to die is an awesome responsibility; one, it may be argued, that no individual or state agency has the right to take. Yet such decisions are inevitable in a world under siege. They will be taken either with profound humility or with arrogance. The principles upon which Israeli intelligence was founded were supposed to accentuate the former. Dan Raviv and Yossi Melman took the title of their history of Israeli intelligence, *Every Spy a Prince*, from the Old Testament story of God's instructing Moses to dispatch spies to scout out the land of Canaan: "of every tribe of their fathers shall you send a man, every one a prince among them" (Numbers 13:1–2). They extrapolate from this notion of the spy-prince to explain Prime Minister David Ben-Gurion's criteria for Israel's spies: "Similarly searching for the 'princes' of the Jewish people, the Ben-Gurion team made stringent demands of its first secret agents: that they be motivated by patriotism, not personal gain; that they represent the best aspects of Israeli society, not the worst; that they obey the unique tenet of self-restraint, which Israel's army calls 'purity of arms,' rather than be triggermen who would glory in bloodshed; and that they remember they are defending democracy, not a monolithic state which ruthlessly crushes its enemies both at home and abroad. Israel employs more than ten thousand citizens in its intelligence community, and obviously not every one can be a prince among men or a princess among women. But they can try, and that is what the state's founding fathers wanted."[8] The conclusion Raviv and Melman reach about Shin Bet, which could be applied more generally across the community, qualifies the idea of IOs living up to a princely standard: "Shin Bet wished to adopt as sacrosanct the principle that, while the nature of the work would often entail lying to the outside world, operatives would speak only the truth to their superiors ... Sooner or later, a person who has been given permission to lie in certain circumstances will permit himself to lie in other circumstances as well."[9]

Spies dispense praise about fellows of their craft sparingly, not an abnormal reaction to come from those who have peeked behind the screen and know how the trick is staged. However, even among such jaded peers there are those who inspire awe, although it is sometimes reluctantly given. And in espionage there are none more awe-inspiring than members of Israel's intelligence community: the legendary external service Mossad, the Shin Bet security service, and military intelligence, known as Aman. Their feats of information gathering and covert action do merit wonderment.

Operating under the relentless stress of crisis-level hostility, against threats worthy of the definition, their agents, I imagine, never doubt the purpose of their vocation. This opinion is not universally held, as evidenced by former Mossad officer Victor Ostrovsky's belittling memoir of several years ago, *By Way of Deception*, which depicts an organization whose early successes opened the way to corruption, just as youthful muscle succumbs to fat. Nevertheless, Mossad is still regarded with esteem as one of few intelligence organizations that can respond efficiently, creatively, and purposefully to its state's national security imperatives. Agreeing that its agent are the best, le Carré nevertheless allows that they have "made awful mistakes, as intelligence services will, but that's because Mossad and Shin Bet are splendidly motivated. If Israel loses a battle, it loses the war; if it loses the war, it loses its country. Everybody in Israel knows what security means, and everybody pulls together."[10]

Their formidable reputation has been built on the strength of several unquestionably brilliant operations, which earned the goodwill and reverence of allies, the fear and loathing of enemies, and the respect of the public. Brief mention of several examples will suffice to illustrate. It was Israel that procured a copy of Nikita Khrushchev's previously secret speech of 20 February 1956, which denounced Stalin before the Twentieth Party Congress, and passed it along to the CIA. In 1960 a team of Israeli operatives located and captured Nazi war criminal Adolf Eichmann in Buenos Aires and brought him back to Israel to stand trial. A major coup was scored in 1966 when efforts to entice an Iraqi pilot to defect with his Soviet-made MiG-21 came to fruition, thus giving the West its first chance to examine what was then among the most sophisticated fighter planes in the Soviet arsenal. The performance of the intelligence community and military establishment in predicting and responding to the Arab threat culminating in the Six Day War in 1967 stunned the world. The 1960s and 1970s saw waves of terrorism against Jewish targets around the globe, including an attack on an El Al airliner in Athens in 1968, the massacre of Israeli athletes at the Munich Olympics in 1972, and the hijacking of an Air France jet to Entebbe Airport, Uganda, in 1976. In each of these cases, daring intelligence efforts resulted in retribution being exacted by Israeli commandos. An audacious 1981 bombing raid destroyed a nuclear reactor under construction in Baghdad, which could have given Saddam Hussein the capacity to construct his own atomic weapons, something that would have spelled disaster a decade later when he invaded Kuwait, precipitating the Gulf War.

Naturally, the record of Israel's secret services has not been one of unqualified successes; there have been failures and scandals. An ill-conceived sabotage campaign unleashed in Egypt in the mid-1950s resulted in the arrest of an Israeli network and the subsequent resignation of Defence Minister Pinchas Lavon. Intelligence's failure to forewarn authorities about Egypt's and Syria's intention to attack in 1973 was costly and very nearly catastrophic. That same year the mission to hunt down those responsible for the Munich massacre ended in disgrace when an innocent man was murdered in a case of mistaken identity (more on this later). The early 1980s brought about a crisis of confidence in the entire state security apparatus as a result of the army's invasion of Lebanon and the eruption of the Intifada in the occupied West Bank and Gaza Strip. In 1984 Shin Bet clumsily tried to cover up its killing of two Palestinian bus hijackers who had been taken into custody. The following year an obscure agency called Lakam, responsible for collecting scientific intelligence, was severely embarrassed – and subsequently disbanded – when a Jewish-American naval intelligence employee, Jonathan Pollard, was arrested and convicted for spying on Israel's behalf. For it to come to light that Israel was running an offensive operation against its most valued ally and biggest financial supporter caused a substantial uproar. And that it was conducted on American soil was a further insult. A year later, in 1986, Mordecai Vanunu, an employee of the top-secret nuclear facility at Dimona, sold details of Israel's atomic program to the British press. He was lured by Mossad from London to Rome, from where he was abducted to Israel and sentenced to life in prison for treason.

This rough balance sheet of achievement and failure is by no means complete. For one thing, one must allow for the frequently overlooked truism: genuine success in intelligence never comes to public attention. A spy who fades unheralded from the scene, an operation that passes unnoticed or without proper attribution – these are the greatest coups. Uncertainty creates more disruption than the knowledge that a particular action has been carried out. For a country or organization to be forever guessing whether, and how deeply, it has been penetrated leaves it in greater disarray than if it feels confident of having thoroughly assessed whatever damage has been inflicted.

Israeli intelligence operates very much within the context of the day-to-day needs of the state. It cannot lose sight of the connection between means and ends. Information collection is prelude to action. Knowledge amassed about a terrorist organization is put to use in pre-emption, interdiction, or, failing that, retribution. Lives are saved or lost in direct proportion to intelligence's success. How often could Cold Warriors make that claim?

The Little Drummer Girl, le Carré's depiction of this world, is a marvelously realized story about conviction and commitment, and whether allegiances are best advanced in relation to people or ideas. It is about the difference between choosing to fight and being obliged to do so, and about determining which fights are open to choice. Broad generalizations work best from a distance, but only someone hardened to the task can be deliberately cruel to those in whom he or she has recognized a spark of humanity. Taking refuge in race may simplify an unmanageable world. By dismissing entire groups as less than human, we can commit any indignity against them with no more remorse than a child feels when burning insects with a magnifying glass.

Love changes all that. Love overwhelms, levelling at random like a tornado, picking people up and depositing them with each other in the most unlikely couplings. Once we are in its grip, it becomes our most savage attachment. It changes us, and we change for it. In *The Little Drummer Girl* the complex chain of events set in motion by Israeli intelligence depends upon this premise. By means of a meticulously conceived plot, le Carré deftly insinuates an Israeli intelligence officer into the life of Charlie, a character based on his stepsister, Charlotte, an actress who was once with the Royal Shakespeare Company.[11] A sideline intellectual leftist, Charlie is for the oppressed, whoever they may be. Naturally that includes the Palestinians, on whose behalf she is stridently vocal. Possessing impeccable radical credentials and physical attractiveness makes her the perfect access agent to set up the Palestinian terrorist behind a series of deadly bomb attacks against Jewish targets. Only her belief in the righteousness of the Palestinian cause stands in the way of her recruitment. To overcome this obstacle, she will have to be manipulated into transferring her allegiance.

Seduction causes abandon. The mysterious Joseph, whose every impromptu appearance is laboriously rehearsed, lures Charlie into putting her feelings for him above her most strongly held

convictions. Before meeting him, "Israel was a confused abstrac-
tion to her, engaging both her protectiveness and her hostility. She
had never supposed for one second that it would ever get up and
come to face her in the flesh."[12] Once it becomes flesh and blood,
it upsets her abstract fanaticism, her lecture-hall rebellion.

"I just want peace,"[13] she implores – a noble sentiment, but a
goal not to be achieved simply in the wishing. The epic paradox
of human history is that peace must be vigorously fought for and
then valiantly defended. And one person's peace may represent
another's oppression, thus spurring that person to fight, and so
on ad infinitum. Of Israel, le Carré has said, "No nation on earth
was more deserving of peace. Or more cruelly condemned to fight
for it."[14]

Charlie's loyalties, then, are linked to a vague longing. She has
to admit that Israel should not be driven into the sea, just as
Palestinians should not be displaced; that Jews should not be
fodder for terrorist bombs, just as Palestinian refugees should not
be bombed from the sky. Racially, she is not bound to either group.
Philosophically, her ideas are not mature enough to be her guide.
Joseph offers her something tangible to replace her slogans: a
human being. He forces her to choose to be loyal or to betray *him*.
Though not taken easily, once she is in love with him, the choice
becomes self-evident. She is no longer acting on concepts she
cannot touch; she recites her lines for him.

Love is not limbo: it is sanctuary or purgatory. If it claims
loyalty without returning it, it becomes manipulation. It is the
field of our loftiest unions or our lowest infidelities. It gives
texture to how we see the world, for it rescues us from isolation.
It draws us into places where we might not venture alone. Charlie
is conveyed from her beliefs, driven to betray what she once
thought she stood for, thus recreating her loyalties.

Kurtz confronts her with her unwillingness to back up her
revolutionary zeal with the appropriate action. "Why don't you
blow up colonialists and imperialists wherever you find them?
Where's your vaunted integrity suddenly? What's gone wrong?"
he demands, chiding her readiness to spout words and yet fear
of engaging in direct action, finally concluding that she is squarely
in the "extreme centre."[15]

Le Carré understands that this is a more difficult position to
occupy than it might appear. He claims it for himself: "I stood –

and stand – wholeheartedly behind the nation-state of Israel as the homeland and guardian of Jews everywhere, and wholeheartedly behind the peace process as the guarantor not only of Israel's survival, but of the Palestinian survival also. And if at first blush this sounds a bit trite – well, in fiction as in politics, the extreme centre is a pretty dangerous place to be."[16] For the participants, however, centre-dwelling is a luxury, one allowed only to those who face no imminent peril.

Being all too aware of the need to fight, Kurtz derides Charlie's politics, with all their superficial high-mindedness but ultimate vacuity. In fact, by questioning her beliefs, he does not intend just to demean her, only to point out the contradictions and the confusion of her childish philosophy and to make her hunger for something more meaningful. He is offering her an opportunity to come in from the sidelines, to abandon the stage on which she pretends to be something in favour of the "theatre of the real," as Kurtz would call it.

Charlie's recruitment is seduction, not coercion. She is broken down for the purpose of being rebuilt. There is no reason to establish the errors of someone's ways unless you intend to offer a better alternative. The trick is to convince the potential source of this, to make her or him come to you willingly: "Volunteers fight harder and longer, he [Kurtz] had argued. Volunteers find their own ways to persuade themselves. And besides, if you are proposing marriage to a lady, it is wiser not to rape her first."[17] And espionage itself is the most mesmerizing of seducers. An invitation into its embrace is irresistibly alluring.

The most effective recruitment does not withdraw a person from what he or she is already a part of, but initiates the person into something familiar. This is precisely how Kurtz lures Charlie: "He had granted her an early glimpse of the new family she might care to join, knowing that deep down, like most rebels, she was only looking for a better conformity."[18] After all, every social bond we form demands a measure of conformity, even when it is ostensibly presented as nonconformity. She cannot survive without a sense of belonging to a troupe, without other actors to play off, without the hope of an audience to applaud her performance.

The objective of the operation is Khalil, the elusive bomb-maker whose outrages have included the killing of the Israeli labour attaché's young son in an explosion at his home in a Bonn suburb.

Terrorism is as crude as it is effective: a single burst, a single victim, an engulfing gust of panic. The act may end only one life, but it may cripple and disrupt multitudes. Whether by randomness or by specificity, it denies everybody the essential comfort of shelter. The first victim of terrorism is the peculiar certainty to which we all cling with a ferocity resembling insanity: that we will survive the day unscathed. Even though we live our entire lives stalked by that one horrible day we will not see to its end, we banish the thought by proclaiming that, no matter what, today is not that day.

Terrorism is inherently difficult to prevent. Because it can be perpetrated by the smallest of groups, even a single determined person, advance warning is tough to achieve. Military strikes, whether preventive or retributive, are inefficient against such an adversary because of their broad-stroke brutality in situations that demand pinpoint accuracy. Arrests are seldom made because borders are easily crossed and sanctuary can usually be found somewhere for any political cause. As a means of political expression, terrorism, for all its crudeness in application, is highly sophisticated in conception. Condemned to respond to violent outrages, counter-terrorism forces give the impression that they are constantly chasing in a foot race from a long way back.

Following the murder of eleven Israeli athletes by Black September at the 1972 Olympics in Munich, Israel decided, as a matter of policy, to move on the attack. It would hunt down and liquidate those individuals directly responsible for terrorist atrocities, thereby eliminating specific enemies and making clear to those who remained their inescapable vulnerability.[19] Mossad teams were dispatched, and over a ten-month period beginning in October 1972, twelve Palestinians were killed. Whether in Rome, Paris, Athens, Cyprus, or Beirut, this time the hunters found themselves hunted. Each assassination was meticulously planned and precisely performed – that is, until the operation collapsed in scandal and tragedy in July 1973 when an innocent Moroccan waiter was gunned down in Lillehammer, Norway. He had been mistakenly identified as Ali Hassan Salameh, the infamous Red Prince, who was responsible for masterminding Munich and other Black September offensives. Five Mossad agents were captured and sentenced to prison terms.[20] The crusade against Salameh was put on hold but not abandoned. He would ultimately be killed by a car bomb in Beirut in 1979. Several books about the post-Munich retributive operation have appeared since *Drummer Girl* was published. However, since much was learned in the aftermath of the Lillehammer tragedy, it could have served to inspire le Carré's idea of sending operatives after Khalil.

It is interesting to note that Shlomo Gazit, a former head of military intelligence, to whom le Carré expresses gratitude in his foreword, questioned the premise of the book. "Let's just say that it is a great thriller. But it is totally unrealistic. I was unhappy from the professional point of view because the chances of such an Israeli plan succeeding are one in 10,000."[21] Perhaps this is so, but Israeli intelligence is the only service that might spin the wheel under such odds.

In their history of Israeli intelligence, Ian Black and Benny Morris assert that the model for Kurtz was Rafi Eitan,[22] whose career scaled the heights of renown and plumbed the depths of disgrace. Israeli-born, he entered the covert world with the Haganah, the pre-independence Jewish underground defence organization in Palestine, at the age of twelve. He went on to command Shin Bet's operations branch and would later serve in the same capacity with Mossad. His greatest glory came from leading the team that captured Eichmann. Following a brief retirement from intelligence in the early 1970s, he returned to serve as the prime minister's adviser on counter-terrorism in the years 1978–84. It was during this period that the Red Prince was found in Beirut by Mossad. In 1981 Eitan assumed the directorship of Lakam, at whose helm he stood when the Pollard scandal erupted. He absorbed much of the blame and embarrassment for the affair.

Upon the enigmatic Joseph does the best-laid plan of le Carré's novel depend. For though Kurtz is the family patriarch, it is to Joseph that Charlie will be wed. "Because he is the middle ground, Shimon," Kurtz tells his right hand, Litvak, by way of explaining why Joseph is the best man for the deed. "Because he has the reluctance that can make the bridge. Because he ponders."[23]

Matching handler to source is a delicate calculation. More often than not, it is a purely administrative decision given little consideration: so-and-so sits on the relevant desk, therefore he or she takes care of the source. However, putting the best handler with a particular source is not unlike casting the right actor to bring a character to life. A source needs constant reassurance, perpetual refuelling of fast-depleted reserves of resolve in order to keep going. Hence Kurtz's sentiment about volunteers: it helps when they convince themselves – that is to say, recruit themselves – for their own reasons, because the bottom line is that sources only coincidentally share their handler's motives.

Joseph is not really Joseph – or not, at any rate, until he is so dubbed by the group of actors with whom Charlie is vacationing on Mykonos, courtesy of Israeli intelligence, although they do not know it. He is really Gadi Becker, to give him the latest name of his choosing, a legendary Israeli fighter. At the same time he plays the part of Michel, the passionate Palestinian terrorist, brother of Khalil. This is for Charlie's benefit, for the fiction of the operation is that she has fallen in love with him. In fact, it will depend on her loving Joseph. Through the fiction of her love for Michel, scripted by Kurtz, brought to life by Joseph, Charlie will take them to Khalil.

Everything is real; everything is contrived. Charlie has never actually met Michel, but she has heard him lecture, and she loves him for his suffering and hates the Israelis on his behalf. Travelling from Mykonos to Thessalonika with Joseph, she will live a love affair with Michel, learning his secrets and sharing every confidence. At his behest she will drive an explosive-laden Mercedes to Salzburg as an initial test of her reliability in order to gain access to Khalil's network beyond Michel. This is crucial, for Michel's fate has already been determined. He is in the Israelis' hands and will be disposed of at the appropriate time.

Throughout this part of the novel, time is ingeniously compressed; past, present, and future are concurrent. With Joseph, Charlie lives her past with Michel, while Kurtz lays the groundwork in order that the future will unfold in their favour. Reality and contrivance blend until fiction is indistinguishable from fact, even upon the most exacting scrutiny. *The Little Drummer Girl* is most successful to this point. Le Carré is particularly fine in crafting Charlie's recruitment and establishing her motivation. He exhibits the patience of a good 10, not hurrying but letting the scene decide his pace. Once she is contacted by Khalil's people, however, the plot changes gears. It speeds up to such an extent that people shown to be obsessed with precautions bring Charlie along with a rapidity threatening sloppiness.

They do continuously test her to reinforce their confidence, sending her to a training camp in Beirut (prior to which Joseph cautions, "You will find them an easy people to love")[24] before she is finally returned to Europe and introduced to the famed Khalil. Trust is so delicate. It is effectively unknown in the terrorist's realm, where survival depends on certainty ("It is better to be inconsistent than to be uncertain,"[25] Joseph advises her). There, trust is an equity that accrues by deed, not word. Charlie will be suspect until she has been bloodied. Only once she has broken those human bonds of which Kurtz has spoken can Khalil be sure of her loyalty, once she no longer has the alternative of turning against him because she has done the unforgivable. From then on, he will not have to trust her, but can rely on her having crossed the point of no return.

Her blooding is to come from delivering the bomb that will kill Professor Minkel, a Jewish philosopher and champion of Arab rights, in Freiburg, where he is to present a lecture. Israeli intelligence has already determined that he is the probable target, and it is in place to intercept Charlie and replace the bomb with a controlled explosion that will convince anyone watching that Minkel has been killed. The plan is then to follow Charlie back to Khalil. Though she pleads with Joseph not to send her back, knowing that Khalil's intention is to bed her, she accedes.

When you keep yourself at the ready, the least significant things can trigger an alert. Khalil dozes with Charlie in the farmhouse where they have taken refuge, secure that her mission has been successfully carried out. But in the morning the silence, the absence of cows and farmers going about their daily routine, alarms him. Something is amiss. At an earlier juncture, Khalil has searched Charlie's purse and surreptitiously removed the batteries from the alarm clock she always carries. Now he demands that she retrieve the clock and give him the time. Dutifully, she does so. Calmly, he asks her to explain how the clock can continue functioning without batteries, and why, when he passes it in front of a radio, it emits the feedback indicative of a transmitter. She has no choice but to confess who and what she is, that her original clock was replaced when she handed the bomb over to Joseph. At that very moment, Joseph and sundry others burst through the door, gunning Khalil down. While he was accusing Charlie, Khalil dumped the batteries from the radio. With that, the transmitter ceased functioning, signalling Charlie's exposure.

Loose ends are gradually tied up in the aftermath. Minor players are killed off. Charlie is taken away for a cooling-off period while her reputation is rehabilitated in England, paving the way for her return. But, it is difficult to cross back to the conventional side of the looking glass. She returns to the stage, but how can it compare with the theatre of the real? Joseph, too, has been affected. Despite all the earlier battles – or maybe because of them – he is ready to surrender. "What am I dreaming of, he wondered, the fighting or the peace? He was too old for both. Too old to go on, too old to stop. Too old to give of himself, yet unable to withhold. Too old not to know the smell of death before he killed."[26]

In the end he goes to Charlie. She sees him in the audience at one of her performances. Mid-act, she abandons the play and exits the theatre. He follows her into the street, and together, with their shared wounds, they set off into the night.

"Why did Pym do it, Tom? In the beginning was the deed. Not the motive, least of all the word. It was his own choice. It was his own life. No one forced him. Anywhere along the line, or right at the start of it, he could have yelled no and surprised himself. He never did."[27]

Why, indeed? What motivates one to aspire to be "a perfect spy"? What lures a person to espionage, to treason, to loyalty, to betrayal? "Love is whatever you can still betray, [Pym] thought. Betrayal can only happen if you love"[28] (shades of Oscar Wilde: "Yet each man kills the thing he loves"). Is this the answer then? Love? Love of what? Just a general, insatiable need to be loved maybe, a need that traitors try to fulfill with whoever happens to be in front of them. They betray love in favour of what they hope will be a better love. As if responding to this conundrum, in *Single & Single*, Alix Hoban's wife explains his duplicity: "Hoban loves nobody, therefore he has betrayed nobody. When he betrays, he is being loyal to himself."[29]

In *A Perfect Spy* (1986), le Carré's next novel, the last task Magnus Pym sets for himself is to find some peace over the question why, if not to definitively answer it. He composes a final letter to his son, Tom, outlining the course and cause of his actions, his treasons and loyalties, how he was bred by his several masters to be the perfect spy of le Carré's title.

His first master was his dear father, Rick, a charming, rapacious con man, constantly suffering problems of liquidity, who saw no reason to dispense cash when a signature would suffice, and who lived on non-existent credit, forever overdrawn against his promises to make things right. His confidence in his wit and the eventual flowering of one or another scheme was undaunted, even by conviction; even when that conviction (for embezzlement) dashed his hopes of sitting as Liberal member of Parliament for Gulworth North; even when it was his best pal, Magnus, who undermined those hopes, gaining surreptitious access to Rick's most closely guarded secrets and revealing them to a sworn enemy, the victim of one of his frauds.

On his father's death, Magnus declares himself free and flees to the secret hideout that he maintains in a rooming house on the Devon coast, there to commit his life to paper, to free himself from the bonds of those other masters he has taken on and, by turn, served or deceived. "You do it once. Once in your life and that's it. No rewrites, no polishing, no evasions. No would-it-be-better-this-ways. You're the male bee. You do it once, and die."[30]

Perhaps le Carré shared this frantic determination to set it down as he composed *A Perfect Spy*, his most autobiographical work. Indeed, the novel was so personal for him that it marked the first time he neglected to submit his work to the authorities for prior approval because "I knew I wasn't going to change it."[31] It is also his most subtle and questing novel, a philosophical sojourn from the battered corpse of the spy and a return to whatever alchemy conjures up aptitudes for the craft. Is the perfect spy born or made? Who, as opposed to what, is a spy? And – always the lurking question – why?

From the days of his youth, Magnus "planned even then a great autobiographical novel that would show the world what a noble sensitive fellow he was compared with Rick."[32] Every son measures himself off against his father. His first standard for success is invariably to surpass his father on whatever plane he deems important: wealth, status, honour. *A Perfect Spy* is le Carré's fulfillment of Magnus's objective. Rick is closely modelled on his own father, Ronnie, a small-time con man who ran a succession of real estate and insurance scams that would see him in jail and bankrupt on several occasions. He was an incorrigible trickster, invariably losing whatever he made by trying for a bigger score. Le Carré's first wife, Ann, said of Ronnie, "If he had a choice between being honest and dishonest, he'd be dishonest. It made him feel clever."[33]

Ronnie loomed large in le Carré's life, as larger-than-life fathers do. Le Carré came to "recognise that my shadowy struggles with the demons of communism might, at least in part, be the continuation of my secret war with Ronnie by other means."[34] For twenty-five years Ronnie overshadowed le Carré's writing career as well, perpetually the subject he could not tackle, the character he could not form. He was his son's mentor in deception, demonstrating by example the lie and the sure-footedness of how to get away with it. In this respect – the domineering father – le Carré sees in Philby his "secret sharer": "I felt, thinking about Philby and his father, and myself and my father, that there could have been a time when I, if properly spoken to by the right wise man or woman, could have been seduced into some kind of underground act of revenge against society."[35]

For le Carré to get the tone he was striving for, to "tell this story and get the humor out of it that I wanted – and through the humor, the compassion – was to make the son, by extension, in many ways worse than the father. So there could be no question of self-pity."[36] Instead of having Magnus use what he has seen of Rick's cons to make himself a better man, he uses what he has learned of deceit and manipulation to charm his way to greater treachery.

Within the secret service Magnus finds refuge from Rick, but also a familiar environment where deception goes rewarded and constant reinvention is essential. This too was where le Carré went to escape Ronnie. But if in real life the son did not turn out to be worse than the father, what he encountered in the secret world was worse than what he had seen in Ronnie's. He elaborates, "I had fled from his delusions only to find them reproduced all around me in the sleeping castles of secret England ... I had met bigger wreckers than Ronnie, bigger hypocrites and bigger liars, dressed in the trappings of high office and still rising, with index-linked pensions and knighthoods to take with them into old age. The difference was, they lied out of obedience to some ill-perceived higher cause, and did their wrecking in the name of service. What broke the code for me was the recognition that it was not the Ronnies who had made such a mess of England, or indeed of the larger world outside – not the dissenters, not the mavericks, heretics, detractors, not even the traitors – but loyal men in grey suits marching blindly to the music of their institutional faiths."[37] Whatever Ronnie's sins, he never pretended to be serving any greater good – small consolation, perhaps, for those he swindled but a way for le Carré to reconcile his private treacheries with those of a more public sort.

Rick is not held against Magnus when the secret service, known in this instalment as the Firm, comes recruiting. On the contrary, his "suspicion is that Rick was an asset. A healthy streak of criminality in a young spy's background never did him any harm."[38] There is nothing like a little larceny in the genes to signal the born spy. A life lived just a desperate wit ahead of ruin can be the best natural training ground for the professional deceiver, apparently. In other words, it is easier to turn the skills of the dishonest man to good purpose than to teach the man of good purpose the traits of dishonour. A life on the run from Rick's creditors is preparation for a life under cover.

Le Carré shared Magnus's formative training in the secret skills. Ronnie's most enduring con, and one in which he enlisted his son's complicity, was to impersonate the proper English gentleman. He also instilled in him the judicious use of secrecy so as to facilitate the juggling of creditors and women. A child forced into lies and secrets turns inward and inhabits a training ground as valuable to the 10 as to the writer. Acknowledging the impact of his unsettled youth upon his later endeavours, le Carré says, "The vagaries and accidents of youth do drive you in upon yourself. That's when you start inventing your secret worlds. When there is absolutely no reason in the adult world around you, then more and more you feed and foster the imagination – secret rooms in the mind all the time."[39] Novelist Arthur Hopcraft, who wrote the screenplay for the BBC adaptation of A Perfect Spy, concluded, "Magnus is fated almost from birth to lead the sort of life he eventually does – he has to learn deviousness, disguise and deception almost from boyhood. The moment he understands that the adults round him aren't to be trusted, that what they're telling him isn't the truth, he has to become a spy to find out what's happening around him."[40]

The novel conjures loyalties that are more soul-wrenching than those aroused by any institution, for at its heart is the relationship of son to father. What loyalty does a son owe to a father he knows to be bad? Magnus is moved by Peggy Wentworth's story of Rick's having embezzled her husband, which leaves her penniless on his death, and he surreptitiously goes through Rick's papers until he finds the proof. She then turns up at a public meeting in Rick's campaign to win election to Parliament and humiliates him by exposing his prison record. As Rick responds to her mellifluously from the podium, Magnus is enthralled, almost believing every word his father utters, seemingly oblivious to having been the architect of his demise.

Without directly accusing Magnus of duplicity, Rick says to him afterward, "We're pals, remember? We don't have to tiptoe around each other looking in one another's pockets, poking in drawers, talking to misguided women in hotel cellars."[41] But Magnus does have to: because he despises his father as much as he loves him; because he feels compelled to betray as much as to honour him. To spy on Rick is the only sure way to the truth about him. Of his relationship with Ronnie, le Carré asked, "Had I loved him or hated him? It no longer mattered. I had done both so amply that the distinctions had disappeared, and with them any thought of judgment."[42]

At the age of sixteen, Magnus Pym runs away from public school and England altogether, lies about his age, and enrols in the University of Berne. It is while holed up in Berne, avoiding the fallout of another of Rick's disastrous adventures, that Magnus chances to find board in a rooming house. There he encounters Axel, whose willing pupil he becomes. Axel has been forced across many borders. Switzerland suits him because of its generous neutrality, its suspicion of choosing a side. Axel is a man of ideas. He schools Pym in, among other things, the great communist masterpieces: "We accept no prejudices, Sir Magnus. We believe everything as we read it and only afterwards reject it. If Hitler hated these fellows so much, they can't be all bad, I say."[43] And so Pym learns at his knee. Together they solve the problems of the world, as idle intellectuals are prone to do.

Along comes Jack Brotherhood. They meet at Berne's English church. A British diplomat, he extends an invitation for a Boxing Day sherry to the English student. It is what idle diplomats do.

But Brotherhood does nothing idly, for he is a British spy and Pym a potential agent. He brings Pym along slowly, semi-consciously, with simple chores for small rewards. He asks about Axel, whose lack of legitimate papers would be taken as sinister by anybody whose own illegitimacy was officially sanctioned.

Doing his duty – to whom or to what? – Brotherhood advises the Swiss and the Americans about Axel, and he is dutifully arrested. Pym is guilt-ridden and resentful toward Brotherhood. In his mind, Axel's "only crimes were his poverty, his illegal presence and his lameness – plus a certain freedom in his way of thinking, which in the eyes of some is what we are there to protect."[44] But still, he does not yell no.

This was how le Carré's own association with intelligence began, at a British Embassy cocktail party in Berne. He was recruited as a source, in which capacity it is rumoured he carried on after his return to England to attend Oxford, where he allegedly spied on leftist students. In response to questions about his university days, he would say only, "I don't want to talk about it. Except to say I can't talk about it. The connections are simply indecipherable." And he added, "It was not as it has been written, but I cannot confirm, deny or refute."[45] In a later interview, he continued to equivocate, but commented that "if that's all I did, I don't know that it's such a disgraceful thing to have done, if you look at the record of people who were recruited at university from the ranks of Communist sympathizers and later turned into traitors to their country." He went on, "Largely the justification for what we did was one I accepted and still accept. That doesn't mean the work was pleasant. It could often be quite disgusting in the sense that you had to penetrate a settled organization of people who trusted each other and invite informants to come forward and say whether their employers and employees were Communists, that sort of stuff … but somebody has to clean the drains, and I found that I did do things that, although they were in some way morally repugnant, I felt at the time, and still feel, to have been necessary."[46]

This is precisely what Magnus does, joining lefty clubs and informing on their members to a succession of moribund handlers, "men who see the threat to their class as synonymous with the threat to England and never wandered far enough to know the difference."[47] It is not entirely fair to accuse such officers of protecting their own class as much as the status quo, and of associating change with threat. After all, working 10s are hardly of the lordly class, though they seek a reflection of themselves in its values. They do not protect anything so much as what they have been schooled to believe in. The system that takes care of its police is well taken care of, regardless of the class origins of the officers.

While doing a stint with a military intelligence field interrogation unit in Groz, Austria, (le Carré likewise did his national service with the Army Intelligence Corps and was stationed in Austria) Pym is told by a Czech translator of a potential defector who is prepared to come over, but only to Pym. At the rendezvous it is Axel who presents himself. But he does not offer himself up as a defector. Instead he tenders Pym an in-place source, Sergeant Pavel of Czech army intelligence, who will pass along reams of valuable information and ensure advancement for Pym. Axel tells him, "A man with a highly regarded source is an admired man and a well-fed one ... He is a cult of one and to know him is to be an insider."[48]

Soon, however, Axel regrets to inform Pym that he has to expose their relationship to his hated superiors for fear of arrest. Now he is in need of some product to justify their contact. Pym is hooked by guilt for Axel's earlier arrest, by love, by the consequences of seeing the fiction of Pavel exposed. "Life is duty, [Pym] reflected. It's just a question of establishing which creditor is asking loudest. Life is paying. Life is seeing people right if it kills you."[49] Thus does Pym enter Axel's service, even as he serves Brotherhood. Thus is his fate sealed. Spies may not stand for much, but they must stand only on one side. It is Pym's "bad habit of protesting loyalty to everyone he met."[50]

Does Pym really believe Axel is giving himself over when they conspire to create Sergeant Pavel? Or does he simply desire to see Axel right – Rick's pledge to everyone he had ever misused – and, plagued by the con man's natural short-sightedness, never pause to consider the question? Maybe Pym does not care. It is easier to surrender to the service of his master than to reason through his deeds, easier to be many Pyms, each serving loyally, than to choose a single Pym, exclusive in his devotion; better to love everyone fully and indiscriminately than to find limits.

Brotherhood believes in Pym for too long. Suspicions about him are affirmed on the basis of an American computer analysis that purports to show that the Czechs are abuzz only where and when

Pym's path crosses that of an identified Czech agent, the one known to Pym as Axel. Otherwise, there is a disconcerting silence. They conclude that Pym is dirty, while Brotherhood insists he is the victim of coincidence or an elaborate Czech set-up, meant to tie them up in knots investigating an effective operative. After all, he argues, the best way to neutralize an incorruptible and effective opponent is to instill doubt within his own circle. In contrast with the dizzying spin out of which Wright and Angleton could never recover, Brotherhood resists the temptation and holds steady on the controls.

"A man can't remember where he was on the night of the tenth? Then he's lying. He *can* remember? Then he's too damn flip with his alibi," Brotherhood marvels.[51] Such are the inherent uncertainties of investigations where everything convicts the guilty and nothing absolves the innocent. Can you remember what you had for dinner last Tuesday? No hesitating; answer NOW. You can't, can you? You have to pause to think; maybe you can't answer at all. Neither can I. I know I had pasta one night, but was it Tuesday? Monday? I would have to think pretty hard to sort it all out. I have no obvious reason to hide what I had for dinner on any particular night, but the suspicion that I'm dissembling will be introduced into some minds. Perhaps on Tuesday I was off some place I shouldn't have been. Maybe I don't want it to be known what I did that night. From now on, all my actions that day will be suspect. Suspicions are nascent conspiracy theories.

When I was conducting investigations, I learned to recognize natural inconsistencies. I was wary about people who could answer to insignificant details too readily. It meant they had rehearsed in preparation for an interrogation. And why should they do that unless they expected to be held to account for their time? Gaps are normal; one day tends to run into the next because most of our days are passed in uninterrupted routine. You don't remember dinner because you eat it every night. People don't act with mathematical regularity. Sometimes the future doesn't seamlessly correspond with its immediate antecedents.

By the time Brotherhood concedes Pym's treachery, it is too late. His consolation is the evidence that indicates the Czechs have lost touch with him as well. Pym has not defected to the opposition; he has chucked them all for something else. In a way reminiscent of Guillam's inability to hate Haydon, Brotherhood feels a strange empathy towards Pym. "Why do I begin to understand him? he wondered, marveling at his own tolerance. Why is it that in my heart if not my intellect I sense a stirring of sympathy for the man who all his life has made a failure of my successes? What I made him do, he made me pay for."[52] Perhaps the sympathy is tinged with regret for being one of the many who fabricated the Pym he has been.

And that includes his wife, Mary. Intelligence services approve of no union so thoroughly as a marriage between spies and indoctrinated support staff. It gives them confidence that, whether in desperation or loneliness, when spies betray secrets to their spouses, the secrets remain in the family. Of course, Mary is not privy to Pym's deepest secret. But it touches her as it never could Brotherhood, haunting their Greek escape, as Pym insisted on hopscotching the country in a vain attempt to elude Axel, who has followed him in an effort to pull him out of the game and behind the Iron Curtain, out of Brotherhood's grasp.

It is significant that in the end only Mary can decode the clues and figure out where Pym has holed up, when neither Axel nor Brotherhood can. For all that those who have created the perfect spy think they know and control him, they are sadly misguided. Like the stubbornly independent Number Six in the classic British television series *The Prisoner*, Pym resolutely keeps a part of himself free, the part that longs to be a writer and is perpetually at work on the great novel. Nobody can get to this part of Pym except Mary, who knows his inner desires. But it's all too late. Pym is too keenly alert to the movements and absences of movement that signal the inevitable end to his run. His despair culminates in a single gunshot that snuffs out his futile endeavours.

"Sometimes, Tom, we have to do a thing in order to find out the reason for it. Sometimes our actions are questions, not answers."[53] Espionage as existential expression: sometimes a thing is done, and still its reasons are a mystery, sometimes even to the person who does it. Fiction at least gives an author the power to imagine characters of his or her own creation in situations of the writer's own invention. It is quite another thing to examine real people and situations that follow their own obscure course. Emotions, errors of judgment, perhaps sincere lapses of common sense, can cause behaviour that defies neat characterization. In a 1991 piece for *Granta*, le Carré stepped away from his own world to explore that of Swiss brigadier Jean-Louis Jeanmaire, one-time chief of Switzerland's air defence, labelled by the press, with its unquenchable fondness for hyperbole, "spy of the century."

As a character study of all the ambiguities and contradictions of espionage, Jeanmaire was worthy of le Carré. He embodied all the perplexity of one who realizes that he has acted inexplicably. Here was a fiercely militarist Swiss patriot, an unwavering anti-communist, a senior military officer, the son of a career soldier, who had nearly forty years of service when he was arrested in 1976. Here too was a man who willingly, without apparent vulnerability to coercion or promise of reward, passed classified military information to Colonel Vassily Denissenko, Soviet military attaché and GRU resident in Berne. How to reconcile the contradictions?

Certainly not in the things he did: Jeanmaire met Denissenko in 1959 while commanding a military demonstration attended by the resident military attachés. Their relationship developed at a snail's pace. Only in June 1963, while they were dining together along with Jeanmaire's wife, Marie-Louise, did Jeanmaire step into the abyss of espionage. Harking back to a conversation they had had months before, in which Denissenko made what, in Jeanmaire's eyes, was a disparaging comment implying that the Swiss military was dependent on NATO's support, Jeanmaire handed him a photocopy of an organization chart that showed no liaison with NATO. The document was classified "confidential." As the evening wore on and the conversation dwelt on Switzerland's battle preparedness, Jeanmaire loaned Denissenko his *Mobilization Handbook*, a "secret" document issued to all company commanders. He also showed the Soviet attaché contingency plans in the event of war, which he would photocopy and pass along at a later date.

As le Carré is able to reconstruct the story using interviews with Jeanmaire and leaked information from his still-secret interrogation and trial of 1976, the Swiss officer was the aggressor in the relationship, pursuing Denissenko more than he was pursued. Why? He was never blackmailed, although he may have realized after his first transgression that he could be threatened with exposure. He angrily refused money, displaying consciousness of how it would look if it were ever said that he had sold his country's

secrets. His accusers claimed that he began spying out of vindic-
tiveness at being passed over for promotion to chief of air defence
and territorial services in 1962. Jeanmaire denies this.

Was it ego? Was the desire not to be politely neutral, to get in
on the game, so fierce that the ground rules were irrelevant?
Neutrality is not synonymous with disinterest. Le Carré has called
Switzerland "the spiritual home of natural spies."[54] Imagine how
unbearable peace must be for a soldier, especially for Jeanmaire
in his orderly fortress when faced with Denissenko, the veteran
of Stalingrad, an officer and representative of a superpower. for
Jeanmarie, keenly aware that he would never have occasion to
fight for his country, spying was a way of exerting influence, of
feeling – if ever so faintly – the glory of battle.

The defence he offered was unoriginal: "All I ever did was give
the Russians harmless bits of proof that Switzerland was a dangerous country to attack! ... My aim was to deter those mad
Bolsheviks at the Kremlin from mounting an assault against my
country! I showed them how expensive it would be! What is
dissuasion if the other side is not *dissuaded*?" He concluded, "I was
never a traitor. A fool maybe. A traitor, never!"[55]

Does it sound familiar? Jeanmaire was hardly the first spy to
claim to have taken matters into his own hands for the purpose
of assisting his country. Excusing his decision to pass the Soviets
highly sensitive information about Germany obtained from
decrypted Enigma signals intelligence during World War ii, John
Cairncross wrote, "Germany was our main enemy, I never considered myself a traitor to Britain, but a patriot in the struggle
against Nazism."[56] Of course, the fact is that it cannot be left up
to every individual with access to restricted information to decide
what should or should not be shared with other countries. To
reveal how a state intends to dissuade its potential enemies does
not necessarily enhance the dissuasion, but it exposes how to
circumvent those obstacles that are in place but unseen.

Whatever his motivation – whether genuine or equivocal –
Jeanmaire was undeniably guilty. He willfully and consciously
passed classified information to an agent of a foreign intelligence
service. But le Carré defined "his greatest crime of all: a luminous,
fathomless gullibility, and an incurable affection for his fellow
man, who could never sufficiently make up to him the love he
felt was owed."[57] He loved Denissenko and would prove it by

betraying the other thing he held dear, his country. And he would forgive Denissenko when the Soviet attaché betrayed him by seducing his wife. The truth that reveals itself through this tangled web is that love and espionage are forever incompatible.

To this day, Jeanmaire remains unrepentant, insisting that Denissenko "is a great and good man. For who, when he has wrecked his life for love and paid everything he possesses, is willing to turn around and say: 'There was nothing there?'"[58] Nothing, not the adultery of his wife, not the public humiliation of his arrest, his demotion, and his terrifically harsh sentence of eighteen years' imprisonment, has shaken this love. Such was the sustenance that he took from their relationship. Jeanmaire was not popular with his comrades: "Partners of the sort he craved were scarce in the ranks of his own kind, and his reputation as a big-mouth didn't help."[59] He will not now forsake the man who bestowed on him the fellowship he craved.

Love between men, le Carré concedes, is a delicate subject. There is nothing to suggest that Jeanmaire had any homosexual leanings, and surely love can be something other than sexual. It can be aesthetic, the expression of admiration for an ideal. Or it can be the product of dependence, of the sort that the spy may come to feel for the handler who is crucial to the spy's identity. Jeanmaire's love for Denissenko may well have been nurtured by both these sentiments.

The prosecution was determined to punish Jeanmaire severely. At the same time as he was arrested, the Americans were expressing concern that sensitive military technology, including the Florida early warning system, they had made available to Switzerland had become known to the East. They threatened to cut off Swiss access unless they were satisfied that the leak had been plugged. Jeanmaire, even though the prosecution could not prove his responsibility in this instance and he convincingly showed he knew nothing about Florida,[60] was a convenient spy on whom to peg all extant security flaws. In passing its sentence, the "Tribunal had done what was needed of it. It had made a big spy of a small one. Such a huge sentence must betoken a huge betrayal."[61]

Just as Jeanmaire despaired at enduring a soldier's life without combat, so the IO feels resentment when a career's worth of surveillance, eavesdropping, and inquiry fails to reveal a spy. In Jeanmaire the real thing had been landed. Unfortunately, the scope of his betrayal hardly lived up to his billing as the spy of the century. Interestingly, I searched through several general books on espionage to see how history has treated his treason. I found only one reference, and that brief and inaccurate. Jeffrey T. Richelson gives Jeanmaire exactly five lines in his book on twentieth-century intelligence and wrongly says he was recruited following his retirement and "probably provided the Soviets with information on Swiss aircraft capabilities, air defense plans, and early warning systems."[62] Denissenko's name does not even come up.

Such is the dreary end to a seamy case. A weak and desolate man finally finds the companionship he craves and gives himself over to it completely, only to be deceived.

CHAPTER SIX

Changing Times

To begin near the end: "The old isms were dead, the contest between Communism and capitalism had ended in a wet whimper. Its rhetoric had fled underground into the secret chambers of the grey men, who were still dancing away long after the music had ended."[1] Bureaucrats will always labour to drive the square peg of new developments into the round hole of the established order, so much do they loathe change. Whatever the dangers or irrationalities posed by the status quo, these have the advantage of being the devil they know. The mistake, however, is to believe that knowing the devil makes him somehow tractable, when in fact the devil remains forever the devil. Confirmation of the world as they understand it is still easier to trust than anything that might call it into question.

The 1990s saw the intelligence lexicon infiltrated by a slew of words and phrases purloined from business-school texts. Maybe if we *sounded* modern and efficient, we would *be*. The ministries to whom we furnished information became our "clients." Our role and capabilities had to be "marketed" across the government. We devised a "mission statement" to embody our function, in case anyone was unclear on the concept. Months of study produced the following: "The people of CSIS are dedicated to the protection of Canada's national security interests and the safety of Canadians." Slick brochures were published to enunciate our "corporate culture." Henceforth, we were to be, not IOs, but captains of the intelligence industry. And yet, *plus ça change* ...

No private business, seeing its industry undergoing the fundamental change that ours experienced with the end of communism, would have survived the years of hand-wringing that intelligence went through. Of course, we had the benefits of a monopoly. It was not as if our marketing efforts were designed to lure clients away from a competitor. At the same time, our most marketable asset – an enemy everyone believed in – had deserted us. We were stubbornly trying to sell typewriters in a computerized marketplace.

A favourite preoccupation in le Carré's work is this desperate effort to make the world conform to expectations. Espionage, then, is not the benign and impartial gathering of information but the selective manipulation of innuendo and suggestion within the context of how the world is perceived – or, more accurately, how the political masters have told the intelligence mandarins to perceive the world. Take the counsel of Scottie Luxmore, the artless chief of section in *The Tailor of Panama*, "Your born intelligencer is the man who knows what he is looking for before he finds it."[2] Ironically, the very nature of secret work argues for this approach. Certain though agents are that a secret smoulders beneath the surface like a dormant volcano, they must probe at just the right spot for the telltale puff of steam to show itself. Failure to reveal the object of their quest is taken as evidence that their probes are misdirected, not misconceived.

"It takes a crafty mind, indeed, Johnny, to hide his tracks from the ears and eyes of modern technology, does it not?" Luxmore offers by way of explaining the suspicious silence of Panama's Silent Opposition. "'No trace' in such circumstances comes close to proof of guilt. These men of the world understand that. They know what it takes to be unseen, unheard, unknown."[3] Indeed, the most damning evidence of the effectiveness of the Silent Opposition is its deafening silence. The best confirmation of a source's value is the snippets that he or she digs out that confirm something is afoot. Thus the less evidence of the plot, the greater is the proof of its being hatched. Since there was once a revolutionary opposition in Panama, it stands to reason that there still is. Russia *was* a potent nuclear threat; hence anything that fails to advance that particular view of the world is suspect. It isn't a matter of selling straight or twisted; it's a question of which represents continuity.

The Russia House (1989) was written as the world teetered on the brink between continuity and momentous change. It contemplates forces that could tip the balance one way or the other. On one level, the book celebrates the promise of glasnost. On another, it laments the temptation to dismiss it as a new mask donned by a familiar face. While threatening optimism, it ultimately surrenders to pessimism.

A tortured Russian scientist – known by several names, including his given, Yakov Savelyev; his chosen, Goethe; and his code, Bluebird – passes to Barley Scott Blair, a shabby English publisher, a manuscript that demonstrates the Soviet nuclear arsenal to be wholly unreliable, a paper tiger buttressed by falsified and exaggerated test results. If this information proves to be accurate, the Western defence establishment, together with its intelligence sidekicks, will be backed into a very tight corner. Thus commences the mad debate over whether Bluebird is the genuine article, passing genuine information, or a Soviet disinformation operation designed to confuse and mislead. What follows is a contortionist's exercise in twisting what is straightforward into a knotted tangle that would confound Houdini.

"He's straight. It's a straight case. Do you remember straight?" Ned, the consummate fieldman, pleads in exasperation. "While you're thinking round corners, Bluebird's going straight for goal."[4] But nothing is ever straight in the secret world. Nothing can be assumed to be fully known. And what is unknown is always confused with what is important. This confusion is the fuel that feeds the machinery of intelligence.

The case bears some resemblance to that of Colonel Oleg Penkovsky, the GRU officer who is lauded by Andrew and Gordievsky as "the most important Western agent of the Cold War," and whose intelligence take proved "of the highest importance."[5] (Le Carré expressed the same evaluation in a 1967 book review.)[6] Penkovsky was so blunt in his efforts to volunteer his services to Western intelligence that he was initially shunned as a likely provocation. However, after finally being accepted and run jointly by the CIA and SIS, he passed on reams of invaluable data about Soviet missile technology and details about decision-making at the highest levels between April 1961 and his arrest in October 1962. Just as Goethe has Blair to carry his secrets, so Penkovsky had a British businessman, Greville Wynne,[7] to transport his. There is no comparison between the two, however, since Wynne had been a wartime intelligence officer and an enthusiastic collaborator in the affair.

Penkovsky was notably influential in convincing the Americans that the missile gap they believed the Soviets had opened up was, on the contrary, in their favour. He told them that the Soviets lacked the number of nuclear warheads, necessary trained personnel, and sufficiently accurate guidance systems to attack the West. The first point was confirmed by evidence from satellite imagery. His greatest impact came during the Cuban Missile Crisis. His assessments of Khrushchev's capabilities and intentions had a direct influence on President John F. Kennedy's decision-making, persuading him that he could achieve his objective of having the missiles withdrawn from the island if he stood firm against the Soviet leader and demonstrated his determination not to back down.[8]

But neither in fact nor in fiction is straight accepted as straight. Penkovsky has his detractors, and it is in their suspicions that his case most closely reflects *The Russia House*. Knightley raises three counter-theories concerning his bona fides: first, that the KGB manufactured an elaborate set-up because it needed to apprehend a Western spy as trade bait for Conon Molody (the illegal Gordon Lonsdale), who had been convicted of espionage in London: Wynne was arrested in Hungary and sentenced to eight years for complicity with Penkovsky, only to be swapped for Molody the next year; second, that Penkovsky was a straightforward purveyor of disinformation intended to lull the West into a false sense of security[9] (direct shades of *The Russia House*); and third, the theory that Knightley professes to adhere to, that wittingly or not, Penkovsky was "used by a faction in the Kremlin to pass a vital message to the West ... What the faction needed, clearly, was a channel through which they could let the West know that whatever Khrushchev might *threaten*, he did not have the *capability* to carry out the threat."[10] Knightley argues the efficacy of this channel on the grounds that the Americans were more apt to believe information coming to them through espionage than that transmitted via diplomatic or political conduits by disaffected officials.

One could expect that Penkovsky's arrest, torture, and execution would have immunized him against charges of being anything but genuine. But there is no such immunity in the secret world. Like some strain of super-virus that infects the imagination, suspicion reveals itself in an infinite diversity of mutations. Even *if* Penkovsky was executed, he could still have been part of some plot. How could he have gained access to so much information? Why was he so anxious to spy for the West? If something looks too good to be true, it is.

Now to return to the beginning. During the darkest nights of Stalinist repression, through Leonid Brezhnev's torpor, well into the uncertain dawn of Mikhail Gorbachev's openness, citizens of the fraternity of socialist states were well advised to follow change at a respectful distance, rather than be caught out in the position of having to backtrack in the event of an official reversal. A society in which disagreement is dissidence is treason encourages an unhealthy allegiance to the prevailing order. For example, Soviet historian Roy Medvedev began work on *Let History Judge*, his account of the Stalin era, in 1962 when Khrushchev sanctioned de-Stalinization. By the time it was completed six years later, Khrushchev was out and Stalin had undergone rehabilitation, the process by which totalitarian states dictate which version of history is to be read on any particular day. Medvedev charged ahead while change stopped short, and he found himself an adherent of a discredited line, a dissident of the newly prevailing orthodoxy. If one leader can write history, another can rewrite it: just as Khrushchev could condemn Stalin and expose his crimes, so Brezhnev could come along and vindicate him. Medvedev was expelled from the Communist Party and condemned to the isolation of an enemy of the state, complete with KGB guard outside his front door to frighten off visitors. His twin brother, Zhores, was confined to a mental institution for his dissidence until Roy raised enough of a hue and cry in the West that he was released and resettled in London.

A powerful tribute to the Russian spirit is its tenacity in the face of all manner of suppression, its ability to approach the present with fatalism but not allow it to sap the energy held in reserve to meet an improved future. Sensitive to this feature of the Russian character, Smiley, upon reviewing Karla's Circus file, "tried but, as so often before, failed to resist his own fascination at the sheer scale of the Russian suffering, its careless savagery, its flights of heroism. He felt small in the face of it, and soft by comparison, even though he did not consider his own life wanting in its pains."[11] It is difficult for a Westerner not to feel humbled before Russians' capacity to endure. The Mongols, Napoleon, the Germans – Russia can plot its history from invasion to invasion, each of which was ultimately repulsed. So much of Russian identity is drawn from periods of collective suffering; the worst of times are remembered nostalgically for bringing out the best in people. In his landmark report *The Russians,* journalist Hedrick Smith writes that many Russians look back with genuine fondness on their perseverance and eventual triumph in World War II.[12] Indeed, in their reminiscing about the Great Patriotic War Smith did not find a false note of propaganda, only a genuine expression of pride.

Attachment to Mother Russia surmounts the excesses of a particular regime and expands the references of patriotism. Russians also have a quality atypical of North Americans: a long view of history. Where we tend to see decades as interminable stretches, they measure time in centuries. Their ability to distinguish between the permanent and the transient is clear from their reverence for the former and the fact that they invest loyalty, accordingly, in land and culture and language. A leader, they know, can inflict demagoguery on them for only so long before succumbing to nature or a rival. Unlike Western defectors, who betrayed both country and regime, Soviets often spied while insisting on their unstinting devotion to Russia. Arkady Shevchenko, who was serving as undersecretary general of the United Nations when he spied on behalf of, and eventually defected to, the United States, articulates this very proposition: "I have never regarded myself as a spy in the true sense of the word, nor have I felt that I betrayed my people or my country. I have always loved Russia and I always will. For a relatively short time in my life I worked with the US government to help it better comprehend the objectives and actions of the Soviet regime – a regime I knew well and had grown to hate. That regime, and the system that props it up, is what I 'betrayed.'"[13]

Savelyev was born in 1938, making him, in the words of the Russia House's Walter, of "the vintage year. Any younger, he'd be brainwashed. Any older, he'd be looking for an old fart's sinecure."[14] Though rather younger than Andrei Sakharov, Savelyev bears a striking resemblance to the great dissident scientist. Both were scientific prodigies, achieving great honours at a young age. Both contributed mightily to Soviet military standing before becoming disillusioned and troubled for having enhanced the power of a leadership of dubious morality to the peril of humanity. Awestruck – perhaps horrified – at the forces he had loosed upon discovering the secret of the hydrogen bomb, Sakharov hoped to strike a balance between the power to destroy and the responsibility not to. Of course, he sought this within a decidedly unbalanced society. For engaging in human-rights activism, he paid dearly: with the loss of his job and the status it conferred, KGB harassment, and ultimately, confinement to internal exile in Gorky in 1980 after he opposed Soviet military intervention in Afghanistan. Abroad openly and in secret at home, he was revered as the uncompromising conscience of Russia for refusing either to leave or to surrender.

Le Carré met Sakharov in 1987 while on a visit to Leningrad in the process of writing *The Russia House*. "Sakharov absolutely fascinated me. Of course, just looking at him, you think: guilt. You must think guilt, because he's the man who gave them the hydrogen bomb, and his opinion of the recipients of his talent was not high," he said. As to whether Sakharov might ever have contemplated espionage, le Carré observed, "I like to imagine that it crossed his mind, in my company, that that was an option that would have been available to him. But the grand contribution of Sakharov, of course, is far, far more significant than a bunch of boring secrets. He took the much braver road of public protest in a closed society. Our spies, our contemptible spies, our traitors, our Kim Philbys and Anthony Blunts and so on, took the secret road in an open society where protest could be voiced and you didn't lose your hide. But Sakharov did lose his hide. I thought he had the stamp of true greatness. He really has contributed to a change in history."[15] The idea for Savelyev emerged from le Carré's musing about what would have happened if Sakharov had indeed gone the other route and become the West's spy deep inside the Russian nuclear establishment.[16]

That Savelyev has christened himself Goethe is undoubtedly in deference to Sakharov's choosing an epigraph from *Faust* – "He alone is worthy of life and freedom / Who each day does battle for them anew" – for the essay "Reflections on Progress, Peaceful Coexistence, and Intellectual Freedom," which won him international attention when it was published in the *New York Times* in 1968. Sakharov explained his motives for writing the piece as being "to alert my readers to the grave perils threatening the human race – thermonuclear extinction, ecological catastrophe, famine, an uncontrolled population explosion, alienation, and dogmatic distortion of our conception of reality. I argued for *convergence*, for a rapprochement of the socialist and capitalist systems that could eliminate or substantially reduce these dangers, which had been increased many times over by the division of the world into opposing camps."[17] Like Sakharov, Savelyev acts with what he perceives to be humankind's best interests at heart. He too is a brilliant physicist made heartsick that his genius is destined to be exploited to wreak havoc on the planet. Neither rejected socialism so much as its totalitarian implementation.

Savelyev would have been thirty during that pivotal moment in communist history, the Prague Spring of 1968, the moment when revolutionary idealism died. Alexander Dubček's experiment in "socialism with a human face" became a test as to whether the Soviets would permit liberalization behind the Iron Curtain. Intellectual freedom sent a warm gust of euphoria through Czechoslovakia, but by the time it risked blowing across to Moscow, it had become a chill wind. Fearing the impact that the Czech reforms would have throughout the East bloc, the Soviets dispatched the Red Army to forcibly crush the Dubček regime. Although Hedrick Smith reports that "many people evidently took pride in the exercise of Soviet power,"[18] this was certainly not the response of anyone who held to the hope that the Soviet system might of its own accord choose anything other than the tyrannical exercise of power. Novelist Vasily Aksyonov called the Czech invasion "a nervous breakdown for the whole generation."[19] Gordievsky refers to the military repression as "that dreadful event, that awful day, which determined irrevocably the course of my own life. Over the past two years I had become increasingly alienated from the Communist system, and now this brutal attack on innocent people made me hate it with a burning passionate hatred. 'Never again would I support it,' I told myself."[20] In his *Memoirs* Sakharov writes that with it, "'real socialism' displayed its true colors, its stagnation, its inability to tolerate pluralistic or democratic tendencies, not just in the Soviet Union but even in neighboring countries ... For millions of former supporters, it destroyed their faith in the Soviet system and its potential for reform."[21] Savelyev greets news of the Soviet invasion with "The system will always win. We talk freedom but we are oppressors."[22]

Before the Russia House christens him Bluebird, Savelyev is feverish, impassioned Goethe, who absorbs and – worse still – believes every word Blair speaks at an impromptu, drunken gathering in Peredelkino, the Soviet writer's village, where Blair ends up following the Moscow book fair. Blair is in brilliant form, holding court on peace, progress, glasnost, utopia, jazz – all that is subversive. His eloquence and imitation of conviction move Savelyev. "Promise me that if ever I find the courage to think like a hero, you will act like a merely decent human being,"[23] he pleads. Without understanding what that decency may entail, Blair promises.

Like the not-peace/not-war that characterized the Cold War, the early days of glasnost were a limbo of change/not-change. Even in Gorbachev's third year, nobody – least of all Gorbachev himself – could anticipate where the Soviet Union was headed, if anywhere. Savelyev wants to do something from which there can be no turning back. Gradualism is all well and good, unless it becomes simply an excuse for indifference.

In time for the following year's audio book fair, Savelyev prepares a manuscript – a heroic act – for Blair to publish – as a merely decent human being. His message is a bombshell: "The American strategists can sleep in peace. Their nightmares cannot be realized. The Soviet knight is dying inside his armour. He is a secondary power like you British. He can start a war but cannot continue one and cannot win one. Believe me."[24] Savelyev provides the diagrams and scientific data to demonstrate that Soviet military strength is a chimera. The calculations that show the trajectory of Soviet intercontinental ballistic missiles to be dead-bang are fudged; in fact, they are all smoke and noise. His manuscript contains the proof that the Soviet arsenal is a fraud.

Never has it been Savelyev's intention that his material should end up in the hands of British intelligence. It is not to help the contemptible grey men of either side that he has made the effort to get it to Blair. His desire is for it to be published for the benefit of world peace, to herald in the new Soviet era with an initiative from which change can never be undone. Unfortunately, Blair fails to show up at the fair, and Savelyev's intermediary, his former lover Katya Orlova, gives the manuscript to Niki Landau, another British publisher, on his promise to take it to Blair. Since it remains dangerous to cross the Soviet border in possession of state secrets, Landau thumbs through it to see what he has gotten himself into. He understands enough of what he reads to know he has been asked to carry nitroglycerine. Nonetheless, he transports the manuscript back to England and even tries to trace Blair to hand it over, but without success. Unable to sit on it forever, he winds up before Ned of the Russia House, and the grey men – never big on acting as decent human beings – have the day.

One might imagine conditions under which the Soviets' rivals would cheer intelligence that pointed to their triumph. But the Cold War presented its own logic, one that both sides had learned and understood. Victory was not the objective of its participants. It was a war to perpetuate indefinitely, not to bring to conclusion. In retrospect, conservative Americans such as former CIA director and president George Bush felt that "American postwar policy toward Europe and the Soviet Union had been successful. The USSR had been contained for four decades and Western Europe had prospered."[25] As American deputy secretary of state Lawrence Eagleburger told a Georgetown audience in 1989, "For all its risks and uncertainties, the Cold War was characterized by a remarkably stable and predictable set of relationships among the great powers."[26] That this occurred with nuclear warheads poised at the ready now seems almost an afterthought. Whether in periods of détente or of crisis, mutually assured destruction – in its appropriate acronym, MAD – made sense under the circumstances. All strategic theorizing – and all strategic thinking was theoretical, for it was impossible to know for certain how a nuclear exchange would play out – took for granted the argument that rational leaders would refrain from launching a first strike because they could count on the dissuasive force of MAD. The reciprocity between strike and counter-strike did more than keep both sides in check; it fuelled the multi-billion-dollar defence industry and its political proponents. The arms race was a game of one-upmanship without limits, between two apparently inexhaustible competitors.

"Moribund on the Sov side means moribund *our* side," complains Russell Sheriton, one of many CIA greys who swarm the Bluebird file. "How do you peddle the arms race when the only asshole you have to race against is yourself? Bluebird is life-threatening intelligence."[27] The question, then, is not simply whether the information is true, but what impact it will have if it is. The effects of easing Cold War tensions were far-reaching; they "threw open the fundamental assumptions on which the entire postwar security structures of Western Europe, and our own strategic planning were based,"[28] writes Brent Scowcroft, national security adviser to two American presidents. As far as much of the American economy and political establishment was concerned, an excuse to halt the arms race was not good news. Therefore an institutional resistance to Bluebird is mounted. Instead of thinking him straight and his emergence an intelligence success, the espiocrats scheme to bring about his failure.

Savelyev is suspect because he is the originator. Katya is suspect because she is his willing intermediary. Blair is suspect because Savelyev chose him. Even Landau is suspect, if for no other reason than that he has the poor taste to be a Pole and to have a sister back in his native land. The whole thing is a Soviet set-up to trick the West into believing it is weaker than is the case, and thus stand down its guard. The Soviets are running Savelyev as a means of eliciting a comprehensive list of strategic questions out of the Americans, for from their questions the Soviets can divine the gaps in their knowledge and even clues as to what and how much they can collect from other sources.

Meanwhile, as the grey men obsess about Bluebird, Blair's concern for Katya and her family grows. He is falling in love. It is certainly not out of the ordinary for spies to fall in love – or something near enough – while out in the cold. It happens to Leamas and it happens to Westerby. None of those watching over Blair's shoulder are unduly troubled by the signs of his growing enchantment with her. Somehow, they all assume it is part and parcel of the operational context; even Ned, who has the best read on Blair's moods, is resigned to this particular need: "Name me a joe in a bad country … who doesn't fall for a pretty face if she's on his side against the world."[29] It's nothing serious – a fling, relief from the loneliness of being far from home, release from the intensity of doing wrong things in a wrong place.

Love is something else though, something true and surprising and untainted by the spy's corrupt outlook on life. Harry Palfrey, the legal overseer of the Russia House and narrator of the book, unfavourably contrasts himself with Blair: "He was believing in all the hopes that I had buried with me when I chose the safe bastion of infinite distrust in preference to the dangerous path of love."[30] Such is the spy's natural choice. Distrust holds open the hatch to escape, a reason to disappear without warning. Love does not conspire for ways out; it marks total capitulation to the mercy and compassion of another. This goes against everything spies' better instincts tell them. Among the axioms le Carré gives us is "Spying is imitating love."[31]

Spying is an excuse for holding love at bay. That's why I would habitually give women false names when I met them. It's why a night out in the bars with Service friends began with a huddle where each chose a name and a profession. It's why wedding bands suddenly disappeared and substitute wives appeared at parties. Like noxious fumes, falsehood is tough to contain. It spreads easily. And don't believe otherwise: a lie is easier to tell than the truth because we invest nothing in the lie. Also, we were absolved of any guilt that would normally accompany lying by virtue of our being spies. For some reason, our commitment of loyalty to our country was licence for every other betrayal.

But Blair isn't a spy. He is a publisher. Notwithstanding his protestation of being the wrong man, he is the only man because Savelyev chose him ("'We're all wrong men,' said Ned. 'We're dealing in wrong things.'").[32] And by any reasonable measure, he is altogether the right man. Unencumbered by the spy's need to fit into a prefab construction of the world, he is totally open to Savelyev and credulous of his motives. If his own designs had not been dissected with the fine scalpels of disbelief that the spies wield with such abandon, he may have stayed right.

But Blair isn't imitating love, and love commands the greatest loyalty of all. When he commits himself to Katya, it is not necessarily at the expense of Britain: "Barley saw it as a question of which England he chose to serve. His last ties to the imperial fantasy were dead. The chauvinist drumbeat revolted him. He would rather be trampled by it than march with it. He knew a better England by far, and it was inside himself"[33] (shades of Maurice Castle). By the time the British, the Americans, and the polygraph machine are satisfied that he is their man, he is no longer.

Only Ned sees it coming. He is disturbed when Savelyev informs Blair he will respond to questions from the intelligence services one time and one time only. The Americans therefore prepare a complete shopping list of all they needed to know. It is too risky to give it to the Soviets in case the situation is a set-up. Ned pleads that the operation be aborted at this point. But the bureaucracy that has replaced the soul of intelligence is a lumbering freight train; once enough cars have been hitched aboard and it has built up a full head of steam, it can't stop abruptly, negotiate sharp turns, or reverse directions. Ned is the only one who sees that the light at the end of the tunnel is from an oncoming train.

However, he has used up his credibility arguing in favour of Bluebird earlier on. In the very macho world of espionage, where courage is so often measured in terms of the risks to which one is prepared to expose someone else, backing out of an approved operation is a sign of losing one's nerve. But Ned knows: he knows when Savelyev is straight and he knows when he has taken a disturbing turn.

The irony is that Savelyev's original manuscript was the sort of treasure for which 10s sift the detritus year after year after year in the cold and isolation and despair of uncertainty and outright failure. Received for what it is worth, it pierces the very heart of the Soviet military, giving the West's leadership the opportunity to accomplish precisely what Sun-tzu had argued, in his sixty-century classic *The Art of War*, was the very purpose of procuring intelligence: "If you know the enemy and know yourself, you need not fear a hundred battles. If you know yourself and not the enemy, for every victory you will suffer a defeat. If you know neither yourself nor the enemy, you are a fool and will meet defeat in every battle."[34] "There was no deception by anyone, except where we deceived ourselves,"[35] insists Ned after all is said and done. Their defeat comes from not knowing themselves.

It is when Savelyev signals to Katya that he has been taken that Blair resolves to do whatever is necessary to save her – because the rule is that, sooner or later, whatever the initial resistance, everybody talks. Savelyev is bound to reveal Katya's involvement. So Blair uses what he has – access to the shopping list – to offer in trade for official forgiveness of her sins in the form of a promise that she will not be punished and that at some unspecified time in the future she will be free to emigrate. The list of questions for Savelyev is duly handed to Blair, who neatly hands it to whoever comes to meet him in Savelyev's stead and proceeds to disappear. Palfrey learns of the arrangement when Blair resurfaces at his *pied-à-terre* in Lisbon, where he intends to await Katya's eventual arrival. Meanwhile, Savelyev's death from natural causes is noted in *Pravda*.

With the collapse of the Soviet Union and the dismantling of its empire, both external and internal, old enemies ceased to exist, at least under recognizable names. The Western intelligence agencies fell into disarray. In order to secure their place within their own government's machinery, they were obliged to identify threats. This was not such a difficult thing to do: threats of varying magnitudes abounded. But the espiocrats were unused to rationalizing their methods, specifying particular objectives, and drawing a linear connection one to the other. And the politicians found the remaining and emergent threats more difficult to pronounce, let alone understand. It took thought to explain how Ukraine or Georgia or Kazakhstan or other Soviet successor states posed a threat to national security, when the old threats had not necessitated their understanding, since they had been inherited from previous decades. Suddenly, a situation calling for leadership and innovative direction had arisen. Nobody was comfortable with that. Lacking a distinctly defined mission, the services were overcome by aimlessness. It was not enough to be guarding national security; they had to guard it against *something*. But nothing presented as menacingly impressive a danger as communism, with its promise to subvert and dominate capitalist democracy. All the new alternatives paled by comparison.

Morale, probably never as high as I had imagined it to be during my first years in csis, deteriorated markedly. While the public debated whether intelligence agencies should be disbanded, officers pondered the possibility of losing what they treasured most: job security and pensions. Furthermore, they were being told flat out what no one would have dared say during the Cold War: their profession was useless. It was a tough message to hear. And those passing as leaders did little to realign the services to the new world order or to convincingly argue the legitimate role that an intelligence service performs under any international conditions. Just as diplomats are necessary under all type of relations, so are spies. While the techniques employed by intelligence services were refined and their usage grew, their essential nature was not a product of the Cold War. Spying is really not about the particulars of politics: its time-honoured methods have served all variety of masters in all manner of causes.

Thanks to the Cold War, we had mastered and entrenched standard operating procedures. Aside from the advances that technology brought about, this bureaucratization was the major innovation of the period. From a political standpoint, it meant that Soviet bloc targets did not need further justification than that they were of the Soviet bloc. Investigations could be predicated on the supportable assertion that past experience had established these states as hostile and thus posing a threat to national security. The evidence upon which this view was based was simple: known intelligence officers were posted around the world under diplomatic and consular cover, as well as with trade missions, on airlines, in tourist bureaus, on academic exchanges, et cetera. The intelligence officers' task was to conduct intelligence operations. Ergo, if they were here, that is what they were doing. Furthermore, decades' worth of examples of offensive operations against the national interest of Canada could be cited, whether they were conducted here or in allied countries.

Whatever moves as slowly as a bureaucracy will be inherently conservative. It establishes processes, hierarchies of authority, policies that spell out selected responses to as many contingencies as are conceivable, and then it adheres to them like a tortoise to its shell. If bureaucracies exhibit any genius – perhaps it is sheer dumb instinct – it is for self-preservation. And here was another of my misperceptions at the outset of my career: I thought that national security could override politics. I likened intelligence to criminal investigations. When a crime is committed, the objective is to identify and apprehend a suspect. The analogy, however, does not hold. When espionage is committed and the spy is identified, his or her expulsion can impact negatively on an impending wheat purchase or adversely affect that ephemeral concept of favourable diplomatic relations. Or the spy's replacement could prove difficult to identify, resulting in a situation in which we were certain the person had been replaced – their bureaucratic law, every bit the equal of ours, so stipulates – but did not know who had taken up the duties. In truth, more often than not, because of another bureaucratic law, slot succession was the rule. This dictated that a departing spy was occupying a diplomatic slot set aside for the intelligence service, so her or his replacement would slide right into that position. It was too cumbersome for the KGB to negotiate new slots with the ministries of foreign affairs or trade or the news agency Tass or Aeroflot. Domestic intelligence services often oppose expulsion on the theory that it is better to tolerate a known io, since such a person is easier to watch and control, than to run the risk of having someone new, without established routines or known methods of operating, running about. Notwithstanding the dictates of tradecraft, spies are as prone to habit as anyone: drinking at the same bar, walking their dog at the same time, taking the same route to and from work. I cannot, however, comment from personal experience on the care with which they handled clandestine meets with agents because I never actually saw one take place.

What I saw were countless contacts with locals that, with a little inventive writing, could be turned into a decent intelligence report. Caution is the watchword for intelligence officers posted on foreign soil, even those enjoying diplomatic immunities. An East bloc IO well knows that expulsion from a Western country is by far the worst mark against his or her career: it makes certain never being accepted *en poste* in the West again. The great attraction of an intelligence career was the promise of living for extended periods outside the suffocating East. Thus, according to former KGB officer Vladimir Kuzichkin, "The fundamental rule is to survive, and to endure until the end of the posting without being expelled from the country ... Another rule flows from this: don't be especially active."[36] These rules did more to control the behaviour of East bloc officers than local defensive services ever could, with the result that their espionage was often remarkably harmless. Nonetheless, their activities had to be monitored and much effort was expended by Western CI to sketch out patterns and build largely vacuous dossiers on the mostly mundane carryings-on of identified IOs. These were then scoured by analysts, who placed great emphasis on deviations from whatever might constitute the usual. More often than not, nothing came of the exercise. Occasionally, support could be found for mounting an operation to approach an IO with the intent of seeing whether he or she would be amenable to passing over information, the culmination of the game.

The work of Soviet spies was greatly facilitated not only by the openness of our society but also by the constricted nature of their own. For instance, information we take for granted could be made to appear the fruit of assiduous work on their part. Telephone directories were never published in the Soviet Union, hence the story – apocryphal for all I know – of KGB agents stealing them in the dead of night from pay phone booths in those countries where they are freely distributed and sending them home. The multitude of publications issued by government departments, research institutions, non-governmental agencies, and even private enterprise were rapaciously collected and slipped into diplomatic bags for safe transport to Centre, where they would be received with great appreciation. Newspaper stories could be rewritten in the agent's hand and reported as insight into developing political conditions. Government officials, journalists, and business leaders could be interviewed completely above-board, only to have the results written up as though they had been induced to provide valuable and hard-to-come by insights – kudos to the spy and no exposure to risk.

But change is disruption. The quandary posed by glasnost at its inception – as with Bluebird – was that it indicated something was over without presenting a definite replacement. Relations with East bloc countries are too complex for them to be cast in stone as either friends or foes. As has been remarked so insightfully, states do not have friends; they have interests. Some new means of productively engaging the East needed to be devised in order that Cold War precepts could be flung aside. Prophets of change are characteristically greeted with trepidation. Scowcroft admits, "I believed that Gorbachev's goal was to restore dynamism to a socialist political and economic system and revitalize the Soviet Union domestically and internationally to compete with the West. To me, especially before 1990, this made Gorbachev potentially more dangerous than his predecessors, each of whom, through some aggressive move, had saved the West from the dangers of its own wishful thinking about the Soviet Union before it was too late."[37] Indeed, Scowcroft may well have been correct regarding Gorbachev's intentions, but events that he unleashed quickly passed beyond his control. Nonetheless, even as the Berlin Wall fell and Poland and Czechoslovakia broke the Soviet stranglehold, Scowcroft held to his skepticism. Only in July 1990, when the Soviets accepted a united Germany within NATO, did he concede that the Cold War was over.[38]

The wariness of the veteran espiocrats in *The Russia House* is an accurate expression of the initial response to glasnost. The book was written well before the outcome of Gorbachev's initiatives could be predicted (even now Russia's transitional tumult is a drama unfinished). Nobody quite understood what it was or was likely to be, or even what the Russians hoped it would be. Did it represent irreversible change or was it simply a ploy, communism with yet another face?

"It's a reason for spying the living daylights out of them twenty-five hours a day and kicking them in the balls every time they try to get off the floor," exclaims the Russia House's Walter.[39] Collecting intelligence need not be perceived as an adversarial activity. It is possible to spy the living daylights out of a target without kicking him in the balls. Spying is about enhancing understanding. It is about finding productive ways of dealing with our surroundings. The tap should not have been shut off after the Cold War; rather, it should have been turned on full force so we could learn about the unprecedented events taking place around us. There was so much to know about the emerging actors on the international stage and about ourselves: how we intended to reinvigorate ourselves for new conditions. Spying is learning the opposition's intentions. Glasnost might have signified a radically new plan or a sophisticated effort to appear so. However, there was a third option, one that offered little prospect for accurate prediction: that glasnost was not a coherent plan at all, but was being shakily constructed ad hoc as circumstance dictated.

Although it will be some time before enough information is declassified to allow for accurate evaluation, by most accounts, the CIA did not do badly in its assessments during Gorbachev's wild ride. In May 1989 a CIA estimate gave him only a fifty-fifty chance of survival beyond the coming three to four years.[40] Unfortunately, such general predictions cannot really be put to much practical use by governments. Besides, how can you be wrong on a fifty-fifty prediction? One way or the other, you're half right. This kind of prediction is the equivalent of a weather forecast: nice to know but too iffy to plan around. Anyway, whether or not the assessment turned out to be correct could not influence Americans' behaviour, since they could hardly treat Gorbachev as a lame duck on the expectation his fall was imminent. Nor did it help them choose a line that might stave off his demise.

The CIA was criticized for failing to predict the coup of August 1991. In fact, Michael Beschloss and Strobe Talbott report that the agency "had indeed suggested a 'low probability' of a hard-line coup, but that was because they did not believe that such a coup could succeed."[41] Only a source among the plotters themselves could have given precise information about their intentions. Moreover, the CIA was correct in assessing the chances of a coup's success as low. Among the reasons that it failed was the fact it was so poorly organized, and therefore none of the usual preparations for such a dramatic act were visible.

When the coup was launched on 18 August, I was on the last day of a vacation in Maine, and I first learned what was up on CNN. The following day, back in Montreal, I decided to drop by the office to see if the crisis demanded that sources be contacted to find out what, if anything, they knew. When I arrived, I found my fellow CI investigators, not out pounding the pavement tracking down human sources for debriefing or even hunched over their computers reading cable traffic from Foreign Affairs or Headquarters that provided first-hand accounts of proceedings, but crowded around the lunch-room television glued to CNN, for it was this source that had the best access and the most field personnel combing the Soviet Union for the story. Quite effectively, the network communicated both the facts and the tenor of the story as it developed.

And this anecdote makes the point that it was not realistic to look to intelligence services to be ahead of the disarray that befell Eastern Europe over this period. After a certain point, events were no longer moving according to the intentions and capabilities of government officials – in other words, those things that IOs are best prepared to discern and analyze. They were subject to a momentum that was as immeasurable as it was unexpected. After decades of confrontation with the West and countless crises, the Soviet Union had turned inward to destroy itself, without reference to its long-standing opponents. Despite all our best efforts, we were irrelevant at the climax. As the playwright, activist, and president of post-empire Czechoslovakia Václav Havel says, "Communism was not defeated by military force, but by life, by the human spirit, by conscience, by the resistance of Being and man to manipulation. It was defeated by a revolt of color, authenticity, history in all its variety, and human individuality against imprisonment within a uniform ideology."[42] Getting at this soul is beyond any espionage method I am familiar with.

Life, given suitable room for expression, will ultimately run its course and carry government along with it. For more than seventy years, communism had suppressed life, until it had morally and economically bankrupted itself. Then life resumed. But how was anyone to know that communism did not have a final gasp left and that it would not expend it on a desperate effort to survive intact? So it is only fair to say that the political result was unpredictable. What we could have had a better handle on was the

Soviets' level of economic disrepair and their proximity to ruin. Their system was doomed to fall by the wayside because of its obsolescence. Theirs was a steel and coal infrastructure trying to compete against fibre optics and microchips. Though we could not foresee precisely when and how the Soviet Union would exhaust itself, we fairly well should have known that it would and why. Based upon our fears, we projected its invincibility, confusing military might with national strength. We had defended ourselves at outlandish cost against an inferior and dysfunctional power. We were deluded into imagining that this hopelessly moribund society had poured all the dynamism and innovation so patently absent from every other walk of life into its military and security sectors.

"The larger and more risky assumption I made after returning from the Soviet Union was that a country so congenitally inefficient, extraordinarily incompetent and frequently lazy could not nurse at its center a flawless, superefficient military capability," le Carré explained, adding, "it's just a human perception that you cannot actually circumscribe incompetence."[43] Kuzichkin made the same point with respect to the KGB: "In the West, the Soviet Union's structure and economy are rightly considered to be stagnant, ineffectual, and inflexible. So why should the KGB be described in quite opposite terms, although this organization is part of the same Soviet system? ... It is absurd to imagine that, in the whole of this rusted machine, there is a component which has remained free from corrosion and is still working perfectly."[44] I suppose we inferred that the Soviets put all the best of themselves into the military and security apparati. We figured that all the inefficiencies overtly in evidence were reversed exponentially in secret, as opposed to being reproduced, and perhaps multiplied, for being carried on under a shroud. As much as the KGB was the watchdog over society, it was also a part of it and therefore its subject.

Discussing the collapse of the Soviet Union in retrospect, Christopher Andrew writes, "At the time the speed of the collapse of the Soviet system took almost all observers by surprise. What now seems most remarkable, however, is less the sudden death of the Communist regime at the end of 1991 than its survival for almost seventy-five years."[45] If we, looking in from the outside, were hoodwinked by the state that Xan Smiley so memorably designated "Upper Volta with missiles,"[46] so too were many insiders.

Writing in October 1984, Shevchenko asserted, "The USSR cannot be erased from the earth or removed from its position at the center of power in the modern world."[47]

Our biggest shortcoming was in misunderstanding human nature and, as a result, failing to take it into account in our interactions with the East bloc. An unmotivated citizenry is a discontented citizenry, and discontented citizens are not dynamic. They don't work hard; they don't innovate; they don't support their government. They subsist and they tolerate. And they resent. These are the emotional precursors to change and were inherent to the Soviet state.

Intelligence officers are supposed to greet change reservedly. This does not make them defensively conservative, in the political sense of the brush-cut, square-jawed, retro-dreamers of some never-was Pleasantville. Change is easier to talk about than to bring about. We invariably fantasized the hidden agenda, the ulterior motive, the prospect of being duped. The periodic portents of coming reform in the East were rarely greeted with applause.

Hence glasnost and its cousin perestroika, like the Khrushchev thaw, the Sino-Soviet split, and Prague Spring before them, were seen for what they might be: theatre got up as reality. Gorbachev certainly never envisioned a Western-style capitalist democracy, with its chaotic markets and unseemly political wrangling. His vision always presupposed the predominance of the Communist Party. As Eduard Sagalayev, producer of *Vremya*, the nightly television news, put it, "They wanted *perestroika* to be a return to Leninism, a purification of the Party from Stalinism and totalitarianism."[48] In other words, it would, ideally, mark a vindication of what Khrushchev had attempted in 1956 and an evolution to a more honest approach to Soviet history. In Gorbachev's mind, the "tragedy of the Stalin era and the farce of the Brezhnev period represented ... not the failure of ideology, but rather its perversion."[49]

However, Lenin was hardly a paragon or proponent of a gentle socialism. David Remnick relates a story told him by Georgian filmmaker Tengiz Abuladze: "A friend of mine met [Stalin's foreign minister Vyacheslav] Molotov before his death and he told Molotov, 'You know, it's a pity that Lenin died so early. If he had lived longer, everything would have been normal.' But Molotov said, 'Why do you say that?' My friend said, 'Because Stalin was a bloodsucker and Lenin was a noble person.' Molotov smiled, and then he said, 'Compared to Lenin, Stalin was a mere lamb.'"[50] Whether or not this story is accurate, it is very telling for it suggests that Stalin was a more natural successor to Lenin than his communist detractors would concede. Christopher Andrew takes up the same argument, writing, "Much of what was later called 'Stalinism' was in reality the creation of Lenin: the cult of the infallible leader, the one-party state and a huge security service with a ubiquitous system of surveillance and a network of concentration camps to terrorize the regime's opponents."[51] Therefore it is not unfair to assume that, had Gorbachev merely redrawn the historical arc of communism from Lenin, around Stalin, and through to himself, the Cold War would not have ended. For, while Gorbachev proved remarkably quiescent when his East European empire pulled away, he was less magnanimous when the Baltic republics asserted their independence. Only because he recognized the extent of the bloodshed and ultimate futility (or, put another way, the probable failure) of resorting to force did he acquiesce.

The fact of the matter was that because Gorbachev was an innovator in a stagnant society, it was not unreasonable to react to his manœuvres hesitantly, even antagonistically. To do otherwise would have required courage, always in short supply when espiocrats gather. He was a Soviet leader whose background was that of the run-of-the-mill communist apparatchik, except that he had the polished manner of a seasoned Western political campaigner. At his disposal were all the perks and the means of repression and munitions that his predecessors enjoyed. Conventional wisdom spoke of the Soviet Union's mightily reinforced armour, not the rust hollowing out its shell. The safe – though short-sighted – reaction was to gasp in awe at the military grandeur of the May Day parades and use it as a framework for assessing any contradictory intelligence. Unpreparedness would never be the product of overestimation. However, our preparedness could well have been undermined by intelligence that would reduce our respect for Soviet offensive capabilities.

I am reminded of a time when I was setting up a rendezvous with an ethnic Russian who had no illusions about the Soviet system. We had agreed to meet on an evening that turned out to be 31 October, Halloween. Since he had young children and I did not know whether trick-or-treating was a Russian custom or something the family might have adopted in Canada, I asked if he would like to reschedule so as to be with his kids that night. He chuckled and said, "October 31 is nothing to me. Our Halloween is May 1."

Le Carré lamented the fact that the West failed to respond generously to the promise of reform in the Soviet Union. Historic moments are often fleeting, presenting opportunities that, once lost, may never be recovered. He feared that this was one of those moments. He shuddered at the prospect that "the 40 years of cold war have bred a silent affinity between the forces of intolerance on both sides," that "after 40 years of being locked into the ice of the cold war, some of us in the West have also lost the will, even the energy, to climb out and face a more hopeful future? That after believing so long we could improve nothing inside the Evil Empire, we have to pinch ourselves before we can accept that we really *can* write tomorrow's script, and help to make it play?"[52]

Times of great flux are also times of decision. More than a decade ago, with the empire of the East dissolved but the Soviet Union still intact, le Carré asked, "What are our Western dreams? Still nightmares? Shall we go on dreaming about more refined ways to kill each other – or do we prefer to dream of a partnership of superpowers that could address itself to tomorrow's enemies rather than to yesterday's?"[53] We have only a marginally better idea of the answers today than we did then. While there has certainly been a scaling down of the quest for new and better means of inflicting harm on one another, we are far from anything approaching partnership. No longer does each side jealously protect an exclusive sphere of influence – the Russians are too destitute to keep that up. However, history has always squared dominant powers off against each other, whether in the absolute terms of bipolarity or in the shifting alliances of a multipolar system. Thus do our dreams retain their nightmare tinge. If Zhou Enlai was sage in saying that it was still too early to assess the French Revolution, how can we be expected to have figured out the events of the past decade?

Perhaps le Carré was overwhelmed by the very questions he was asking, or maybe he merely sensed a need to take stock of the upheaval and catch his breath. In either event, he slipped *The Secret Pilgrim* (1990) into his body of work after *The Russia House* almost as an interlude, a chance to recall the past and dig in for the future. The book is essentially a collection of short stories, linked through Ned's memory. The spies Ned has run or run to ground over the course of his career are an unseemly collection of misfits, sadists, and charlatans, as well as the downright pathetic; the happy, well-adjusted spy is a distinct rarity. Do only the maladjusted become spies, or is it the spying that throws off their adjustment? Probably some combination of the two.

Everything in the covert world takes place in such confined quarters that it gets easily magnified. The weak are doubly vulnerable, since someone is always trying to sniff them out for the very purpose of taking advantage. Ben Cavendish was all that Ned was: a model recruit. Upon graduation from Sarratt, while Ned did the rounds through Headquarters, he gets the prize assignment of Berlin. His superior, jealous of his sources and resentful at having been ordered to turn his network over to his junior, rides Ben hard. There is just too much to absorb, too many details, too many fallback procedures – just too much: a moment's carelessness, suppressed desires, omnipresent fear, and the clear knowledge that people have died, not by your own hand, but just as certainly by your fault.

Unable to commit to memory all the nuances he needs at his fingertips when he crosses into East Berlin to meet his principal agent, Ben breaks every rule of tradecraft, not to mention common sense, and carries a crib sheet, from which the locals would be able to identify his agents. At some point during his run in the East, he loses the sheet. Without any reasonable explanation for doing as he has, and fully aware of the consequences, he disappears. Sure enough, the network is rolled up. There was no orchestrated treason, just banal negligence.

Smiley interrogates Ned because of their known friendship and the suggestion of something more contained in an unmailed love letter discovered during a search of Ben's flat. When an IO goes bad, those closest to him are cast either as informants or in a bad light. Until very recent times, homosexuality was as suspect as Marx in security circles. Condemned as deviance or weakness of character, it was seen as indicative of a greater tendency towards unreliability. Homosexuals were supposed to be susceptible to blackmail; it hardly occurred to anyone that, to the extent that this may have been so, it was the attitude that forced gays to hide their sexuality which brought about the susceptibility. To be on the receiving end of homosexual love, whether requited or not, was an uncomfortable place to find oneself.

In the dimmest recesses of his memory, Ned recalls Ben telling him of his distant cousin and regrettably platonic love, Stefanie. Out of loyalty to his friend, Ned evades surveillance and, cautious all the way, ventures to her isolated cottage to find his friend and an explanation. Of course, the student has not outlearned his masters, and he is successfully followed. Ben is taken into custody.

Strikingly similar to the other, Ben is Ned under pressures he cannot bear; Ben is Ned with a secret desire. Ben is anyone's panicked reaction to an inexcusable mistake that can never be corrected. To Stefanie, who might have loved either of them, Ned is "a callow boy, another Ben, unversed in life, banishing weakness with a show of strength, and taking refuge in a cloistered world."[54]

Cyril Frewin is the saddest of spies. He is very reminiscent of Jeanmaire, the Swiss general who turned to a Soviet IO to fill a void in his life. Sergei Modrian is Frewin's Denissenko. Ned recalls, "A traitor needs two things, Smiley had once remarked bitterly to me at the time of Haydon's betrayal of the Circus: somebody to hate and somebody to love."[55] Frewin hates his colleagues in the Foreign Office cypher unit where he works. He hates their mocking, their lewd jokes, their fun at his expense, their taunting nickname for him, St Cyril, because he doesn't participate in their vulgar sex banter.

Modrian is different, a "magical person, custom-trained to provide the good company Frewin had so loudly craved."[56] Frewin desperately needs a friend, appreciation, reprieve from loneliness, and Modrian comes out of nowhere to give him all that. Frewin has been taking Russian-language courses offered by Radio Moscow. He submitted essay assignments to the Academy, including one describing his work. This makes him a prize pupil and the prize is Modrian – Modrian, who isn't interested in secrets, but in furthering cultural friendship; Modrian, who wouldn't have asked Frewin to share information about his work, if it were not for the philistines he answered to; Modrian, who can only continue their relationship if Frewin will pass him a little bit to satisfy those who cannot understand the value of purely cultural contact. Well, of course, he will. What is the value in guarding paltry secrets with thoroughly nasty people who treat him with disdain when compared with the opportunity to help Modrian? "It was sickening to me that a trickster like Modrian had contrived to turn Frewin's loneliness to treachery. I felt threatened by the notion of love as the antithesis of duty,"[57] cries Ned after prying the truth out of Frewin.

After Modrian breaks contact with him, Frewin submits a denunciation of himself to the security service, knowing full well that it will have to send someone to speak to him. He only hopes it will be someone as grand as Modrian. "I was empty. I didn't know you, but I needed you," Frewin tells Ned.[58] He knows no cure for his solitude other than spying. He has nothing to offer other than his secrets. In exchange for them, he is able to command the company he craved. Perhaps anything is better than isolation, for to avoid that, Frewin is prepared to betray even himself.

One interpretation of the outcome would have it that Ned has succeeded brilliantly in extracting Frewin's confession and so expunged a dangerous traitor from a highly sensitive post. But triumphant isn't how Ned feels. Indeed, he is left conflicted over the callous disregard with which the professional manipulators – both himself and Modrian – have engineered Frewin's treason and destruction, much as Smiley felt as the engineer of Karla's downfall. Explaining his reluctance to turn in his confession, Ned says, "I was on his stupid side, not theirs. Yet what side was that? Was love an ideology? Was loyalty a political party? Or had we, in our rush to divide the world, divided it the wrong way, failing to notice that the real battle lay between those who were still searching, and those who, in order to prevail, had reduced their vulnerability to the lowest common factor of indifference? I was on the brink of destroying a man for love. I had led him to the steps of his own scaffold, pretending we were taking a Sunday stroll together."[59]

There are those spies who defy all motive, for whom there is no easy explanation. Colonel Jerzy, the chief of operations for Polish Security, lures Ned to Gdańsk with a message from a long-lost source, given up for dead in Haydon's wake. In fact, he is dead, and Ned is arrested when he shows up for the meet. Jerzy has him brutally beaten and then offers to spy for him. Why? Recognizing that Ned will need a reason to give to his superiors, Jerzy proposes, "Tell them I'm bored. Tell them I'm sick of the work. Tell them the Party's a bunch of crooks. They know that anyway, but tell them. I'm a Catholic. I'm a Jew. I'm a Tatar. Tell them whatever the hell they want to hear."[60]

We consider a source's motives and comfort ourselves with the fiction that we will be able to spot the false informant if only we have a checklist to verify motivation: mercenary, adventure, vengeance, ideology. It's like reading a murder mystery. The whodunit is really *why*dunit. Unless we are satisfied about the *why*, we doubt the *who*. And if we doubt the *who*, we doubt *what* they provide. This confusion is at the heart of *The Russia House*. Spies are uncomfortable with the complexities of human motivation. We like to categorize, to tick off the appropriate box on the form. Whatever doesn't fit is cause for round upon round of uncertainty.

But sure motive does not guarantee anything. The Hungarian Professor Teodor is not guilty of subtlety. For fifteen years he has spearheaded a remarkably innocuous operation. His output of productive intelligence is nil, but he remains Toby Esterhase's star agent on the basis of little more than the fact that he fled Hungary during the 1956 Soviet invasion, forever establishing his dissident credentials. The operation runs trouble-free and is the source of no embarrassing controversy. Why not let it run indefinitely? The more operations that stand on the books, the more activist the intelligence service appears – all the better at such crucial moments as budget allocation time, when appearances count for so much. Such considerations explain why intelligence operations turn like an old vinyl record with a deep scratch that keeps pushing the needle back a few grooves to replay the same bars over and over. The record keeps spinning and the music keeps playing, but it's all sound and motion that goes nowhere.

I once infuriated a supervisor, sending him into a veritable frenzy of memo writing, when, following more than a year's worth of uneventful investigation on my part, tacked on to more than a decade's work by various predecessors, I suggested terminating our efforts against a target that we supposedly knew from defector reports and historical data to be involved in espionage operations. My rationale was that, having failed to uncover any definitive evidence of espionage – the kind that threatened Canada's security – our resources could be better expended elsewhere. Alternatively, we could undertake far more aggressive action against the target. By that, I meant something more than running the low-level sources we were recruiting. We regularly saw an impressive number of people who were in casual daily contact with the target, testament to our success in recruiting sources. But none of them were on such intimate terms that they could be counted upon to learn whether it was engaged in clandestine acts. Unless one of these sources ended up being approached by a target to serve as one of its assets, no advances were likely. Such a thing *could* happen, but what were the chances?

I hoped my report might stir the pot enough that a concerted effort would be launched to take a run after a high-level access agent. Confronted with a choice of continued monitoring along established patterns or writing a new playbook, monitoring, I was sorry to discover, won out. At the insistence of my supervisor, who became as effective a creative writer when his back was at the wall as a man with a gun to his head becomes talkative, existing sources were handed over to someone else and maintained. To everybody's relief, I was transferred.

Discussing how real intelligence differs from the spy novel, le Carré said, "To abstract, to take a spy novel out of the uncoordinated, messy secret world and make stories, is bliss. In the secret world of reality you never finish a case. They just trickle on. You never know half of what you're doing, because they never tell you. But when you make a fiction, you can see everybody's point of view, and actually put an end on a story."[61]

Set to assume control of Teodor, Ned seeks an assessment of the value of the intelligence he has provided from those more familiar with the case. He fails to discover substance beneath Esterhase's vague platitudes. The files are crammed with Teodor's meagre offerings, operational time is filled by them, and budgets are bloated because of them. His subagents have everything going for them: "they are not expensive, they are not conclusive, they don't necessarily lead anywhere – but then neither does political stalemate – they are free of scandal. And each year when the annual audit is taken, they are waved through without a vote, until their longevity becomes their justification."[62] Because of their immortality, these operations outlast any one handler and are passed from officer to officer. Never does the same one start as finish the case. In the time it takes to familiarize yourself and become convinced of the wastage, the case becomes a justification in your arsenal, as it was in your predecessor's. Soon after, you move to another assignment, and your successor begins the process anew.

When Ned's American counterpart assures him that Teodor has never been of any use, he immediately advises Esterhase. Conveniently, one week later, Teodor summons Ned for an emergency meet. Upon arriving, he is introduced to one Latzi Kaldor, who has been dispatched by the Hungarian secret service to assassinate the dangerous dissident. It takes Ned hardly any time to decide that Kaldor's story doesn't add up and that the scenario is a fabrication enacted both to enhance Teodor's prestige and to indicate that he has been blown, which will be enough to convince the British and Americans to resettle him out of the game.

"A Hungarian assassination attempt – that's a *Good Housekeeping* certificate for the target, I would say," raves Esterhase.[63] That is to say, targeting him for assassination is the highest confirmation of the threat he poses to the Hungarian regime. He is so important that the opposition will stop at nothing to foil his efforts. That it is all a ruse Teodor has invented himself, or perhaps in concert with Esterhase, doesn't stand in the way of a successful book deal and the perpetuation of the fiction that Teodor is an active and effective spy. The incident bears a striking resemblance to a real event in 1954, when KGB assassin Nikolai Khokhlov called at the Frankfurt home of Ukrainian dissident Georgi Okolovich. Rather than killing his intended victim, Khokhlov confessed to him and defected to the CIA. He was subsequently presented to the world at a sensational press conference, where he exposed the plot.[64]

And sometimes the value of a spy is destined to twist forever on a frayed rope of doubt – whether information or disinformation, agent or double agent, and if double, perhaps triple. Sea Captain Brandt has been recruited to run a supply line out of Hamburg to the Baltic coast during Haydon's time. It is dangerous and ultra-secret work. Regardless of what is at stake, Brandt insists on having his young girlfriend, Bella, constantly by his side. Haydon casts doubt on her reliability, citing her father's dubious survival of and alleged complicity with a bloody Russian assault on a group of Latvian patriots, of which he was supposedly a member. If he was bad, the reasoning goes, she is likely bad as well.

Brandt's absence on a mission is the perfect opportunity for Ned to draw her out and assess where she stands. With Brandt gone, she quickly betrays him by sleeping with Ned at a safe house. That is not enough for her. She wants him to come to the farmhouse she shares with Brandt: "she wanted to be able to look at all the places in the house where we had made love, and think of me."[65]

Ignoring how she relishes deceiving Brandt, Ned responds with the judgment of a hormonally charged man: "If I had ever suspected her of anything, the sight of her naked body convinced me of her innocence."[66] Despite such circumstantial evidence, after Brandt's landing party comes under fire and he, along with the other survivors, is spirited to Sarratt for questioning, she surges to the top of the list of suspects, propelled by an appearance in a class photo from a Centre-run language school in Kiev.

In the end, Brandt and Bella are declared clean. Haydon, for whose protection Centre implicated Bella, has betrayed the network. However, in 1989, when Toby and Peter are given a glasnost-spirited tour of Centre, they are sure they spot Brandt at a distance. "Nothing goes away in the secret world; nothing goes away in the real one."[67] Is Haydon the only mole? Has he been protecting Brandt? When did Brandt go bad? Are Esterhase and Peter mistaken? Who knows?

IOs deal in the unseen. Their concept of reality is tenuous because what is evident may be illusory, a meticulous deception. The metaphor of the wilderness of mirrors is most appropriate. What is real and what is reality's reflection? What should you trust? And if you can't trust what you see, can you trust anything? It is a common human trait to want most what you cannot have. IOs are constantly plagued by uncertainty. Hence what they most want is certainty. Schooled to withhold and conceal, they dream of the utterly candid relationship. Incapable of trust, they desperately want to believe. Ready to accept betrayal at every turn, they long for loyalty. That is why they give themselves so hopefully to their service, and why, when the service disappoints them, it's so devastating. Most begin with idealism; none of them embarks a cynic. None whom I've seen escapes the transformation.

For some, the cynicism is liberating, releasing them from all bonds of caring or decency. They happily become the coldest of bureaucrats, enthusiastically adapting to the rules of the hierarchy and, like rats on a sinking ship, contentedly claw their way to the highest attainable perch. Others, those who have yearned for more, finding a terrifying emptiness at the core of all the secrets and deceits, wallow in distress and disappointment. And others still, having something or someone else to care about, leave.

Ned decides, "Life was to be a search, or nothing! But it was the fear that it was nothing that drove me forward."[68] Yes, above all, 10s are afraid – afraid to find that all those secrets they guard so assiduously are really about nothing; that there is no righteous purpose for the betrayals. The search is for what, a cause? Ned makes Hansen his quest.

The wilderness of mirrors is not dissimilar from the true wilderness of forests or jungles. The effect of either on a person is as Joseph Conrad wrote: "He had to live in the midst of the incomprehensible, which is also detestable. And it has a fascination, too, that goes to work upon him. The fascination of the abomination – you know, imagine the growing regrets, the longing to escape, the powerless disgust, the surrender, the hate."[69]

During one of my first drinking binges with a group of colleagues, one of them leaned towards me over his whisky. I could smell the alcohol thick on his breath. He fixed me with dulled, blood-shot eyes and sneered, "Kid, what makes a good 10?" The words were slurred nearly to incoherence. I stared back at him, rapt, urging him to tell me, to initiate me into the mystery of how to succeed at my profession. There is an old adage in intelligence: the truth comes out of the last third of the bottle. If that was the case, he was ready to impart the truth. "He wants to *know*." He punched out each word carefully, handing me the keys to the universe. He paused as if there was more to say, then gave a wise half-nod and in a single motion leaned back and drained his glass. Never taking his eyes off me, he wagged a finger in my direction, got up, and staggered out. I was filled with gratitude. That was it: I just needed to *want to know*.

Ned wants to know Hansen. In his abilities, appetites, and passions, Hansen is larger than life. A disgraced Jesuit, he finds redemption in the hermitage of the secret service. He plies the jungles of Southeast Asia, as he did in his missionary days, making his way to the remotest tribes in the most inaccessible tangles, gathering information that the British can trade to the Americans in support of their overt and covert wars in Vietnam, Cambodia, and Laos. Hansen burrows into the countryside and directs American bombers to the villages that give comfort to the Viet Cong – until he vanishes, only to turn up a year and a half later in a Bangkok brothel, reportedly mad but with his head full of secrets intact. Ned is dispatched to find out what has happened to him and whether his condition puts those secrets in jeopardy.

Hansen tells Ned his story. He is certain as to his loyalty: it is to the daughter he fathered in a Cambodian village. All else is inconsequential. Like Conrad's Kurtz, ultimately overwhelmed by the horror, he is revolted by the role he has played in the bombers' indiscriminately murderous campaigns, by his complicity with the West's sin against Asia, just as Kurtz was with the sins against Africa. His solace is to have a daughter into whom he can pour all the devotion and allegiance others might try to direct back to the service.

Returning home one day to find his village deserted, he sets off into the jungle in pursuit of his daughter and her Khmer Rouge captors. He is single-minded in his quest. When he catches up with them, he is taken captive, tortured mercilessly, and forced to watch helplessly while his daughter is transformed into a Khmer militant. Even after she forsakes him, Hansen gives her the gift of unconditional love. Inexplicably, the troops decamp one day, leaving him where he has passed out after a final interrogation. He doggedly sets off after his daughter once again, tracing her to the Thai brothel. Because she is unwilling to leave, he stays, assuming the role of her protector.

Ned promises Hansen that he will reveal little of his story to his service masters. It is an act of loyalty on his part, not unlike Marlow's withholding Kurtz's story from the company agent: "I did not betray Mr. Kurtz – it was ordered I should never betray him – it was written I should be loyal to the nightmare of my choice. I was anxious to deal with this shadow of myself alone."[70] In Hansen, Ned "had found what I was looking for – a man like myself, but one who in his search for meaning had discovered a worthwhile object for his life; who had paid every price and not counted it a sacrifice; who was paying it still and would pay it till he died; who cared nothing for compromise, nothing for his pride, nothing for ourselves or the opinion of others; who had reduced his life to the one thing that mattered to him, and was free. The slumbering subversive in me had met his champion. The would-be lover in me had found a scale by which to measure his own trivial preoccupations."[71] This is what Marlow sees in Kurtz: "I saw the inconceivable mystery of a soul that knew no restraint, no faith, and no fear, yet struggling blindly with itself."[72]

Other Wars

Leonard Burr pops up from an indeterminate background to head
the Service after the housecleaning brought about by Blair's defection. Refreshingly blunt, he is a results-over-rules man. Sending
Ned off to vet Frewin, he is pointed and succinct: "So get on with
it, then. Keep me informed, but not too much – don't bullshit me,
always give me bad news straight."[1] Ned's final mission in *The
Secret Pilgrim* is to appeal to Sir Anthony Joyston Bradshaw to
stop feeding the appetite for arms in all the world's hungry little
conflicts. He initially undertook this lucrative venture at the
behest of the Service when it deemed it in the Service's interests.
However, the tides have shifted, and it has been decided to ease
off on the firepower made available.

But Bradshaw totally lacks anything to which one can appeal –
patriotism, conscience, decency, even prudence. He is all class and
status, and willing to go to any extreme to maintain them. He has
found a commodity in endless demand, and he sees no logic in
abandoning its supply. Ned is at a loss: "it was as if my whole
life had been fought against the wrong enemy. Then it was as if
Bradshaw had personally stolen the fruits of my victory."[2] Is this
what the Cold War was won for? If those excesses that were
justified by the necessities of the times are to continue unabated,
what was the point? The prospect of thoughtlessly persisting with
the old behaviour in the absence of the old pretext portends a
world of greater depravity than the one being forsaken.

Le Carré was angered by how some interests in the West held
on for dear life to the Cold War mentality, fervently denying that
a radically new international dynamic was possible, not to mention preferable. He said, "There was a time when we were outraged by the cruelties of history that had split our world down

the middle. Have we now entered a new time, where we *need* the old divisions to justify our galloping materialism?" The prospect left him disheartened: that we might fail the moment "where human imagination, and human creativity, unleashed in time, may yet sweep us above the slough of hopelessness to which we have been condemned for too long."[3] He wrote these words in 1989 following the release of *The Russia House*. The actual dissolution of the Soviet Union was not yet even imagined. Le Carré hoped that, with an end in sight, we could rekindle the purposes for which the Cold War had ostensibly been joined.

Four years later, he had succumbed to pessimism: "We have squandered the peace that we've won with the cold war. We had some kind of vision in the cold war; we got a crusade going even when we were mistaken and crude about it," he said in a 1993 interview. "I see at the moment, and I hope it's only an intervening moment in our history, a time of absolute moral failure by the West to perceive its own role in the future."[4] The Cold War had become a global Jarndyce versus Jarndyce, in which we were bound in a tangle of red tape, long-forgotten objectives, fully compromised ideals, and force of habit – a bad habit against which no willpower was summoned.

Faced with truly radical changes, nobody knew quite what to do. The United States had never recognized the Soviet annexation of the Baltic republics, but it felt unsure in the wake of their declarations of independence, beginning with Lithuania in 1989. Formal American policy had always been in favour of an eventual reunification of Germany, but had informally harboured concerns about Germans' mustering the wherewithal to again dominate the continent. In other words, it was all well and good to champion what was never expected to come to pass.

But somewhere beneath the rubble of the Berlin Wall and the assertive nationalism of the Soviet satellites and territories lurked opportunity. Suddenly, in le Carré's words, "we are shorn of all our old excuses for not addressing the real problems of the earth – that we can no longer put our humanity on hold, in order to defend humanity. The *difficult* is finding a better name for the compassionate aspects of communism: because we need them as much today as we ever did. They just got into the wrong hands."[5] Now was the time to show that ours had been the right hands all along, that we were worthy of our own hype. We would have to define our society in terms other than rhetorical; no longer would it be enough to speak theoretically about openness, freedom, compassion. Time had come for our values to be taken out of wraps. The tinpot desperados and self-styled rebels who had been invited to sit at our table strictly because they seemed a better alternative to something worse became untenable allies. It was time to embrace something better in recognition that the worst had been transcended. Or had it? The discomforting fact is that we had to come to terms with another question: was the worst really inside ourselves and must we look inward to face our dread?

Le Carré thought so: "The fight against communism diminished us. That's why we were unable to rejoice at our victory. It made us less than the sum of our parts. It left us a state of false and corrosive orthodoxy. It licensed our excesses, and we didn't like ourselves the better for them. It dulled our love of dissent, and our sense of life's adventure."[6] It made us less than our ideals would have had us be. Thus the issue became whether or not those ideals could be recovered in the Cold War's aftermath.

I will not deny that I was perfectly comfortable with the Cold War. East-West confrontation was the only international order I had known, the only one that seemed remotely possible in my lifetime. I had been educated in its rationale and intricacies. I was not particularly unsettled by the massive nuclear arsenals, ready and awaiting the launch order, with which the superpowers held each other at bay. Indeed, their stable oversight seemed a sane alternative to the anarchy that was certain if they were not positioned to reign in irresponsible allies and to hold each other's ambitions in check.

I cannot say I was overly troubled by the plight of those living under repressive regimes. It was a shame that their lot was so difficult, but the world's divisions were a *fait accompli*. When the Berlin Wall went up, le Carré remembers, "I felt angrier than I had felt before about any political event, and the anger gave wing to my writing."[7] The Cold War never made me angry. The Berlin Wall was there; so be it. I did not bother to imagine a different or better world.

Neither compassion nor optimism are in evidence in *The Night Manager* (1993), le Carré's first authentic excursion into the post-Cold War wilderness. The opposition had rarely been a fully

drawn participant in le Carré's stories. As in real Cold War espionage, it dwelt just over the horizon, a presence felt (or imagined)
rather than observed. Karla, for example, is barely glimpsed at the
conclusion of the trilogy preoccupied with his seizure. Nor do we
meet those who capture Leiser. And, while Leo Harting turns out
not to be an enemy, he too lives beyond the ken of his pursuers.

Nonetheless, looking into the mirror, we could recognize the
face of our enemies, even though we condemned their methods.
We were not resolute policemen chasing a monstrous serial killer;
we were bureaucrats pursuing our opposite numbers. As often as
not, the specific offence our target had committed was less than
certain. We were in the upside-down position of finding a suspected culprit before we had witnessed a crime. New Soviet and
East bloc diplomats would arrive at their embassy or consulate,
accompanied by a formal notice to External Affairs listing such
particulars as name, date of birth, previous postings, spouse and
children, and so on. These details would be telexed to friendly
services for traces. Depending on the responses and whether the
new person was replacing an intelligence agent, he or she would
be labelled suspect 10, known 10, or clean – or, more accurately,
clean with qualifications. The most positive vetting would be one
of NKT (no known traces) or NRT (no reportable traces) – in other
words, no ... but maybe.

The game was one long continuum. We watched and waited:
observing, identifying contacts, year after year, monitoring and
collecting, adding to the files. To what purpose? More intelligence
to evaluate and collect and evaluate further – the temptation of a
more spectacular payoff somewhere around the next bend was
constant and irresistible. We were like out-of-control gamblers
who keep doubling down, expecting the hand that is never dealt
to pay the jackpot.

Supposedly, when we stepped out from the other end of the
Cold War tunnel, the futility of the endless upmanship would
become apparent. Theory, at least, argued so. In the world to
which *The Night Manager* belongs, the secret conclave has been
split between Pure Intelligence and Enforcement. The former, run
by Geoffrey Darker out of the River House in close collaboration
with its American counterpart in Langley, "meant turning a blind
eye to some of the biggest crooks in the hemisphere for the sake
of nebulous advantages elsewhere. It meant operations inexplica-

bly abandoned in midstream and orders countermanded from on high. It meant callow Yale fantasists in button-down shirts who believed they could outwit the worst cut-throats in Latin America and always had six unbeatable arguments for doing the wrong thing"[8] – not, it should be said, unlike the British diplomats in *A Small Town in Germany*, faced with Nazi war criminals. "For you and me there are always a dozen good reasons for doing nothing," Alan Turner accuses Bradfield. "Leo's made the other way round. In Leo's book there's only one reason for doing something: because he must. Because he feels."[9] The bureaucrat has no feelings to consider.

Shamelessly corrupt and fiercely protective of all that was theirs in spying's heyday, the Purists and others within the establishment elite who share their benefits – Bradshaw and his kind – will not easily concede Enforcement's ascendancy. Burr, who has forsaken the preserve of intelligence to head up Enforcement, underestimates the lengths to which Darker and his forces will go to further their interests. And Jonathan Pine, the guilt-plagued, service-devoted night manager of an extravagantly posh Zurich hotel, is ignorant of all the forces that will conspire against him once he agrees to set off after "the worst man in the world"[10] – Richard Onslow Roper.

Roper is the personification of all the evil le Carré found so obscure in the Cold War, the manifestation of all the worst instincts that freedom and capitalism can produce. There is not, in *The Night Manager*, the equivalency between hunter and hunted that distinguishes his earlier spies versus spies. Roper has the cut-throat single-mindedness that belies ambivalence. His interests are clearly defined: whatever makes him wealthier, enhances his status, attracts the youngest and most beautiful women. His philosophy is predicated on a refusal to acknowledge limits: "Promise to build a chap a house, he won't believe you. Threaten to burn his place down, he'll do what you tell him. Fact of life."[11] This is not substantively different from the mentality that drove the Americans to destroy villages in Vietnam for the purpose of saving them. How to behave is not a moral conundrum, but a simple matter of most expediently exacting compliance.

There is nothing subtle about Roper's transgressions. He is putting together his biggest score: a barter trade of the latest in American and British arms to the Colombian drug cartels for

cocaine, which he will distribute on the lucrative Central and
Eastern European markets. Burr knows what Roper is up to, but
he needs a source, a human penetration, inside Roper's circle in
order to secure proof that can be used to charge, prosecute, and
incarcerate him; for this is to be the Enforcers' day. They are
police-oriented, identifying a problem and taking the steps necessary to put it out of commission. Information on one player will
not be gathered in the fantastical hope of its leading to even bigger
criminals in due course. Roper is *it*, the end-game. He will not be
recruited as a conduit to someone worse because there is nothing
worse than the worst man in the world.

But not even the worst of men can succeed in isolation. Roper
depends on the complicity of others who stand to profit from his
scheme, among whom are officials purchased with a commission
on arms sales. In *The Night Manager* le Carré confronts two
contiguous, unscrupulous foes: the captain of commerce who
trades in corruption and the politician who trades in venality.
These are the enemies we ignored during the Cold War because
our attention was diverted elsewhere. In our mania for *national*
security, we neglected *human* security. It was the classic us-
versus-them syndrome; we were so engrossed in the fight against
them and so ignoring of the criminals among *us*. Besides, the
criminals were invariably valiant opponents of *them*. Men like
Roper and Bradshaw were encouraged and cultivated by (not
necessarily secret) elements within government in the misguided
conceit that they could be tamed like house pets to serve the
master's whims. What the cultivators were too oblivious to take
into account was how wealth is the real currency of power and
influence. It was the Ropers who were the actual masters and
could cause the politicos to jump to their call. It was not a
question so much of the tail wagging the dog as of figuring out
where the tail ended and the dog began.

The Night Manager commences as a straightforward thriller.
Roper's arrival at the Hotel Meister Palace triggers within Pine
painful memories of an earlier, indirect brush with the man while
he was in the employ of Freddie Hamid at the Queen Nefertiti
Hotel in Cairo. Hamid and Dicky Roper did dirty deals together.
Details of their trade in arms and chemicals were entrusted, in a
sealed envelope, to Pine by Sophie, Hamid's woman, with whom
he ill-advisedly fell in love. Instead of guarding her confidence

for all it was worth, he took it to the British Embassy. Pine's compulsion for duty caused Sophie to be beaten to death, most probably by Hamid. But it was Roper, tipped off by friends in London that the authorities were on to his business with Hamid, who encouraged his suspicions of her. "I loved you but betrayed you instead, to a pompous British spy I didn't even like,"[12] Pine lamented. Sophie was what he betrayed that was more important than a country, the friend he failed to choose over the state.

Roper's appearance at Meister's is Pine's chance to seek revenge in the only way he knows how: he spies. He obtains lists of the long-distance numbers rung up and copies the faxes passing through the hotel for Roper's party and takes them all to the appropriate British Embassy spook. Thus does he come to Burr's attention as a candidate for more delicate spying. Burr pitches him the offer of a better life: "Not better for you maybe, but better for what you and I are pleased to call the common good. A five-star unimpeachable cause, guaranteed to improve the lot of mankind or your money back in full"[13] – exactly what we were fantasizing about during the Cold War, but could so rarely find.

Pine, the perennial volunteer perpetually looking for more noble service, is unable to resist the call. Given what befell Sophie, this may seem strange, but it is absolutely in keeping with his character. "For the trained soldier, trained however long ago, there is nothing startling about the call to duty."[14] The call has an overwhelming appeal for anyone who feels, as Pine does, that his term of service has been incomplete. Pine's officially ended on a nasty note in Ireland when he opened fire on a kid who turned out to have been unarmed, and his unofficial efforts against Hamid resulted in Sophie's death.

Roper is a sophisticated operator. He does not speak indiscreetly on the telephone; he does not send incriminating documents through the post; no satellite reconnaissance can possibly track his business. Burr's hopes depend on what only a human infiltration can provide: first-hand observance to identify the deal and how it is to be done. Pine – perfectly mannered in the way of the good servant, soldier, sailor, climber, painter, chef, skier, tennis player – is altogether ideal for the role.

He is painstakingly prepared with a legend, à la Leamas. First, he departs quickly from Meister's on the heels of a theft of funds from the safe. After being set up as Jack Linden on the Cornish

coast, he departs suddenly following the disappearance and presumed murder of his drug-running business partner. He surfaces
as Jacques Beauregard in a northern Quebec mining town, where
he seduces the daughter of the innkeeper for whom he works and
uses her to obtain a genuine Canadian passport by means of her
fiancé's birth certificate. Run out of town by her father, he next
reappears as Thomas Lamont, itinerant cabin crewman and chef
in the Caribbean, putting him directly in the path of Roper's yacht
when it docks at Roper's favourite restaurant. A robbery is staged
in which Roper's son is taken hostage and Pine has been cast to
come to his rescue, earning him the great man's everlasting gratitude and a passage to Crystal, his private island. There he begins
to worm his way into the inner circle in earnest.

Pine is once again smitten with the wrong woman when he
becomes infatuated with Jed, Roper's infuriatingly beautiful con-
sort. She is a terribly shallow girl who was enticed by Roper's fantastic wealth and power, as young women often are by older men.
Until other people let her in on the secret, she has no inkling that
his affairs are illegal, for she is every bit as dim as she is gorgeous.

Enforcement's ability to run this case assumes that Pure Intelligence's power has waned. It had not. Thus *The Night Manager* does
not proceed according to the usual plan expected of a common
thriller. In the best tradition of le Carré, the tension does a U-turn
from the rather straightforward question of whether Roper will
be brought to justice to follow whether Burr can fight off the
Purists in a desperate effort to extricate Pine and shut down the
operation while minimizing the damage. The failure of the operation is the triumph of the Pure Intelligence approach to the world.
Those who remember straight are not well served by the memory.
Twisted wins the day, its convolutions somehow more pragmatic
than what straight has to offer.

Geoffrey Darker has nothing to learn from the worst man in the
world when it comes to ruthless manipulation in the cause of
self-betterment. The bureaucrat whose empire is at risk will be as
vicious as a cornered rhinoceros protecting its pup. And the
Purists feel their backs against a wall. As Harry Palfrey, survivor
extraordinaire and now legal adviser at the River House, explains,
"Couple of years ago, they were top-notch Cold Warriors. Best
seats in the club, all that. Hard to stop running, once you've been
wound up like that. You keep going. Natural."[15] The loss they feel

most acutely is their place at the table. "Still got the *power*, of course. Nobody's taken *that* away from them. Just a question of where to put it," Palfrey says.[16]

The trauma they experience was very real and intensely felt throughout the intelligence world. The Cold War bureaucracy was in advanced middle age and had become comfortably settled in its routine. Employment was gainful; budgets were automatic; an enemy was in place; the world made sense. What mattered to the purists (and the Purists) was what to do next. They scrambled for reasons to continue their mission. Political indecision accounted for much of the dilemma.

Le Carré draws a complex conspiracy between his Purists, their Whitehall allies, and the British arms industry, along with their Langley counterparts – all of whom figure to profit from Roper's transactions – on the one hand, and American and British enforcers with their champion, Rex Goodhew, on the other. Goodhew, adviser to the minister in charge of security coordination, has an epiphany at the end of the Cold War that, "in the misused name of freedom, he had been sacrificing scruple and principle to the great god of expediency, and that the excuse for doing so was dead … He must mend his ways or perish in his soul. Because the threat outside the gates had gone."[17] Supporting the aims of Enforcement is his way of atoning.

However, the forces arrayed against him are monumental. Burr is astonished to find how susceptibility to corruption has permeated the power structure. Despite all evidence to the contrary, including a blatant threat from a Darker emissary, Goodhew convinces himself to believe otherwise. He insists, "We mustn't condemn the barrel because of a few bad apples. My master is persuadable. This is still England. We are good people. Things may go amiss from time to time, but sooner or later honor prevails and the right forces win. I believe that."[18] Whether he truly believes it – whether anybody really does – at the end is open to some doubt, but there is no question he *needs* to believe it – as do we all.

Pine, out in the cold, is helpless in the face of infighting that has put him in harm's way. As elaborate as the steps taken to backstop him and establish an impenetrable cover to cloak his true identity are, there is no way that Burr can protect him from enemies even he does not know are colluding for their failure –

a failure, which for Burr would be a professional catastrophe, but for Pine would mean death.

When it turns out that Palfrey, who has been feeding Goodhew intelligence about the schemes hatched within the River House, has been double-dealing Goodhew back to Darker, Burr realizes his agent is in mortal danger. Palfrey has learned that the Americans have been running Dr Paul Apostoll, legal counsel to the Colombian cartels, as an agent. Apo is ordered to raise suspicions about Roper's factotum, Major Corkoran, so that he will fall out of favour, opening the way for Pine to step in as a replacement. When Apo is found dead wearing a "Colombian necktie" – the quaint expression for having one's throat slit and one's tongue pulled out through the opening – Burr knows that Pine is blown. Apo would not have known that Pine is an agent, but he must have revealed his mission to undermine Corkoran. Why do that except to cement Pine's position?

With the arms-for-drugs exchange completed, the ships loaded with each cargo have put to sea, bound for Colombia and Poland respectively. By this time Roper is conscious of Pine's espionage and holds him captive, hoping to learn for whom he is working and how much he has revealed. In fact, Pine has already managed to pass Burr meticulously detailed intelligence about the shipments. Conceding that his case is lost, all that is left for Burr is to win his release. He uses Palfrey to help fabricate Darker's arrest in order to convince Bradshaw to contact Roper and tell him that he will be next unless he agrees to release Pine along with Jed, in which case no charges will be pursued and the shipments currently en route will be allowed to proceed unmolested. This is a deal not to be missed, and the two are freed.

By the conclusion of *The Night Manager* it is clear that Enforcement has been supplanted – if, indeed, it was ever ascendant. Otherwise put, the world is back at square one. Le Carré's follow-up novel, *Our Game* (1995), is his bluntest expression of disgust (but not surprise) at the West's failure to implement the principles for which the Cold War was allegedly contested.

The final betrayal, in his view, is of whatever ideals were espoused to justify its excesses. He is, in this respect, not unlike Harting. Tim Cranmer, a warrior forcibly retired to a comfortable,

bourgeois vineyard he has inherited in Somerset with his beautiful, disgracefully young mistress, Emma, epitomizes the utter
contempt of the intelligence bureaucracy towards any inclination
to do right. As Larry Pettifer, his sometimes loyal agent and
friend, expresses it, "Timbo is also fireproof, since the man who
believes in nothing, and therefore has space for everything, has a
terrible advantage over us. What passes for a kindly tolerance in
him is in reality a craven acceptance of the world's worst crimes"[19]
(recall those Yale fantasists of *The Night Manager*). During the deep
freeze there was a reason for failing to stand up to our professed
principles on behalf of anyone but ourselves. Le Carré writes, in
Cranmer's voice, "All through the Cold War it was our Western
boast that we defended the underdog against the bully. The boast
was a bloody lie. Again and again during the Cold War and after
it the West made common cause with the bully in favour of what
we call stability, to the despair of the very people we claimed to
be protecting. That's what we're up to now."[20]

The hypocrisy of the Cold War was that the West's enmity
towards the Soviet Union masked our dependence on its stability.
For all the rhetoric and propaganda, the bloodshed and despicable
allies in the Third World, unmanageable and unpredictable
domestic upheaval and hardship within Russia proper and ethnic
atrocities in the Balkans were the real nightmares. So we competed at the outer edges, compromising at the core, and accepted
the notion of unassailable spheres of interest, impregnable back-
yards. This was simple discretion. Only so far could a nuclear
superpower be pushed. Being undermined in their less-than-vital
interests was something to which both sides were prepared to
accede. Recognizing in each other the maturity to retreat from the
brink was what gave us confidence in the nuclear stalemate. So
long as we probed the periphery and skirted the frontal assault,
all was forgiven.

Russia is not the formidable adversary that the Soviet Union
was. Impoverished and disheartened, it fails to make its subjects
cower. First, the states of Eastern Europe dared to speak with their
own voices, then the Baltic republics insisted on independence,
and finally the ethnic-based republics of the south and the Slavic
republics to the west asserted their right to pursue sovereign
futures. In the end, Russia faced the prospect that even national

minorities within what remained of its territory would agitate for autonomy. The Caucasian region of Russia is a quagmire of ethnic fragmentation and unfulfilled national aspirations involving people invisible to outsiders: Ingushetians, Chechens, Dagestanis, Abkhazians, Ossetians, Azeris, Armenians, Georgians. Theirs are causes the Western powers would just as soon ignore, happily leaving them to the Russians to dispose of as they may. The West is reluctant to champion the cause of troublesome nationalities. This is the Russians' home field, and whatever they can do to quell the nastiness is gratefully appreciated. Of his purpose for undertaking a novel set in this confusing mess of obscure blood feuds and seething nationalist aspirations, le Carré writes, "I wanted to say something rather bitter about the repression of small nations, and about the unfashionable wars that politicians may safely ignore."[21]

Troubled Ingushetia of *Our Game* is not dissimilar from the real-life conflict that engulfed Chechnya between December 1994 and August 1996 and presaged the related problems that arose in Dagestan in August 1999. This latest conflagration quickly spread into Chechnya proper and by October had escalated into a full-scale, if undeclared, war to crush the Chechen independence movement once and for all. Russian president Vladimir Putin, who was then prime minister, said at the time, "We don't have a border with Chechnya. Chechnya is part of the Russian Federation."[22] There have been hints of murky connections between Russian intelligence and Chechen rebels. It has been suggested that *if* several terrorist bombings of Moscow apartment blocks were the work of Chechens, Russian forces may have somehow conspired with them so as to give Putin, himself a former lieutenant-colonel in the KGB, an excuse to attack and thus boost his political popularity in anticipation of his presidential run.[23] If so, the trick worked. In March 2000 Putin was indeed elected president. The Chechen capital, Grozny, has been bombarded, pummelled by air and artillery with no regard for civilian life or property, such that the term "genocide" has been bandied about. The West has watched, issuing periodic expressions of horror and dismay, but all the while conceding Russia's freedom to continue.

Putin's emergence from obscurity to power owes much to his unflinching conquest of Chechnya. When appointed prime minister by Boris Yeltsin, his popularity stood at 2 per cent. It soared to 60 per cent following his promise to "wipe the terrorists out wherever we find them, even if they are sitting on the toilet"[24] His approach appeals to that substantial segment of the Russian population whose pride is sustained by demonstrations of national power, a pride that cannot assimilate any more erosion of Russia's territory or brook further evidence of military impotence or international marginalization.

Simmering resentments and unrealized aspirations nonetheless keep the region in tumult. The Ingush and Chechens are closely associated, ethnically and historically. Their traditional home-lands were once joined in a single "autonomous region," that administrative fiction employed by the Soviets to create the impression that they respected minority rights. Both suffered at Stalin's hands: a merciless pogrom in 1937 that, on a single day, left 3 per cent of the Chechen-Ingush population dead, followed by a brutal deportation in 1944 that saw half a million people forcibly transported from the North Caucasus to central Asia. Krushchev allowed the survivors to return in 1957 as part of his de-Stalinization efforts. In 1991 the Ingush held a referendum and elected to form their own republic within the Russian federation, while the Chechens declared independence.

Fearing the consequences of unchecked nationalism fragment-ing the world into incomprehensible enclaves, the West suddenly put itself on the side of Russia's upholding of the Soviet concep-tion of its territory, opposing the aspirations of those we had once looked upon as oppressed. "The self-determination of oppressed nations was a cornerstone of our anti-Communism. For half a century we preached that on the day democracy replaced tyranny the victim would be raised above the bully and small nations would be free," le Carré asserts. Notwithstanding such professed intentions, we are meekly resigned to the idea that "a nation is a people tough enough to grab the land it wants and hang on to it. Period."[25] Thus it has always been.

Surely the emergence of a plethora of micro-states of dubious viability breaking away from existing states like an unsolved jigsaw puzzle poses its own serious problems. The Caucasus alone could easily fragment into a half a dozen states. The idea may be more idealized than practical. Were it the case that these indepen-dent nations would be peaceful and content within agreed-upon borders, that would be one thing. But if, as is probable, they became feuding, dictatorial fiefdoms raging in perpetual conflict, it would be quite another – and not an illegitimate cause for concern.

Cranmer's sedate wine-making is rudely disrupted when Pettifer is reported to have done a runner with £37 million bilked from the Russian Embassy in collusion with Konstantin Checheyev, a KGB officer native to the breakaway republic of Ingushetia. Also missing is the delectable Emma. Suspected by both his old Office and the local constabulary of being in league with their game, Cranmer is compelled to set off to find his agent, not to mention his lover. Lending urgency to the quest is Cranmer's certain knowledge that Pettifer is dead, knowledge gained when Cranmer killed him with his bare hands.

Like Ned and Smiley, Cranmer is a Cold War anachronism adjusting to a new world. His time past, he has been unceremoniously defrocked of his secret vestments. "Done your job, Tim, old boy," announces Jake Merriman, head of personnel, in consigning him to pasture. "Lived the passion of your time. Who can do more? … It was there, it was evil, you spied the hell out of it, and now it's gone away."[26] Hooray! We won! And that's that.

Pettifer is wonderfully subversive. As a classy English intellectual without communist ties, but also without hostility to the party's ideals, he was a perfect candidate to be dangled in front of the Soviet Embassy in the days when such a person was considered a prize catch. He could build the Soviets a network of like-minded sorts on their way up through British society. The problem is that Pettifer is not using an actor's guile to play a role, but is putting his real self into the spy game; the game is uncannily suited to who he is. It is, on the one hand, the handlers' conceit that the source is their creation; on the other, their impending fear that the source will develop a mind of his or her own. Pettifer always has a mind of his own.

"When I send him out into the world, I intend that he should come back to me more mine than when he left me,"[27] Cranmer avows. To the staid world of the espiocrat, Pettifer is a natural enemy: a free-spirited intellectual with a rebellious soul, boundless curiosity, an affinity for the underdog, a romantic predisposition for hopeless causes, and a proclivity for acting on his beliefs. He is taken with the Ingush cause because of the purity he sees in it, or at least, that he so badly wants to see in it. Those who want most sincerely to believe are susceptible to romantic tripe.

Checheyev delivers to Cranmer an elegy (or perhaps an eulogy) contrasting the free spirit of the Ingush and of Pettifer with the tired resignation of the English: "And when you Western whitearses decide it's time for us to be crushed – which you will, Mr. Timothy, you will, because no compromise is beyond your English grasp – part of you will die. Because what *we* have is what you used to fight for when you were men. Ask Larry."[28]

The danger of the free thinker as agent is that it might come into the person's head to think freely. Pettifer is utterly smitten with Checheyev. The Ingush has a cause, passion, commitment, ideals. In his memory of the atrocities endured by his people he carries what is in real life the "common memory of attempted genocide [that] underlay the process of the Chechens' nation-building. It added an extra fear to their mistrust of the outside invader and gave them a kind of recklessness as they defied Russia."[29]

Cranmer has none of the suffering-bred fire of the fierce mountain people. Expounding on his beliefs to Marjorie Pew, head of internal security, when he is being interrogated in the wake of Pettifer's disappearance, he sums it up simply: "I was a professional, Marjorie. I didn't have the time to share views or reject them. I believed whatever was necessary to the job at the time."[30] Such detachment is bred over the years when conflict continues tiredly beyond remembrance of there being anything at stake – indeed, when nothing personal is threatened at all. Pettifer, however, never ceases to believe in his hopeless causes. To Cranmer, he says, "I mean it's all right for *you*, selling your soul. You haven't got one. But what about mine?"[31]

People do not actually sell their soul; it is one thing to which they are inextricably bound. They may, however, deny it, tame it, or dampen its resolve in a ceaseless current of self-control. When he chooses Emma, Cranmer casts off a lifetime's worth of suppression. She is his impulse, his grand risk, and, ultimately, his great discomfort, because more than anything else, the aversion to risk, and the excuse that the secret life allows for every retreat, is comfortable. Life is so much safer lived with an unerring commitment to being uncommitted. Reflecting on his own reasons for entering secret life, le Carré recounts how secrecy is "a means of outgunning people we would otherwise be scared of; of feeling superior to life rather than engaging in it; as a place of escape, attracting not the strong in search of danger, but us timid fellows, who couldn't cope with reality for one calendar day without the structures of conspiracy to get us by."[32] Pettifer taunts Cranmer as the embodiment of all life's possibilities when it is lived with abandon. Spying is about thinking and rethinking every contingency. Freedom is about impulsiveness. In a fit of regret, self-loathing, even, Cranmer swears:

> And after I had cursed the England that had made me, I cursed the Office for being its secret seminary, and Emma for luring me from my comfortable captivity.
> And then I cursed Larry for shining a lamp into the cavernous emptiness of what he called my dull rectangular mind and dragging me beyond the limits of my precious self-mastery.
> Above all I cursed myself.[33]

Finding Pettifer becomes Cranmer's cause. When it becomes clear that he did not, in fact, kill him, Cranmer becomes determined to warn him of the hounds on his trail, and to save Emma, towards whom he still feels protective, despite her betrayal. He follows a suitably complex trail through Bristol to Paris, to Moscow, and finally to Ingushetia. In Bristol he finds the house where Pettifer and Emma holed up and learns of their operation to purchase arms for shipment to the rebel fighters. Paris is where Emma awaits Pettifer's return or a call to join him, and where Cranmer realizes that she is irretrievably lost to him. In Moscow he connects with Ingush mobsters, who take him to Checheyev, Pettifer's target, hero, and accomplice. Checheyev brings him to Ingushetia, where he learns that Pettifer has died the death he always wanted for the cause he always hoped to serve.

With his next book, *The Tailor of Panama* (1996), le Carré brilliantly revives the classic agent-recruitment plot that flourished during the Cold War. In so doing, he shows that, notwithstanding a changing cast of players, the game retains its enviable durability – all the more so for the novel's echoing of Graham Greene's 1958 spy satire, *Our Man in Havana*, whose inspiration le Carré acknowledges. But there is a meaner, more vindictive atmosphere to *The Tailor*, reflective of a different time, one with a harder edge. The fatalism of the 1950s was a comfort in which Greene's Dr Hasselbacher took solace, dismissing "long term worry" as "not worth calling a worry. We live in an atomic age, Mr. Wormold. Push a button – piff bang – where are we? Another Scotch please."[34] Unable to find refuge in the prospect of imminent destruction, the players of the 1990s suffer the prospect of the future more.

Greene's seedy pre-Castro Cuba has become le Carré's seamy post-Noriega Panama. The enemies are less obvious, but there is a prevailing certainty of their presence. Like divers in murky water, the nefarious backroom cabal behind British intelligence – known rather vaguely as Planning and Application, of which Ambassador Maltby comments wryly, "It never occurred to me we were capable of either function"[35] – frantically casts its beam about to reveal those creatures it fantasizes as being just the other side of the darkness. And as in Greeneland, there are the small fish caught swimming in the twilight between, who are destined to perish, oblivious of why.

Incidentally, Greene knew Panama well, having developed a somewhat offbeat friendship with its populist dictator, General Omar Torrijos, who had seized power in a bloodless coup in 1968 and was killed in a mysterious plane crash in 1981. In his short memoir of their relationship, *Getting to Know the General*, Greene expresses a surprisingly uncritical admiration for a man who, for all his reported benevolence, was a military dictator and was not above profiting personally from his position. Drugs were transshipped via Panama to the United States with the complicity of high officials, including the general's older brother. Indeed, John Dean told the Senate Watergate Committee that the White House had contemplated assassinating Torrijos because of his intransigence on canal treaty negotiations and for permitting the drug trade.[36]

What intrigued Greene about Torrijos was his *cohonjes* in dealing with the Americans, always a sure ticket to Greene's heart. It was Torrijos who signed the 1977 treaty providing that control over the canal would be transferred to Panama at the end of 1999. Greene, who for many years was denied entry to the United States as a suspected communist, was included as a member of the official Panamanian delegation attending the signing ceremony in Washington, something that obviously appealed to the mischievously seditious side of his character. He reported that the two provisions of the treaty which "stuck in his gullet"[37] were the need to wait until the eve of the millennium – 31 December 1999 – for control and the Americans' retention of the right to intervene beyond that time should the canal's neutrality be threatened. Both of these clauses figure in the plot of *The Tailor*.

Torrijos was responsible for giving Manuel Noriega the opportunity to develop a power base and consolidate his influence. It was Torrijos who protected Noriega when he was accused of brutality and rape as a young national guardsman. And it was Noriega's loyalty that was key to Torrijos surviving a coup attempt in 1969. As a reward, Noriega was appointed head of G2, the national intelligence service. Although Greene mentions meeting the future leader, it is only in passing, and the distinctively pockmarked little man made no apparent impression. Noriega, however, would end up making a distinct impression on a broader audience.

A cunning manipulator, he courted his friends and their enemies with equal conscientiousness, finding a secure place for himself at the vortex of others' rivalries. Noriega really raised double agency (in fact, multiple agency) to new heights of duplicity. He was not only a long-standing CIA asset, dating back to the Torrijos era, when he was perceived as a counterweight to the general's socialism, but was on the intelligence payrolls of several sworn enemies of the United States, including Cuba, Nicaragua, and Libya.[38] One might have expected the Americans to be leery about pursuing a covert relationship with him when they knew of his closeness to the Castro regime, but they believed the quality of intelligence he supplied them about Cuba outweighed what he could give the Cubans about the United States,[39] quite a daring – or irresponsible – attitude considering that Panama was being used as a base for training and arming the Contras, Nicaraguan rebels engaged in a guerrilla war against the Cuban-supported Sandanista government. Noriega also moved drugs for the Colombian cartels while collaborating with the Drug Enforcement Agency.

By the time the United States launched Operation Just Cause to unseat him in December 1989, his drug trafficking, gun-running, money laundering, and violent – sometimes murderous – suppression of opponents had finally turned him into more of a liability than an asset. In particular, his involvement with drugs, a major domestic issue, became a *cause célèbre*. A Florida indictment in February 1988, the first ever issued against a friendly foreign leader, officially made him a fugitive from American justice. With his especially ham-fisted interference in elections in May that year and subsequent harassment of American soldiers, culminating in one being killed at a Panama Defence Forces roadblock, the Americans had more than enough excuse to take offensive action to remove Noriega by arrest. Also, they expressed concern for the security of the canal, asserting that the invasion was meant to protect its unhindered functioning. Though the military situation was quickly brought under control – not, however, without considerable losses: as many as a thousand Panamanian and twenty-five American lives, plus $1.5 billion in damages – Noriega's arrest was sloppy. He evaded capture by taking refuge with the papal nuncio, where he hid out for ten days before surrendering and being taken into custody.

The Panama in which *The Tailor* is set is lurching from the turmoil of Noriega's reign and the American military operation that deposed him towards asserting control over the canal, which remains an important economic and strategic thoroughfare. Some in the international community doubt whether the Panamanians are up to administering it to their satisfaction. Notwithstanding that this is the Americans' backyard, British intelligence is intent upon finding some influence for itself. Indeed, the prospect of scooping the Yanks in their own realm is particular cause for gloating. The scenario appealed to le Carré because "it's a brand-new country from lunchtime on the thirty-first of December, 1999 ... The canal will revert to their own possession. And we have the fascinating sight of a small country identifying itself, finding out who it will be ... I tried to play one perception of the country against my own domestic concerns."[40]

English expatriate Harry Pendel is in turmoil, plagued by impending financial doom and guilt for the suffering of friends. Add to that the burden of being a fabricator, of living a life stitched together from a textured weave of lies, every bit as meticulously fashioned as the fine men's clothing he tailors under the mark of "Pendel & Braithwaite, Tailors to Royalty." The problem with living a lie is that someone may come along who will discover the truth. The lengths to which a person goes to maintain the facade are the measure of their desperation.

Enter Andy Osnard, who thrives on turmoil, that predicament which intelligence services by turn exploit or foment. In espionage he has found "his true Church of England, his rotten borough with a handsome budget."[41] Charming, manipulative, and cruel as a well-bred English public school bully (a character familiar to readers of Greene), Osnard is determined to squeeze the most out of his first foreign posting. He has put in his time playing foil to his chief, Scottie Luxmore, for whom he has utter contempt, only to secure the opportunity to run a one-man station in Panama, where he will have ample freedom to disburse funds – to his sources and himself – and from which his reports will find their way to the dispensers of future sinecures. All Osnard needs is an agent in a position to supply him with information concerning the tumultuous inner workings of, and interrelations between, the Panamanian government, the American military and canal zone administration, and the revolutionary students and workers who are so deviously clever in their clandestine organization that nobody knows of their existence until Pendel brings it to Osnard's attention.

Pendel shows every sign of being a natural recruit. Best of all, he is vulnerable to the carrot that Osnard wags and the stick he wields: help the mother country and earn a way out of debt, or have the disgraces of his past revealed, with the resultant unravelling of the life in exile he has so carefully crafted for himself. He desperately needs the money, given that his investment in a rice farm is drying up. He also needs to keep from his wife, Louisa, the truth of his past: that P&B never tailored for royalty: that he is only a convicted arsonist who has reinvented himself as respectable in far-off Panama. So he succumbs.

Tailoring is a clever metaphor for what Pendel does. The careful measuring, cutting, stitching, and finishing of a fine garment is no different than what he does in assembling sources and information. Indeed, "It was tailoring. It was improving on people. It was cutting and shaping them until they became understandable members of his internal universe. It was fluence. It was running ahead of events and waiting for them to catch up. It was making people bigger or smaller according to whether they enhanced or threatened his existence."[42]

Everyone who is anyone in Panama City has his clothes custom tailored by P&B, and all, according to Pendel, naturally confide in him their most pressing and private preoccupations during the intimacy of a fitting. He dresses the president and the American general in charge of Southern Command. He measures the rich and the influential. As well, Louisa is assistant to the esteemed Ernesto Delgado, the government's forward-planning adviser on the canal.

Only, his access is nothing like what he suggests. The ideal man of service, he goes barely noticed. He actually hears nothing but idle banter, the odd snippet of gossip, a few meaningless remarks. It is for him to spin this lint into finery. But intelligence services, he learns, only pay for what they want to hear. Embroidering with uninformed speculation and pure invention, Pendel, fabricator of his own history, satisfies Osnard and his masters in London, for he confirms their worst expectations regarding Panamanian stability. And much to their delight, none of the information that he supplies is known to the Americans.

Panama is the quintessence of what Americans think of as their Latin American bailiwick. After all, they did effectively create the country, excising the narrow strip of land from Colombia in 1903, and engineered the canal, keeping a suitably wide belt along both sides for themselves, along with a sufficient military presence to ensure uninterrupted shipping. The Zone, as it is known, is America, inhabited by soldiers, administrators, and descendants of Americans who have lived there since its creation. It is the world from which Louisa comes, a world described by journalist Frederick Kempe as "a red-neck preserve of baseball fields, country-and-western bars, and Southern Baptist churches, where racism had a good name and political lobbying against the treaties was most reactionary ... They [the Zonians] considered the waterway American property in perpetuity. They stole it fair and square, they liked to laugh to each other. Zonians' salaries were higher, few spoke Spanish, and they swaggered through Panama with the arrogant air of colonial masters when they weren't in their spacious homes attending to well-groomed lawns."[43] All this privilege stood to be lost with the surrender of the canal.

Jim Wormold, Greene's man in Havana, is cautioned by his confidant, Hasselbacher, "But remember, as long as you lie you do no harm."[44] Quite the opposite turns out to be the case in that instance, as with le Carré's tailor. Intelligence officers are a contradictory amalgam of paranoid disbelief and childlike gullibility.

Tell them that all is well and they imagine the chaos to be erupting just beyond their view. Hint that things are worse than they ever dreamt and they feel their nightmares to be justified and sleep easier. Furthermore, a lie does not behave like a lie when those to whom it is told believe it wholeheartedly and act upon it as they would the truth. Like Pendel, Wormold is in need of funds, since his desultory vacuum cleaner concession is not sufficient to provide his pubescent daughter with private education, stable fees for the horse she covets, or country club membership to give her a suitable place to ride. A rather buffoonish recruitment by Hawthorne of the Secret Service convinces him that he can acquire steady cash with a few well-placed inventions. He builds an entire network of imaginary agents and submits sketches of enlarged vacuum cleaner components to illustrate the construction of a non-existent military installation. It is all so absurd that he fully expects to be found out fairly quickly.

But he isn't. The chief is so enthusiastic about the exciting intelligence emanating from Havana that Hawthorne curbs his own suspicions over how much the military installation resembles a vacuum cleaner. Then, when one of Wormold's agents is killed in a suspicious car accident, Hasselbacher is shot to death, and a plot to terminate Wormold is discovered, he is relieved: "You see, that really proves the drawings are genuine."[45] – shades here of *The Looking Glass War*, where Taylor's death is evidence of something significant stirring. When nobody plays the comedy for laughs, it becomes deathly serious. There is indeed an attempt made on Wormold's life, by Carter in the employ of unidentified parties. Wormold is left with no choice but to shoot Carter and finally confess his fraud. Far from being punished, he is awarded a decoration and an appointment to training branch. A final report is issued declaring, not that the installation was a figment of his imagination, but that it has been dismantled. In this way no one looks any the more foolish. On the contrary, it appears as though a threat has been well monitored and contained.

Markus Wolf refers to *Our Man in Havana* as the "classic espionage book ... That is the best."[46] According to a story related by le Carré, Greene came very close to being prosecuted under the Official Secrets Act for it. He learned from the service's in-house lawyer that it was especially perturbed by his accurate representation of the relationship between a field 10 and his agent.[47] I suppose the service was doubly embarrassed to have an accurate portrayal given in the cause of such a bungled caper.

Osnard's career and expense account cannot be served by an all's-well; he needs an all's-not-as-it-appears. He needs an enemy where none existed, a conspiracy in the absence of conspirators. Pendel is only too willing to oblige, hence the beauty of the Silent Opposition. It is out there opposing, only silently. And the loudest silence emanates from Mickie Abraxas, upon whom Pendel has bestowed leadership. Abraxas suffered horribly in Noriega's prisons in his youth, only to emerge a battered and defeated drunk. For that, Pendel owes him, because he has taken his punishment without ever naming Pendel, who was with him, along with Marta, his assistant and almost-lover, when they were stopped by Noriega's thugs. Marta was beaten to disfigurement, while Pendel got away with the guilt of those whose fortune it is to escape. So why choose Abraxas? To "make a gift of love to Mickie, build him into something he could never be, a Mickie redux, dried out, shining bright, militant and courageous,"[48] in other words, all the things Abraxas neither is nor aspires any longer to be. As le Carré has posited elsewhere, you only betray what you love, and Pendel loves Abraxas.

Everyone – except the Panamanians, with whom nobody consults – has an interest in the veracity of Pendel's intelligence. Therefore nobody looks too closely for the lie. The thing is said, reported, and acted upon. When Ambassador Maltby sees the opportunity to take over from young Osnard as Pendel's paymaster, he gladly does so, in the interest of seeing that a more senior man will take responsibility and to finance his impending divorce. Secret disbursements are, after all, difficult to account for. He muses on "how I yearned to take part in a British plot. Well, here it is. The secret bugle has sounded."[49] He adds that, "it's absolutely nothing to do with you or me or anyone else in this embassy, with the possible exception of young Andy, that the BUCHAN [Pendel's codename] stuff is the most frightful tosh."[50]

However, it does have much to do with Abraxas. He is paid a visit by the Panamanian police, who, much to his mystification, accuse him of being a spy and remind him of the unpleasantness of the local penal system. Rather than suffer gaol again, he commits suicide. Pendel answers Abraxas's mistress's call and goes to help her with the body. He trusses it up and dumps it in an isolated spot, making it appear as though the beloved leader of the Silent Opposition has been executed – proof positive of a gravely deteriorating situation.

Meanwhile, suspicious of Pendel's behaviour, his odd comings and goings, sightings outside pay-by-the-hour motels, Louisa goes through his papers and finds all sorts of strange scraps addressed to Osnard regarding the canal and Delgado that she knows to be false. Confused, outraged, frightened, she goes to Osnard to confront him or be consoled. Osnard, lacking any concept of propriety or shame, proceeds to bed her, if only because "screwing one's friend's wives is never less than interesting."[51] The conquest is not without intelligence value either, for he learns conclusively that Louisa has no idea what Pendel was up to, whereas Pendel told him that he was using her as a source. He therefore realizes that the BUCHAN has been a con from the outset. He summarily packs his things and departs Panama forthwith.

Thanks to the *murder* of Abraxas, the Planners and Appliers and their American sympathizers are presented grounds on which to arouse public outrage and a peg upon which to hang a military invasion, both to preserve democracy and to secure the precious canal. Nothing else matters, and since the details are all concealed behind a shroud of secrecy, nothing else will be known of the machinations of the Silent Opposition. Operation Safe Passage is launched, and once more Panama comes under the helter-skelter bombardment of precision weapons.

Le Carré is in his usual fine form throughout *The Tailor of Panama*. His pacing is crisp and his insights are as revealing as ever. Pendel joins Barley Blair and Larry Pettifer among his great bemused subversives. Osnard is the alter ego to George Smiley and Ned; he is self-serving and mean-spirited, a survivalist espiocrat for the nineties, living in "a world without faith or antifaith,"[52] as le Carré terms it in *Our Game*. Like that book, *The Tailor* deals with a potentially emergent hot spot where the powers that be – and those that were – may next turn in their search for a suitable enemy. As he puts it, "all the world's vultures were gathering over poor little Panama and the game was guessing who was going to get the prize."[53]

Who gets caught in the way of events is of utmost importance to him. Elephantine powers butting heads concentrate on too broad a field to bother with what they pulverize in every stride.

There is the image that recurs to Leamas in *The Spy Who Came in from the Cold* of the station wagon about to be crushed on the autobahn between giant transport trucks, while children laugh and wave, oblivious to their impending demise.

With *The Tailor of Panama* le Carré brought his post-Cold War trajectory full circle. The hope of *The Russia House* – that decent human beings would behave courageously – having been disappointed, was succeeded by the prospect that Enforcement would impose some rationality on the business of pursuing the worst men in the world, only to be dashed too. *Our Game* allowed for the consideration that small conflicts might arouse some moral concerns, but to no avail. Finally, with *The Tailor*, the Cold War text was reopened and its teachings reapplied, but without any pretended zeal of mission.

Greene and le Carré paint pictures of IOs too dim or venal to be able, or to want, to catch out amateur fabricators. Could a Wormold or a Pendel really run rings around the intelligence establishment? Certainly not to anything like the same extent. An Osnard would not be able to dole out cash as he does, for secret funds are much more closely accounted than le Carré makes it appear. But if we take a less literal view of the fabricator, the question stands as to whether an IO can be led a ride?

Certainly, handlers *want*, and *urge*, their sources to be good and productive. They are predisposed to want to believe – which is different from believing – a source. This inclination can lead, perhaps, to more patience than a source deserves, some harmless exaggeration of the source's access or potential, but rarely to colluding in the dissemination of patently false information or failing to double check. In the end, spies are judged on the usefulness of what they provide, whether or not it is put to any use. Most operations that drag on year after year after decade do not do so because of a steady haul of premium intelligence, but because of the sheer hope of something to come. It takes a brave person or an order from on high to close a file. Even then, the terminology speaks of hope: cases are not terminated, they are classed as "dormant" – in other words, placed in a cryogenic freeze, forever anticipating revival.

In the view of Aiden Bell, a former Ireland hand in *Single & Single*, a "joe was a joe for him. You paid him what he was worth and dropped him down a hole when he wasn't worth it anymore.

If he was leading you up the garden, you had a quiet word with him in a backstreet."[54] In my service, there were never quiet words in back streets. A dishonest source was cut loose, plain and simple. However, you really did everything you could not to drop a source. Once you had undertaken the preliminary work to identify a likely informant, the background checks to make sure he or she had no questionable antecedents, the wooing until the person responded to tasking, you dropped him or her with supreme reluctance.

Handler and source develop a mutual dependence. It's in the handler's interest to have valuable sources, to churn out reports based upon their revelations. It certainly isn't collusion or fabrication – more like optimism. You wouldn't turn an inconsequential occurrence into something of consequence, but you'd look for the possibility of forthcoming advantages. I had inherited sources whose value had long since dissipated, but they had proved their worth in the past and would always prove valuable in the event that anything came their way. I had also handled sources at the extreme margins of very difficult to penetrate groups, particularly in counter-terrorism. You'd cling to them in the hope that they would somehow, eventually, penetrate deeper. There was no future in an abandoned source. This is not an irresponsible or wasteful approach, but it does exponentially increase the number of hours expended on every bit of genuinely useful intelligence.

In the absence of faith, corruption and narcissism are what motivate. Sacrifice is disavowed where society has been degraded. What supplants the notion of community is free enterprise run amok; or, as Burr proclaims, "Boredom and greed, they're the only motives left these days. Plus getting even, which is eternal."[55] In the West the corruption embodied by the Darkers and the Osnards and, in le Carré's next book, by Tiger Single is constrained only by the regime's legitimacy and a functioning legal establishment. But where law and legitimacy have dissolved, along with community, all restraints disappear and corruption reigns supreme. In today's Russia, extortion is a normal element of doing business. The *mafiya* is so pervasive that a 1994 report by Moscow's Analytic Center for Social and Economic Policies said that nearly 80 per cent of private businesses and commercial banks paid up to 20 per cent of their earnings to racketeers for protection.[56] This is the new Russia, where gangsters and government officials conspire to plunder the resources that were once under the monopoly control of the state, but are now up for grabs in the awkward transition to market capitalism. Real wealth is to be had from moving Russian commodities to the West in exchange for luxury items and hard cash. To facilitate such transactions, those with connections to exportable property enlist the services of Western financiers.

The great House of Single is the most reputable of disreputable upmarket investment advisers, specializing in cleansing illicitly made money so that it may be enjoyed conspicuously. Founder and senior partner Tiger Single embodies the courage, vision, and, yes, larceny necessary to find and exploit untried opportunities. As he explains to his son and junior partner, "Single's exists to say yes where others say no, Oliver. We bring vision. Know-how. Energy. Resources. To wherever the spirit of true adventure leads."[57]

Beginning five years before the action of *Single & Single* (1999) takes place, that spirit found no greater outlet than in the frontier badlands of the Soviet Union, where everything was up for grabs *if* you had the right connections. Yevgeny Orlov, his brother Mikhail, and son-in-law Alix Hoban were connected to everything for which there was a demand, including scrap metal, oil, even human blood. It was in their power to ensure which bidder, paying how much and to whom, would get the concessions to these and other, worse commodities – like weapons, like drugs.

Bribery is the one dependable in a chaotic system. The old Soviet order was not so much replaced by a new order as left in disorder. The old bureaucrats who inherited positions of influence were in an excellent position to collude with gangsters. Bureaucrats thrived on the corruption; hence it flourished without check. In his study *Comrade Criminal*, journalist Stephen Handelman argues, "The most successful entrepreneurs in post-Soviet society were those who knew how to make their way through the treacherous maze created by the working relationship between organized crime and the corrupt bureaucracy. More to the point, they knew how to use the new system while managing to stay alive."[58] This comment calls to mind an expression that le Carré uses in both *The Night Manager* and *Single & Single*: "It's either we make you rich or we make you dead."[59] That is how it appears to be in Russia. By no means is every businessman a gangster, but many of the successful ones have come to an understanding with the *mafiyas* in order that all may prosper.

Handelman and others make the point that the corruption in Russia is just a more open form of the black market that thrived in the Soviet Union. Because the black market was such an integral part of the communist economy, criminal gangs were an inseparable part of the state structure. Indeed, Hedrick Smith claims there was not so much a black market as a "full-fledged shadow economy, and one on which the nation depended."[60] What had been underground moved to the foreground as the Russian version of the free market spawned a free-for-all to accumulate wealth. No more is there an oppressive police apparatus to control the gangsterism. Gone are the privileges that the apparatchiks depended upon to ensure that they lived better than the masses, a measure that helped keep their avarice in check. Thanks to the monumental inefficiency of the command economy, virtually nothing happened without bribery, leading Remnick to conclude that the "Communist Party apparatus was the most gigantic mafia the world has ever known."[61] The difference in post-Soviet Russia is that the party has lost its monopoly on graft, as it has lost all its other monopolies. Thus has carefully managed corruption become anarchic.

The apparatchik-driven mafia of Soviet society spun in a dizzying circle: where privilege turned on power imposed by fear, from which not even the most powerful were immune. In the words of poet and novelist Yevgeny Yevtushenko, "Power – small, medium and big – did not save you from the biggest power of all, and that biggest power did not belong to someone, it was something even bigger than Stalin himself – fear."[62] In the new Russia, as Yegor Gaidar, once Yeltsin's crusading reformist prime minister, lamented, "The Russian bureaucrat has today been given ideal conditions for getting rich: the conversion of power into property. (He) has unlimited possibilities to take individual, uncontrolled decisions, handing out quotas to export produce, credits and subsidies, support for individual banks, and so on."[63]

Keeping the fiction of legitimate business, Tiger declares, "House of Single does not bribe, of course. That's not what we do at all. If legitimate commissions are to be paid, they will be paid."[64] "Oliver likes it, hates it, thinks it is good business, disgusting business, not business at all but theft. But he had no time to set his revulsion into words. He lacks the age, the sureness, the address, the space."[65] At the time, he lacked the lack of conscience. The complex relationship between father and son is as prominent in *Single & Single* as it is in *A Perfect Spy*. Is the son bound to blindly honour the father, or is he obliged to betray him in the event that the father is so dishonourable as to make that impossible? Le Carré admits that prior to writing *A Perfect Spy*, he tried to address his relationship with his father in other guises, with "proxy father-figures ... and weighed them down with my unfocused broodings about love and loyalty."[66] Foremost among them is Smiley. Another he mentions is Westerby's newspaper magnate father in *The Honourable Schoolboy* and Charlie's father in *The Little Drummer Girl*, about whom she tells outrageous lies that were the truth about Ronnie. Finally, in *Single* le Carré imagines how things might have turned out between himself and his father if Ronnie had been a wildly successful cheat. Tiger is a Ronnie whose schemes pay off. And Oliver is le Carré drawn against his best judgment into his birthright.

Oliver's choices eventually become clear, if agonizing: continue to further the interests of Single & Single or initiate measures to set matters right. Taking the latter course, he contacts Her Majesty's Customs and so becomes an informant to Nat Brock, an officer who lives by the credo "you did best to think dirty and double it."[67] He is after money launderers and the indictable British – not untouchable offshore – officials they corrupt in return for impunity. For all the promise of Oliver's privileged access at Single's, however, four years after resettling him under a new identity, Brock is still without the evidence he needs. And then Single lawyer Alfred Winser gets his head blown off. After receiving a gruesome videotape of Winser's execution and the promise of a similar fate, Tiger goes missing. The suspense revolves around who will find him first: his nemeses, who believe that Single's double-cross has resulted in a shipload of their heroin being seized and a loss of £200 million, or Brock, who will offer him haven in exchange for information.

Tortured by guilt and loyalties guided and misguided in turn by Brock and by filial duty, Oliver agrees to resurface as the junior Single and to attempt, if it is not already too late, to find Tiger. Brock tries to salve his conscience: "It's not betrayal, Oliver. It's justice. That was what you wanted, if you remember. You wanted to put the world to rights. That's what we're doing."[68] But, of course, it is not as simple as a dichotomy between betrayal and justice. Sometimes, in the world of intelligence, the former is precursor to the latter. So it is not betrayal *or* justice; it is justice as consequence of betrayal. And often, despite the best of intentions, justice gets away. To succeed, Brock needs Oliver. "You can feel him, guess him, live him, just by breathing in. You know him better than you know yourself,"[69] he pleads, somewhat overdramatizing his argument, since Oliver has had no contact with Tiger in the four years since he has gone to ground.

Just as Magnus Pym is forever serving several masters at once, so is Oliver. In scenes reminiscent of *A Perfect Spy*, where Magnus gains surreptitious access to the cellar in which Rick keeps his guarded file cabinet, Oliver penetrates the partners' strongroom at the House of Single and conducts a search of Tiger's apartment. Though he does this in the guise of rescuing Tiger from the Orlovs' clutches, he is ever acting at the behest of his other master, Brock. When Oliver shakes Brock's leash and takes off after Tiger under his own steam, Brock acknowledges, "I was pushing him, but Tiger was pulling him, and Tiger's pull was harder than my push."[70] This, then, is the answer le Carré arrives at in the end: that the father – be it through love or through obligation – exercises the strongest hold over the son.

Though his concern in this novel, as in *A Perfect Spy*, is with crooked fathers and responsible sons and their duties to each other, this time le Carré does not make the son worse than the father. Schooled in the law, as Rick had intended for Magnus, Oliver has an aversion to descending too far below the line of rectitude. Tiger, on the other hand, sees the law as either shield or inconvenience. Oliver's dilemma is how to both protect his father and serve the higher loyalty urged by norms and values that highlight his villainy. Oliver answers these questions, though not necessarily to his own satisfaction, when he allows, "I may be a traitor but I'm not a criminal."[71] For the son of Tiger Single, as for the son of Rick Pym, this is what the choices come down to.

Interestingly, Timothy Garton Ash asked le Carré whether he had ever betrayed his father, to which the novelist replied, "The betrayal, I suppose, was falling out of love with him. And actually telling him I didn't want to see him again."[72] He had come to feel that everything he did with Ronnie made him an accomplice to fraud, thus precipitating the break.

Attentive readers of le Carré will notice much that is familiar in *Single & Single*. For example, Charmian, the uncommon name that Aggie, the customs agent assigned to pose as Oliver's wife, adopts as an alias belongs to the activist actress Charlie. Brock shares with Kurtz the habit of telephoning his long-suffering wife on the eve of battle, taking comfort in listening to her ridiculous ideas about how to resolve the question of Northern Ireland or the scandalous affair between the village postmistress's daughter and the local builder. As a type, Brock is not dissimilar to Ned. He understands the bent loyalties of his source ("Brock's distrust of Oliver was as absolute as his affection for him"[73]) and the sleep-robbing compromises of the job ("I hunt a man for fifteen years. I conspire against him, hair goes white, I neglect my wife. Fret and worry how to catch him with his pants down. Next thing I know, he's cringing in a ditch with the hounds after him and all I want to do is reach out for him, give him a hot cup of tea and offer him total amnesty").[74] Tiger and his cronies could have stepped directly off the pages of *The Night Manager* and substituted for Dickie Roper. And Oliver, physically imposing, more than a little scraggly, and necessarily vague about his past after he takes on the guise of Uncle Ollie, magician for children's parties, bears more than a passing resemblance to Jonathan Pine.

With Oliver, female characters fall too readily and too conveniently in love, giving him just the edge he needs at any particular time. Aggie is one of them, prepared to risk her career and quite conceivably her life for his sake. As their pretended intimacy begins to resemble the real thing, they have the following exchange over dinner. Oliver says:

"It's a bit of a tall order."

"What is?"

"Being one person all day and somebody else in the evening. I'm not sure who to be anymore."

"Be yourself, Oliver. Just for once."

"Yeah, well, there's not that much left to be, really. Not after Tiger and Brock have finished with me."

"Oliver, if you're going to talk like that, I think I'll eat alone."[75]

This exchange reads like hackneyed le Carré, not something original to these characters. It is an awful lot like sentiments expressed by Magnus to Mary about the tug-of-war waged over his self between Rick, Brotherhood, and Axel. Or it could be Charlie speaking to Joseph, or the reluctant, lovelorn Barley Blair addressing Katya, or maybe Pine with Jed. And therein lies the central problem with the novel: it seems too much the product of work le Carré had already done.

Le Carré professed relief when the Cold War ended, saying that he had grown tired of it, and he expressed the hope and expectation that a new world would present refreshing challenges. He criticized politicians for getting too cozy, "hiding behind a huge nuclear arsenal than to be stepping out of our bunkers, offering a helping hand to our former enemies and taking on such headaches as world famine, global pollution, arms proliferation, brushfire wars in far-off places and the rights of small nations to self-determination – even though such headaches have much more to do with our long-term survival than the Cold War ever did."[76] But the Cold War was so pervasive, it would have been difficult for him to abandon it as long as it persisted. "If the spy novelist of today can rise to the challenge," he told *Time* in 1991, "he has got it made. He can sweep away the cobwebs of a world grown old and cold and weary ... and take on any number of new hunting grounds."[77]

And so he has, finding betrayal in new guises: among arms traders and in the Caucasus and Panama; with fashionable London bankers and their Georgian clients-partners he addresses the "eternal enemy," "human wickedness."[78] The difference is that this enemy is drawn far more starkly than were Cold War adversaries. There is little ambivalence to the wickedness of Single's world.

It is hard to discuss recent le Carré novels without comparison to his earlier work, and by that impossibly high standard, *Single & Single*, his seventeenth offering, falls short. Neither bearer of that name will be remembered with his most resonant creations, – Smiley, of course, Alec Leamas, Pym, Blair, Jerry Westerby, or Pendel. Unfortunately, the conclusion that Oliver reaches about Tiger is not inapplicable to the book as a whole: when he "had arrived at the last, most hidden room of his search, he had prized open the most top-secret box, and it was empty. Tiger's secret was that he had no secret."[79]

That is not to say that there is not some merit to recommend the book. The narrative is tautly constructed and tension is deftly created through seamless cuts between the present and flash-backs. And there are some genuinely great moments, not the least of which is the opening: the execution of Winser is positively terrifying and will pull readers in before the first page has been turned. Murder is how dissatisfied customers make the point when illegal enterprises fail to yield promised returns. With cold straightforwardness that is vintage le Carré, Hoban, Winser's killer, explains to him, "Sure, it's a vengeance killing too. Please. We would not be human if we did not exact vengeance. But also we intend this gesture will be interpreted as formal request for recompense."[80] Now what could be more reasonable than that?

For Yevgeny Orlov, the issue is more serious than the loss of a single ship. His beloved brother was aboard and had been killed during the seizure, turning his dispute with Tiger into an old-fashioned Georgian blood feud. Not only does this complicate matters, but it begs the question of why that particular boat was seized and how Mikhail came to be in the crossfire. What could Tiger have possibly stood to gain from undermining the Orlovs? Oliver is not the culprit; he was far removed from the business of Single by this point. In truth, a far more elaborate plot was being hatched between Hoban and Tiger's chief of staff, Randy Massingham, whereby they would wrest control of Single's holdings for themselves, using the demand of payment for the ship's loss and Mikhail's death as leverage.

Unfortunately, the hunt becomes fairly predictable, twisting down a path that le Carré has taken before. The shootout ending, in which the cavalry swoops in at the last second to save the day, disappoints for having been heavy-handedly manipulated to arrive at a particular outcome, as opposed to fulfilling the natural flow that is his customary achievement. I find it very difficult to believe in how this final scene plays out, with all ending well and the hero getting the girl.

What le Carré has done with *Single & Single*, as with his three previous works, is to signal from which direction our next generation of antagonists will emanate. We no longer have to look so far afield to find those who threaten our well-being. They are not across frontiers or at some indiscernible place over the horizon. They are among us and they are ruthless. They are criminal and corrupt. They utterly lack the enobling quality of philosophy. They do not even pretend to have vision. Le Carré relates a wonderful story about meeting with the leader of one of Moscow's bloodiest gangs. Challenging him, le Carré said, "You're a robber baron, Grigori. Congratulations. That's what people say of Carnegie and J.P. Morgan and Rockefeller. But they ended up building hospitals and art galleries for the society they'd exploited. When are you going to start putting something back, Grigori?" Grigori's response was to advise the impertinent Englishman to "Bug off," which he hastily did.[81] In this generation of robber barons, we have endless exploitation without redemption. We have complete lack of restraint. Consequently, we have some very dangerous people to face up to.

Discussing the connection between his post–Cold War novels, le Carré says he has been "trying to document this mysterious search for identity that we're all going through," affirming his "fascination with what will happen to capitalism now that there's no opponent."[82] Accordingly, he has replaced his cast of spies with corporate villains, supplanting those who acted lamentably in the name of national security and ideology with those acting in the name of profit and position; the latter appear capable of much greater damage. Le Carré's spies at least had the virtue of irrelevance, even if they stubbornly refused to recognize it in themselves. Basically, they manoeuvred and conspired against one another. Only occasionally did their plots spill over to engulf anyone who had not somehow agreed to play (the glaring example being *The Tailor of Panama*).

Le Carré's new villains prey on innocents as a matter of course. The globalization of the economy has opened a wealth of nefarious opportunities: for Western corporations poised to plunder, along with the corrupt locals positioned to hinder or facilitate their efforts. The pursuit of profit – the closest thing we now have to universal dogma – goes untempered by better instinct, except in the form of those few individuals unwilling to compromise for the sake of their own comfort. It is all well and good to condemn corporate greed, but there is a more pervasive human trait at work – selfishness – the instinct that demands constant increases in stock values because *I* need to ensure my retirement, or an immediate cure for the debilitating, possibly fatal, disease that *I* risk contracting, no matter whether others get hurt along the way. We all share a measure of complicity.

In a world that generally gives itself quickly and easily to cynicism, a measure of optimism is reserved for the health-care industry. Call it wishful thinking. Much as we acknowledge the industry's monetary underbelly, we shudder at the prospect that access to or quality of care could be compromised by so crass a consideration as finances. It is intimidating enough to be sick and left without any alternative but to place your trust in someone else's expertise and compassion. We take a leap of faith, believing that when we are ill – at our weakest, most vulnerable – we will be rendered assistance in a spirit of altruism, in the tradition of Hippocrates, where the only issue is restoring our well-being, where the dispensation of remedies is dictated by nothing save what constitutes the most effective treatment.

How unsettling it is, then, to have the pharmaceutical industry branded "the *most* secretive, duplicitous, mendacious, hypocritical bunch of corporate wide-boys it's been my dubious pleasure to encounter"[83] by a character in le Carré's latest novel, *The Constant Gardener* (2001). This trade may be his most unsavory antagonist, yet because of our delusion – duly encouraged by the pharmas themselves – that profits are merely a happy afterthought, an unintended (if not unwelcome) consequence of helping people. To them we consign our health – in effect, our lives. When we are prescribed pills, we gulp them down, usually without a second thought, certainly not for how rich we are making the manufacturers or whether they, in turn, are compensating the doctor for what is, however you look at it, a sale. Disquieting as that idea is to contemplate, it is worse to think that scientific endorsements for a medicine can be purchased, as opposed to being the outcome of rigorous research and objective analysis. Along the way, contradictory evidence may be buried, together with those who loudly call attention to them, quite literally.

Literally? People getting killed to ensure silence and protect corporate earnings? "I am sure people have died," le Carré told an interviewer.[84] Furthermore, in the Author's Note to the novel he wrote, "As my journey through the pharmaceutical jungle progressed, I came to realise that, by comparison with the reality, my story was as tame as a holiday postcard."[85] *The Constant Gardener* opens with the grisly murder of Tessa Quayle, crusading human-rights lawyer and beautiful young wife of Justin, enthusiastic gardener and undistinguished diplomat at the British High Commission in Nairobi. She is discovered, throat slit, beside the headless body of her driver near the shore of Lake Turkana. Missing and presumed guilty is Dr Arnold Bluhm, the Congolese-born, Belgium-raised aid-agency physician ("the Westerner's African")[86] who shared her mission to protect hapless Africans from the boundless inhumanity and avarice of pharma-profiteers, rapacious government officials, and unscrupulous scientists, all of which abound in Kenya.

Le Carré based Tessa, a woman of heroic qualities not to be dissuaded by death threats or the knowledge that all power and apathy were aligned against her, upon Yvette Pierpaoli, a tireless relief worker he met back in the 1970s when he travelled Indochina gathering material for *The Honourable Schoolboy*. Along with her husband, she ran a trading company, the profits from which she poured into aiding the sick, the starving, and the stateless. He claims that she, "like almost no one else, had opened my eyes to constructive compassion, to putting your money and your life where your heart was."[87] Although, like Tessa, Pierpaoli would die tragically prematurely – in a car accident while helping refugees in Albania – *The Constant Gardener* makes clear that living life on any other terms is cheating. Struck most forcefully by this premise is Justin, who, in setting out after Tessa's ghost to find out who killed her and why, sheds the tattered cloak of his professional duty – "I serve, therefore I feel"[88] – for the less comfortable garb of involvement.

"I am thinking I don't believe in me any more, and all I stood for," he reproaches himself.[89] His life is suddenly and rudely tossed about like a small boat on rough seas. To some observers, he brought upheaval upon himself by recklessly surrendering his middle-aged bachelorhood to a girl in her twenties – a girl who, unlike the pliable civil servant, had not yet conceded victory to those forces that inevitably defeat idealism. Prior to her murder, Justin "had regarded strongly held convictions as the natural enemies of the diplomat, to be ignored, humoured or, like dangerous energy, diverted into harmless channels. Now to his surprise he saw them as emblems of courage and Tessa as their standard-bearer."[90] With this vision in mind, he embarks "to extinguish his own identity and revive hers; to kill Justin, and bring Tessa back to life."[91]

Tessa and Arnold had collected evidence that Dypraxa, a fictional treatment for the drug-resistant strains of tuberculosis that flourish in Africa and elsewhere, was killing Kenyans who were being used as unwitting guinea pigs to test it. Tuberculosis is an interesting choice on le Carré's part because it is not now a significant health issue in Western Europe or North America, where patients can actually afford to pay for medication and where, therefore, huge money stands to be made. However, there is an ever-present threat that "if it hasn't done so already, it will hitch a ride on an airplane, a bus, a train and escape into the rest of the world."[92] Tuberculosis frequently shows up in conjunction with AIDS, preying on sufferers' ravaged immune systems. In 1992 New York City experienced a mini-epidemic in which 3,800 new cases were reported.

Data on the deadly side effects of Dypraxa are being suppressed by the manufacturer, Karel Vita Hudson (KVH) of Basel, Vancouver, and Seattle, and its African distributor, the ubiquitous British conglomerate House of ThreeBees. Their motive is to use the drug's reputed success in Kenya, where controls over testing and licensing are far less rigorous than in the West, to rush it to market worldwide. Whomever gets trampled over in the stampede is incidental – but not to Tessa or Arnold, unwilling to jettison African lives as natural effluence for advancing the corporations' constant quest for higher returns on investment.

With the current cost of bringing a drug to market estimated at $500 million,[93] it is no wonder a manufacturer would aggressively pursue avenues down which savings are to be found. But at the cost of how many lives? Glowing reports of Dypraxa's performance in its African trials are essential for its international acceptance. All the more enervating in le Carré's conception is the unanimous opinion that Dypraxa would in fact be a very good drug after appropriate refinement.

Tessa's vulnerability to those who would silence her is heightened because she insists on voicing her concerns through the system. She is determined not to bypass it to rant and rail publicly, but to force the system to work as it theoretically should.[94] To this end, she submits a detailed report to the British Foreign Office through Head of Chancery Sandy Woodrow, ignoring the fact that he is the *fonctionnaire par excellence*, the embodiment of a bureaucracy that allows no lies to be so blatant, no transgressions so unconscionable, that they cannot be accommodated under Her Majesty's banner as necessity decrees. Woodrow dutifully posts her report to Sir Bernard Pellegrin, the FO's Africa major-domo, who has very carefully laid out plans for his post-civil service career. As he points out to Justin over a club lunch, "Plenty of plums out there for a chap who's got himself sorted. Plenty of places I wouldn't be seen dead in,"[95] leaving absolutely no doubt that he is bound for the plums. Accordingly, he promptly proceeds to lose Tessa's submission, thereby advancing his prospects for directorships on the boards of KVH and ThreeBees.

The system to which Tessa gives the benefit of the doubt is Justin's: where he is thought of as Old Office, reliable; whose interests he has served around the world; whose lies he believed and sold as his own. Through Tessa he had learned, however, that these are not his interests. When unsuspecting people suffer dizziness, blindness, internal bleeding, liver failure, death, he is not being served. Nor could he any longer subsume himself to those who are.

He transforms himself from unassuming diplomat to spy, adopting the spies' ways: "This is the watchfulness they learn from their cradles. This is how they cross a dark street, scan doorways, turn a corner: are you waiting for me? Have I seen you somewhere before?"[96] He goes to ground, emerging in Italy, northern Germany, and the bitter, barren cold of Saskatchewan and returning to Africa as he recreates Tessa's case against Dypraxa. Pursuing and impeding him all the way are the same powerful forces that put an abrupt, vicious end to her efforts.

Novelists sometimes reach for extremes to illustrate a point or for the benefit of narrative excitement. So it was uncanny to happen upon a *Washington Post* investigative report that bears an astonishing resemblance to *The Constant Gardener*. In 1996 Pfizer, the American pharmaceutical giant, opened a clinic in Kano, Nigeria, during a meningitis outbreak to test the as yet unapproved drug Trovan. There is no Tessa Quayle in this story, but there are doctors from the Nobel prize-winning humanitarian group Médecins sans Frontières. Allegedly, there were no formal ethics-approval protocols in place for testing Trovan on children; nor were the patients properly advised that they were participating in an experiment; nor was proper long-term follow-up implemented. Consequently, of two hundred children treated, eleven died, while others suffered serious meningitis-related symptoms, such as deafness, lameness, blindness, seizures, and disorientation.[97] Patients deteriorating on Trovan were not taken off it and given another antibiotic. "This is a mistake," said Marc Gastellu-Etchegorry of MSF. "When the patient is declining step-by-step, you try to give them a fighting chance. It can look like a murder if you don't."[98] The mortality rate in its clinic, a Pfizer doctor claimed, was as low as, or lower than, at the MSF clinic. Regardless, that claim fails to respond to the ethical question of giving children an untested drug and the choices made about how to treat individuals who were on it. The Pfizer attitude resembles that of Sandy Woodrow: "We're not killing people who wouldn't otherwise die. I mean, Christ, look at the death rate in this place. Not that anybody's counting."[99] Indeed, as concerns Trovan, nobody counted until sixteen months after the U.S. Food and Drug Administration had approved it and 140 cases of liver problems were reported, including at least 6 deaths. Lawsuits are pending.

No allegations are made that those speaking out against Trovan have been threatened. However, le Carré's Dr Lara Emrich, one of the discoverers of the molecule for Dypraxa and Justin's destination in Saskatchewan, bears striking similarities to Dr Nancy Olivieri, who blew the whistle in 1993 against the drug deferiprone while at Toronto's Hospital for Sick Children. Emrich is under contract to conduct research for KVH, but is bound by a confidentiality clause against revealing anything negative she might turn up. Dr Olivieri, too, was restricted by such a clause, but violated it to publicize the negative side effects of the drug in the *New England Journal of Medicine*. Like Emrich, Olivieri was the recipient of threatening notes.[100] Given such real-life parallels, it seems ill-advised to underestimate *The Constant Gardener*.

There is a rich cast of finely sketched characters here: diplomats and their families, frustrated Scotland Yarders burdened with investigating a murder beyond their jurisdiction, corporate types, and rough-and-ready aid workers. Each has his or her own objectives. Nameless and faceless on the periphery are the teeming masses of Africans, powerless and impoverished, sick and neglected. If they get food, it is only after a horde of corrupt agents has extracted a cut. If they get medicine, it is only because of the promise for profits elsewhere. When they die, it goes unnoticed. What the majority of le Carré's characters share is regret.

Justin, of course, regrets all. Woodrow has a marriage that leaves him anxious for alternatives that do not exist. In a letter he ought never have sent, he proclaims his undying love for Tessa and would surely regret treating her cause in so cowardly a fashion. Markus Lorbeer, who has been instrumental in marketing Dypraxa to ThreeBees, regrets how his actions amount to a sin against God and condemns himself to an aid outpost in southern Sudan as penance. Rob and Lesley of the Yard regret being stone-walled and subsequently removed from the investigation into Tessa's murder, their careers in shambles for failing to compre-hend that they were never meant to solve the case. For the aged and ill British intelligence man in Nairobi, Tim Donahue, the "only regret, looking back, was that he had spent so little of his life on kids' football, and so much of it on spies."[101] Only when it is already too late, do most of us recognize how skewed our priorities somehow become when we are not looking. Only Tessa and Arnold could be – or deserved to be – free of regret. They saw a wrong and worked relentlessly to redress it, to the ultimate price. In so doing, they assumed a responsibility we would be mistaken to presume some government to take on. Governments have already abdicated, leaving us to fend for ourselves with whatever conscience and courage we can muster. This, I think le Carré might agree, is what has happened to capitalism in the absence of an opponent.

Conclusion

Myths, like rumours, originate from some basic parable of truth. From that point of origin, however, they assume a life of their own, undermining reality, sometimes usurping it altogether. So it is in intelligence, where myth is inseparable from whatever truth seeps up from the clutches of secrecy. No matter what we are told about espionage – or, in my case, what I experienced of it – it is impossible to silence those dissonant voices that insist there is something more. Are these the voices of reason or of myth? Hard to tell. They sound so much alike.

Looking back over the six years since I left the Service, I still try to discern some tangible accomplishment out of what I did that contributed to protecting Canada's security, and regrettably I come up empty. The most it would be honest to say is that I helped to monitor several situations. Nothing remotely cata-strophic happened on my watch, but neither did I personally collect any particular piece of intelligence that saved the day. Perhaps none of the sources I handled were in a position to provide day-saving intelligence. Is it possible the day was never in as much danger as I had hoped? Yes, indeed, hoped: an intel-ligence officer is only ever as valuable as the threat is imminent.

One hopes that all the manipulation, deceit, and false seduction is carried out in the cause of something – dare I say – noble. I don't think there has ever been an intelligence officer who didn't sign on with the expectation of making a difference, however ill-defined that cliché might be. Much though we might like to believe or expect otherwise, few of us really change things; mostly, we become the way things are. I remember my first mentor in the Service, with whom I worked closely for a year and became good friends. When I was transferred over to another unit, he began waxing nostalgic in the realization that we were destined not to see as much of each other in the future: "I remember how you came in here your first day, all high in the saddle of a white charger, shield polished, lance held out straight and firm," he chuckled. "I thought, 'Another asshole gonna fix all the wrongs with the world.' Then I got to know you, watched that charger slow down, your shield get dented, and the lance bend. And I saw how you were just like the rest of us."

I've always suspected that I had reminded him of how he had been in his early days, and he expected I would end up much like him as well. He was one of those volunteer-for-anything types. Every organization has them. It's not all altruism; it's every bit as much a personal need for involvement. You want to be in the middle of everything, afraid that the one thing you miss will be *the* most exciting thing. But time after time after time, the big thing becomes the next thing or maybe the thing after that. Soon you stop pushing for the sheer futility of it.

Notwithstanding my frustrations and disappointments, I feel privileged to have been able to explore le Carré's landscape first-hand. What I found was different but easily recognizable, in the way that reality always deviates from representation – more banal and less tortured, I would say; less successful, too, in many respects. The big cases during my tenure were fewer and farther between, and often they were never truly big except in the minds of those with a stake in perpetuating them. The production-line processing of paper, robotically moving reports and forms from in-tray to out to the next in up the line was priority one. It was all about bureaucracy's manic craving for volume: more paper, more files, more personnel. It's like an all-you-can-eat buffet: a hundred choices, each as tasteless as the next. Only once the frenzy of shovelling down all you can devour has diminished, do you realize how dissatisfying the experience was.

An interview with a potential source could be put off, but be tardy in submitting the monthly log on which were recorded how many hours per day had been devoted to which designated targets, and the keepers of the gates of hell would descend in all their wrath. Bureaucratic absurdity is the defining feature of the civil service, the kind of absurdity that Greene lampoons in *Our Man in Havana* and le Carré takes up in *The Tailor of Panama*. But as they both demonstrate, the absurdity can often overshadow, but never quite obliterate, the potentially serious consequences of secret men doing things in secrecy.

One question keeps coming back to me: could we do better? It is a question with which to judge the past and one which ought to guide us as we look forward. Certainly, in order to do better, we must think differently. We must step outside the confines of routine and take a broader view. Unfortunately, you do something the same way for so long, nobody bothers to ask why, or how it might be done differently.

Le Carré has argued, "It's very dangerous to approach the peace with the same people who've been fighting the cold war. In fact, the cold war happened because we moved from the hot war to the cold war with the same team on both sides. The manners of open hostility became the manners of covert hostility."[1] It was, in large part, from the heroics of open hostility that we purloined our myths and brought them down into the caverns of secrecy with us. There they fermented like fine wine, becoming the object of romance and fantasy. Our world was like the dark forest of primordial fear: anything could be imagined. And anyone who has braved the dark will always be looked upon with – what? Admiration? Respect? Gratitude?

The myths of espionage are too entrenched in our culture to be debunked. Le Carré may have tried, but I am sure he inspired more of us than he disillusioned. He showed those of us who were so inclined a place where we could hide, a place where we could pretend to be some kind of hero, where we could play act our importance. It was quite an awakening to come out of that forest and just be me, and to have to relearn how to be that person without cover or sanctuary. To suffer reality devoid of myth is where the potential for true heroism resides – to live the life of a merely decent human being.

Epilogue

I'm sitting in my office one day in August 1999, four years and a month after quitting CSIS, clicking away on my keyboard, working on this very book. It's a little after 9:00 a.m. The telephone rings, something of a rarity. A writer lives in an infrequently disturbed cocoon. I don't attend meetings or consult with anyone on a regular basis about what I intend to do. Particularly when I'm engrossed in a lengthy book project, particularly as deadlines storm up in force, the solitude becomes more profound and welcome. So a telephone call is a jarring, disruptive intrusion.

"Hello." I give no sign of irritation. You never know when it might be an assignment from that editor who's been refusing to take your calls for months.

"Hi. What's up?" It takes me a minute to adjust to the deadpan voice of my friend Phil. He was an early partner when I began at Quebec Region and one of the few of my former colleagues with whom I keep in touch.

"Not much. You?" Almost unconsciously, I slip into a cadence matching his.

"Nothing." Pause. "I thought maybe we could get together for a drink."

"Sure."

"How about tonight?"

"Nope. No good." Softball night. Sacrosanct. "I'm busy tomorrow also. Any night's good next week."

"Um, well, I was hoping to see you this week." Pause. "It's sort of official business."

I'm surprised, unable to think up any official reason why he might want to see me – maybe a dormant source I'd run was returning to life, and they needed a familiar face to make contact. But surely they could do better than to call on an ex-member.

"Official, how?"

"Well, you know, it's one of those things that we say we'd prefer not to discuss over the phone."

Oh, yes, I know the drill well. And what I'd forgotten quickly comes back.

"If it's official, I can see you this afternoon."

"Great," he replies.

"How's 3:30," I suggest.

"Perfect. That way I can leave the office early and get an overnight car." Ever the pragmatist.

And I get a free beer if it's official, I think.

There's a popular legend about spies – once in, never out – the premise being that, unless 1os depart in utter disgrace, they never *really* leave the secret service. Ready, trained, and indoctrinated, they remain forever a valuable resource, available at the beck and call of their masters to use whatever position they've moved on to as cover for their country's needs. Smiley, with his successive retirements and returns, and Westerby, Leiser, and Pine have all helped to nurture this completely erroneous conception. Truth is: once out, out. Leaving with equal parts regret and bitterness, I knew my departure was irrevocable, mutually so. I wouldn't forgive being put in the position of choosing an arbitrary transfer or abandoning my career, and they, I was sure, wouldn't seek a relationship with someone who had proven his independence and had written some less-than-flattering commentaries.

We meet at the appointed time and place, an ill-lit, friendly, out-of-the-way neighbourhood bar we both know. A little small talk. A bit of catching up because we haven't spoken in at least a month.

"So, I understand now the effect I had when I'd call people out of the blue and tell them csis wanted to see them on official business," I say, leading the conversation to the point. "All day, my stomach's been in knots. I've been sweating, my hands shaking. What did I do?"

"Oh, nothing, it's nothing like that," he replies, smiling.

"I can see it now," I laugh and quote the report I envision him writing the following morning: "Subject tried to give impression of being at ease by making self-deprecating comments about how nervous approach from this Service made him."

"It's tough dealing with a guy who knows the system," Phil laughs, quickly adding, "No, no, I'm not writing a report about this. I just wanted to sound out your reaction to an idea we've been kicking around. If you're not interested, there's no point in going to the trouble of writing anything up. If you are, then we'll put it on paper and get the necessary approval." He's lying, I think – maybe not. I don't know. The consummation of any meeting was the report, if only as evidence of having done something that, with a little creativity, could be made to seem productive.

"It occurred to us that you, as a genuine writer, can go places we can't, unless we go through the procedures for getting approval, and you know how long that takes," he begins.

"Man, this is sounding vaguely illegal." Sometimes even I can't curb the bureaucrat in me.

"No, not if it's done properly. All I'm suggesting is that you, being conscious of our interests and mandate, able to move about freely interviewing and meeting people you might intend to write about, and being open about your past affiliation with csis, might be in a position to make some contacts of interest to us. And if we learn of someone who might be open to an approach, you could be someone they'd see as a useful, unofficial conduit to us."

I'll admit here what I wouldn't admit to Phil then – I was intrigued. I got a definite jolt in the operational part of me that had gone dead when I left all that behind. No matter how thoroughly my illusions about espionage had been perforated by the ugly tentacles of reality, the thought of being back dealing at the table was enticing. But I quickly force that aside and remember why I'd left it behind – how I'd been full-time operational until some grey suit in a grey office was inspired to cast me as an HQ researcher, a part I was never inclined to play. I think about the last words from my DG before I walked out of his office, my letter of resignation on his desk: "I expect you'll regret this."

Yes, I have regrets, but not of the sort he anticipated. Now here is the Service calling on me. Maybe they had cause to regret my departure more than I did. No, on second thought, I doubt that. Somebody was filling my slot, and that's all that ever really counted.

"I can't," I say with a heavier heart than I hope I let on. There's no reason to. Becoming a freelance soul has instilled a certain wariness at the call to service; finding meaning outside the system fosters reluctance to re-enter it.

To his credit, Phil didn't try to talk me into it. I walked away feeling petty. I felt too good turning him down, too vindictive. After a day's reflection, however, I knew there was no other response. I had a new career and new interests. Living in the open again, I would quickly suffocate back in the covert world. I don't want to learn secrets, and I don't want to keep them. I don't want to be false with anyone – not for any reason.

Only then did it hit me that csis had inadvertently given me the conclusion for this book, not to mention – finally – a definitive end to those lingering disappointments of my career.

I was out.

Notes

PREFACE

1 Le Carré, *The Russia House*, 58.
2 Quoted in Barber, "John le Carré," 9.
3 Quoted in Kaplan, "The Author Who Came in from the Cold."
4 Le Carré, *A Perfect Spy*, 250.
5 Le Carré, "The Unbearable Peace," 44.

CHAPTER ONE

1 Quoted in Hodgson, "The Secret Life of John le Carré."
2 Graham Greene, "Kim Philby," in Philby, *My Silent War*, 1.
3 Forster, *Two Cheers for Democracy*, 78.
4 Le Carré, "Spying ... the Passion of My Time," 270.
5 Quoted in Collins, "The Secret Worlds of John le Carré."
6 Quoted in Sanoff, "The Thawing of the Old Spymaster," 59.
7 Le Carré, *Single & Single*, 46.
8 Wolf with McElvoy, *Man without a Face*, 174.
9 Le Carré, *Call for the Dead*, 138.
10 Le Carré, *The Secret Pilgrim*, 321.
11 Le Carré, *The Spy Who Came in from the Cold*, 120–2.
12 Le Carré, *The Honourable Schoolboy*, 457.
13 Wolf with McElvoy, *Man without a Face*, xi.
14 Knightley, *Philby*, 187.
15 Quoted in Isaacson and Kelly, "We Distorted Our Own Minds," 26.
16 Canadian Security Intelligence Service, *Public Report 1992*, 10.
17 Vienneau, "CSIS: More Deskwork than Derring-do."

18 Andrew and Mitrokhin, *The Mitrokhin Archive*, 543.

19 Bindman, "Spy School" B1.

20 Ellroy, *Crime Wave*, 106.

21 Le Carré, *The Secret Pilgrim*, 247.

22 Ibid., 28.

23 Ibid., 9.

24 Le Carré, *Call for the Dead*, 10.

25 Le Carré, *The Secret Pilgrim*, 12.

CHAPTER TWO

1   Fleming, "From Russia, With Love," 65.

2   Pearson, *The Life of Ian Fleming*, 199.

3   Ibid., 266.

4   Fleming, *Casino Royale*, 188.

5   Burgess, "The James Bond Novels: An Introduction," in Fleming, *Casino Royale*, 4–5.

6   Burgess, *You've Had Your Time*, 110.

7   Quoted in Sanoff, "The Thawing of the Old Spymaster," 59.

8   Quoted in Lane, "Of Human Bondage," 150.

9   Fleming, "From Russia, with Love," 113.

10 Lane, "Of Human Bondage," 151.

11 Le Carré, *A Murder of Quality*, 83.

12 Le Carré, *Call for the Dead*, 7.

13 Colby and Forbath, *Honorable Men*, 98.

14 Stafford, *The Silent Game*, 170–1.

15 Fleming, *Casino Royale*, 29.

16 Le Carré, *Call for the Dead*, 11.

17 Granatstein and Stafford, *Spy Wars*, 72.

18 Cave Brown, "C," 158–61.

19 John Pearson denied this link, arguing that "there is little – apart from the initial and the position in the intelligence service – which really corresponds ... and although while at the Admiralty Fleming knew him and had some contact with him he never seems to have been particularly deeply impressed by him." See Pearson, *The Life of Ian Fleming*, 198.

20 Deacon, "C," 252.

21 Ibid., 216.

22 Le Carré, "A Mission into Enemy Territory," preface to Guinness, *My Name Escapes Me*, vii.

23 Ibid., viii.
24 The letter appeared in the *Times* of London, 17 MARCH 1981. Quoted in Deacon, "*C*," 250–51.
25 Quoted in Knightley, "Dinner with the Spymaster."
26 Quoted in Plimpton, "John le Carré," 55.
27 Quoted in Abley, "John le Carré's Trail of Terror," 51.
28 Stafford, *The Silent Game*, 207.
29 See Diemert, *Graham Greene's Thrillers and the 1930s*, 62–3.
30 Quoted in Plimpton, "John le Carré," 56.
31 Le Carré, *Call for the Dead*, 26.
32 Doyle, "*A Study in Scarlet*," 27.
33 Ibid., 33.
34 Le Carré, *Call for the Dead*, 13.
35 Ibid., 45–6.
36 Knightley, *The Second Oldest Profession*, 225.
37 Le Carré , *Call for the Dead*, 12.
38 Knightley, *The Second Oldest Profession*, 243.
39 Starnes, *Closely Guarded*, 158.
40 Ibid., 159.
41 Sevunts, "A Spy in the Office," A2.
42 Le Carré, *Call for the Dead*, 145.
43 Ibid., 156.
44 Ibid., 119.
45 Quoted in Coleman, "Le Carré on Writing," 25.
46 Le Carré , *A Murder of Quality*, 9. Wormwood, with its implication of decay and rot, is something that le Carré associates with the upper classes. In *Call for the Dead* he writes of the residents of suburban Merridale Lane, who "wait patiently for the years to endow these treasures with an appearance of weathered antiquity, until one day even the beams on the garage may boast of beetle and wormwood" (23), suggesting that even the pests of the rich confer status.
47 Ibid., 14.
48 Quoted in Coleman, "Le Carré on Writing," 25.
49 Le Carré, *A Murder of Quality*, 51.
50 Ibid., 15.
51 Quoted in "Bibliophile," 30.
52 Le Carré, *A Murder of Quality*, 35.
53 Ibid., 145.
54 Ibid., 135.

CHAPTER THREE

1 Ash, *In Europe's Name*, 14.
2 Murphy, Kondrashev, and Bailey, *Battleground Berlin*, 146.
3 Ibid., 329.
4 Le Carré, *The Spy Who Came in from the Cold*, 74.
5 Le Carré, *A Perfect Spy*, 441.
6 Ash, *The File*, 84.
7 Ibid., 32.
8 Ibid.
9 Andrew and Mitrokhin, *The Mitrokhin Archive*, 120.
10 Ibid., 124–5.
11 Ibid., 278.
12 Quoted in Coleman, "Le Carré on Writing," 25.
13 Cave Brown, "C," 10.
14 Stafford, *The Silent Game*, 200.
15 Le Carré, "Smiley's People are Alive and Well," 21.
16 Mitrovica, "Spy Probe of China Was Aborted,"
17 Bronskilll, "CSIS Boss Denies Burying Spy Study."
18 Mitrovica and Sallot, "China Set up Crime Web in Canada, Report Says," A1.
19 Mitrovica and Sallot, "Mounties Blamed CSIS for Sanitizing Sidewinder," A1, A6.
20 Le Carré, *The Spy Who Came in from the Cold*, 126.
21 Ibid., 18–19.
22 Ibid., 93.
23 Ibid., 51.
24 Quoted in Plimpton, "John le Carré," 57–8.
25 Le Carré, *The Spy Who Came in from the Cold*, 209.
26 Ibid., 112.
27 Ibid., 156.
28 Ibid., 210.
29 Ibid.,
30 Quoted in Sherry, *The Life of Graham Greene*, 2: 49.
31 Wolf, *Man without a Face*, 102.
32 Le Carré, "Don't be Beastly to Your Secret Service," 41.
33 Le Carré, *The Looking Glass War*, 41.
34 Security Intelligence Review Committee, *Annual Report 1986–87*, 27.
35 Moore, "Spy Agency – RCMP Turf War Threatens Security: Report."

36 Mitrovica and Sallot, "Spy Agent Blasted over Secret Slips."

37 Pearson, KAL 007, 87–8. Oliver Clubb comes up with a similar international list in *KAL Flight 007*, 84–6.

38 Pearson, KAL 007, 97.

39 Ibid., 109.

40 Ibid., 17.

41 Hersh, *"The Target is Destroyed,"* 7.

42 Ibid., 30.

43 Johnson, *Shootdown*, 265–6.

44 Pearson, KAL 007, 48.

45 Le Carré, *The Looking Glass War*, 22.

46 Ibid., 36.

47 Ibid., 106–7.

48 Ibid., 93.

49 Ibid., 54.

50 Carroll, *Alice in Wonderland*, 13.

51 Le Carré, *The Looking Glass War*, 80.

52 Ibid., 199–200.

53 Ibid., 80.

54 Ibid., 77.

55 Ibid., 122.

56 Le Carré, *The Secret Pilgrim*, 154.

57 Le Carré, *The Looking Glass War*, 146.

58 Ibid., 229.

59 Ibid., 131.

60 Ibid., 251.

61 Greene, *The Human Factor*, 117.

62 Epigraph to Knightley *The Second Oldest Profession*.

63 Quoted in Plimpton, "John le Carré," 70.

64 Le Carré, *The Looking Glass War*, 264–5.

65 Ibid., 277–8.

66 Le Carré, *A Small Town in Germany*, 20–1.

67 Ibid., 334.

68 Ibid., 336.

69 Ibid., 66.

70 Ibid., 321.

71 Le Carré, *A Perfect Spy*, 14.

72 Le Carré, *A Small Town in Germany*, 264.

73 Ibid., 53.

74 Ibid., 114.

75 Andrew and Mitrokhin, *The Mitrokhin Archive*, 10.
76 Le Carré, *A Small Town in Germany*, 56.
77 Ibid., 130.
78 Stafford, *The Silent Game*, 202.
79 Le Carré, *A Small Town in Germany*, 301.
80 Ibid., 321.
81 Ibid., 300.
82 Breitman, *Official Secrets*, 213–4.
83 Kennaway and Kennaway, *The Kennaway Papers*, 19.
84 Ibid., 16.
85 Kennaway, *Some Gorgeous Accident*, 3.
86 Le Carré, *The Naïve and Sentimental Lover*, 11.
87 Ibid., 61.
88 Kennaway, *Some Gorgeous Accident*, 58.
89 Le Carré, *The Naïve and Sentimental Lover*, 320.
90 Kennaway and Kennaway, *The Kennaway Papers*, 105.
91 Le Carré, *The Naïve and Sentimental Lover*, 25.
92 Kennaway, *Some Gorgeous Accident*, 7.
93 Le Carré, *The Naïve and Sentimental Lover*, 203.
94 Conrad, "The Secret Sharer," 662.
95 Le Carré, *The Naïve and Sentimental Lover*, 91.
96 Ibid., 176.
97 Ibid., 204.
98 Ibid.
99 Kennaway and Kennaway, *The Kennaway Papers*, 17.
100 Ibid., 18.
101 Le Carré, *The Naïve and Sentimental Lover*, 255.
102 Ibid., 455.
103 Kennaway and Kennaway, *The Kennaway Papers*, 23–4.
104 Kennaway, *Some Gorgeous Accident*, 103.
105 Le Carré, *The Naïve and Sentimental Lover*, 457.
106 Ibid., 462.
107 Kennaway and Kennaway, *The Kennaway Papers*, 120.

CHAPTER FOUR

1 Rosenbaum, "Kim Philby and the Age of Paranoia," 31.
2 Le Carré, *The Secret Pilgrim*, 114.
3 For instance, Yuri Modin, who was the KGB analyst who handled intelligence emanating from the Cambridge ring and also handled

Burgess, Blunt, and Cairncross from the Soviet Embassy in London, wrote, "if one considers that the aim of espionage is to furnish governments and heads of state with information that will assist them in their decisions, then the spy of the century has to be Donald Maclean. He gathered the political, economic and scientific intelligence that guided the strategy of our leaders for over ten years." See Modin, *My Five Cambridge Friends*, 270.

4   Le Carré, "Introduction," in Page, Leitch, and Knightley, Philby 10.
5   Woodward, *Veil*, 43.
6   Knightley, *Philby*, 262.
7   Le Carré, "Introduction," in Page, Leitch, and Knightley, Philby, 15.
8   Le Carré, *A Small Town in Germany*, 149.
9   Trevor-Roper, *The Philby Affair*, 75.
10 Knightley, *Philby*, 118.
11 Quoted in Hoffman, "Infinite Suspicion," 248.
12 Greene, "Kim Philby," *in Philby, My Silent War*, 3.
13 Gordievsky, *Next Stop Execution*, 126.
14 Ibid., 8.
15 Mathews, "In from the Cold," 55.
16 LeCarré, "Introduction," *in Page, Leitch, and Knightley, Philby*, 11.
17 Knightley, *Philby*, 265.
18 Philby, *My Silent War*, 10.
19 Cave Brown, *Treason in the Blood*, 507.
20 Ibid., 506.
21 A full account of his escape is given in Gordievsky, *Next Stop Execution*, 1–24.
22 Cave Brown, "C," 712.
23 Quoted ibid., 712.
24 Ibid., 744.
25 Ibid., 746.
26 Powers, "The Truth About the CIA," 53.
27 Knightley, *Philby*, 265.
28 Cave Brown, *Treason in the Blood*, 605.
29 Sherry, *The Life of Graham Greene*, 494.
30 Ibid., 496.
31 Ibid., 494.
32 Quoted in Cave Brown, *Treason in the Blood*, 504.
33 Greene, *Ways of Escape*, 228.
34 Greene, *The Human Factor*, 121.

35 Ibid., 119.

36 Ibid., 187.

37 Ibid., 110.

38 Malan, *My Traitor's Heart*, 18.

39 Ibid., 73.

40 Greene, *The Human Factor*, 16.

41 Knightley, *Philby*, 80.

42 Greene, *The Human Factor*, 253.

43 Rosenbaum, "Kim Philby and the Age of Paranoia," 54. Knightley's account of Philby's reaction is rather more benign. He writes, "Philby, no doubt looking around his own pleasant apartment, said that the man's flat in Moscow was too drab." See Knightley, *Philby*, 245.

44 Modin, *My Five Cambridge Friends*, 267.

45 Sherry, *The Life of Graham Greene*, 494.

46 Wright, *Spycatcher*.

47 Mangold, *Cold Warrior*, 45–8.

48 Andrew, *For the President's Eyes Only*, 401.

49 Mangold, *Cold Warrior*, 277.

50 Weiner, Johnston, and Lewis, *Betrayal*, 131.

51 Wise, *Nightmover*, 200.

52 Kuzichkin, *Inside the KGB*, 147.

53 Greene, *The Human Factor*, 107.

54 Downie, "The Spies Have It."

55 Le Carré, *Tinker Tailor Soldier Spy*, 354.

56 Rosenbaum, "Kim Philby and the Age of Paranoia," 34.

57 Le Carré, *Tinker Tailor Soldier Spy*, 365.

58 Ibid., 98.

59 Ibid., 188–9.

60 Ibid., 350.

61 Ibid., 362.

62 Ibid., 365.

63 Ibid., 153.

64 Ibid., 305–6.

65 Hoffman, "Le Carré Weaves through Greeneland," 509.

66 Le Carré, *Tinker Tailor Soldier Spy*, 338.

67 Ibid., 343.

68 Fleming, *Casino Royale*, 147.

69 Le Carré, *Tinker Tailor Soldier Spy*, 208.

70 Ibid., 210.

71 Najman, "Stasi 'Spy with a Heart' Wants to Meet le Carré."

72 Le Carré, "The Lawnmower That Came in from the Cold."
73 Quoted in Gedye, "Le Carré Got Me Wrong."
74 Le Carré, "The Lawnmower That Came in from the Cold."
75 Le Carré, *The Honourable Schoolboy,* 63–4.
76 Ibid., 71.
77 Ibid., 181.
78 Ibid., 175.
79 Interview on *Pamela Wallin & Company,* CBC Newsworld, 11 JUNE 1999.
80 Le Carré, *The Honourable Schoolboy,* 457.
81 Ibid., 470–1.
82 Ibid., 116.
83 Ibid., 334.
84 Le Carré, *Tinker Tailor Soldier Spy,* 216.
85 Le Carré, *Smiley's People,* 284.
86 Ibid., 371.
87 Ibid., 205–6.
88 Ibid., 371.
89 Ibid., 21.
90 Ibid., 68.
91 Ibid., 275.
92 Ibid., 321.
93 Ibid., 351.
94 Ibid., 374.
95 Bell, "Groups Act as Fronts for Terror: CSIS," A13.
96 Sengupta, "Canadian Cash Fuelling Revolt in Sri Lanka?"
97 Bell, "Canadian Cash Flow Confirmed as Tigers Kill 21," A1.
98 Ondaatje, *Anil's Ghost,* 54.
99 Le Carré, *The Honourable Schoolboy,* 75.
100 Le Carré, *Smiley's People,* 44.

CHAPTER FIVE

1 Quoted in Bragg, "A Talk with John le Carré," 22.
2 Quoted in Isaacson and Kelly, "We Distorted Our Own Minds," 26.
3 Le Carré, "Dark Side of the Star."
4 See "West Bank Uneasy over le Carré Filming," 17.
5 Le Carré, *The Little Drummer Girl,* 223.
6 Ibid., 107.
7 Osnos, "Le Carré's Drumbeat."
8 Raviv and Melman, *Every Spy a Prince,* 2.

9 Ibid., 284.

10 Quoted in Plimpton, "John le Carré," 64–5.

11 O'Connor, "Le Carré on Channel 13 Discusses Himself and His Writing."

12 Le Carré, *The Little Drummer Girl*, 104.

13 Ibid., 105.

14 Le Carré, "Dark Side of the Star," 5

15 Le Carré, The Little Drummer Girl,. 128–129.

16 Le Carré, "Dark Side of the Star," 5.

17 Le Carré, *The Little Drummer Girl*, 142.

18 Ibid., 108.

19 Among others, see Ben-Zohar and Haber, *The Quest for the Red Prince*, 135–7. There were a few examples of earlier hits against specific terrorist targets, but 1972 marked the watershed for the policy. See Black and Morris, *Israel's Secret Wars*, 272–3.

20 Several books have been written about the post-Munich retributive operation, including Tinnin and Christensen, *The Hit Team*; Ben-Zohar and Haber, *The Quest for the Red Prince*; and Jonas, *Vengeance*.

21 Abley, "John le Carré's Trail of Terror," 48.

22 Black and Morris, *Israel's Secret Wars*, 419.

23 Le Carré, *The Little Drummer Girl*, 39–40.

24 Ibid., 327.

25 Ibid., 400.

26 Ibid., 219.

27 Le Carré, *A Perfect Spy*, 273.

28 Ibid., 276.

29 Le Carré, *Single & Single*, 308.

30 Le Carré, *A Perfect Spy*, 22.

31 Quoted in Collins, "The Secret Worlds of John le Carré."

32 Le Carré, *A Perfect Spy*, 205.

33 Quoted in Lelyveld, "Le Carré's Toughest Case," 40.

34 Le Carré, "Spying on My Father."

35 Quoted in Plimpton, "John le Carré," 65–6.

36 Quoted in Lelyveld, "Le Carré's Toughest Case," 40.

37 Le Carré, "Spying on My Father," 34.

38 Le Carré, *A Perfect Spy*, 416.

39 Quoted in Collins, "The Secret Worlds of John le Carré."

40 Quoted in Caudwell, "The Curtains Part on Murder Most British," 1.

41 Le Carré, *A Perfect Spy*, 310.

42 Le Carré, "Spying on My Father," 34.

43 Le Carré, *A Perfect Spy*, 206.

44 Ibid., 225.

45 Quoted in Heller, "Behind an Iron Curtain."

46 Quoted in Franks, "Tinker, Tailor, Writer, Spy."

47 Le Carré, *A Perfect Spy*, 271.

48 Ibid., 367.

49 Ibid., 370.

50 Ibid., 356.

51 Ibid., 162.

52 Ibid., 408.

53 Ibid., 22.

54 Ibid., 159.

55 Le Carré, "The Unbearable Peace," 14.

56 Cairncross, *The Enigma Spy*, 8.

57 Le Carré, "The Unbearable Peace," 28.

58 Ibid., 45.

59 Ibid., 48.

60 Ibid., 56–8.

61 Ibid., 71.

62 Richelson, *A Century of Spies*, 343.

CHAPTER SIX

1 Le Carré, *The Russia House*, 286.

2 Le Carré, *The Tailor of Panama*, 170.

3 Ibid., 239.

4 Le Carré, *The Russia House*, 255.

5 Andrew and Gordievsky, *KGB*, 389–90.

6 Le Carré called Penkovsky "the most important spy in history" in "Wardrobe of Disguises,"31.

7 Wynne wrote of his role in the Penkovsky affair in *The Man from Moscow*.

8 Andrew, *For the President's Eyes Only*, 270.

9 Knightley, *The Second Oldest Profession*, 316.

10 Ibid., 325.

11 Le Carré, *Smiley's People*, 281.

12 Smith, *The Russians*, 402–404.

13 Shevchenko, *Breaking with Moscow*, v-vi.

14 Le Carré, *The Russia House*, 188.

15 Quoted in Whitney, "Russians Warm to le Carré," C13.

16 Mathews, "In from the Cold," 56.

17 Sakharov, *Memoirs*, 282. The article referred to appeared in the *New York Times* on 22 July 1968.

18 Smith, *The Russians*, 417.

19 Quoted in Remnick, *Lenin's Tomb*, 18.

20 Gordievsky, *Next Stop Execution*, 172.

21 Sakharov, *Memoirs*, 289–90.

22 Le Carré, *The Russia House*, 167.

23 Ibid., 87. Le Carré paraphrased the epigraph he took from May Sarton: "One must think like a hero to behave like a merely decent human being."

24 Ibid., 18.

25 Bush and Scowcroft, *A World Transformed*, 42.

26 Quoted in Beschloss and Talbott, *At the Highest Levels*, 106.

27 Le Carré, *The Russia House*, 245–246.

28 Bush and Scowcroft, *A World Transformed*, 230.

29 Le Carré, *The Russia House*, 296.

30 Ibid., 352.

31 Ibid., 302.

32 Ibid., 100.

33 Ibid., 286.

34 Quoted in Polmar and Allen, *The Encyclopedia of Espionage*, 541.

35 Le Carré, *The Russia House*, 341.

36 Kuzichkin, *Inside the* KGB, 106.

37 Bush and Scowcroft, *A World Transformed*, 13.

38 Ibid., 299.

39 Le Carré, *The Russia House*, 99.

40 Andrew, *For the President's Eyes Only*, 506.

41 Beschloss and Talbott, *At the Highest Levels*, 424.

42 Havel, *The Art of the Possible*, 90.

43 Quoted in Sanoff, "The Thawing of the Old Spymaster," 61.

44 Kuzichkin, *Inside the* KGB, 107.

45 Andrew and Mitrokhin, *The Mitrokhin Archive*, 730.

46 Quoted in Remnick, *Lenin's Tomb*, 199.

47 Shevchenko, *Breaking with Moscow*, v.

48 Quoted in Remnick, *Lenin's Tomb*, 146–7.

49 Ibid., 149.

50 Ibid., 45.

51 Andrew and Mitrokhin, *The Mitrokhin Archive*, 51.
52 Le Carré, "Why I Came in from the Cold."
53 Ibid., C3.
54 Le Carré, *The Secret Pilgrim*, 66.
55 Ibid., 297.
56 Ibid., 301.
57 Ibid., 309.
58 Ibid., 314.
59 Ibid., 317.
60 Ibid., 168.
61 Quoted in Streitfeld, "Debriefing John le Carré."
62 Le Carré, *The Secret Pilgrim*, 122.
63 Ibid., 146.
64 Andrew and Mitrokhin, *The Mitrokhin Archive*, 466–7.
65 Le Carré, *The Secret Pilgrim*, 92.
66 Ibid., 91.
67 Ibid., 109.
68 Ibid., 178.
69 Conrad, *Heart of Darkness*, 9.
70 Ibid., 92.
71 Le Carré, *The Secret Pilgrim*, 245.
72 Conrad, *Heart of Darkness*, 95–6.

CHAPTER SEVEN

1 Le Carré, *The Secret Pilgrim*, 264.
2 Ibid., 334.
3 Le Carré, "Why I Came in from the Cold."
4 Quoted in Isaacson and Kelly, "We Distorted Our Own Minds," 26.
5 Le Carré, "Spying … the Passion of My Time," 269.
6 Ibid., 272.
7 Le Carré, "Smiley's People Are Alive and Well," 21.
8 Le Carré, *The Night Manager*, 55.
9 Le Carré, *A Small Town in Germany*, 301.
10 Le Carré, *The Night Manager*, 7.
11 Ibid., 237.
12 Ibid., 17.
13 Ibid., 78.
14 Ibid., 15–6.
15 Ibid., 210.

16 Ibid.

17 Ibid., 60.

18 Ibid., 359.

19 Le Carré, *Our Game*, 179.

20 Ibid., 183.

21 Le Carré, "My New Friends in the New Russia," 33.

22 Quoted in Quinn-Judge, "Back to the Inferno," 22.

23 Ibid., 24.

24 Quoted in McGeary, "The Spy Who Came in from the Crowd," 40.

25 Le Carré, "Demons Dance as the West Watches."

26 Le Carré, *Our Game*, 19.

27 Ibid., 32.

28 Ibid., 283.

29 Gall and de Waal, *Chechnya*, 75.

30 Le Carré, *Our Game*, 53.

31 Ibid., 33.

32 Le Carré, "Don't Be Beastly to Your Secret Service," 42.

33 Le Carré, *Our Game*, 134.

34 Greene, *Our Man in Havana*, 5.

35 Le Carré, *The Tailor of Panama*, 100.

36 Dinges, *Our Man in Panama*, 61.

37 Greene, *Getting to Know the General*, 123.

38 Kempe, *Divorcing the Dictator*, 281.

39 See Dinges, *Our Man in Panama*, 233; and Woodward, *Veil*, 256.

40 Quoted in Plimpton, "John le Carré," 61–2.

41 Le Carré, *The Tailor of Panama*, 165.

42 Ibid., 52.

43 Kempe, *Divorcing the Dictator*, 29–30.

44 Greene, *Our Man in Havana*, 63.

45 Ibid., 180.

46 Quoted in Benjamin and Jackson, "Tales of a Master Spy from the Other Side."

47 Le Carré, "Don't be Beastly to Your Secret Service," 41.

48 Le Carré, *The Tailor of Panama*, 59.

49 Ibid., 258.

50 Ibid., 261.

51 Ibid., 298.

52 Le Carré, *Our Game*, 12.

53 Le Carré, *The Tailor of Panama*, 156.

54 Le Carré, *Single & Single*, 230.

55 Le Carré, *The Secret Pilgrim*, 265.
56 Handelman, *Comrade Criminal*, 147.
57 Le Carré, *Single & Single*, 114.
58 Handelman, *Comrade Criminal*, 147.
59 Le Carré, *Single & Single*, 75.
60 Smith, *The New Russians*, 266.
61 Remnick, *Lenin's Tomb*, 183.
62 Yevtushenko, *Don't Die Before You're Dead*, 106.
63 Quoted in Handelman, *Comrade Criminal*, 285–6.
64 Le Carré, *Single & Single*, 113.
65 Ibid., 119.
66 Le Carré, "Spying on My Father," 34.
67 Le Carré, *Single & Single*, 74.
68 Ibid., 91.
69 Ibid., 96.
70 Ibid., 321.
71 Ibid., 95.
72 Quoted in Ash, "The Real le Carré," 39.
73 Le Carré, *Single & Single*, 165.
74 Ibid., 95.
75 Ibid., 259.
76 Le Carré, "Demons Dance as the West Watches."
77 Quoted in Kanfer, "When Spies Become Allies," 50.
78 Le Carré, *Single & Single*, 81.
79 Ibid., 337.
80 Ibid., 11.
81 Le Carré, "My New Friends in the New Russia," 32.
82 Gussow, "In a Plot from the Cold, le Carré Sums up the Past."
83 Le Carré, *The Constant Gardener*, 182.
84 Treneman, "Out of the Shadows."
85 *The Constant Gardener*, 506.
86 Ibid., 31.
87 Le Carré, "The Constant Muse," 74.
88 *The Constant Gardener*, 370.
89 Ibid., 370.
90 Ibid., 148.
91 Ibid., 235.
92 Nash, "The Antibiotics Crisis," 60.
93 Lemonick, "Brave New Pharmacy," 37.
94 *The Constant Gardener*, 445.

95 Ibid., 204.

96 Ibid., 317.

97 Stephens, "Did Patient 6587-0069 Have to Die?"

98 Quoted ibid., B4.

99 Le Carré, *The Constant Gardener*, 444.

100 Roberts, "Le Carré's Olivieri Lookalike."

101 Le Carré, *The Constant Gardener*, 412.

CONCLUSION

1 Quoted in Sanoff, "The Thawing of the Old Spymaster," 59.

Bibliography

Abley, Mark. "John le Carré's Trail of Terror." *Maclean's*, 7 March 1983, 47–52.

Andrew, Christopher. *For the President's Eyes Only: Secret Intelligence and the American Presidency from Washington to Bush*. New York: Harper-Collins 1995.

– and Oleg Gordievsky. KGB: *The Inside Story of Its Foreign Operations from Lenin to Gorbachev*. London: Hodder and Stoughton 1990.

– and Vasili Mitrokhin. *The Mitrokhin Archive: The* KGB *in Europe and the West*. London: Allen Lane/*Penguin* Press 1999.

Ash, Timothy Garton. *The File*. New York: Random House 1997.

– *In Europe's Name: Germany and the Divided Continent*. London: Jonathan Cape 1993.

– "The Real le Carré." *New Yorker*, 15 March 1999, 36–45.

Barber, Michael. "John le Carré: An Interrogation." *New York Times*, 25 September 1977, 9, 44–5.

Bell, Stewart. "Canadian Cash Flow Confirmed as Tigers Kill 21." *National Post* (Toronto), 8 June 2000, A1, A12.

– "Canadian Funds Back Terror: Elcock." *National Post* (Toronto), 2 June 2000, A1, A10.

– "Groups Act as Fronts for Terror: CSIS." *National Post* (Toronto), 9 December 2000, A1, A13.

Benjamin, Daniel, and James O. Jackson. "Tales of a Master Spy from the Other Side." *Time*, 25 November 1991, 26.

Ben-Zohar, Michael, and Eitan Haber. *The Quest for the Red Prince*. New York: William Morrow 1983.

Beschloss, Michael R., and Strobe Talbott. *At the Highest Levels: The Inside Story of the End of the Cold War*. Boston: Little Brown 1993.

"Bibliophile." *New Yorker*, 24 May 1993, 30.

Bindman, Stephen. "Spy School: A New Breed Emerges in Intelligence Service." *Ottawa Citizen*, 13 August 1988, B1.

Black, Ian, and Benny Morris. *Israel's Secret Wars: The Untold Story of Israeli Intelligence*. London: Hamish Hamilton 1991.

Bragg, Melvyn. "A Talk with John le Carré." *New York Times Book Review*, 13 March 1983, 1, 22.

Breitman, Richard. *Official Secrets: What the Nazis Planned, What the British and Americans Knew*. New York: Hill & Wang 1998.

Bronskill, Jim. "CSIS Boss Denies Burying Spy Study." *Gazette* (Montreal), 25 April 2000, A11.

Burgess, Anthony. *You've Had Your Time*. London: Heinemann 1990.

Bush, George and Brent Skowcroft. *A World Transformed*. New York: Alfred A. Knopf 1998.

Cairncross, John. *The Enigma Spy*. London: Century 1997.

Canadian Security Intelligence Service. *Public Report 1992*. Ottawa: Minister of Supply and Services 1993.

Carroll, Lewis. *Alice in Wonderland*. Edited by Donald J. Gray. New York: W.W. Norton 1971.

Caudwell, Sarah. "The Curtains Part on Murder Most British." *New York Times*, 9 October 1988, Section 2, 1, 36.

Cave Brown, Anthony. *"C": The Secret Life of Sir Stewart Menzies, Spymaster to Winston Churchill*. New York: Macmillan 1987.

– *Treason in the Blood: H. St. John Philby, Kim Philby, and the Spy Case of the Century*. Boston: Houghton Mifflin 1994.

Clubb, Oliver. *KAL Flight 007: The Hidden Story*. Sag Harbor, NY: The Permanent Press 1985.

Colby, William and Peter Forbath. *Honorable Men: My Life in the CIA*. New York: Simon & Schuster 1978.

Coleman, Terry. "Le Carré on Writing." *Guardian* (London),17 July 1993.

Collins, Dan. "The Secret Worlds of John le Carré." *Los Angeles Times*, 12 November 1996 E1.

Conrad, Joseph. *Heart of Darkness*. Harmondsworth: Penguin Books, 1902.

– "The Secret Sharer" (1912). In *The Portable Conrad*, ed. by Morton Dauwen Zabel. Penguin Books 1975.

Deacon, Richard. *"C": A Biography of Sir Maurice Oldfield*. London and Sydney: Macdonald 1984.

Diemert, Brian. *Graham Greene's Thrillers and the 1930s*. Montreal and Kingston: McGill-Queen's University Press 1996.

Dinges, John. *Our Man in Panama: How General Noriega Used the U.S. – and Made Millions in Drugs and Arms*. New York: Random House 1990.

Downie, Leonard, Jr. "The Spies Have It." *Washington Post*, 29 September 1980, vol. D1.

Doyle, Sir Arthur Conan. "A Study in Scarlet" (1888). In *The Complete Sherlock Holmes*, vol. I. Garden City, NY: Doubleday (n.d.).

Ellroy, James. *Crime Wave*. New York: Vintage Crime 1999.

Fleming, Ian. *Casino Royale*. London: Coronet Books 1953.

– "From Russia, with Love" (1957). In *James Bond 007: Five Complete Novels*. New York: Avenel Books 1988.

Forster, E.M. *Two Cheers for Democracy*, London: Edward Arnold, 1951.

Franks, Alan. "Tinker, Tailor, Writer, Spy." *Globe and Mail* (Toronto), 25 March 1999, C1–2.

Gall, Carlotta, and Thomas de Waal. *Chechnya: Calamity in the Caucasus*. New York and London: New York University Press 1998.

Gedye, Robin. "Le Carré Got Me Wrong." *Daily Telegraph* (London), 5 May 1993, 10.

Gordievsky, Oleg. *Next Stop Execution*. London: Macmillan 1995.

Granatstein, J.L., and David Stafford. *Spy Wars: Espionage and Canada from Gouzenko to Glasnost*. Toronto: Key Porter Books 1990.

Greene, Graham. *Getting to Know the General: The Story of an Involvement*. Toronto: Lester & Orpen Dennys 1984.

– *The Heart of the Matter*. Harmondsworth: Penguin Books 1948.

– *The Human Factor*. Harmondsworth: Penguin Books 1978.

– *Our Man in Havana*. New York: Viking Press 1958.

– *Ways of Escape*. Harmondsworth: Penguin Books 1980.

Guinness, Alec. *My Name Escapes Me*. London: Hamish Hamilton 1996.

Gussow, Mel. "In a Plot Far from the Cold, le Carré Sums up the Past." *New York Times*, 19 December 2000, B1, B9.

Handelman, Stephen. *Comrade Criminal: The Theft of the Second Russian Revolution*. London: Michael Joseph 1994.

Havel, Václav. *The Art of the Possible: Politics as Morality in Practice, Speeches and Writings 1990–1996*. Translated by Paul Wilson. New York: Alfred A. Knopf 1997.

Heller, Zoe. "Behind an Iron Curtain." *Independent* (London), 1 August 1993, 2.

Hersh, Seymour M. *"The Target Is Destroyed": What Really Happened to Flight 007 and What America Knew About It*. New York: Random House 1986.

Hodgson, Godfrey. "The Secret Life of John le Carré." *Washington Post,*
    9 October 1977, E1.
Hoffman, Tod. "History as Conspiracy." *Queen's Quarterly* 105 (fall 1998)
    392–404.
– "Infinite Suspicion: The File on Herbert Norman." *Queen's Quarterly*
    106 (summer 1999) 247–57.
– "The Informants." *Queen's Quarterly* 105 (winter 1998) 529–40.
– "The KGB: Ballet or Farce?" *Globe and Mail* (Toronto), 9 October 1999, D16.
– "Le Carré's Latest Gospel of Betrayal." *Ottawa Citizen,* 28 February
    1999, C1, C12.
– "Le Carré Weaves through Greeneland." *Queen's Quarterly* 104 (fall
    1997) 499–509.
– "The Mystery of Aldrich Ames." *Queen's Quarterly* 103 (summer 1996)
    385–96.
– "Treasons and Loyalties." *Queen's Quarterly* 104 (spring 1997) 31–45.
Hoy, Claire, and Victor Ostrovsky. *By Way of Deception.* Toronto: General
    Paperbacks 1991.
Isaacson, Walter, and James Kelly. "We Distorted Our Own Minds." *Time,*
    5 July 1993, 26–7.
Johnson, R.W. *Shootdown: Flight 007 and the American Connection.* New
    York: Viking 1986.
Jonas, George. *Vengeance: The True Story of an Israeli Counter-Terrorism
    Team.* Toronto: Lester & Orpen Dennys / Collins 1984.
Kanfer, Stefan. "When Spies Become Allies." *Time,* 19 August 1991, 50–1.
Kaplan, Fred. "The Author Who Came in from the Cold." *Boston Globe,*
    5 November 1996, C1.
Kempe, Frederick. *Divorcing the Dictator: America's Bungled Affair with
    Noriega.* New York: G.P. Putnam's Sons 1990.
Kennaway, James. *Some Gorgeous Accident.* Edinburgh: Mainstream Pub-
    lishing 1967.
– and Susan Kennaway. *The Kennaway Papers.* New York: Holt, Rinehart
    and Winston 1981.
Knightley, Phillip. "Dinner with the Spymaster." *Sunday Times* (London),
    15 March 1981, 13.
– *Philby: KGB Masterspy.* London: Andre Deutsch 1988.
– *The Second Oldest Profession: The Spy as Patriot, Bureaucrat, Fantasist and
    Whore.* London: Pan Books 1986.
Kuzichkin, Vladimir. *Inside the KGB: Myth and Reality.* Translated by
    Thomas B. Beattie. London: Andre Deutsch 1990.

Lane, Anthony. "Of Human Bondage." *New Yorker*, 14 June–1 July 1996, 148–53.

le Carré, John. *Call for the Dead*. Harmondsworth: Penguin Books 1961.

– *The Constant Gardener*. Toronto: Penguin Viking, 2001.

– "The Constant Muse." *New Yorker*, 25 December 2000 and 1 January 2001, 66–74.

– "Dark Side of the Star." *Guardian* (London), 15 November 1997, "The Week," 5.

– "Demons Dance as the West Watches." *Observer* (London), 18 December 1994, 21.

– "Don't Be Beastly to Your Secret Service." *Sunday Times* (London), 23 March 1986, 41–42.

– *The Honourable Schoolboy*. London: Pan Books 1977.

– "The Lawnmower That Came in from the Cold." *Guardian* (London), 6 May 1993, 1.

– *The Little Drummer Girl*. London: Hodder and Stoughton 1983.

– *The Looking Glass War*. Harmondsworth: Penguin Books 1965.

– *A Murder of Quality*. Harmondsworth: Penguin Books 1962.

– "My New Friends in the New Russia: In Search of a Few Good Crooks, Cops, and Former Agents." *New York Times Review of Books*, 15 February 1995, 3, 32–3.

– *The Naïve and Sentimental Lover*. Harmondsworth: Penguin Books 1971.

– *The Night Manager*. Toronto: Viking 1993.

– *Our Game*. Toronto: Viking Penguin 1995.

– *A Perfect Spy*. New York: Alfred A. Knopf 1986.

– *The Russia House*. New York: Viking 1989.

– *The Secret Pilgrim*. New York: Viking 1990.

– *Single & Single*. New York: Viking 1999.

– *A Small Town in Germany*. Harmondsworth: Penguin Books 1968.

– *Smiley's People*. New York: Alfred A. Knopf 1980.

– "Smiley's People Are Alive and Well." *Manchester Guardian*, 16 November 1989, 21–2.

– "Spying on My Father." *Sunday Times* (London), 16 March 1986, 33–4.

– "Spying ... the Passion of My Time." *Queen's Quarterly* 100 (summer 1993) 269–72.

– *The Spy Who Came in from the Cold*. Harmondsworth: Penguin Books 1963.

– *The Tailor of Panama*. New York: Viking 1996.

– *Tinker Tailor Solder Spy*. Harmondsworth: Penguin Books 1974

– "The Unbearable Peace." *Granta* 35 (spring 1991): 11–76.

– "Wardrobe of Disguises." *Sunday Times* (London), 10 September 1967, 31.
– "Why I Came in from the Cold." *Sunday Times* (London), 24 September 1989, C3.
Lelyveld, Joseph. "Le Carré's Toughest Case." *New York Times Magazine,* 16 March 1986, 40–6, 79, 90–1.
Lemonick, Michael, D. "Brave New Pharmacy." *Time,* 15 January 2001, 32–43.
McGeary, Johanna. "Death Stalks a Continent." *Time,* 12 February, 2001, 28–37.
– "The Spy Who Came in from the Crowd," *Time,* 3 April 2000, 37–41.
Malan, Rian. *My Traitor's Heart.* New York: Atlantic Monthly Press 1990.
Mangold, Tom. *Cold Warrior: James Jesus Angleton, the* CIA's *Master Spy Hunter.* London: Simon & Schuster 1991.
Mathews, Tom. "In from the Cold." *Newsweek,* 5 June 1989, 52–7.
Mitrovica, Andrew. "Spy Probe of China Was Aborted." *Globe and Mail* (Toronto), 30 September 1999, A1–2.
– and Jeff Sallot. "China Set up Crime Web in Canada, Report Says." *Globe and Mail* (Toronto), 29 April 2000, A1, A7.
– "Mounties Blamed CSIS for Sanitizing Sidewinder." *Globe and Mail* (Toronto), 6 May 2000, A1, A6.
– "Spy Agency Blasted over Secret Slips." *Globe and Mail* (Toronto), 21 October 2000, A5.
Modin, Yuri, with Jean-Charles Deniau and Aguieszka Ziarek. *My Five Cambridge Friends.* Translated by Anthony Roberts. Toronto: Knopf Canada 1995.
Monaghan, David. *Smiley's Circus: A Guide to the Secret World of John le Carré.* London: Orbis 1986.
Moore, Dene. "Spy Agency – RCMP Turf War Threatens Security: Report." *Gazette* (Montreal), 18 October 1999, A9.
Murphy, David E., Sergei A. Kondrashev, and George Bailey. *Battleground Berlin:* CIA *vs.* KGB *in the Cold War.* New Haven and London: Yale University Press 1997.
Najman, Maurice. "Stasi 'Spy with a Heart' Wants to Meet le Carré." *Sunday Times* (London), 3 November 1991, 29.
Nash, J. Madeleine. "The Antibiotics Crisis." *Time,* 15 January 2001, 60–2.
O'Connor, John J. "Le Carré on Channel 13 Discusses Himself and His Writing." *New York Times,* 12 July 1985, C26.
Ondaatje, Michael. *Anil's Ghost.* Toronto: McClelland and Stewart, 2000.
Osnos, Peter. "Le Carré's Drumbeat." *Washington Post,* 6 April 1983, B1.

Page, Bruce, David Leitch, and Phillip Knightley. *Philby: The Spy Who Betrayed a Generation*. London: Andre Deutsch 1968.

Pearson, David E. *KAL 007: The Cover-up*. New York: Summit Books 1987.

Pearson, John. *The Life of Ian Fleming*. London: Jonathan Cape 1966.

Philby, Kim. *My Silent War*. New York: Ballantine Books 1968.

Plimpton, George. "John le Carré." *Paris Review* 39 (Summer 1997), 51–74.

Polmar, Norman, and Thomas B. Allen. *The Encyclopedia of Espionage*. New York: Gramercy Books 1998.

Powers, Thomas. "The Truth About the CIA." *New York Review of Books*, 13 May 1993.

Quinn-Judge, Paul, "Back to the Inferno," *Time*, 11 October 1999, 22–4.

Raviv, Dan, and Yossi Melman. *Every Spy a Prince: The Complete History of Israel's Intelligence Community*. Boston: Houghton Mifflin 1990.

Remnick, David. *Lenin's Tomb: The Last Days of the Soviet Empire*. New York: Vintage Books 1994.

Richelson, Jeffrey T. *A Century of Spies: Intelligence in the Twentieth Century*. New York and Oxford: Oxford University Press 1995.

Roberts, Siobhan. "Le Carré's Olivieri Lookalike." *National Post* (Toronto), 9 December 2000, A1, A9.

Rosenbaum, Ron. "Kim Philby and the Age of Paranoia." *New York Times Magazine*, 10 July 1994, 28–37, 50, 53–4.

Sakharov, Andrei. *Memoirs*. Translated by Richard Lourie. New York: Alfred A. Knopf 1990.

Sanoff, Alvin. "The Thawing of the Old Spymaster." *US News and World Report*, 19 June 1989, 59–61.

Security Intelligence Review Committee. *Annual Report 1986–87*. Ottawa: Minister of Supply and Services 1987.

Sengupta, Somini. "Canadian Cash Fueling Revolt in Sri Lanka?" *Gazette* (Montreal), 16 July 2000, A7.

Sevunts, Levon. "A Spy in the Office." *Gazette* (Montreal), 23 July 2000, A1, A2.

Sherry, Norman. *The Life of Graham Greene*. Vol. 2, *1939–1955*. London: Jonathan Cape 1994.

Shevchenko, Arkady N. *Breaking with Moscow*. New York: Ballantine Books 1985.

Smith, Hedrick. *The New Russians*. New York: Avon Books 1991.

– *The Russians*. New York: Ballantine Books 1976.

Stafford, David. *The Silent Game: The Real World of Imaginary Spies*. Toronto: Lester & Orpen Dennys 1988.

Starnes, John. *Closely Guarded: A Life in Canadian Security and Intelligence.* Toronto: University of Toronto Press, 1998.

Stephens, Joe. "Did Patient 6587–0069 Have to Die?" *Gazette* (Montreal), 20 January 2001, B1, B4.

Streitfeld, David. "Debriefing John le Carré." *Washington Post*, 8 November 1992, X15.

Tinnin, David B., and Dag Christensen. *The Hit Team.* Boston: Little Brown 1976.

Treneman, Ann. "Out of the Shadows." *Gazette* (Montreal), 17 December 2000, C1, C2.

Trevor-Roper, Hugh. *The Philby Affair.* London: William Kimber 1968.

Updike, John. "Le Carré's Game." *New Yorker*, 20 March 1995, 102–3.

Vienneau, David. "csis: More Deskwork than Derring-do." *Gazette* (Montreal), 29 July 1989, B4.

Weiner, Tim, David Johnston, and Neil A. Lewis. *Betrayal: The Story of Aldrich Ames, an American Spy.* New York: Random House 1995.

"West Bank Uneasy over le Carré Filming." *New York Times*, 5 November 1983, 17.

Whitney, Craig R. "Russians Warm to le Carré." *New York Times*, 22 May 1989, C13, C18.

Wise, David. *Nightmover: How Aldrich Ames Sold the cia to the kgb for $4.6 Million.* New York: HarperCollins 1995.

Wolf, Markus, with Anne McElvoy. *Man without a Face.* New York: Times Books 1997.

Woodward, Bob. *Veil: The Secret Wars of the cia, 1981–1987.* New York: Pocket Books 1987.

Wright, Peter. *Spycatcher.* Toronto: Stoddart 1987.

Wynne, Greville. *The Man from Moscow: The Story of Wynne and Penkovsky.* London: Hutchinson 1967.

Yevtushenko, Yevgeny. *Don't Die before You're Dead.* Translated by Antonina W. Bouis. Toronto: Key Porter Books 1995.

Index

Ames, Aldrich, 130–1, 134

Andrew, Christopher, 26, 185, 202, 204

Angleton, James Jesus, 128–30, 177

Ash, Timothy Garton, 61, 64, 244

Avery, John, 82, 87, 91–2, 95, 107. *See also The Looking Glass War*

Axel, 174–8, 246. *See also A Perfect Spy*

Ben-Gurion, David, 160

Bingham, John, 47–8

Blair, Barley, 185, 190–1, 193–5, 215, 238, 246. *See also The Russia House*

Blunt, Anthony, 112, 189

Bond, James, 26, 40, 41–5, 46, 47, 77, 138, 144

Bradfield, Rawley, 97–8, 101, 113–14, 219. *See also A Small Town in Germany*

Bradshaw, Anthony Joyston, 114, 215, 219–20, 224. *See also The Secret Pilgrim and The Night Manager*

Brandt, Captain, 211–12. *See also The Secret Pilgrim*

Brimley, Ailsa, 59. *See also A Murder of Quality*

British Secret Intelligence Service (MI6), 8, 46, 47, 69, 112, 119, 120, 122, 123, 126, 129, 185

British Secret Service (MI5), 8, 14, 123, 128, 129

Brock, Nat, 243–5. *See also Single & Single*

Brotherhood, Jack, 174–8, 246. *See also A Perfect Spy*

Browne, Anthony Montague, 121

Burgess, Anthony, 43

Burgess, Guy, 112, 115, 123

Burr, Leonard, 215, 219–24, 240. *See also The Night Manager*

Bush, George, 192

Cairncross, John, 112, 180

Call for the Dead, 4, 44, 48–9, 55, 71

Canadian Security Intelligence Service (CSIS), 9, 21–3, 25, 27, 36, 40, 41, 53–4, 78–9, 99, 140, 183, 196, 259–62; and business cards, 17–20; and China, 69–70, 79; CSIS Act, 71; and internal security, 67; public report, 21; Research Analysis Production (RAP), 34, 35, 36; security screening, 13–16, 67–8; training, 17, 23–4, 27–8, 29, 35, 39

Carne School, 56–7, 59–60. *See also A Murder of Quality*

Carroll, Lewis, 86

Casino Royale, 42, 45, 138

Cassidy, Aldo, 103–10. *See also The Naïve and Sentimental Lover*

Castle, Maurice, 92, 124–5, 126, 127–8, 132, 194. *See also The Human Factor*

Cave Brown, Anthony, 46, 69, 119, 120, 121, 123

Cavendish, Ben, 206–7. *See also The Secret Pilgrim*

Central Intelligence Agency (CIA), 44, 45, 51–2, 80, 113, 131, 161, 185, 192, 200, 211, 232; and Philby, 121, 128–9, 130

Charlie, 159, 163–5, 167–70, 243, 246. *See also The Little Drummer Girl*

Chechnya, 226–7, 229

CNN, 86, 201

Colby, William, 44

Cold War, 4, 13, 55, 62, 63, 66, 75–7, 107, 115, 137–8, 141, 152, 158, 185, 191–2, 219–21, 223, 225, 230; aftermath, 5, 11, 85, 196, 199–200, 204, 215–17, 218, 223–4, 239, 246, 257

Connery, Sean, 41, 42

Conrad, Joseph, 213–14

conspiracy theory, 16–17, 131

Constant Gardener, The, 114, 249–53

Cornwell, David, x–xi, 47, 48. *See also* le Carré, John

Cornwell, Ronnie, 171–4, 243, 244

counter-intelligence, 5, 6, 26, 65, 128, 130, 135, 198, 201

Cranmer, Tim, 224–6, 228–30. *See also Our Game*

Cumming, Sir Mansfield, 46

Czechoslovakia, 134, 138, 199, 201; Prague Spring, 116, 129, 190, 203

Denissenko, Vassily, 179–82, 207

Donovan, Wild Bill, 51–2

double agent, 69–70, 70–1, 118, 120, 128

Doyle, Sir Arthur Conan, 51

Dulles, Allen, 45

Eco, Umberto, 58

Eitan, Rafi, 167

Elcock, Ward, 70

Ellroy, James, 28

Esterhase, Toby, 153, 209–11, 212

Fennan, Elsa, 49–51, 55. *See also Call for the Dead*

Fennan, Samuel, 49–51, 76. *See also Call for the Dead*

Fiedler, Jens, 12, 73–7, 142. *See also The Spy Who Came in from the Cold*

Fielding, Terence, 56–7, 59–60. *See also A Murder of Quality*

Fleming, Ian, 42–5, 46, 47

Forster, E.M., 3–4

Frewin, Cyril, 207–8, 215. *See also The Secret Pilgrim*

Frey, Dieter, 55–6. *See also Call for the Dead*

From Russia, with Love, 43

Germany, 63, 64, 76, 96, 98, 216–17; Berlin, 62–3, 69, 71, 96, 206; Berlin Wall, 63, 138, 153, 199, 216–17; and Cold War, 62

Getting to Know the General, 231

Golitsyn, Anatoly, 129–30

Gorbachev, Mikhail, 187, 191, 199–200, 203–4

Gordievsky, Oleg, 116–18, 120, 185, 190

Gouzenko, Igor, 25–6, 45

Green, Vivian, 48

Greene, Graham, 3, 69, 77, 92, 133, 230–2, 233, 235, 239; on Philby, 115–16, 122, 124, 127, 128, 132

GRU (Soviet military intelligence), 25, 65, 179, 185

Guillam, Peter, 135–6, 138, 144, 146, 147–8, 153, 177, 212

Guinness, Alec, 47

Gulf War, 86, 162

Haldane, Adrian, 87, 90–2. *See also The Looking Glass War*

Handelman, Stephen, 241–2

Hansen, 213–14. *See also The Secret Pilgrim*

Harting, Leo, 97–8, 100–3, 106, 113, 218, 224. *See also A Small Town in Germany*

Havel, Václav, 201
Haydon, Bill, 111, 132–3, 134–8, 141, 143–5, 149, 177, 207, 211–12. *See also Tinker Tailor Soldier Spy*
Heart of the Matter, The, 133
Helen, 105–9. *See also The Naïve and Sentimental Lover*
Helms, Richard, 113
Hiss, Alger, 25
Hoban, Alix, 170, 241, 247. *See also Single & Single*
Hollis, Sir Roger, 123, 128–9
Holmes, Sherlock, 51, 55
Honourable Schoolboy, The, 6, 142, 145, 147, 157, 243, 250
Human Factor, The, 93, 124, 127
HVA (East German intelligence), 10, 64

Israel, 158–67

Jeanmaire, Jean-Louis, 179–82, 207
Jerzy, Colonel, 208–9. *See also The Secret Pilgrim*
Joseph, 163–4, 167–70, 246. *See also The Little Drummer Girl*

Karfeld, Klaus, 96, 101–2. *See also A Small Town in Germany*
Karla, 43, 46, 100, 134–7, 140–50, 152–3, 157, 187, 218
Kennaway, James, 103–10
Kennaway, Susan, 103–9
KGB (Soviet intelligence), 26, 42, 65, 98–9, 112, 116–17, 119, 120, 127, 129, 130, 131, 135, 186, 189, 198, 202, 211, 226
Khalil, 159, 165, 167–9. *See also The Little Drummer Girl*
Khokhlov, Nikolai, 211
Khrushchev, Nikita, 161, 186, 187, 203, 227
Kissinger, Henry, 129
Knightley, Phillip, 52, 113, 118, 121, 186
Ko, Drake, 144–8. *See also The Honourable Schoolboy*

Korean Air Lines (KAL), 80–2
Kurtz, Marty, 159, 164–5, 167–9, 245. *See also The Little Drummer Girl*
Kuzichkin, Vladimir, 131, 198, 202

Leamas, Alec, 12, 71–7, 87, 193, 221, 239, 246. *See also The Spy Who Came in from the Cold*
le Carré, John, 3, 44, 47, 48, 52, 56–7, 63, 68–9, 75, 77, 87, 96, 97, 138, 141–2, 146, 149, 202, 205, 215–17, 223, 225, 226–7, 230, 233, 237, 239, 246, 248–9, 254, 257; on Bond, 43; and Jeanmaire, 179–81; and joining intelligence service, 175–6; and Kennaways, 103, 104–9; on loyalty, 94; and Middle East, 158–9, 161, 163–5, 167; on Philby, 111–14, 118, 124, 132, 172; on Sakharov, 189; on secrecy, 17, 229–30, 236–7; on spying, 5, 90, 100, 153, 157, 184, 193; on writing, ix, x, 3, 7–8, 48–9, 60, 147, 210; youth, 4, 171–4, 243–4
Leclerc, 78, 82, 85–7, 90–2, 95. *See also The Looking Glass War*
Leiser, Fred, 87, 91–2, 95, 101, 218. *See also The Looking Glass War*
lie detector, 15
Little Drummer Girl, The, 158–9, 163, 168, 243
Looking Glass War, The, 77, 79, 82, 85, 100, 105, 151, 236

Maclean, Donald, 112, 115, 123
Macmillan, Harold, 123
Malan, Rian, 125–6
May, Allan Nunn, 25
Medvedev, Roy, 187
Mendel, Arthur, 50, 136
Menzies, Sir Stewart, 46, 69, 120
Mitel Corporation, 54
Mitrokhin, Vasili, 64–5, 98–9
Modin, Yuri, 127–8
Moore, Roger, 42

Morden, Reid, 21
Mossad, 160–2; and Munich Olympics, 166–7
Mundt, Hans-Dieter, 50, 55–6, 71, 73–7, 142. *See also Call for the Dead* and *The Spy Who Came in from the Cold*
Murder of Quality, A, 48, 56, 59–60
My Traitor's Heart, 125

Naïve and Sentimental Lover, The, 103, 104–5
NATO, 25, 179, 199
Ned, 28–9, 30, 38, 111, 185, 192–5, 206–8, 210–14, 215, 228, 238, 245. *See also The Russia House* and *The Secret Pilgrim*
Night Manager, The, 114, 217–20, 224, 225, 241, 245
Noriega, Manuel, 231–3
Norman, Herbert, 115

Office of Strategic Services (OSS), 51–2
Oldfield, Sir Maurice, 46–7
Ondaatje, Michael, 156
Orlova, Katya, 191–5, 246. *See also The Russia House*
Osnard, Andy, 233–5, 237–8, 239, 240. *See also The Tailor of Panama*
Our Game, 224, 226, 238, 239
Our Man in Havana, 230, 236, 256

Panama, 184, 231–3, 235, 246
Pendel, Harry, 233–8, 239, 246. *See also The Tailor of Panama*
Penkovsky, Oleg, 185–6
Perfect Spy, A, x, 63, 97, 170–3, 243, 244
Pettifer, Larry, 225, 228–30, 238. *See also Our Game*
Petty, Clare, 130
Philby, Kim, 64, 69, 112–24, 127–30, 132, 134, 135, 137, 172, 189; death of, 26; defection, 26, 111; *My Silent War*, 118
physical surveillance, 30, 153

Pierpaoli, Yvette, 250
Pine, Jonathan, 219–24, 245, 246. *See also The Night Manager*
Prisoner, The, 178
Putin, Vladimir, 226
Pym, Magnus, x, 63, 170–8, 244, 246. *See also A Perfect Spy*
Pym, Rick, 171–4, 176, 244. *See also A Perfect Spy*

Quayle, Justin, 250–4. *See also The Constant Gardener*
Quayle, Tessa, 249–54. *See also The Constant Gardener*

Remnick, David, 203, 242
Riemeck, Karl, 71, 74. *See also The Spy Who Came in from the Cold*
Rode, Stella, 59–60. *See also A Murder of Quality*
Rodenbaum, Ron, 111, 134
Roper, Richard Onslow, 114, 219–24, 245. *See also The Night Manager*
Royal Canadian Mounted Police (RCMP), 11, 27, 45, 58, 70, 78, 79; and October Crisis, 53; Security Service, 8–9
Russia House, The, 184, 186, 189, 199, 205, 209, 216, 239
Ryan, Operation, 65

Sachs, Connie, 144, 146, 148, 149
Sackville, Lady Avice, 41
Sakharov, Andrei, 188–90
Savelyev, Yakov, 185, 188–91, 193–5. *See also The Russia House*
Saving Private Ryan, 13
Scowcroft, Brent, 192, 199
Secret Pilgrim, The, 28, 38, 114, 205, 215
Security Intelligence Review Committee (SIRC), 78, 79
security screening, 15–16, 66–7, 114
Sercomb, Lady Ann, 45–6, 137, 141, 149

Shamus, 105–10. *See also The Naïve and Sentimental Lover*
Sherry, Norman, 122
Shevchenko, Arkady, 188, 203
Sidewinder, Operation, 70, 79
Single, Oliver, 242–5. *See also Single & Single*
Single, Tiger, 114, 240–6. *See also Single & Single*
Single & Single, 8, 114, 170, 239, 241–7
Skardon, William, 14
Small Town in Germany, A, 96, 100, 113, 219
SMERSH (Soviet intelligence) 42
Smiley, George, 11, 29, 38, 43, 44–51, 54–5, 59–60, 74–5, 91, 95, 134–8, 140–50, 152–3, 157, 158, 187, 206, 228, 238, 246
Smiley's People, 47, 149, 152, 157
Smith, Hedrick, 188, 190, 242
Some Gorgeous Accident, 104–5
South Africa, 124–6
Soviet Union (USSR), 42, 46, 62–3, 64, 84, 115, 117, 121, 190–1, 195, 198, 199, 201–5, 216, 225
Spy Who Came in from the Cold, The, 7, 12, 46, 50, 68, 71, 75, 100, 103, 142, 147, 239
Sri Lanka, 154–6; Liberation Tigers of Tamil Eelam (LTTE), 154–6; Tamils, 154
Stalin, Joseph, 42, 43, 55, 62, 65, 115, 117, 161, 187, 203–4, 227, 242

Starnes, John, 53
Stasi (East German security), 64
Stettinius, Edward, 25
Study in Scarlet, A, 51
Sun-tzu, 195

Tailor of Panama, The, 184, 230, 232, 233, 238, 239, 248, 256
Taylor, Wilf, 82, 86, 236. *See also The Looking Glass War*
Teodor, Professor, 209–11. *See also The Secret Pilgrim*
ThreeBees, 114, 251–4. *See also The Constant Gardener*
Tinker Tailor Soldier Spy, 47, 132, 138, 149, 152, 157
Trevor-Roper, Hugh, 114
Turner, Alan, 97–8, 100–1, 106, 113, 219. *See also A Small Town in Germany*

Vivian, Valentine, 126
Volkov, Konstantin, 135

Westerby, Jerry, 12, 145–8, 193, 243, 246. *See also The Honourable Schoolboy*
Wolf, Markus, 10, 13, 77, 142, 236
Woodward, Bob, 113
World War II, 45, 55, 65, 102, 119, 180, 188
Wright, Peter, 128, 177
Wynne, Greville, 185–6

Yevtushenko, Yevgeny, 242